SWING IT, SUNNY

JENNIFER L. HOLM & MATTHEW HOLM
WITH COLOR BY LARK PIEN

graphix

AN IMPRINT OF

📖 SCHOLASTIC

Library of Congress data available

ISBN 978-0-545-74170-5 (hardcover)
ISBN 978-0-545-74172-9 (paperback)

10 9 8 7 6 5 4 3 2 1   17 18 19 20 21

Printed in Malaysia 108
First edition, September 2017
Edited by David Levithan
Lettering by Fawn Lau
Color by Lark Pien
Book design by Phil Falco
Creative Director: David Saylor

For Neelam and Neeta

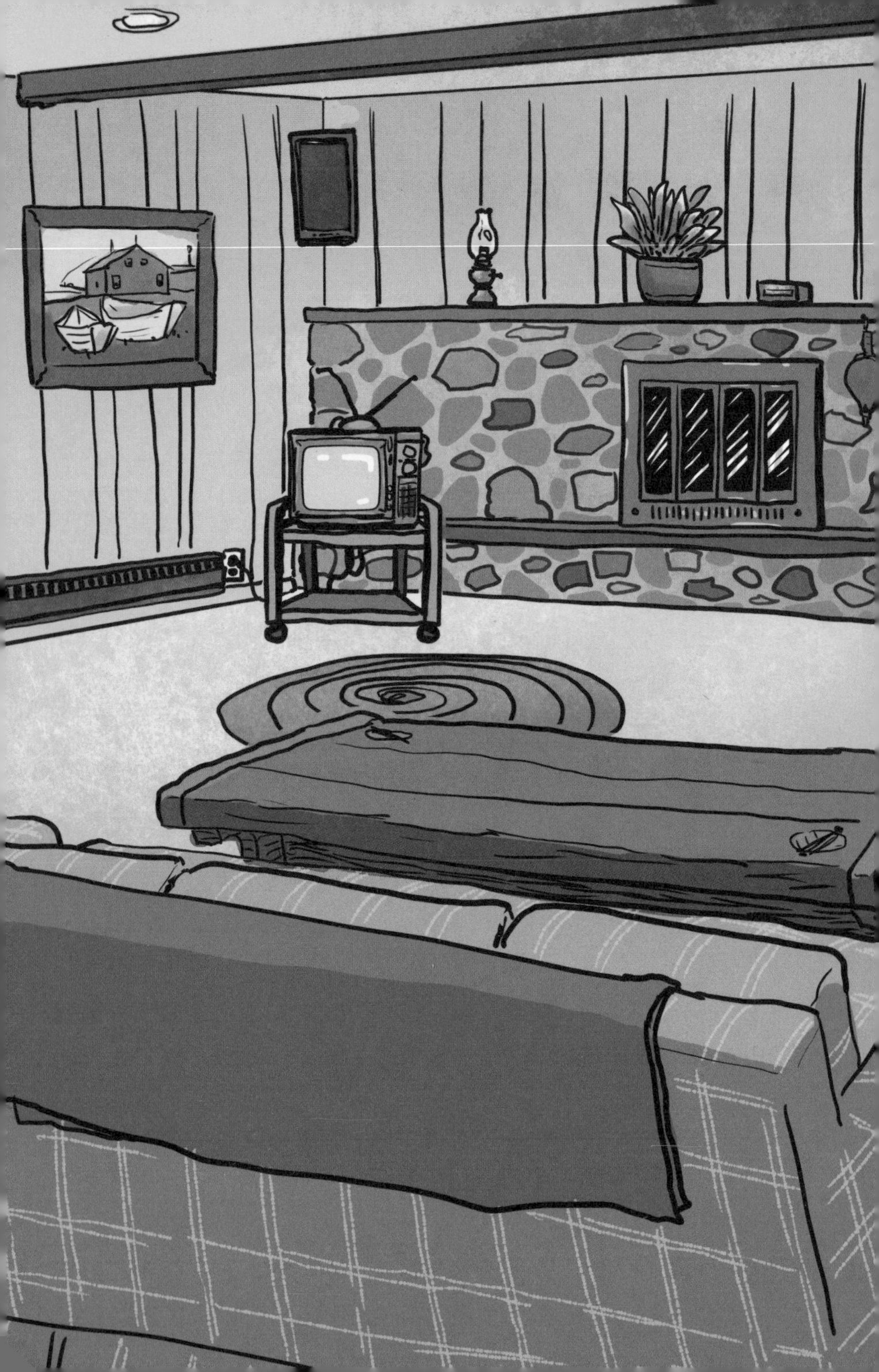

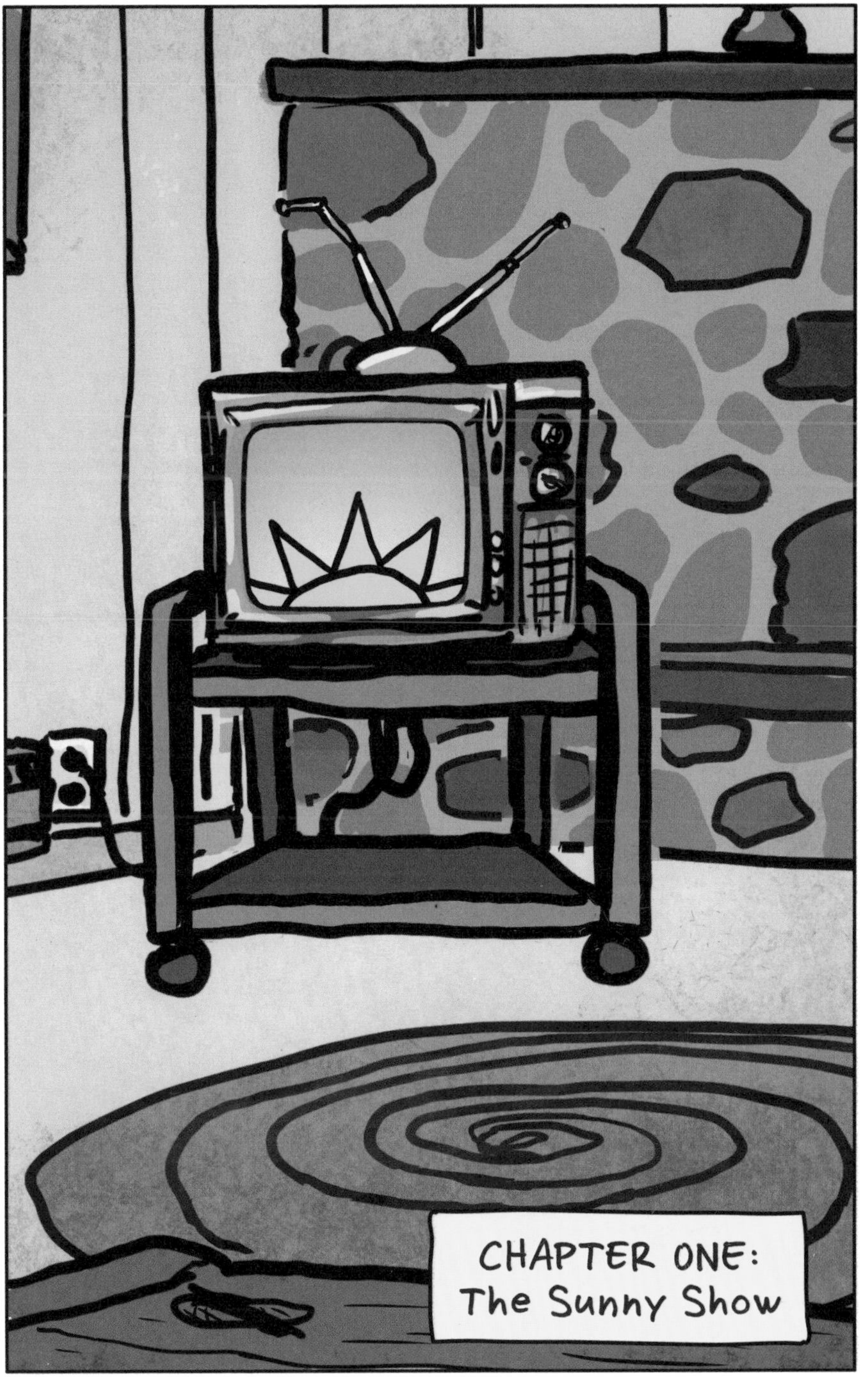
CHAPTER ONE:
The Sunny Show

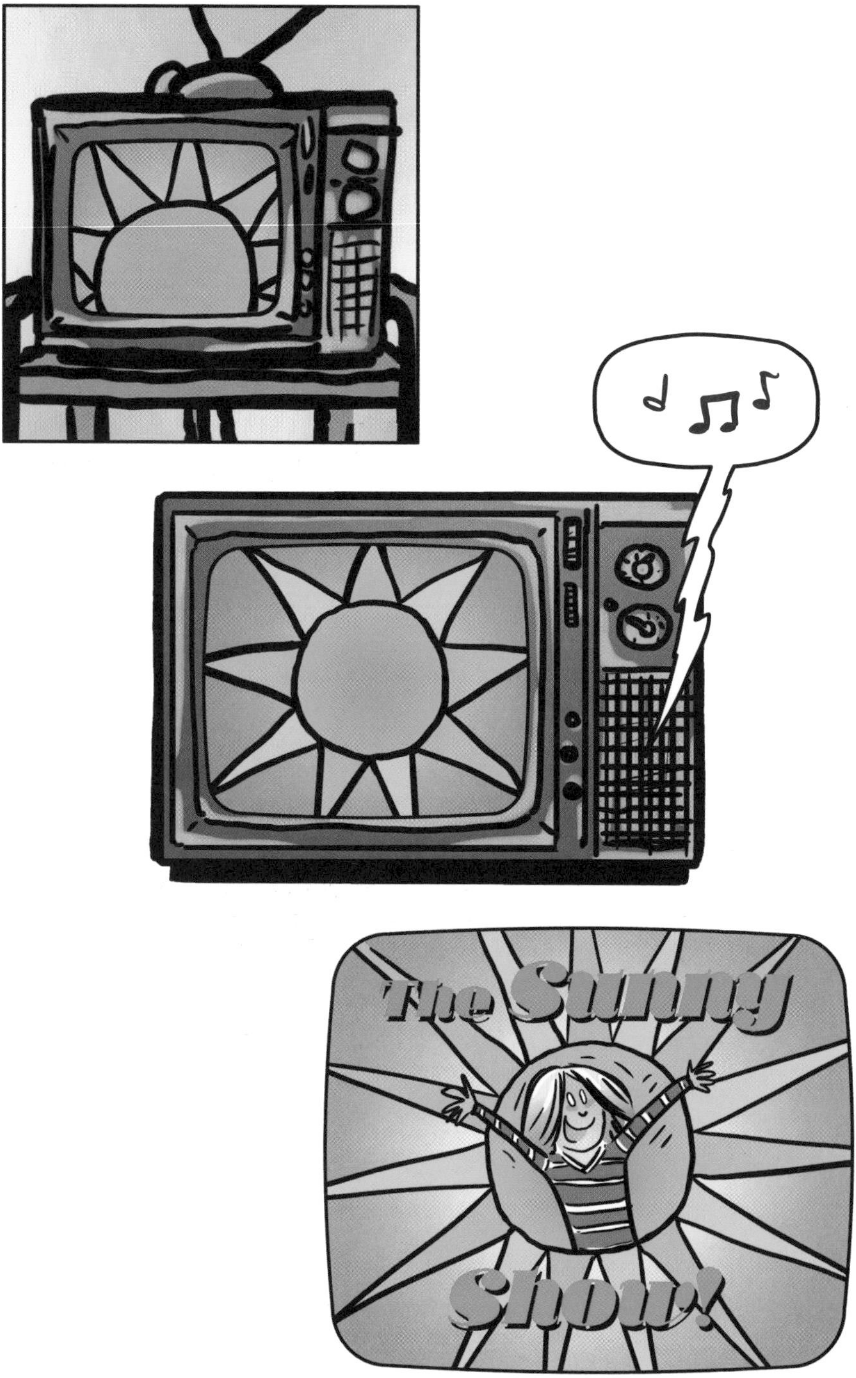
The Sunny
Show!

Starring Sunny!
(as herself)

♫

She's just a **regular girl** in a regular **world!**

♫ Her **MOM'S** always **busy**

♩

♪

♫ Her **dad's** always **groovy!**

Her little brother's always silly!

There's her best friend, Deb!

And don't forget Gramps!

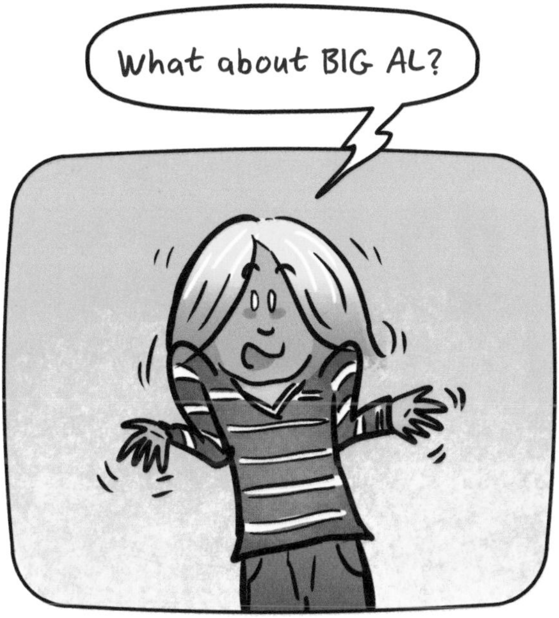
What about BIG AL?

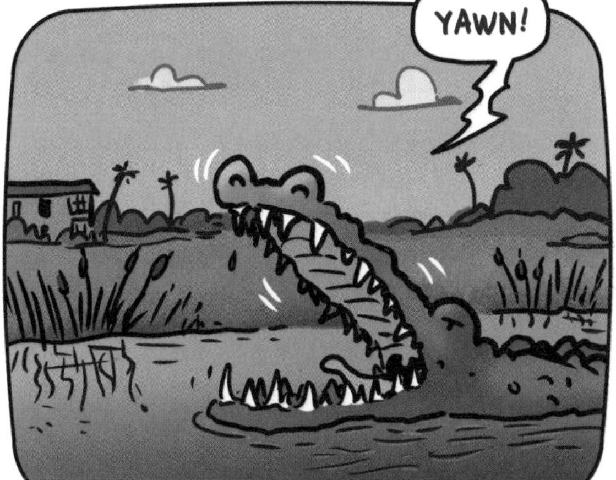
YAWN!

♫ And her favorite alligator! ♪

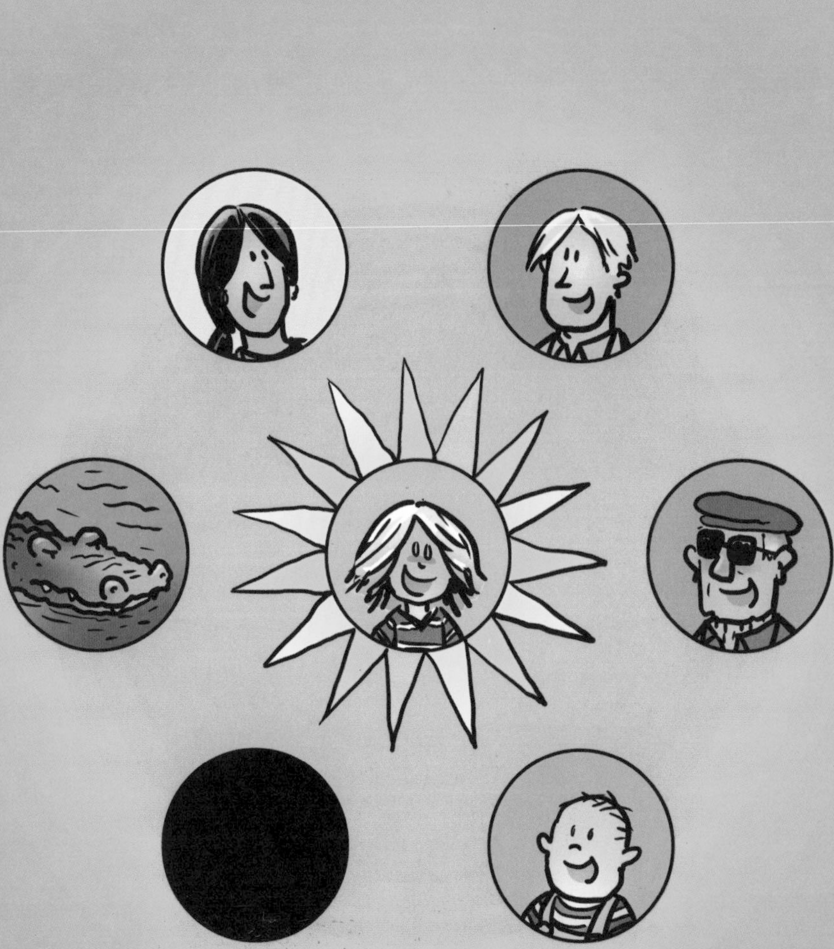

It's The Sunny Show!

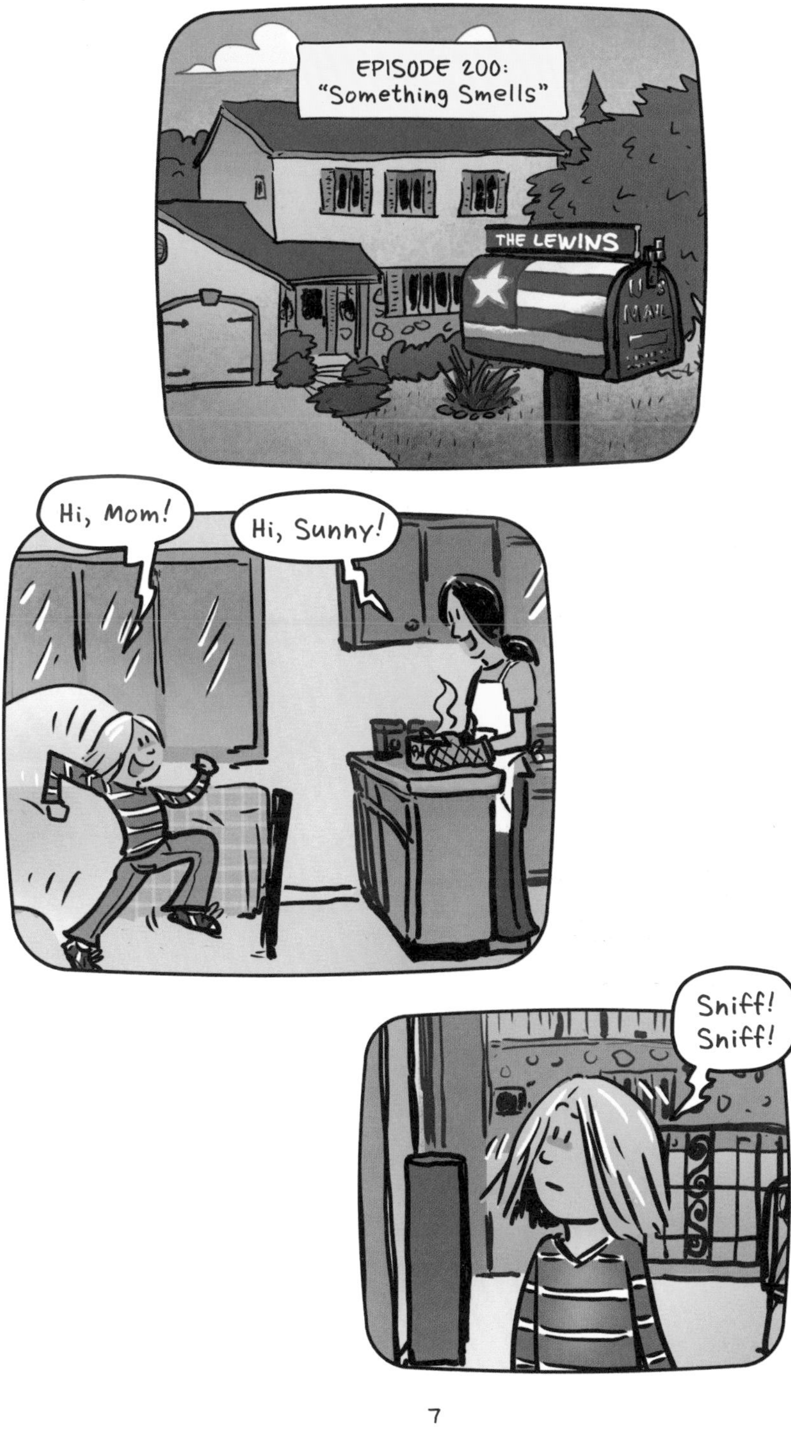
EPISODE 200:
"Something Smells"
THE LEWINS
U.S. MAIL
Hi, Mom!
Hi, Sunny!
Sniff!
Sniff!

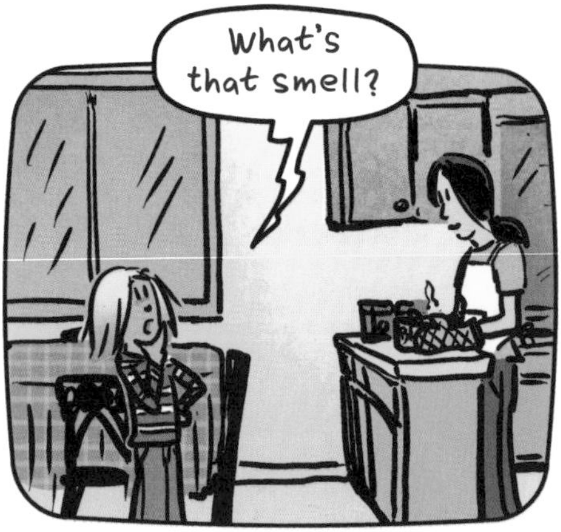
What's that smell?

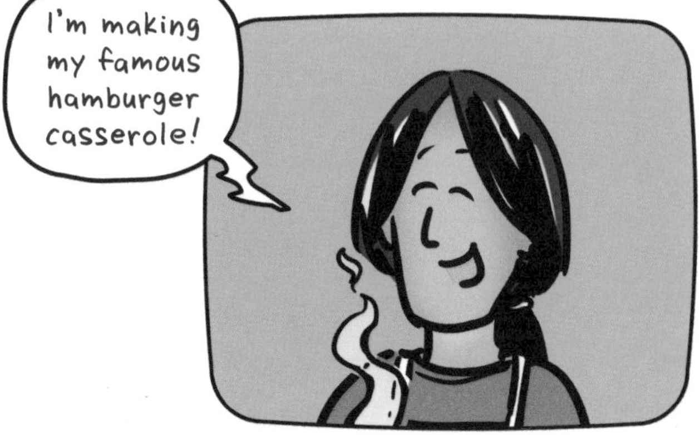
I'm making my famous hamburger casserole!

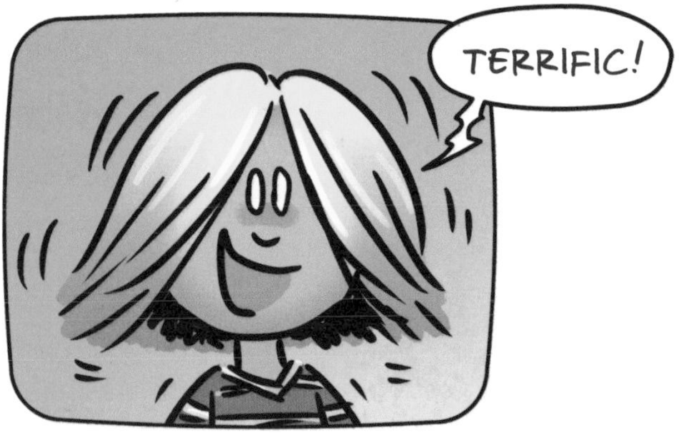
TERRIFIC!

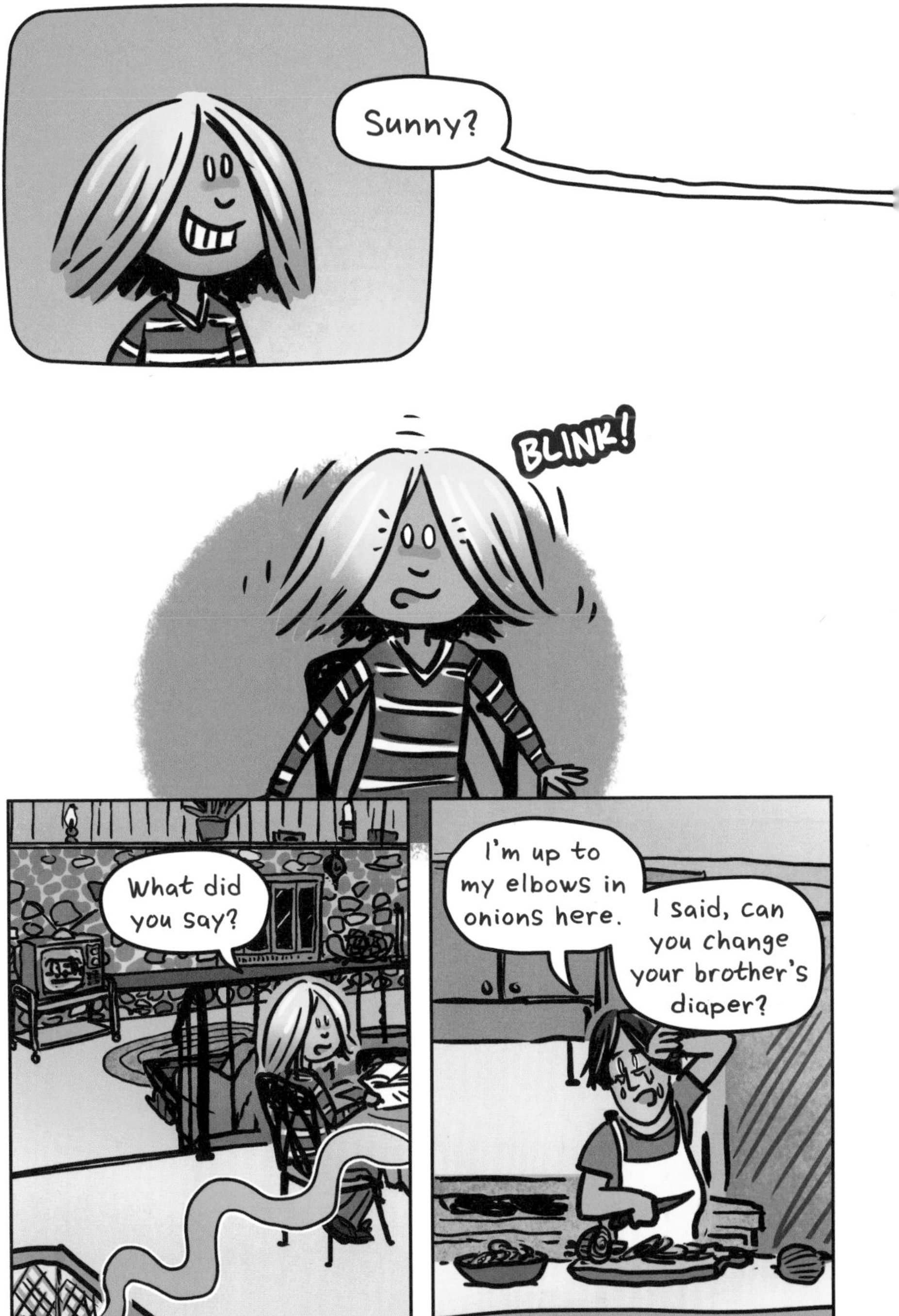
Sunny?
BLINK!
What did you say?
I'm up to my elbows in onions here.
I said, can you change your brother's diaper?

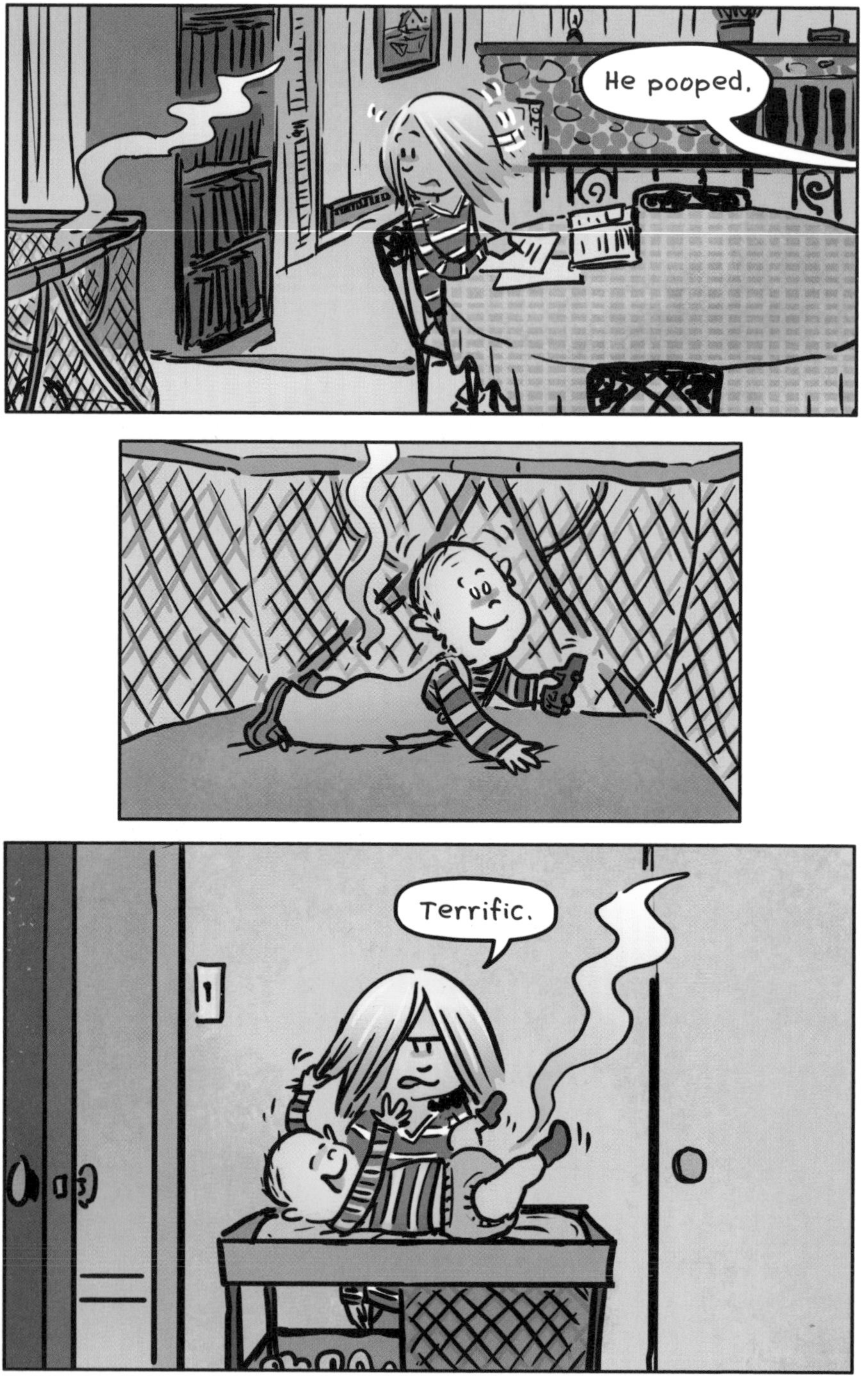
He pooped.
Terrific.

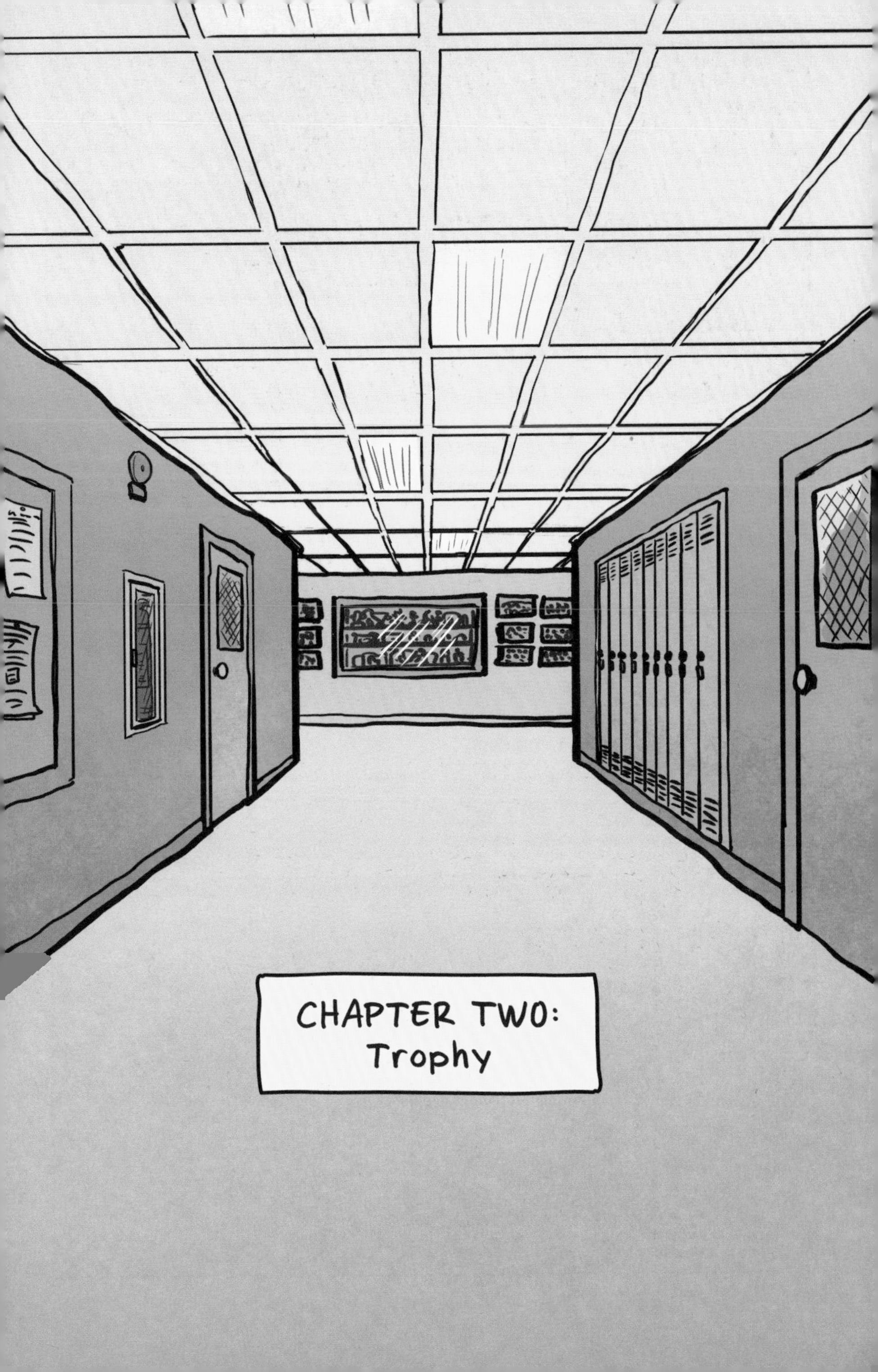
CHAPTER TWO:
Trophy

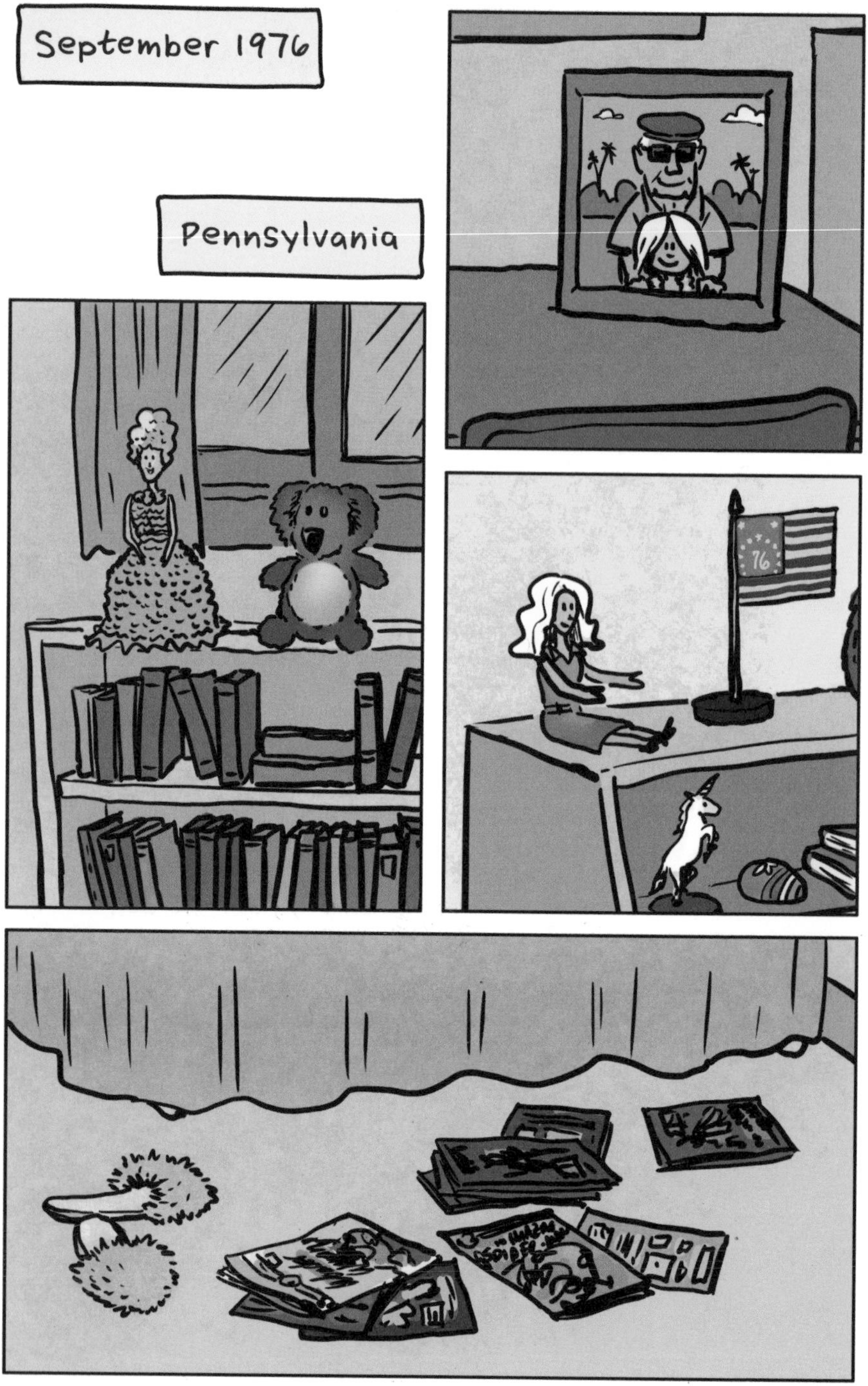
September 1976
Pennsylvania
76

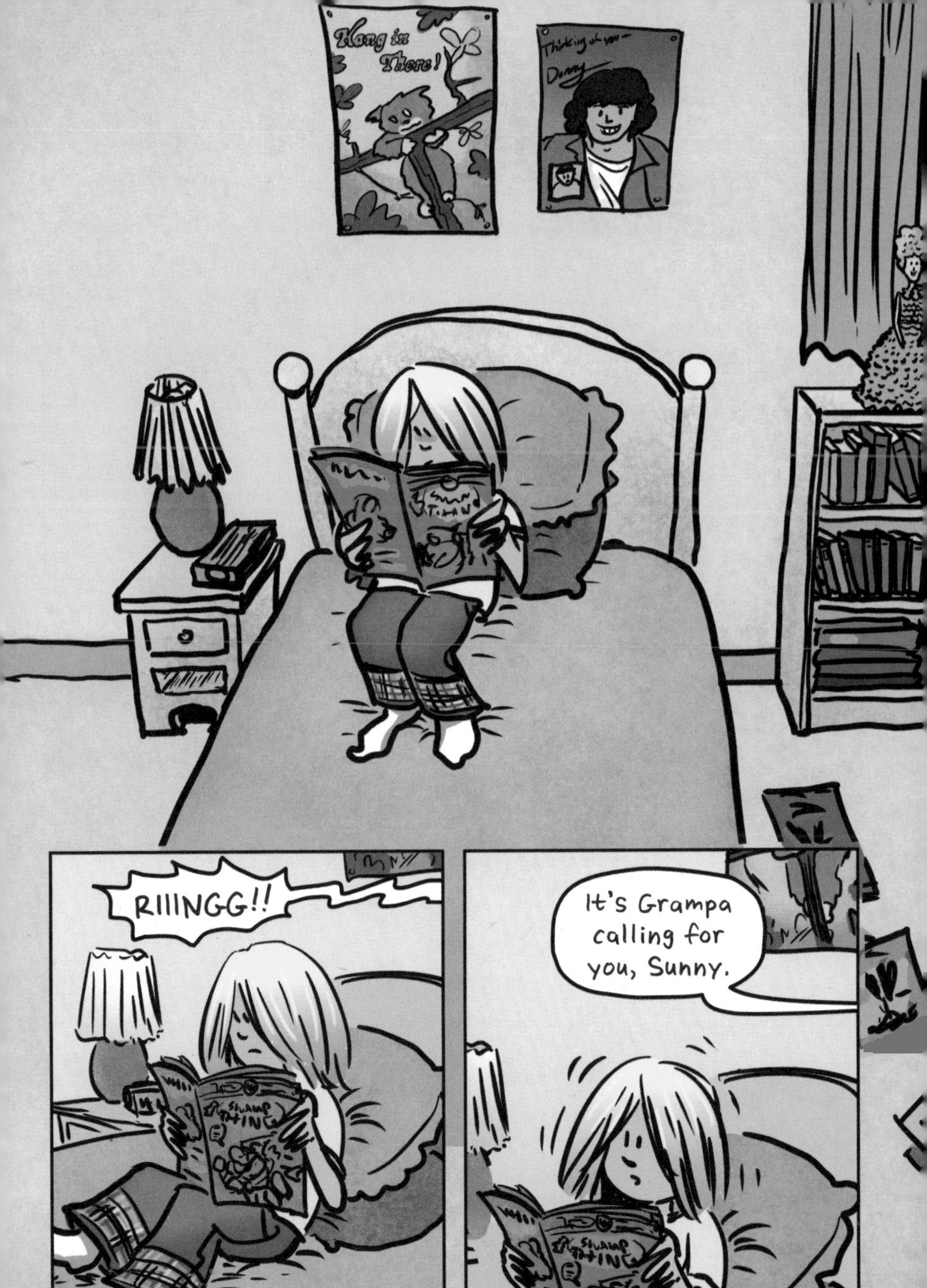
Hang in There!
Thinking of you—
Donny
RIIINGG!!
It's Grampa calling for you, Sunny.

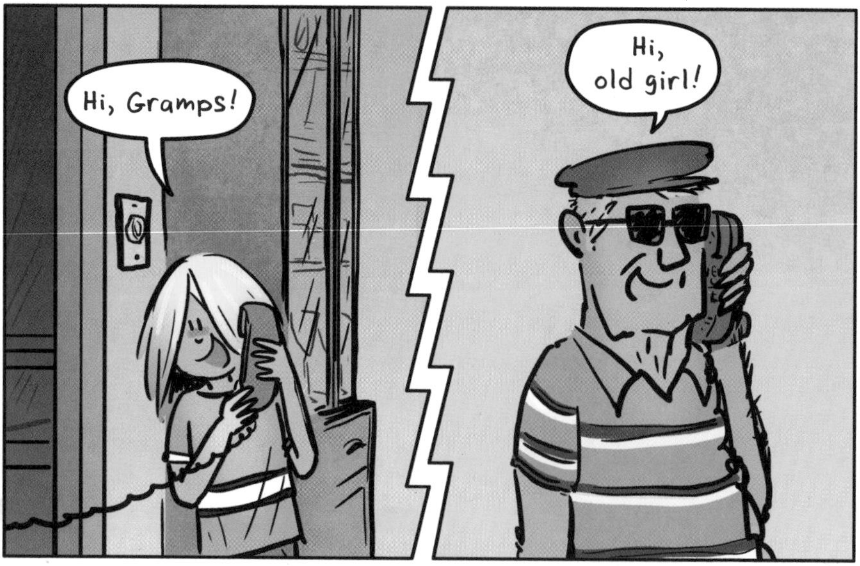
Hi, Gramps!
Hi, old girl!

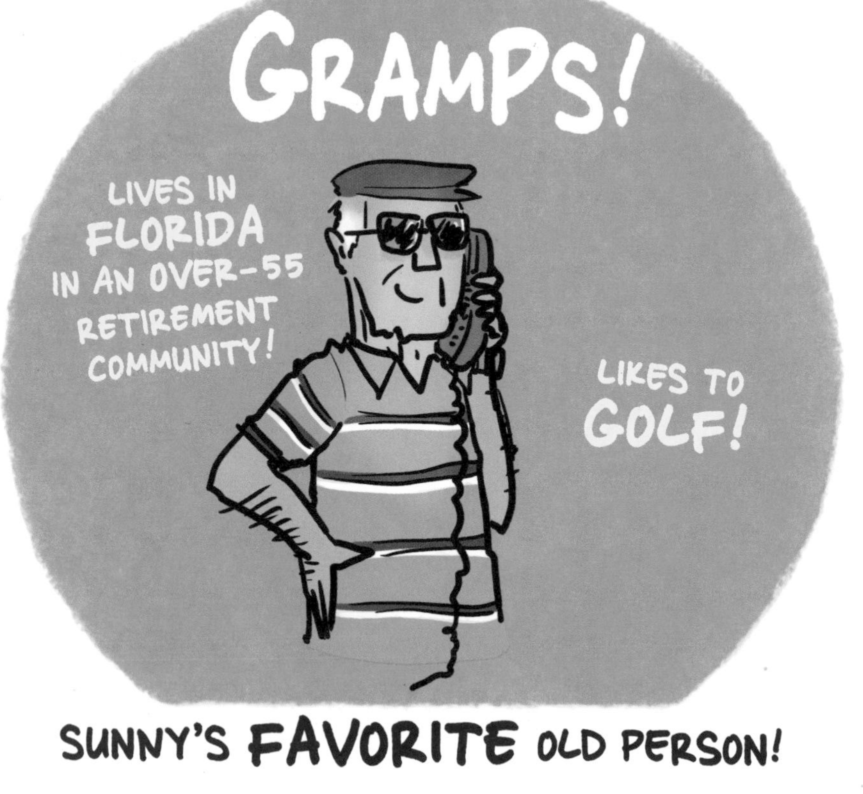
GRAMPS!
LIVES IN FLORIDA IN AN OVER-55 RETIREMENT COMMUNITY!
LIKES TO GOLF!

SUNNY'S **FAVORITE** OLD PERSON!

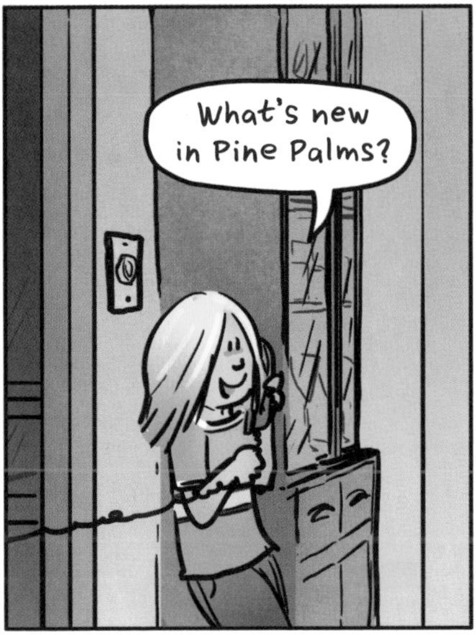
What's new in Pine Palms?

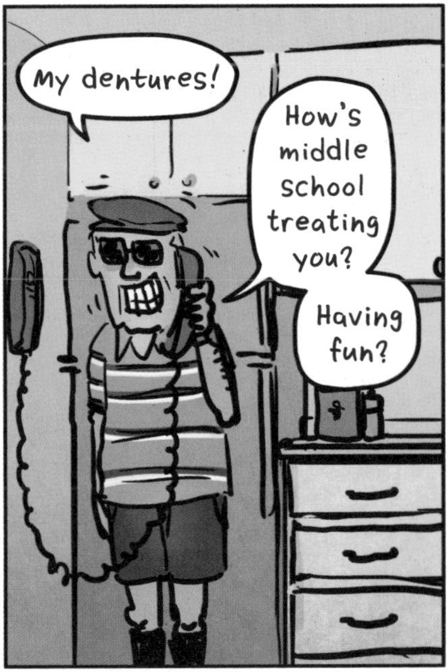
My dentures!
How's middle school treating you?
Having fun?

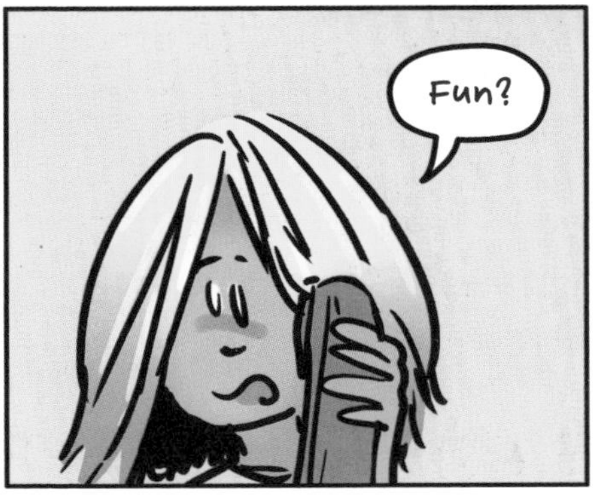
Fun?

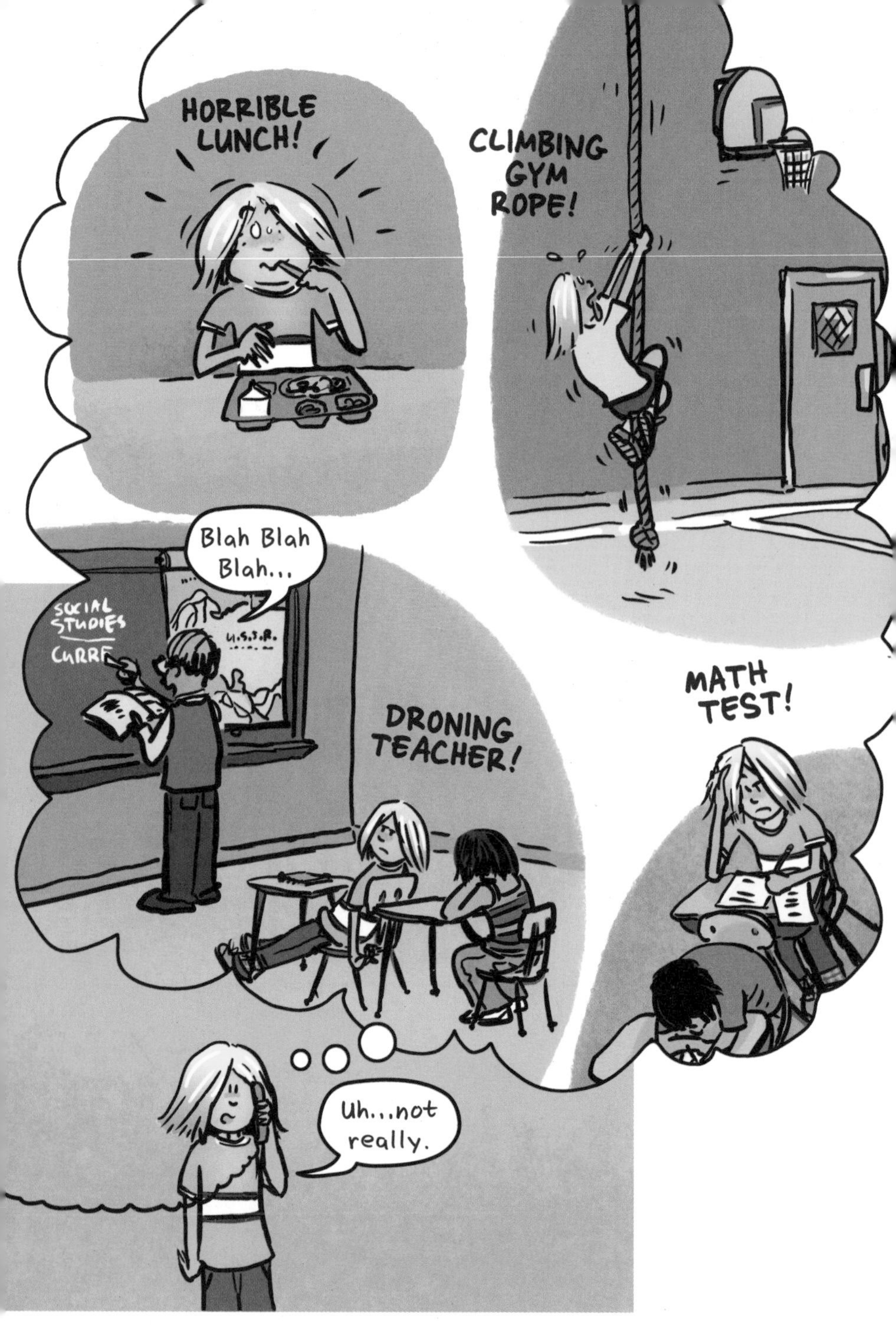
HORRIBLE LUNCH!
CLIMBING GYM ROPE!
Blah Blah Blah...
SOCIAL STUDIES
CURRE
U.S.S.R.
DRONING TEACHER!
MATH TEST!
Uh...not really.

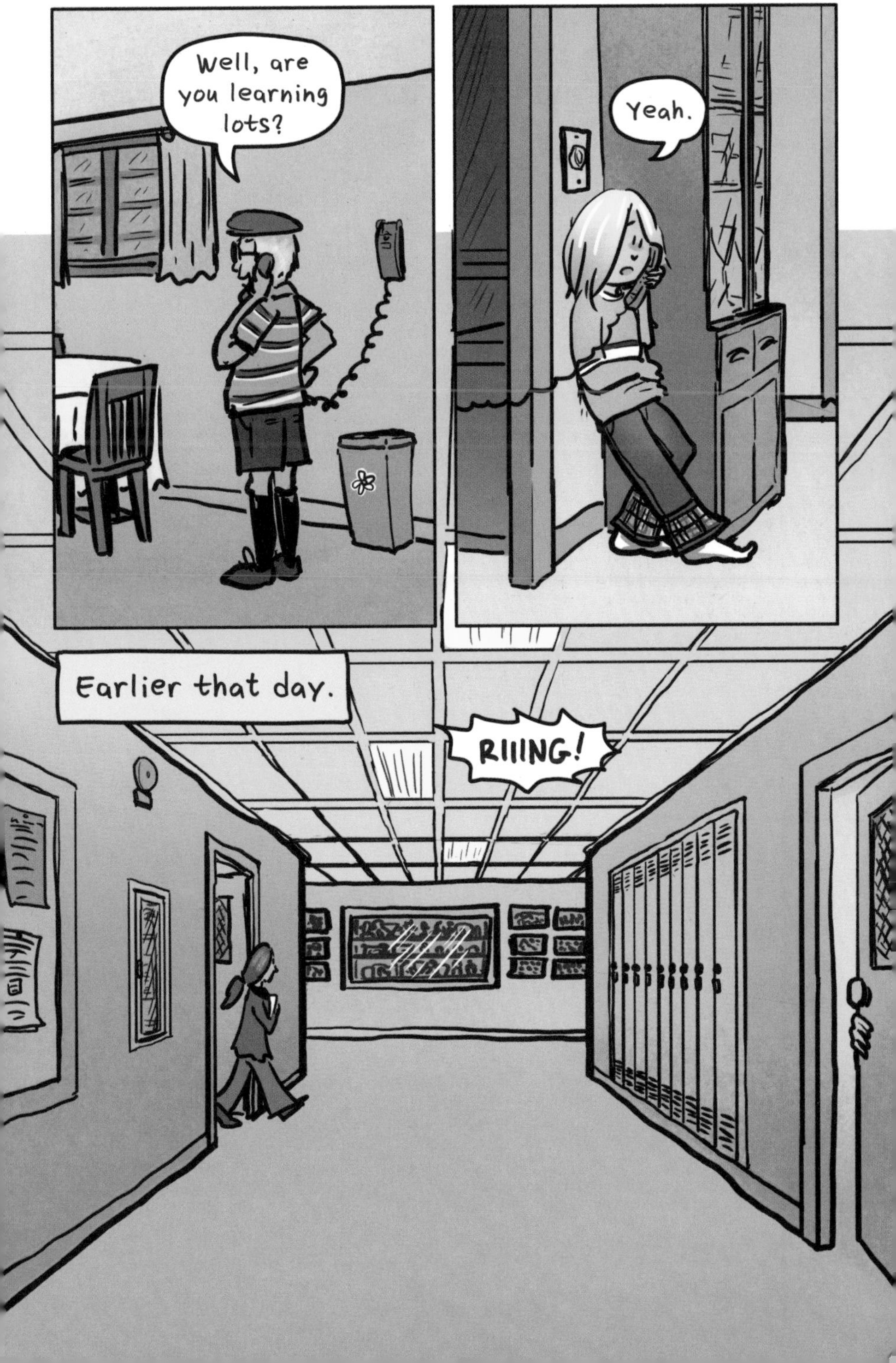
Well, are you learning lots?
Yeah.
Earlier that day.
RIIING!

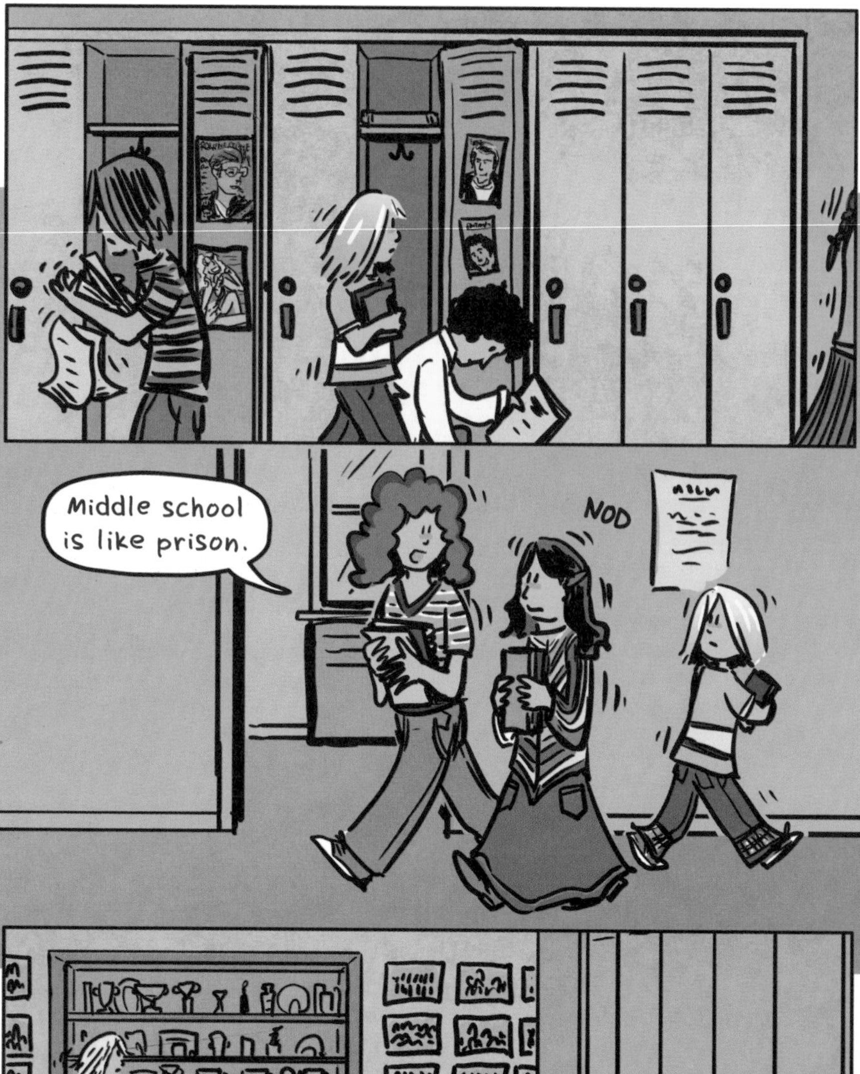
Middle school is like prison.
NOD

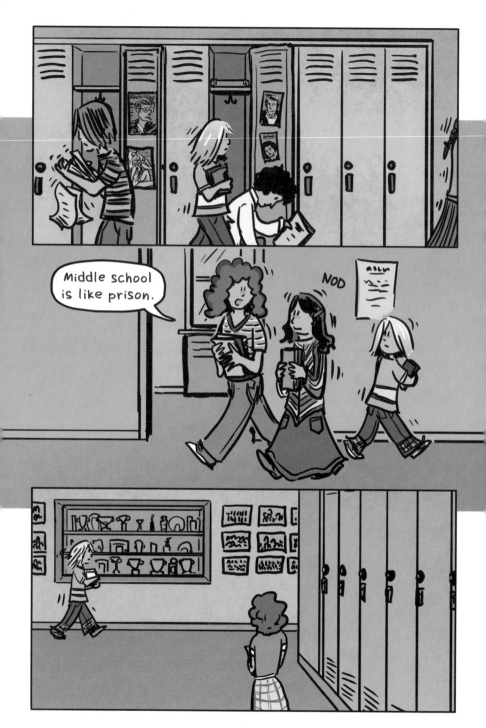

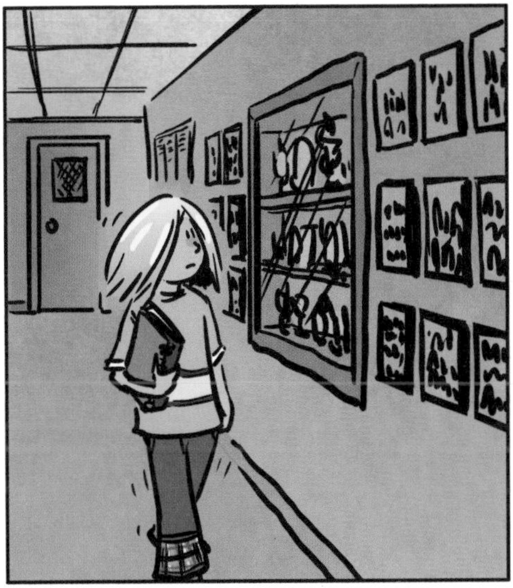

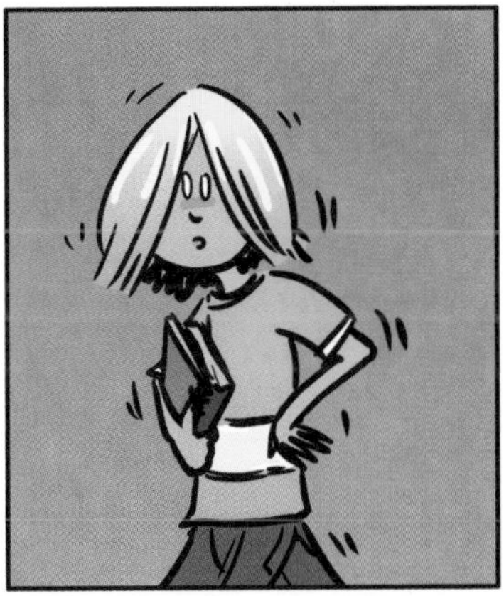

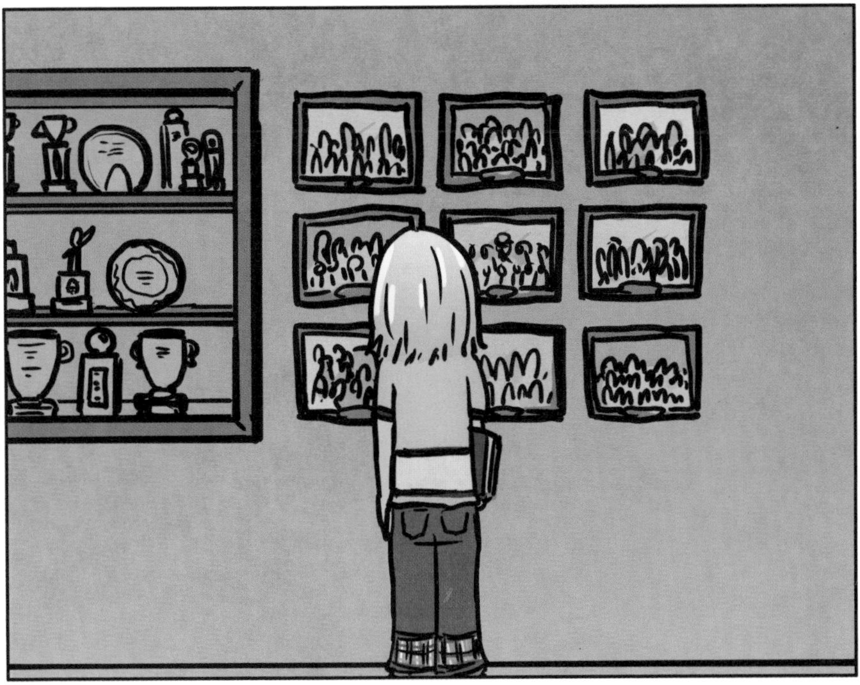

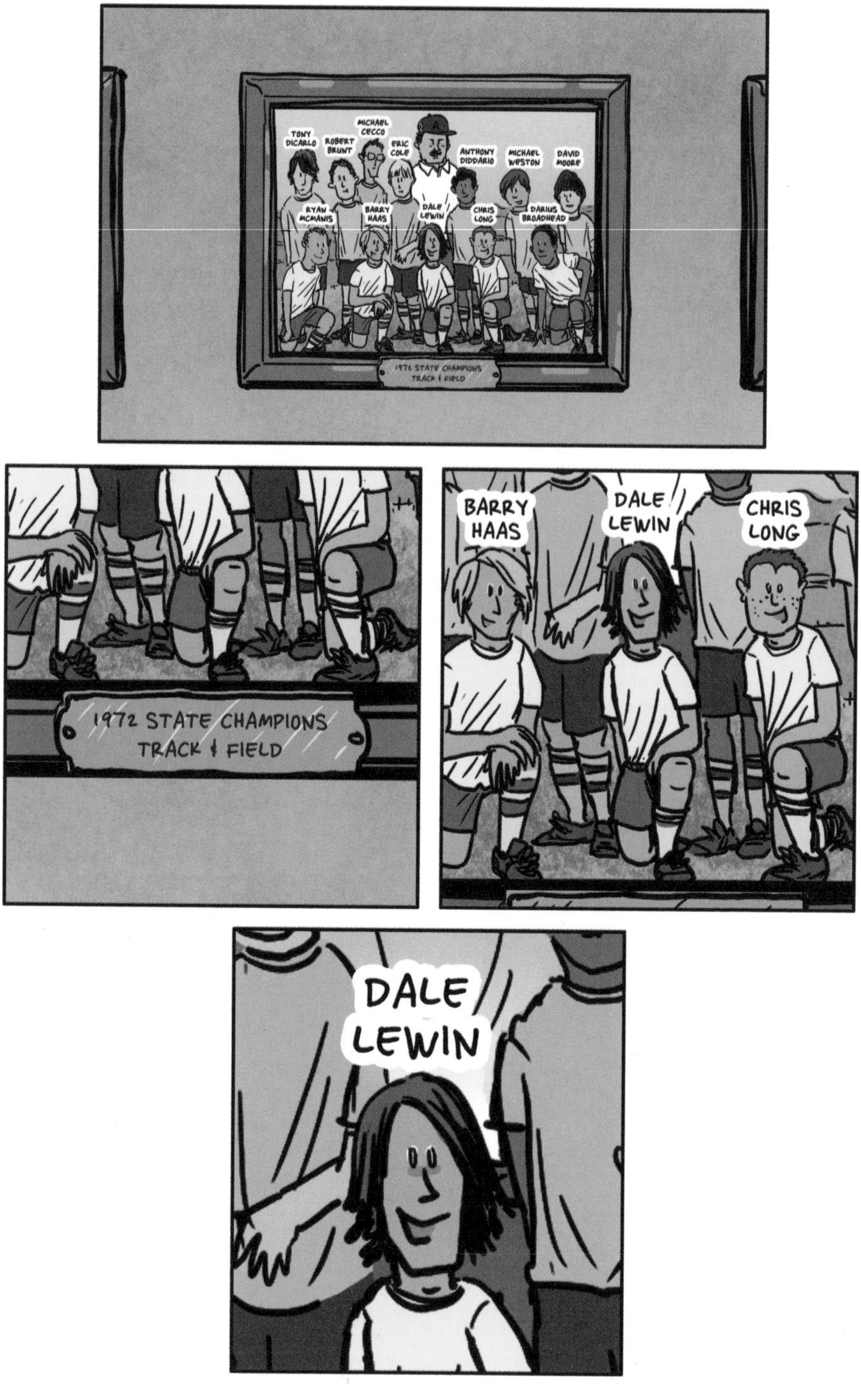
TONY DICARLO
ROBERT BRUNT
MICHAEL CECCO
ERIC COLE
ANTHONY DIDDARIO
MICHAEL WESTON
DAVID MOORE
RYAN MCMANIS
BARRY HAAS
DALE LEWIN
CHRIS LONG
DARIUS BROADHEAD
1972 STATE CHAMPIONS TRACK & FIELD
1972 STATE CHAMPIONS TRACK & FIELD
BARRY HAAS
DALE LEWIN
CHRIS LONG
DALE LEWIN

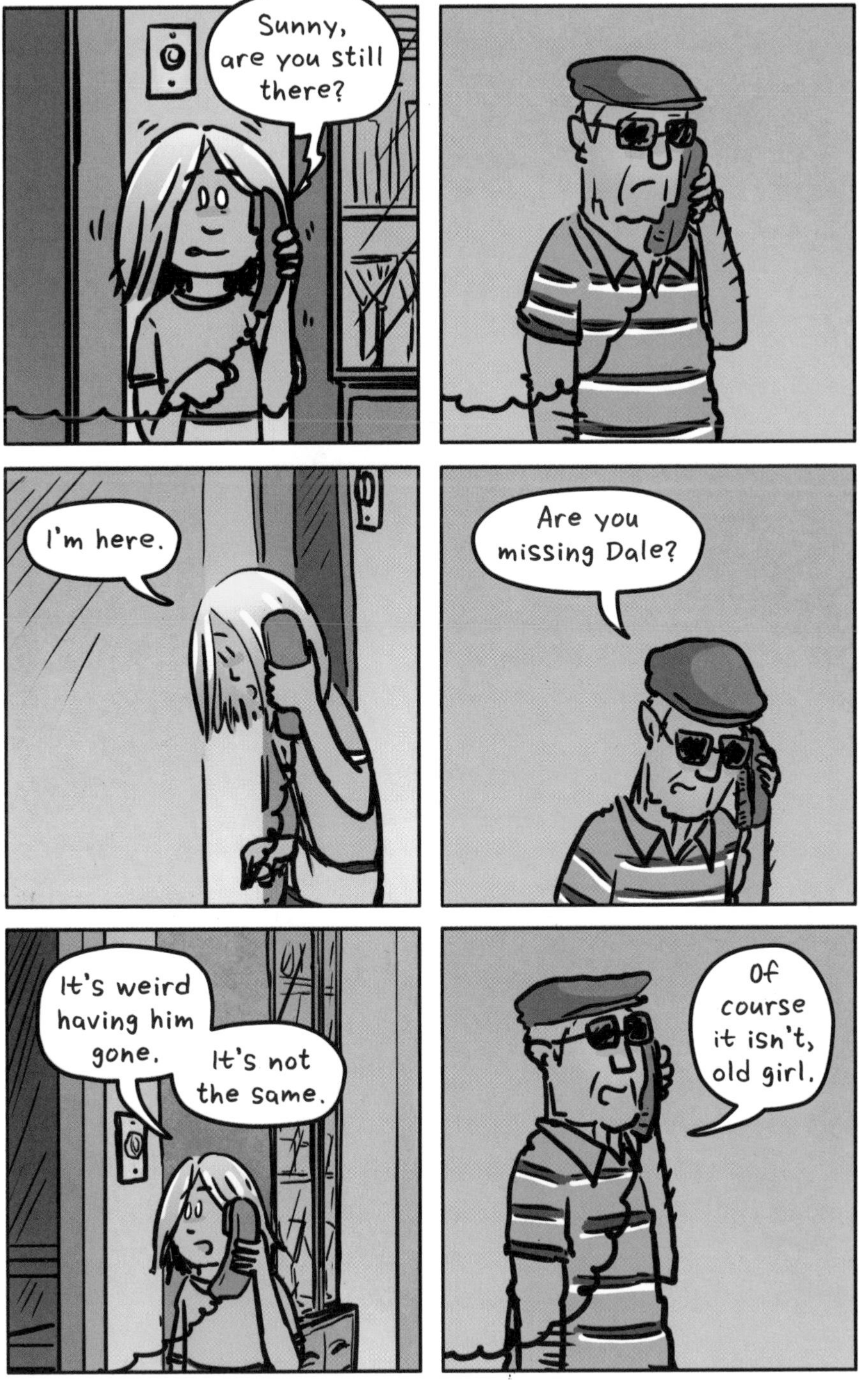
Sunny, are you still there?
I'm here.
Are you missing Dale?
It's weird having him gone.
It's not the same.
Of course it isn't, old girl.

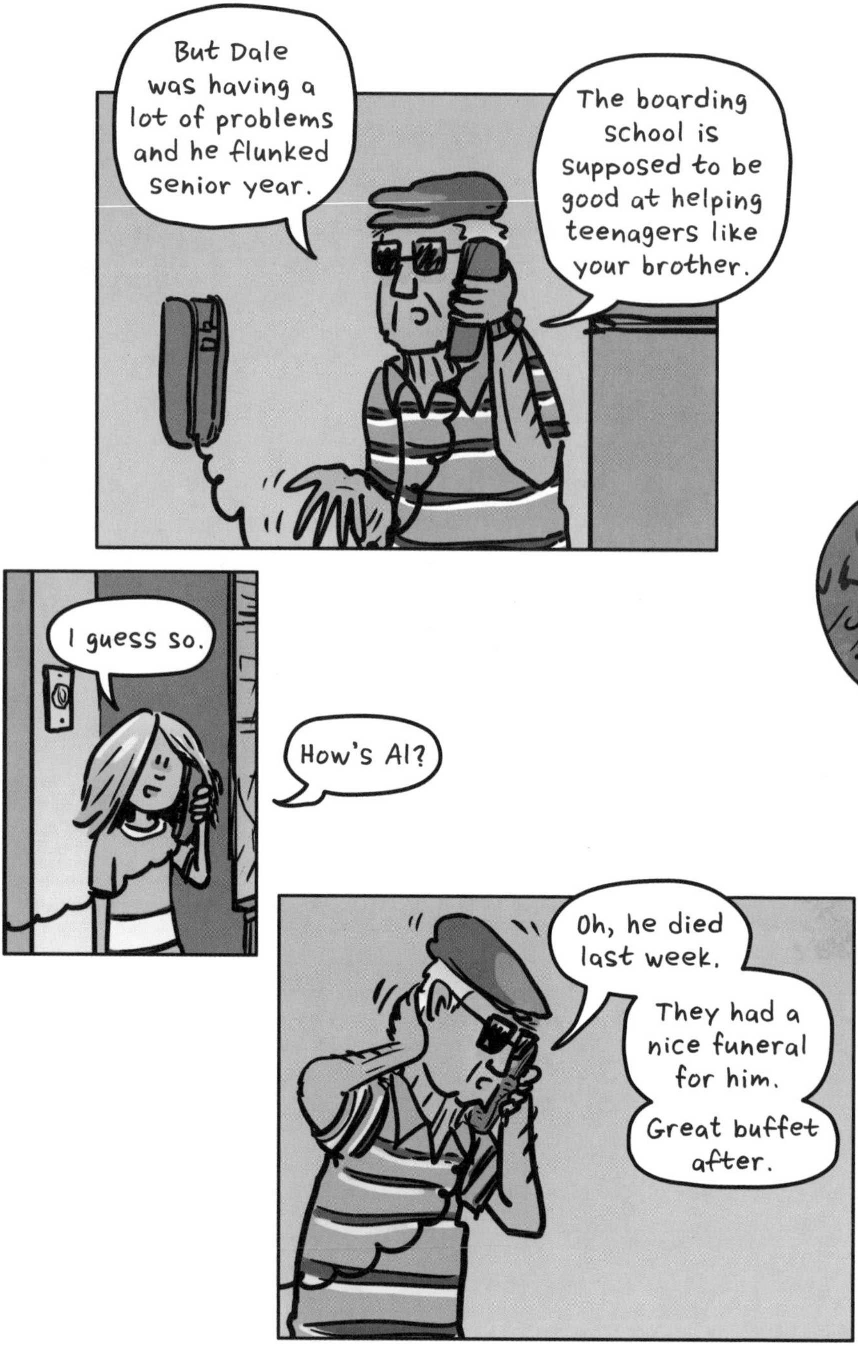
But Dale was having a lot of problems and he flunked senior year.
The boarding school is supposed to be good at helping teenagers like your brother.
I guess so.
How's Al?
Oh, he died last week.
They had a nice funeral for him.
Great buffet after.

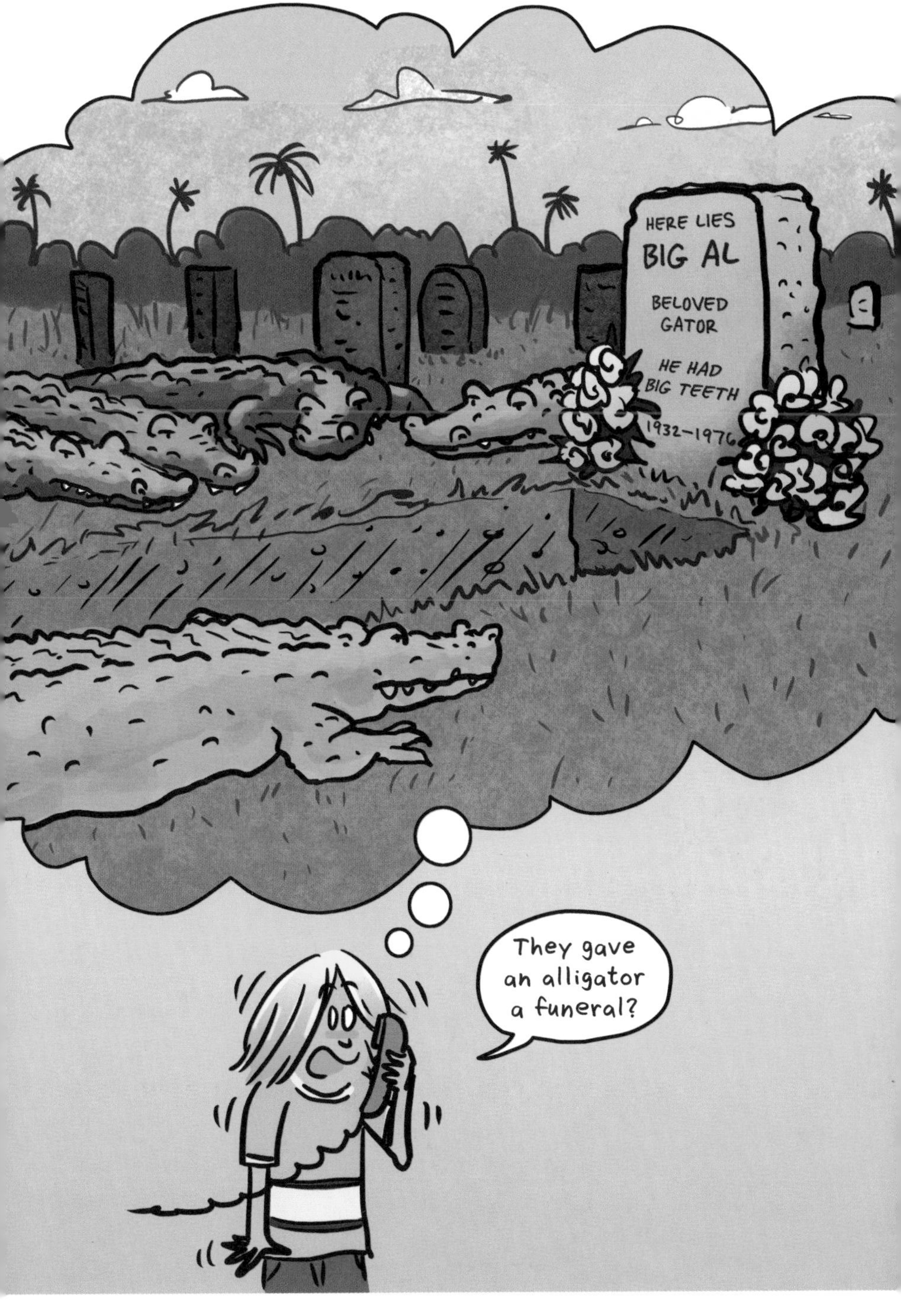
HERE LIES
BIG AL
BELOVED
GATOR
HE HAD
BIG TEETH
1932–1976
They gave an alligator a funeral?

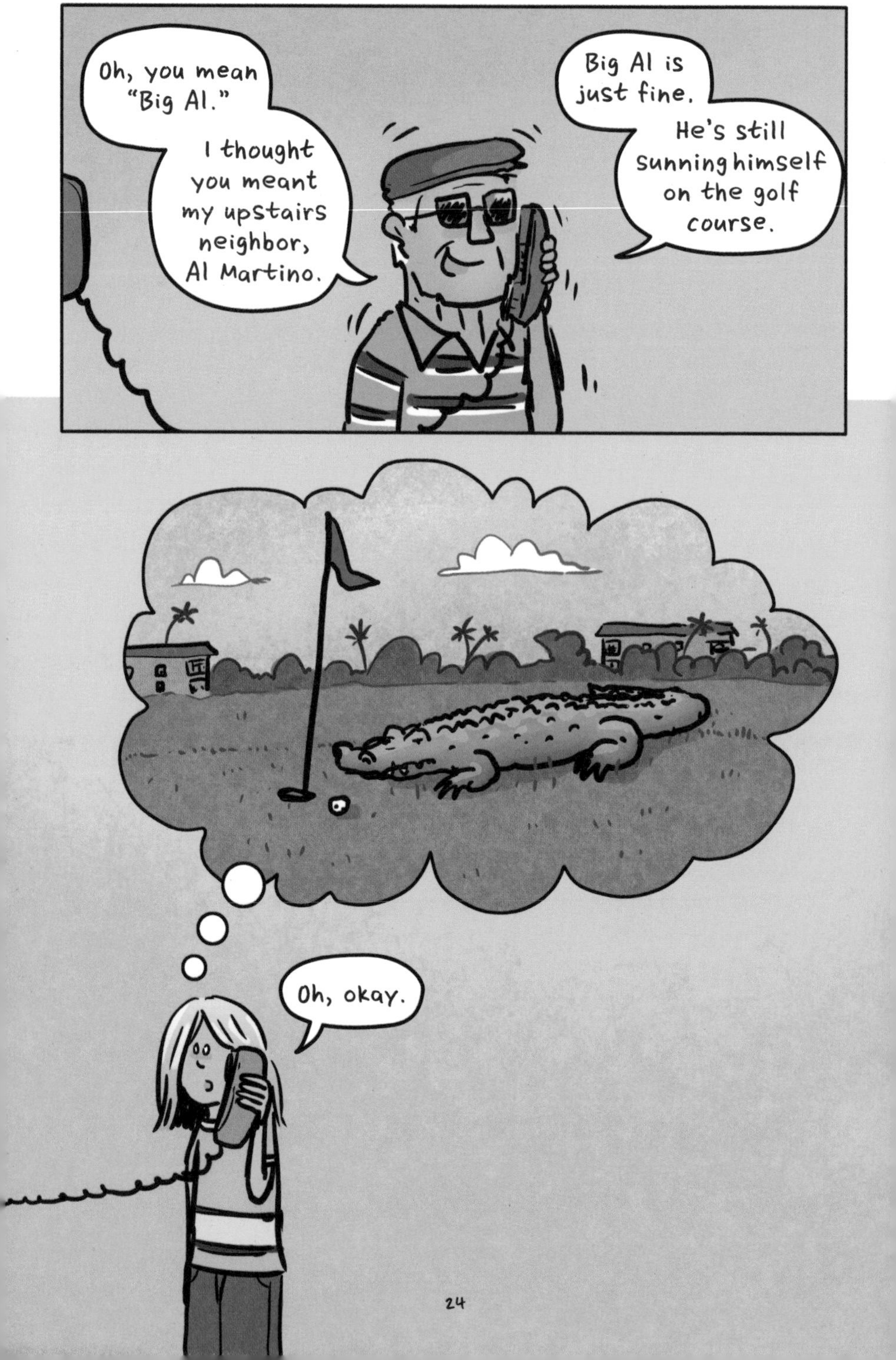
Oh, you mean "Big Al."
I thought you meant my upstairs neighbor, Al Martino.
Big Al is just fine.
He's still sunning himself on the golf course.
Oh, okay.

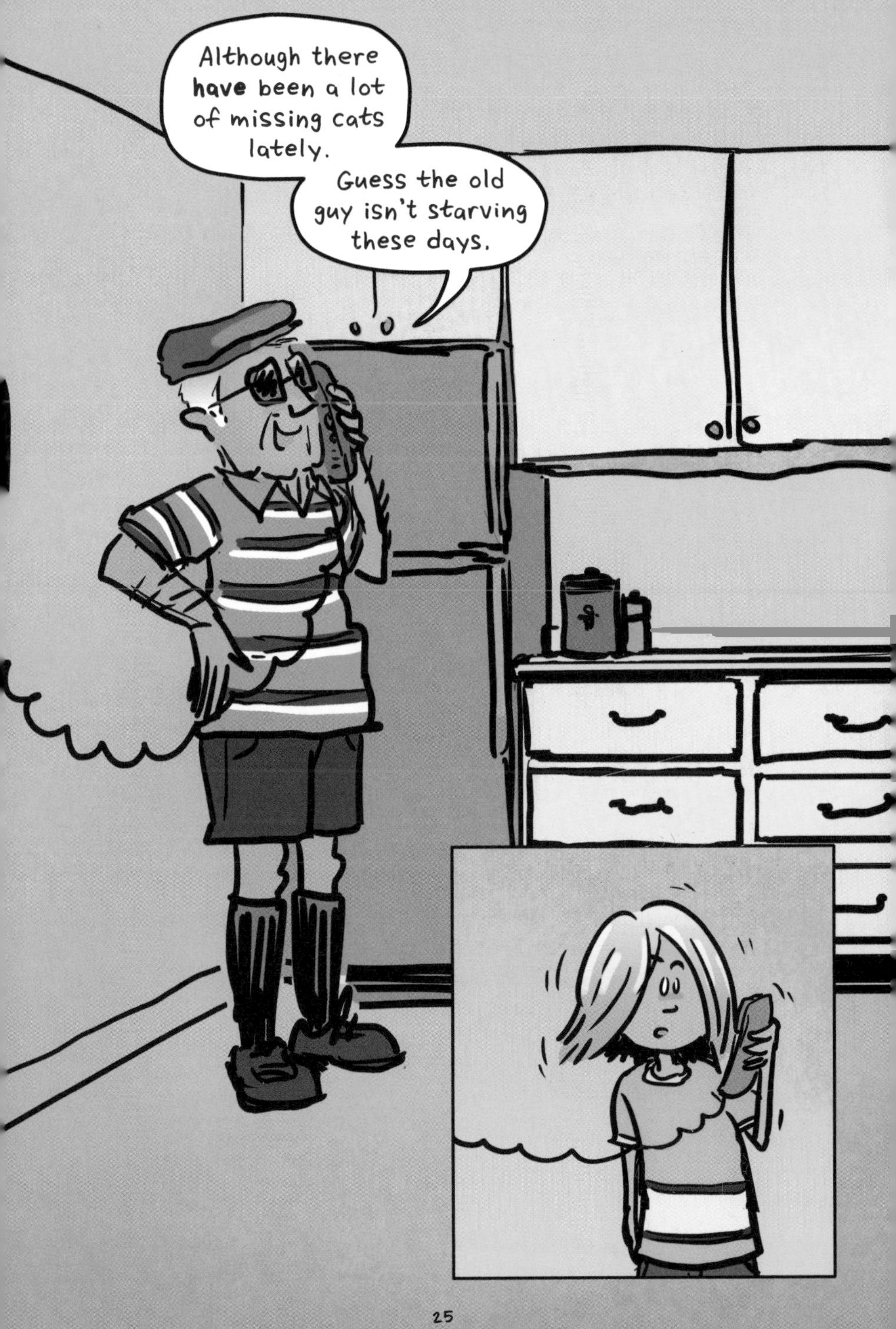
Although there **have** been a lot of missing cats lately.
Guess the old guy isn't starving these days.

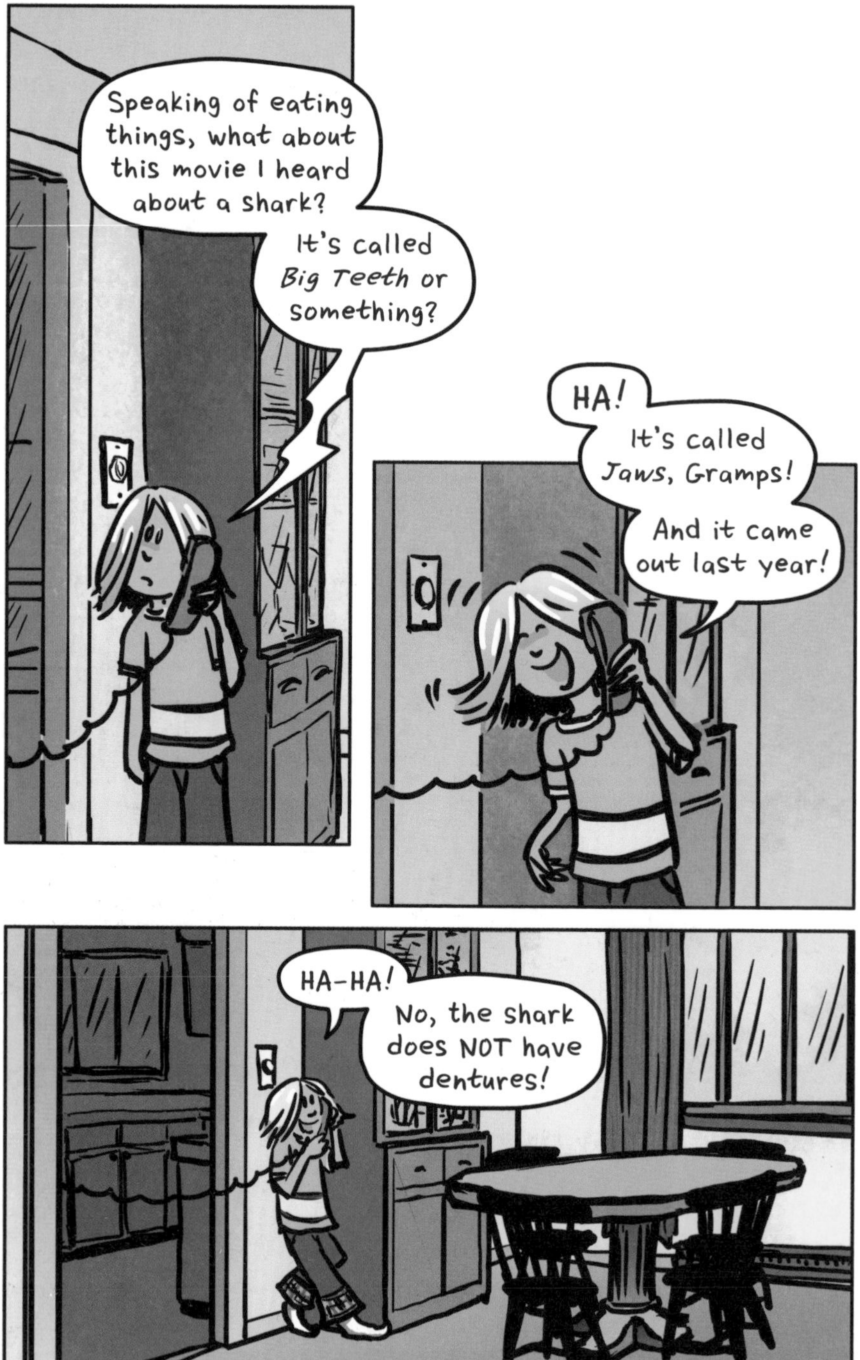
Speaking of eating things, what about this movie I heard about a shark?
It's called *Big Teeth* or something?
HA!
It's called *Jaws*, Gramps!
And it came out last year!
HA-HA!
No, the shark does NOT have dentures!

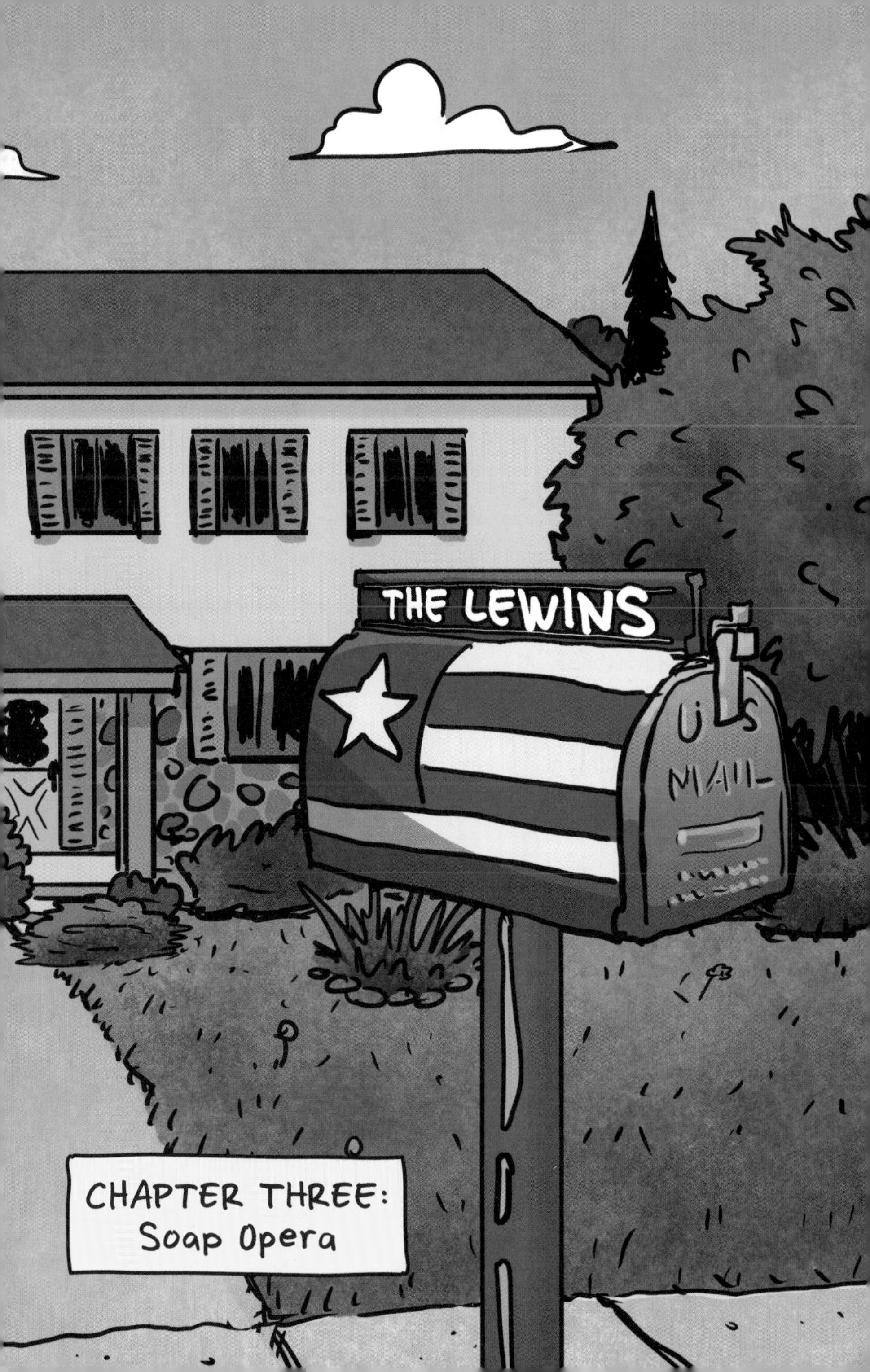
THE LEWINS
U S MAIL
CHAPTER THREE:
Soap Opera

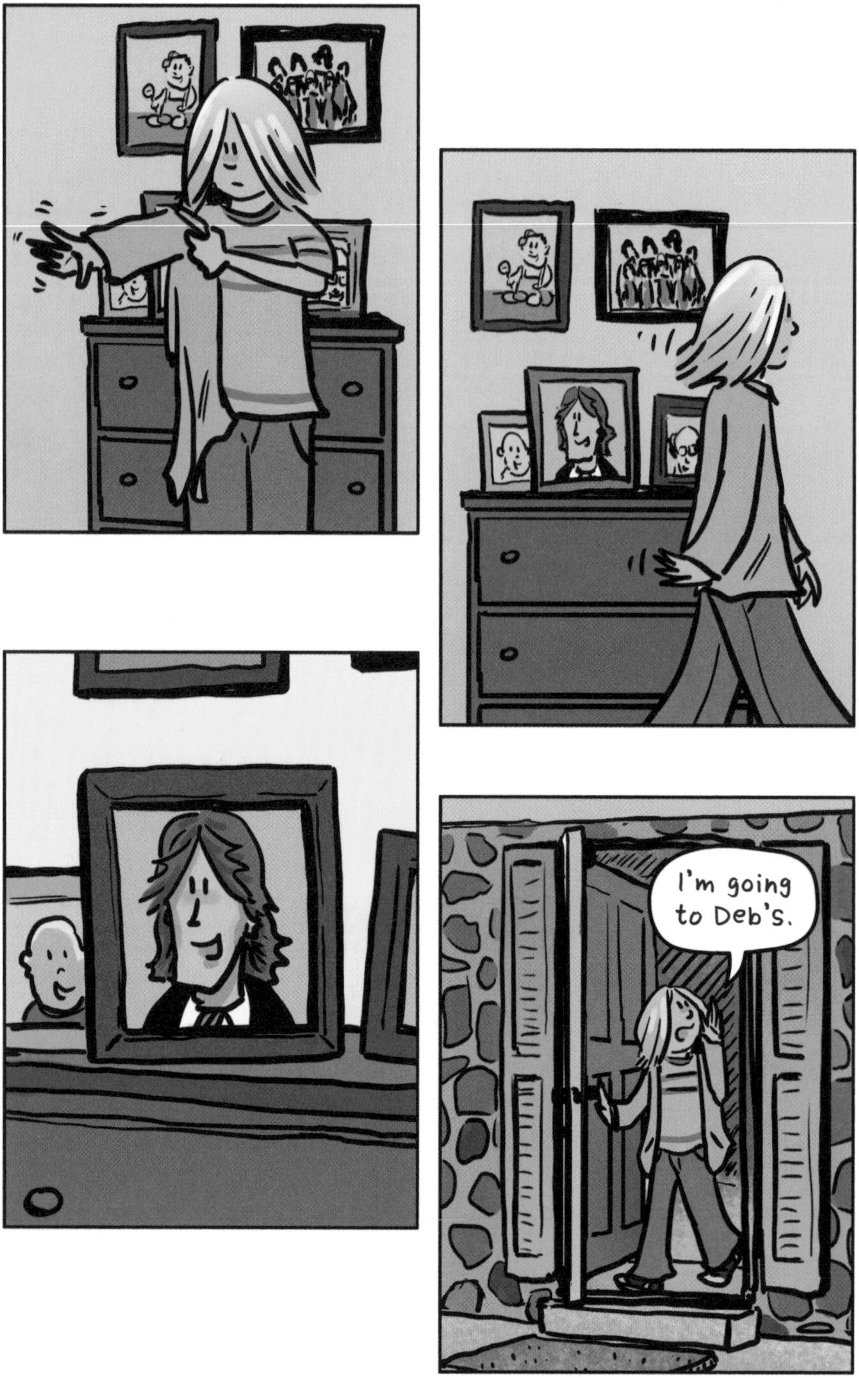
I'm going to Deb's.

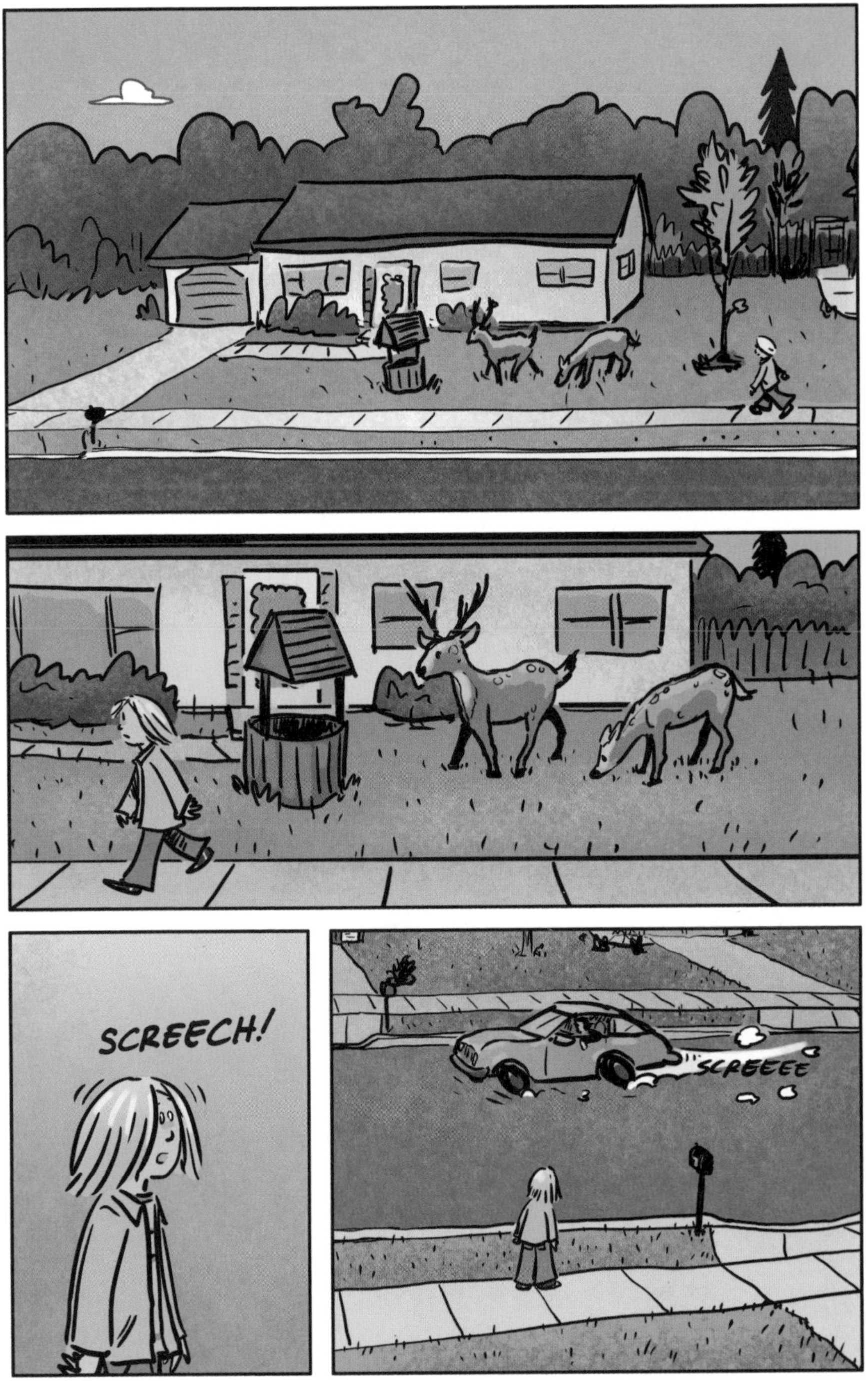
SCREECH!
SCREEEEE

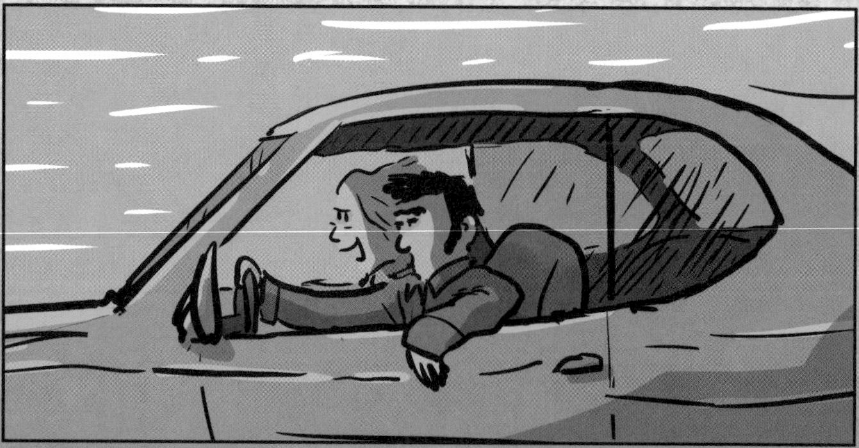

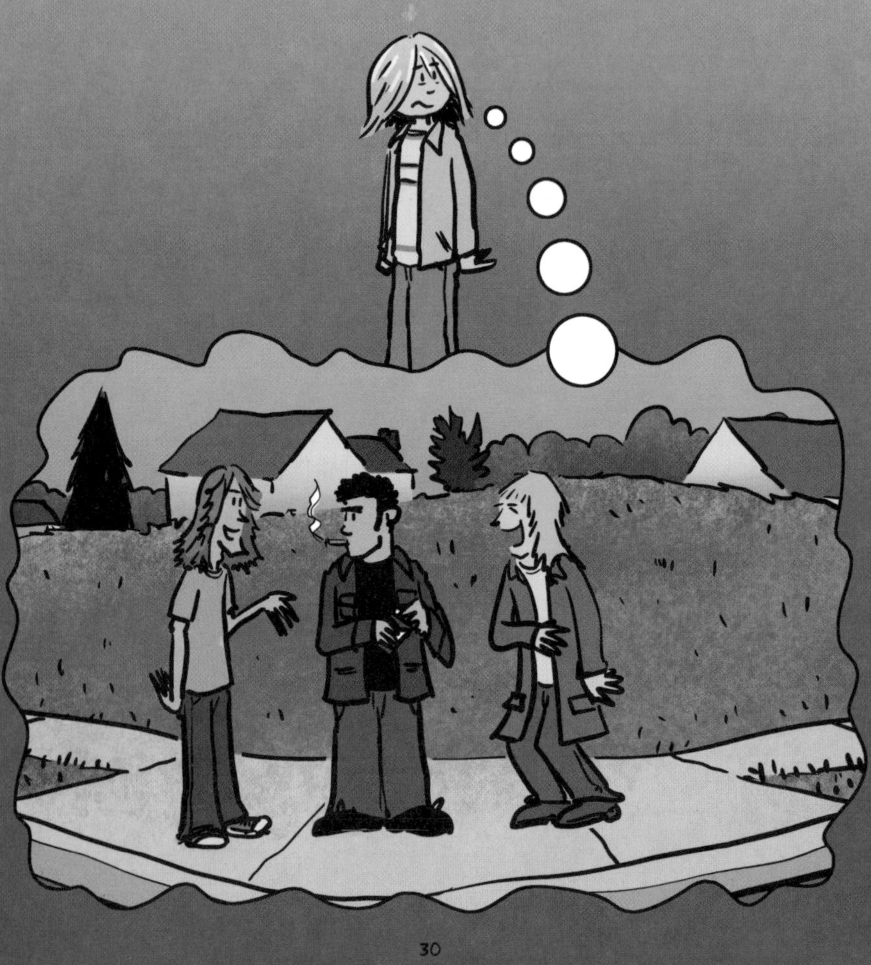

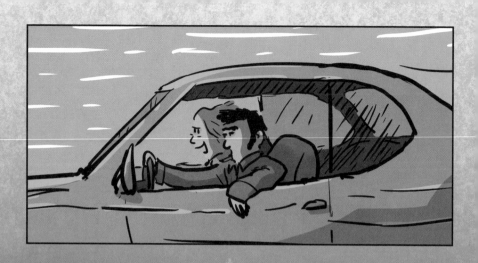

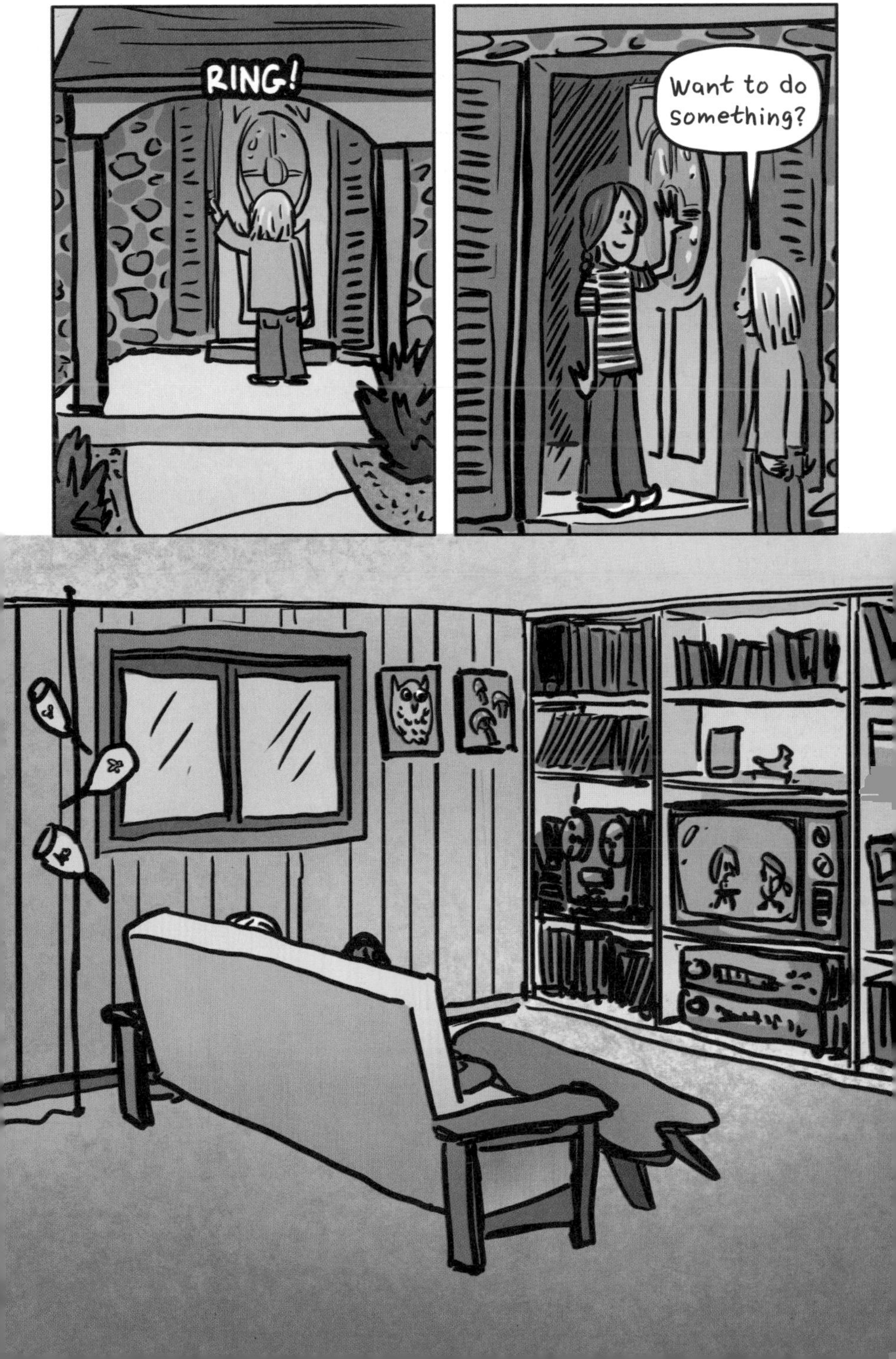
RING!
Want to do something?

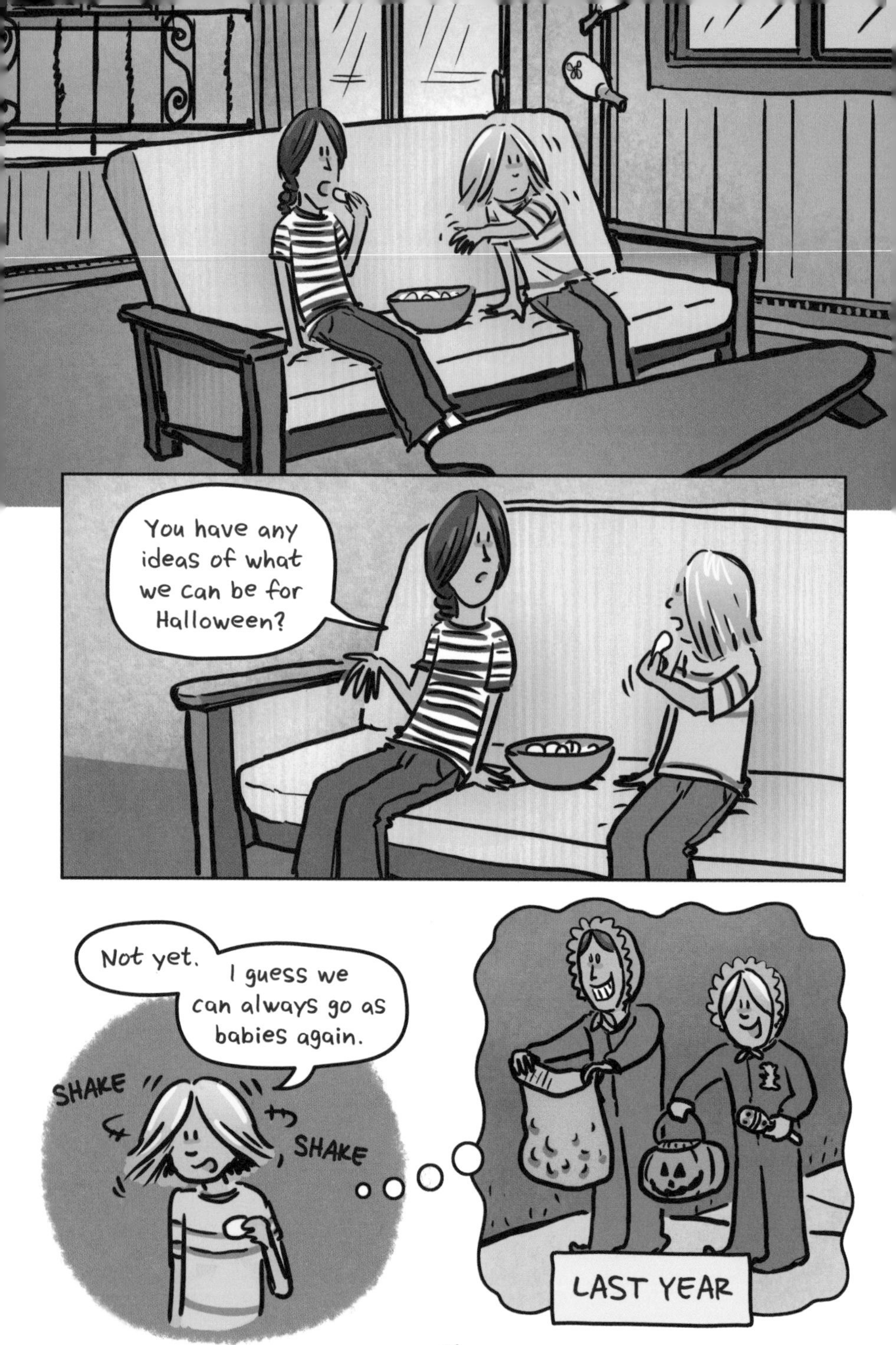
You have any ideas of what we can be for Halloween?
Not yet.
I guess we can always go as babies again.
SHAKE
SHAKE
LAST YEAR

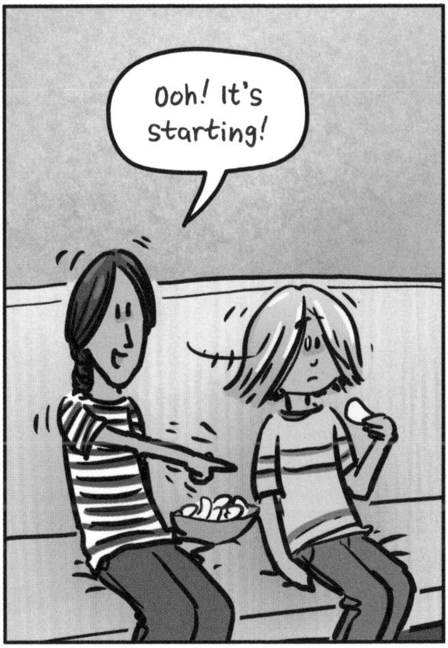
Ooh! It's starting!

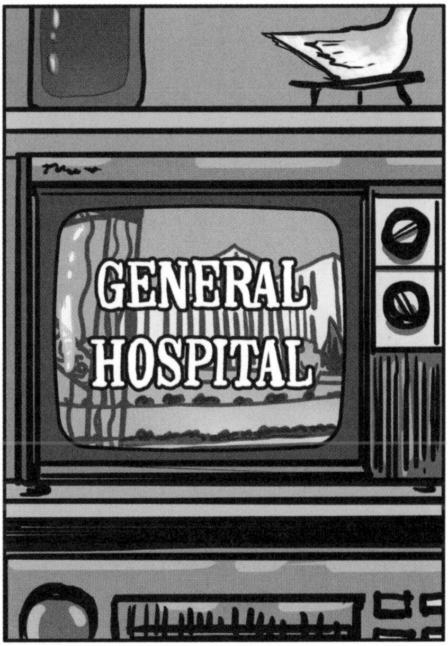
GENERAL HOSPITAL

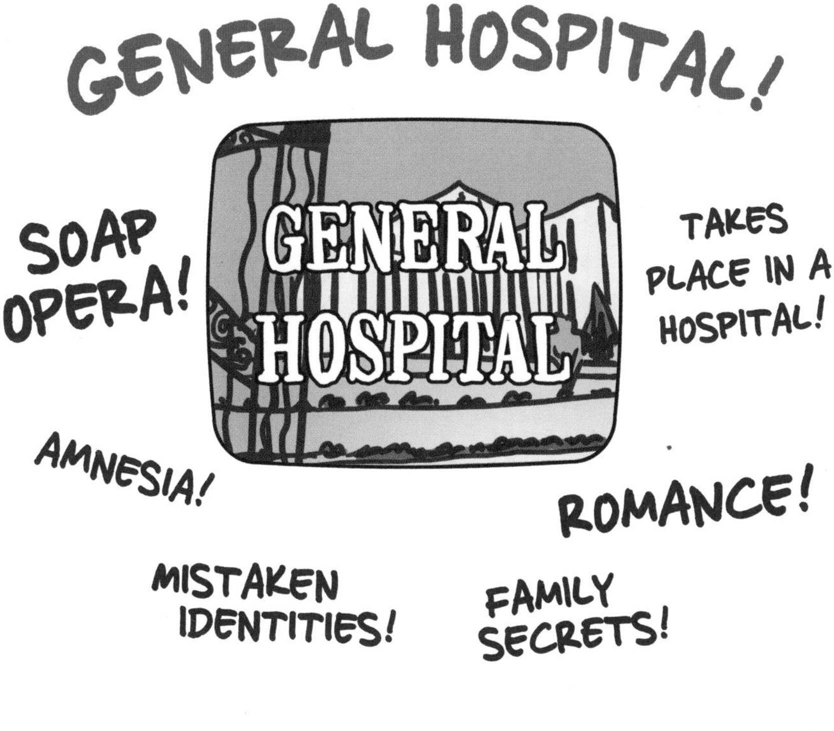
GENERAL HOSPITAL!
SOAP OPERA!
GENERAL HOSPITAL
TAKES PLACE IN A HOSPITAL!
AMNESIA!
ROMANCE!
MISTAKEN IDENTITIES!
FAMILY SECRETS!

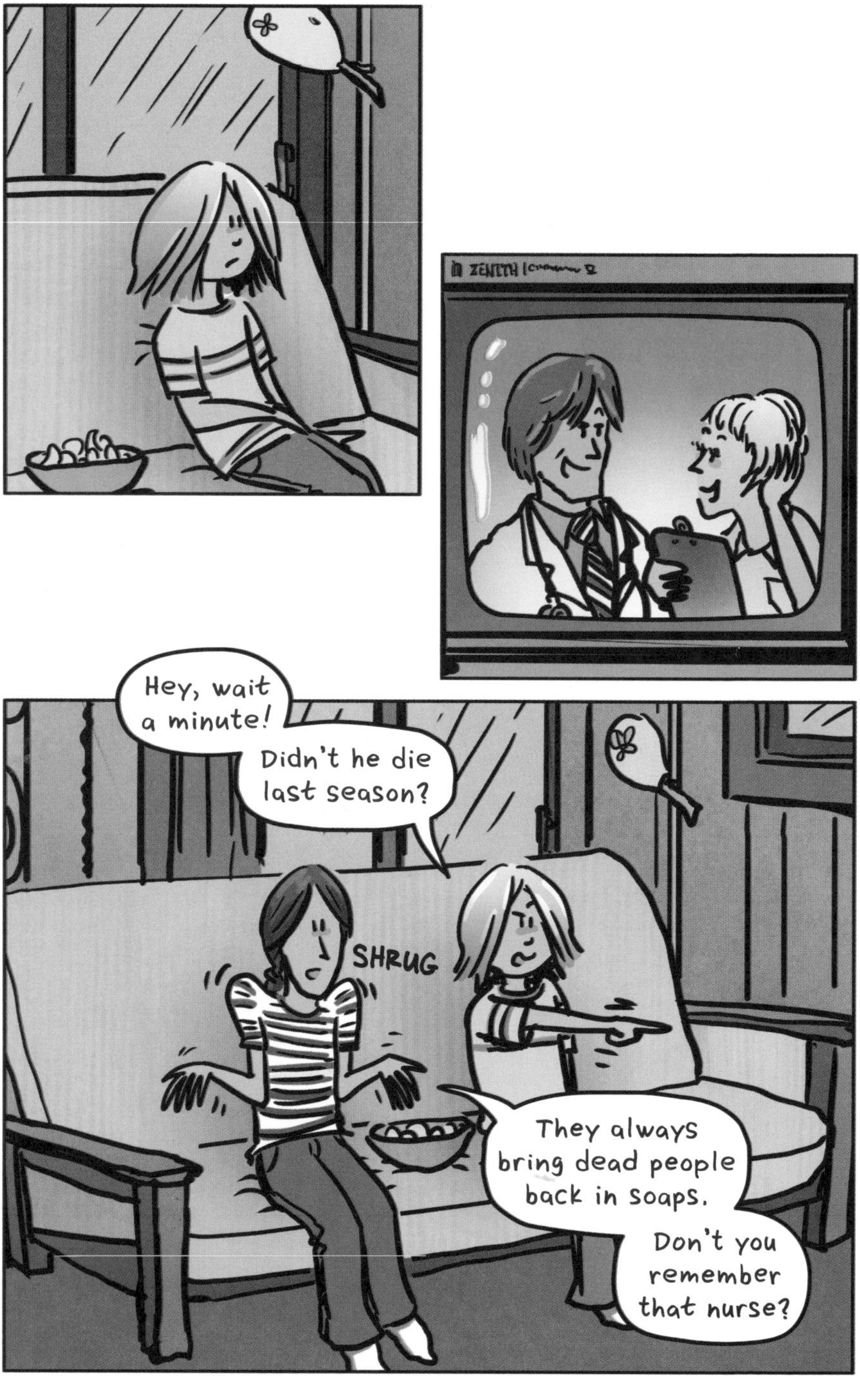
ZENITH
Hey, wait a minute!
Didn't he die last season?
SHRUG
They always bring dead people back in soaps.
Don't you remember that nurse?

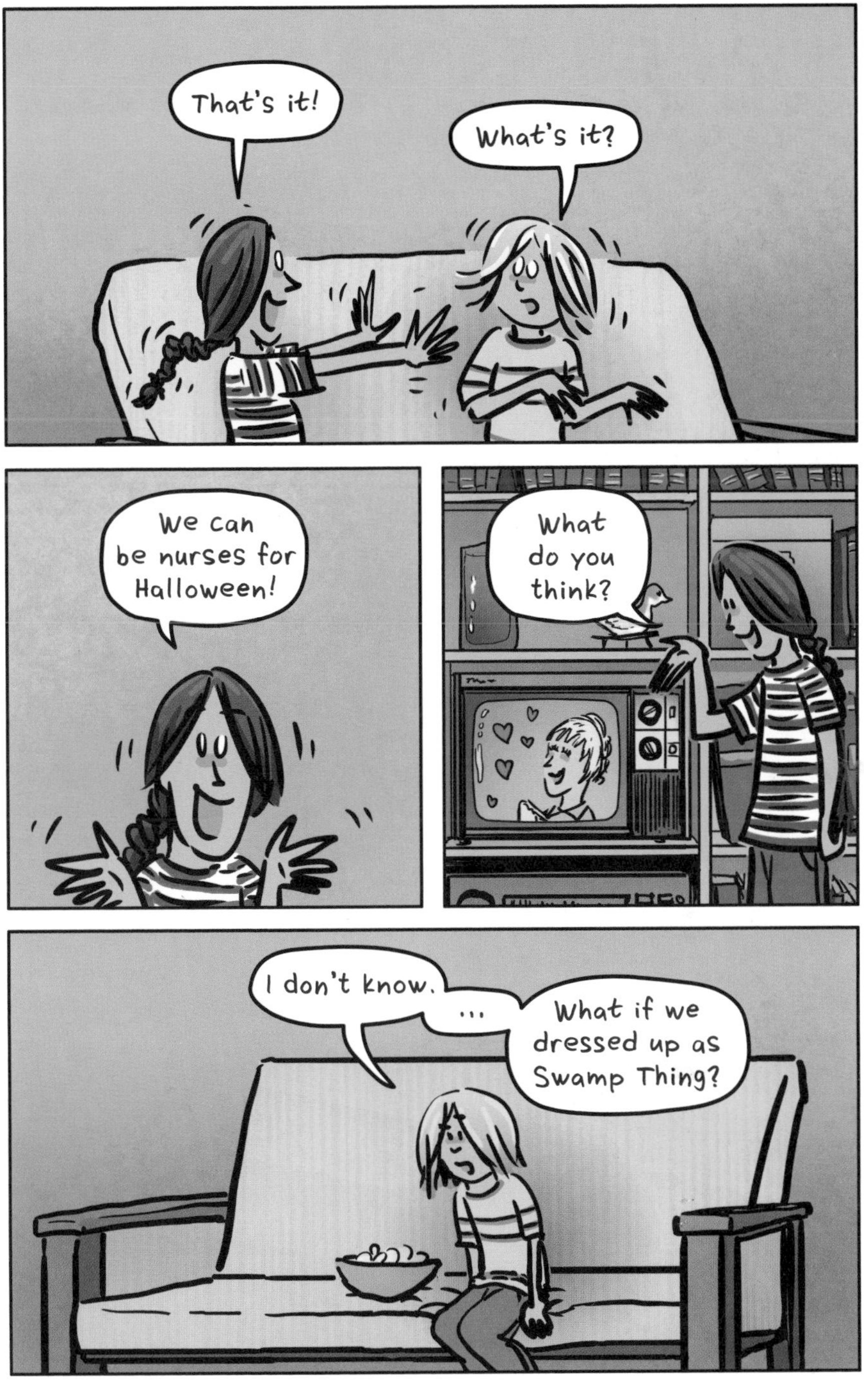
That's it!
What's it?
We can be nurses for Halloween!
What do you think?
I don't know.
...
What if we dressed up as Swamp Thing?

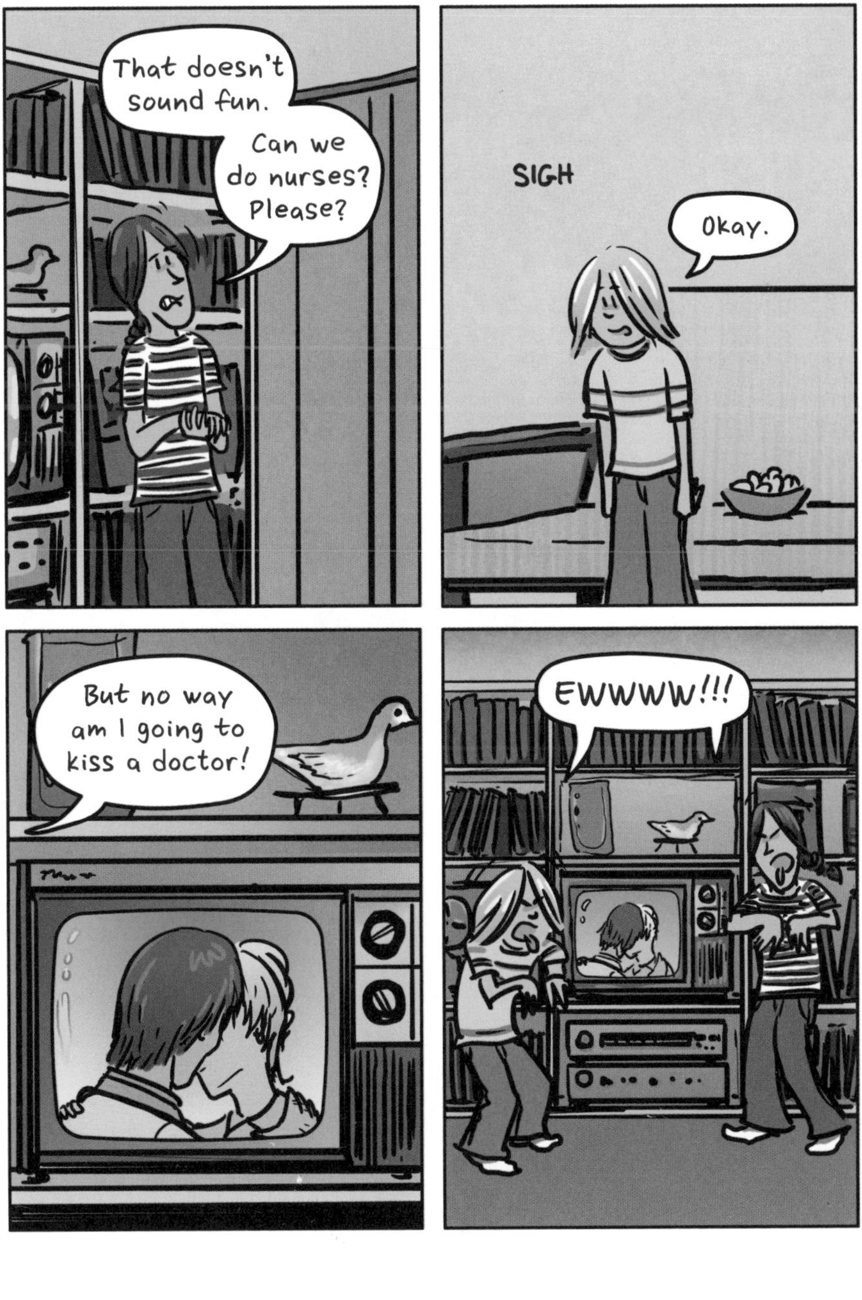
That doesn't sound fun.
Can we do nurses? Please?
SIGH
Okay.
But no way am I going to kiss a doctor!
EWWWW!!!

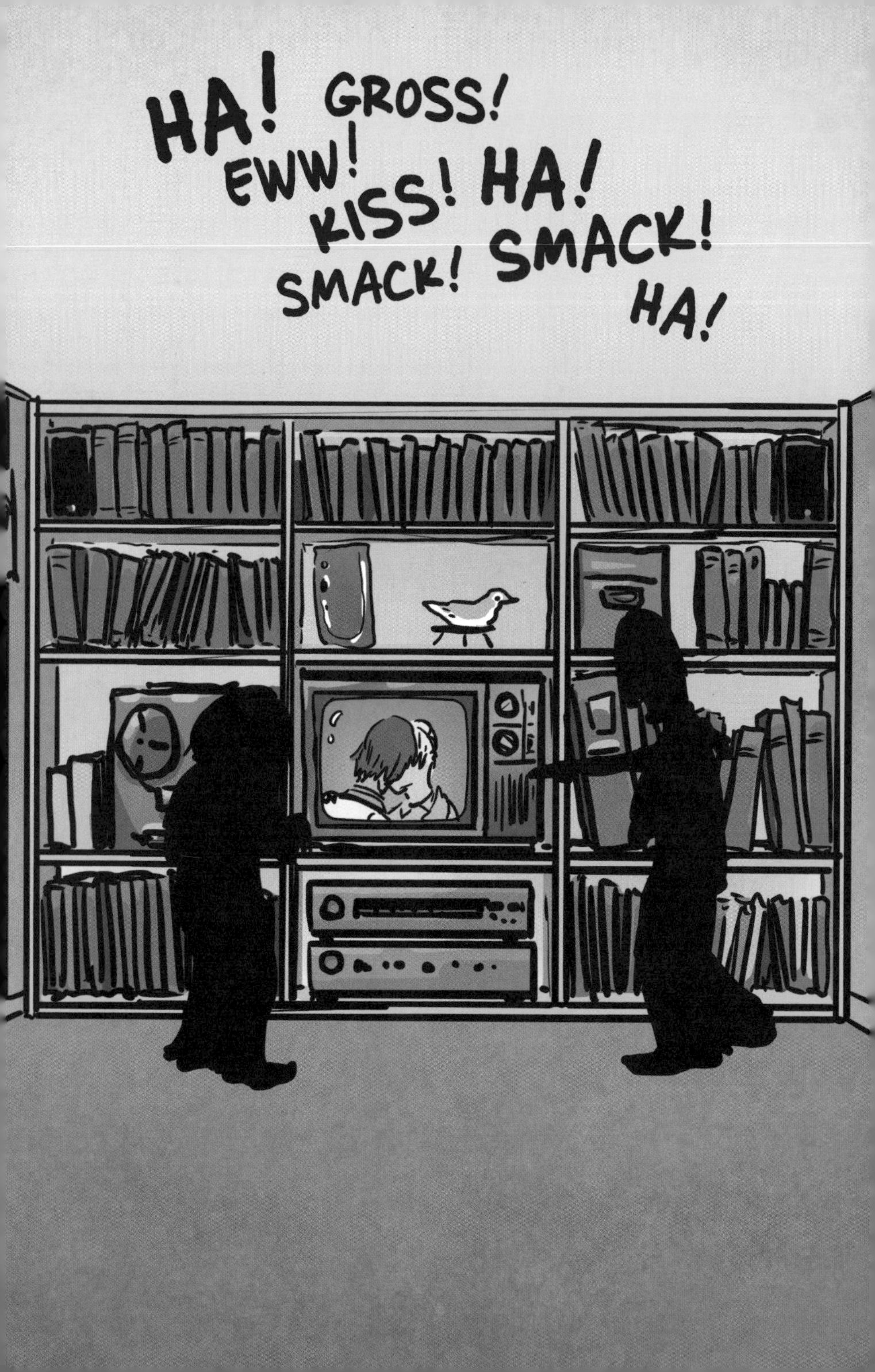
HA!
GROSS!
EWW!
KISS!
HA!
SMACK!
SMACK!
HA!

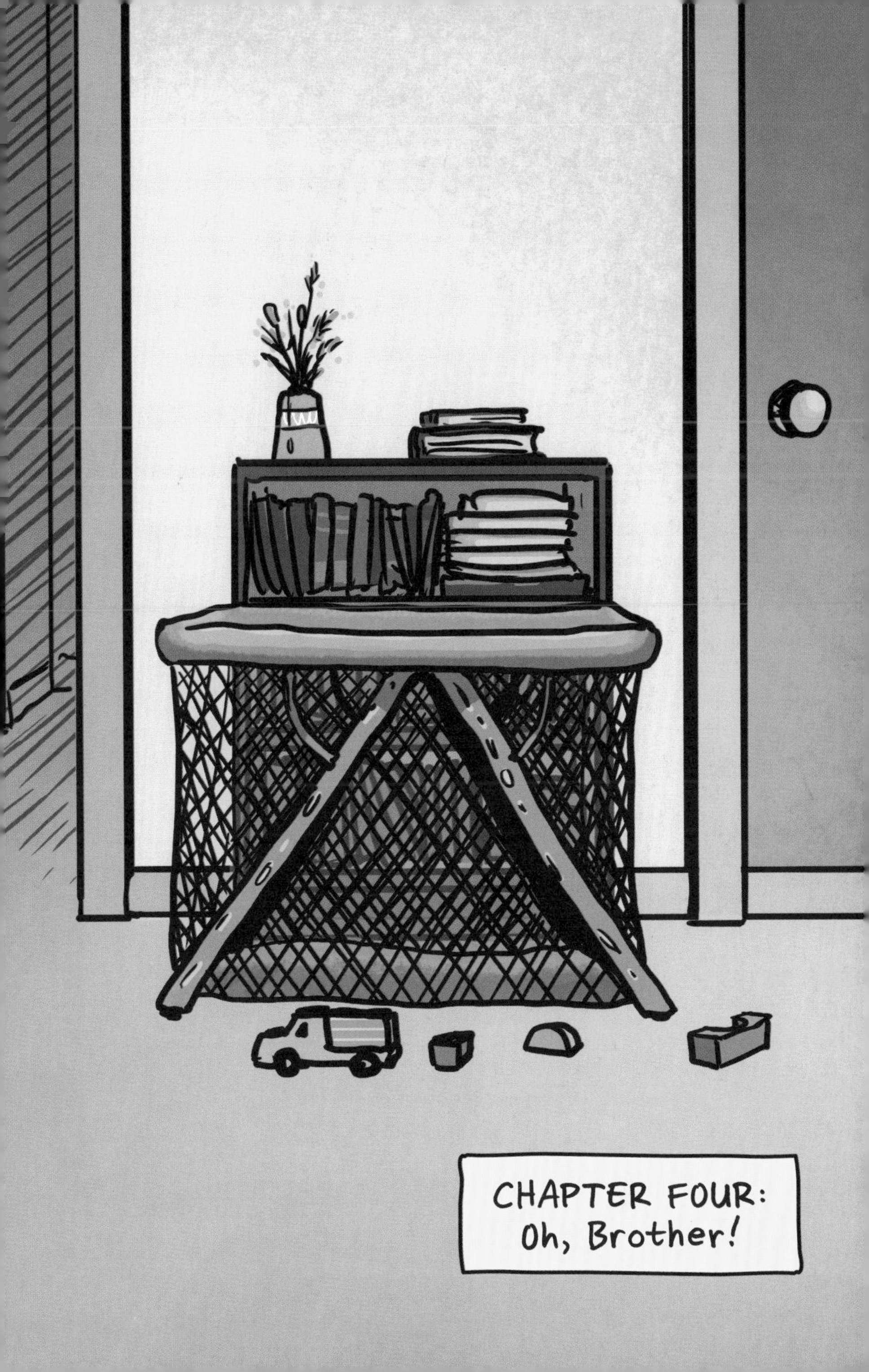
CHAPTER FOUR:
Oh, Brother!

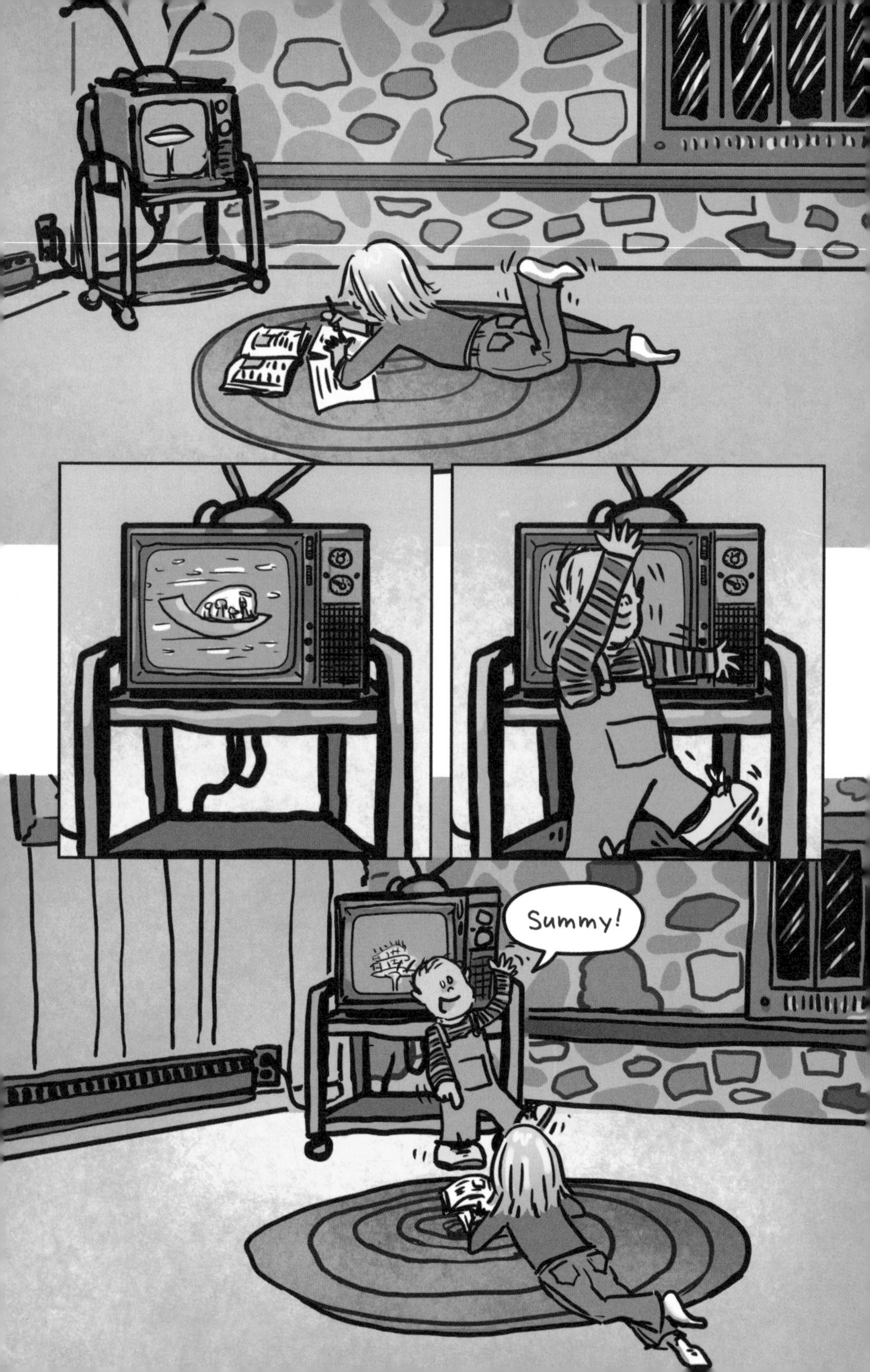
Summy!

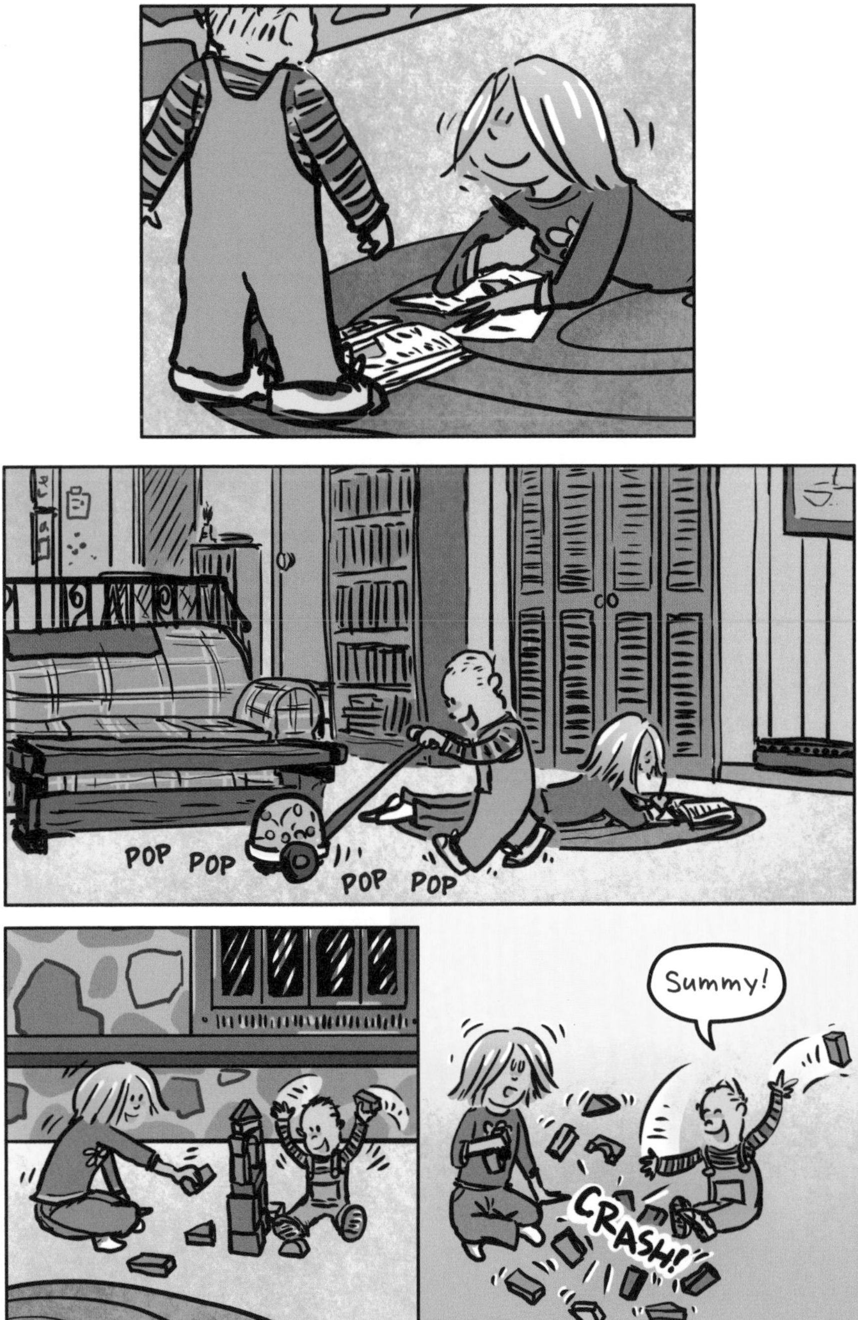
POP POP POP POP
Summy!
CRASH!

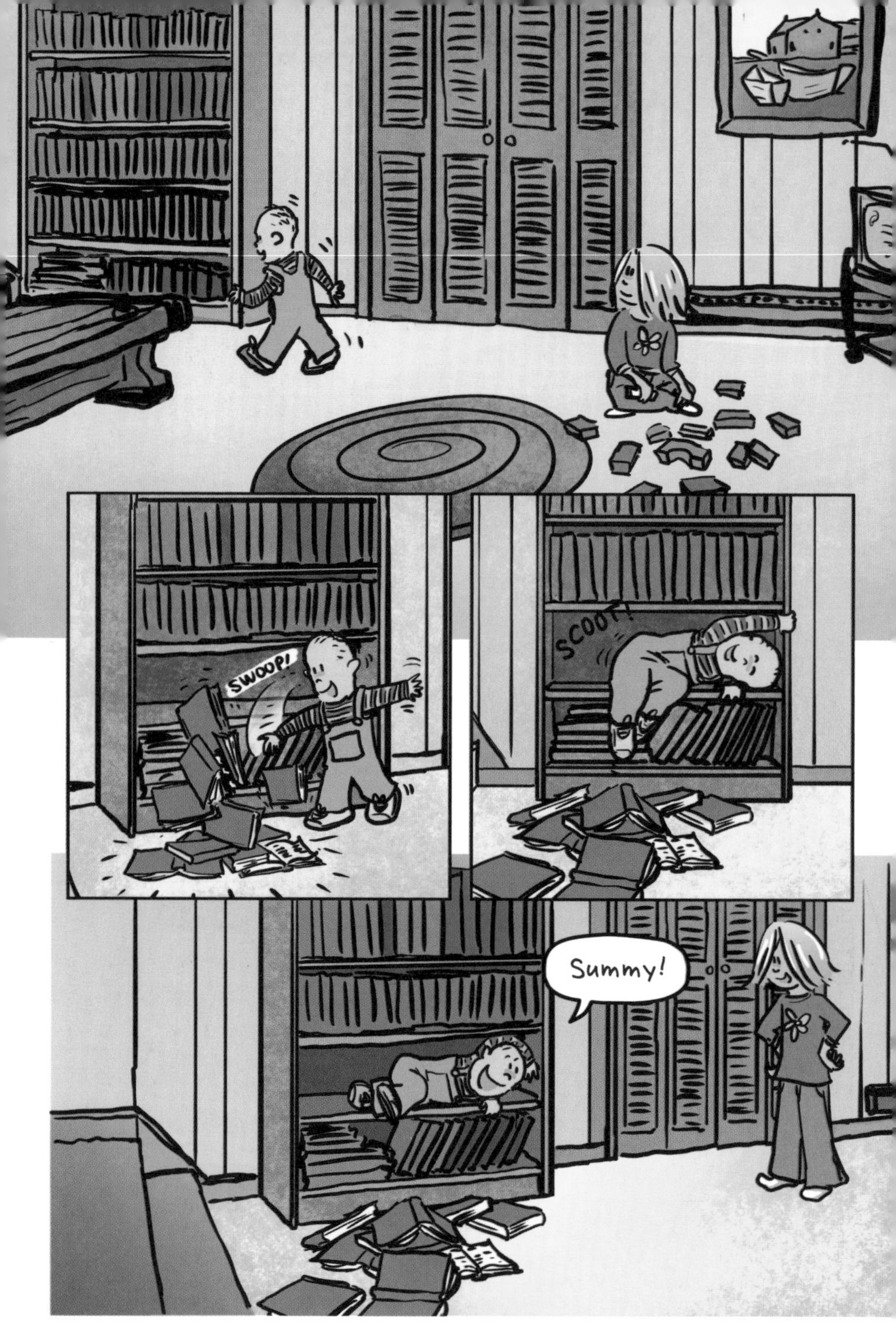
SWOOP!
SCOOT!
Summy!

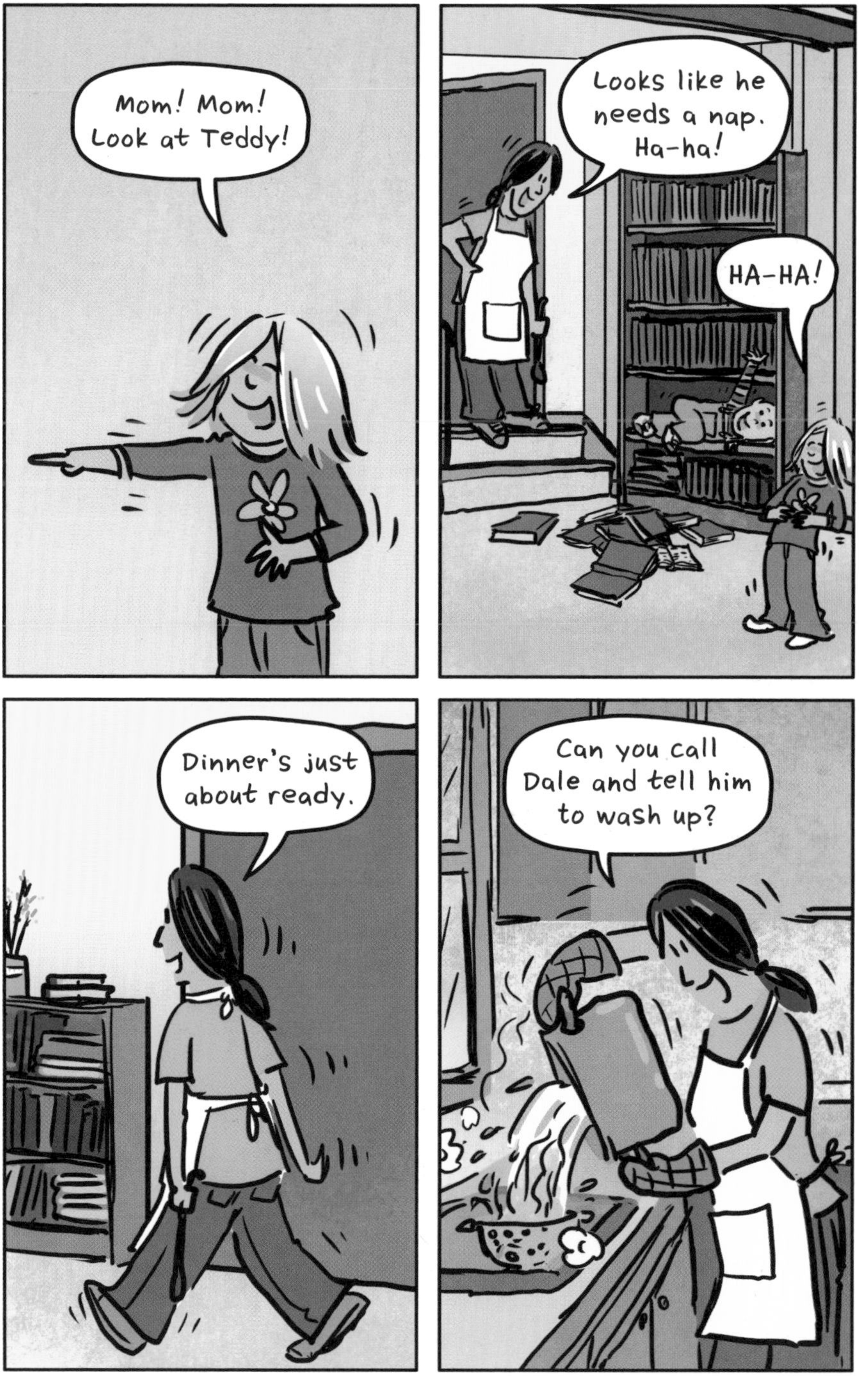
Mom! Mom! Look at Teddy!
Looks like he needs a nap. Ha-ha!
HA-HA!
Dinner's just about ready.
Can you call Dale and tell him to wash up?

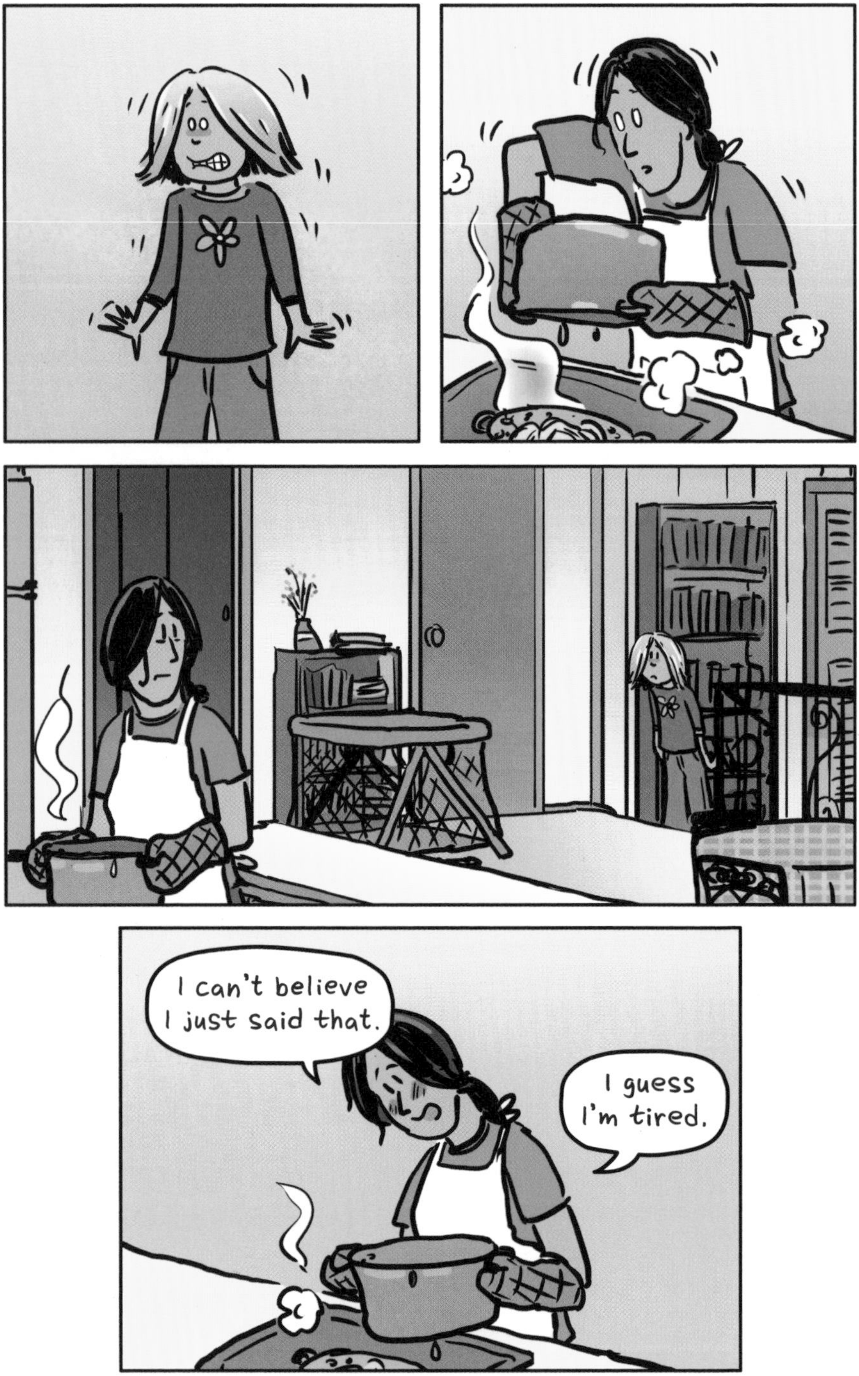
I can't believe I just said that.
I guess I'm tired.

That night.

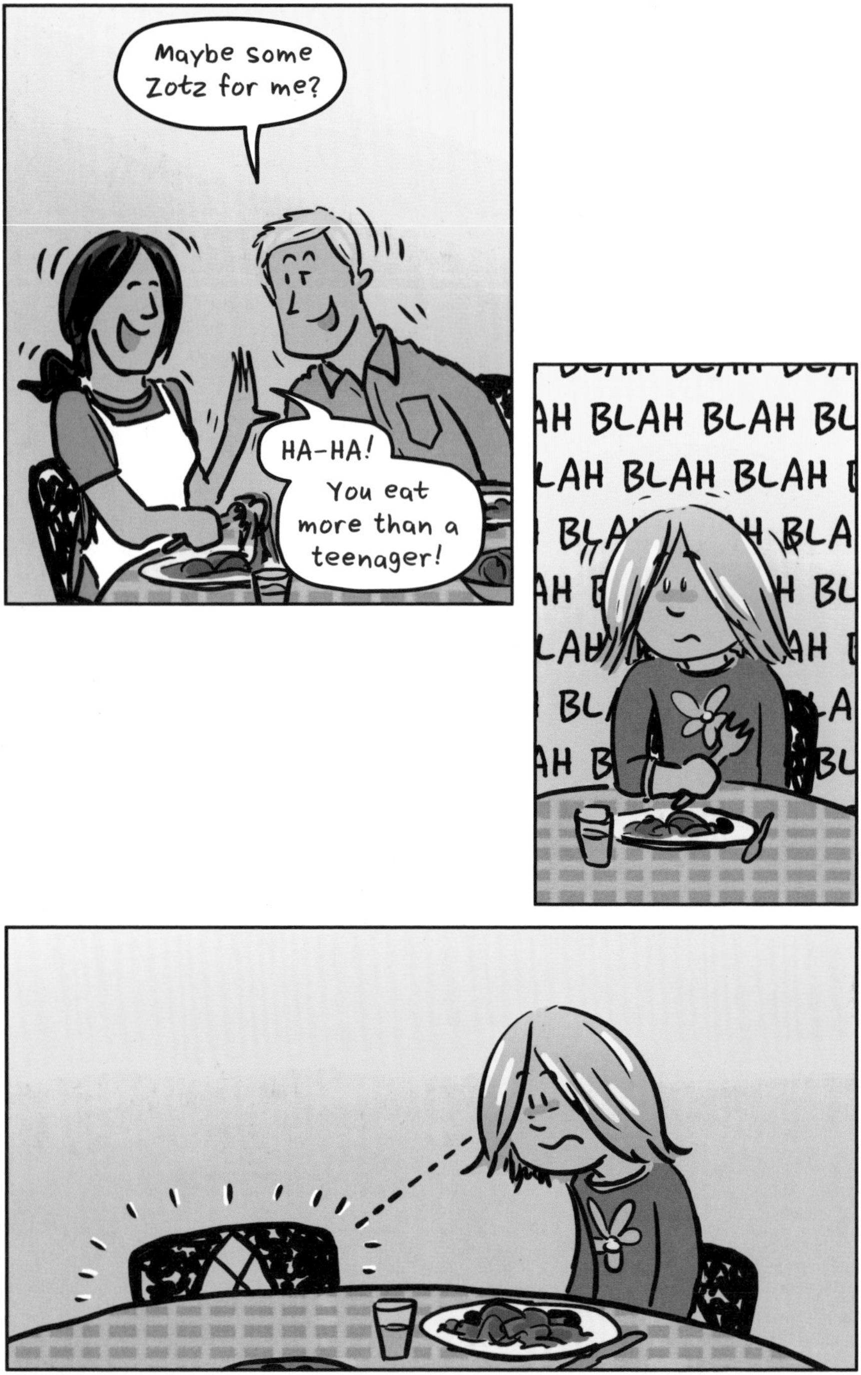
Maybe some Zotz for me?
HA-HA! You eat more than a teenager!
BLAH BLAH
BLAH BLAH

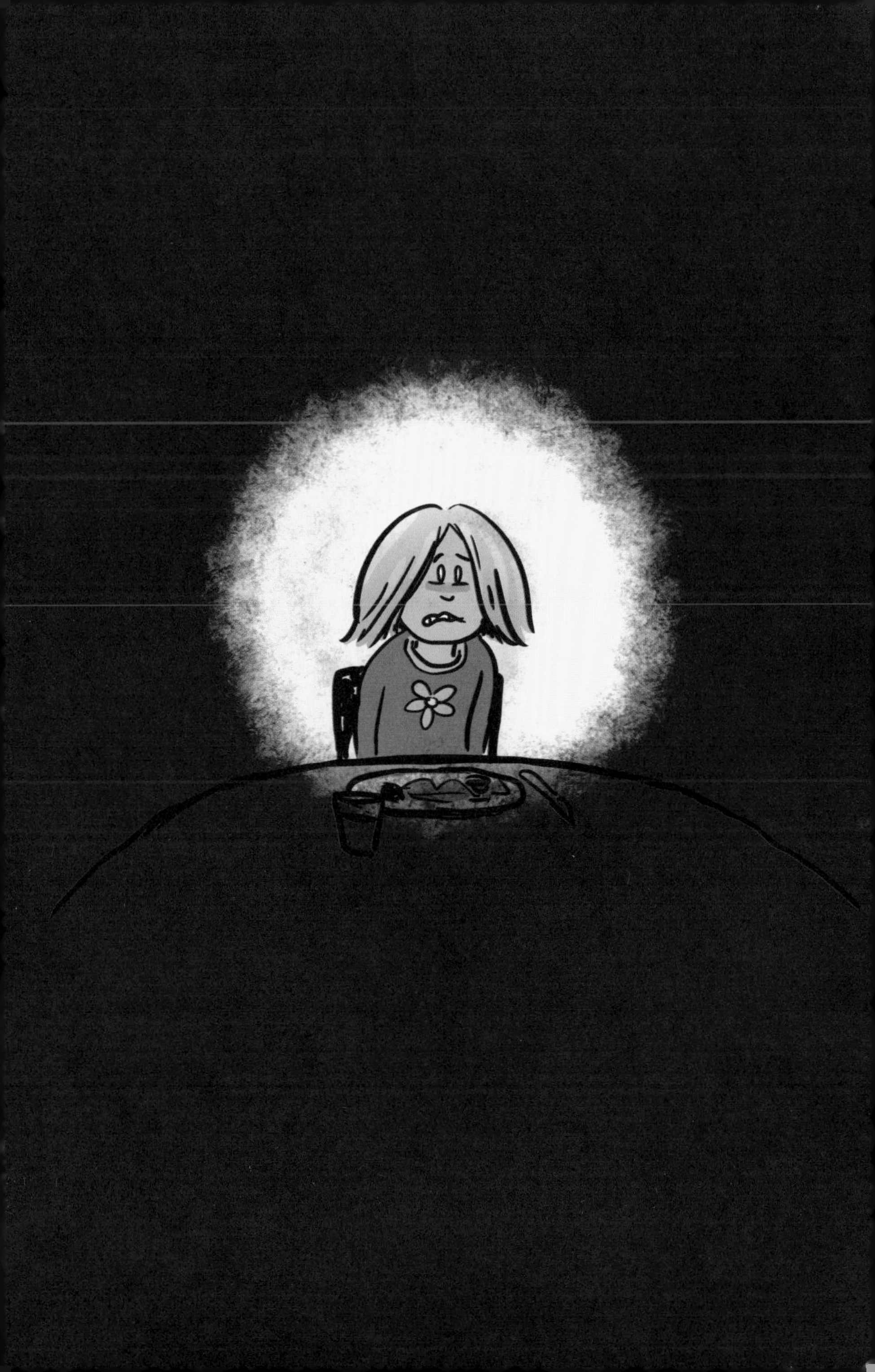

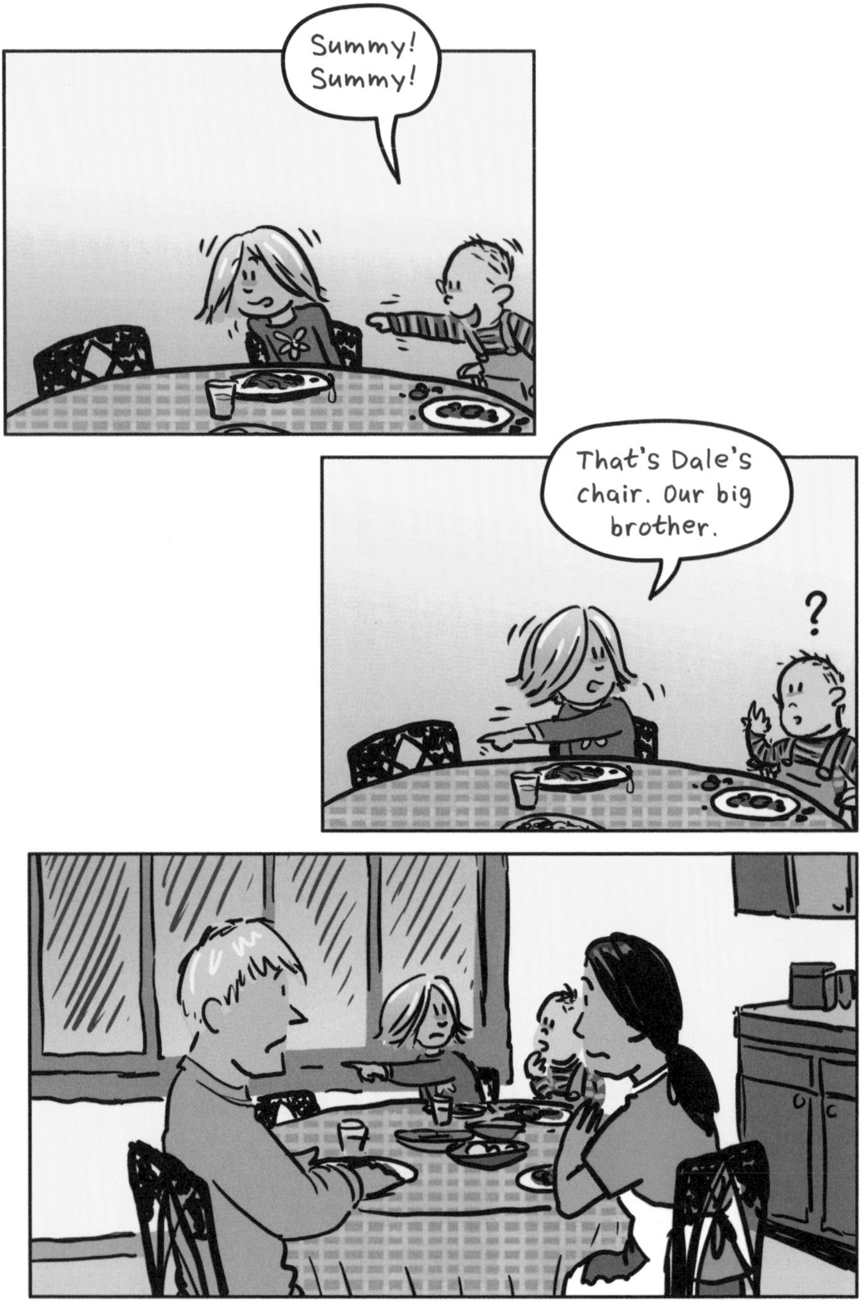
Summy! Summy!
That's Dale's chair. Our big brother.
?

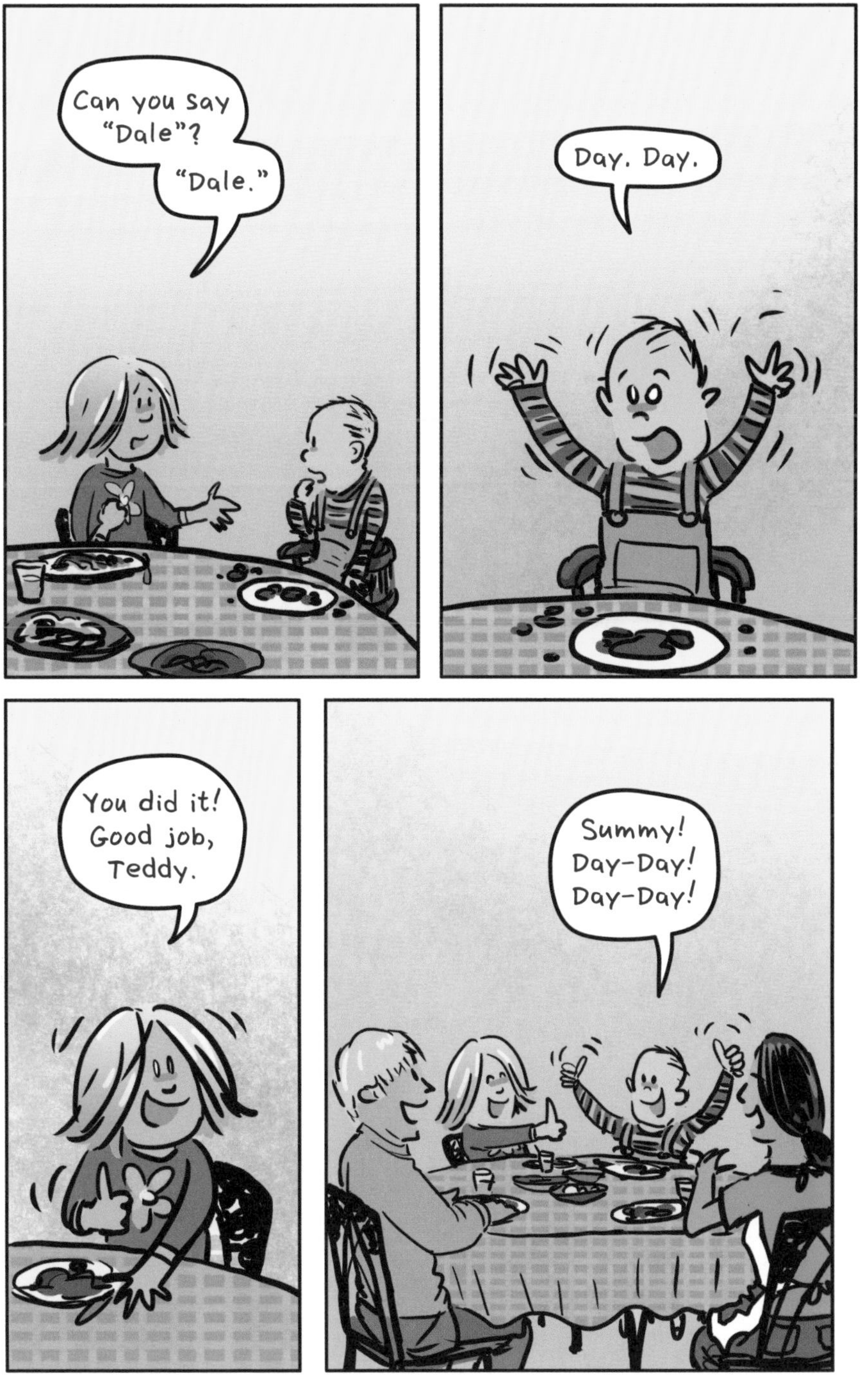
Can you say "Dale"?
"Dale."
Day. Day.
You did it! Good job, Teddy.
Summy! Day-Day! Day-Day!

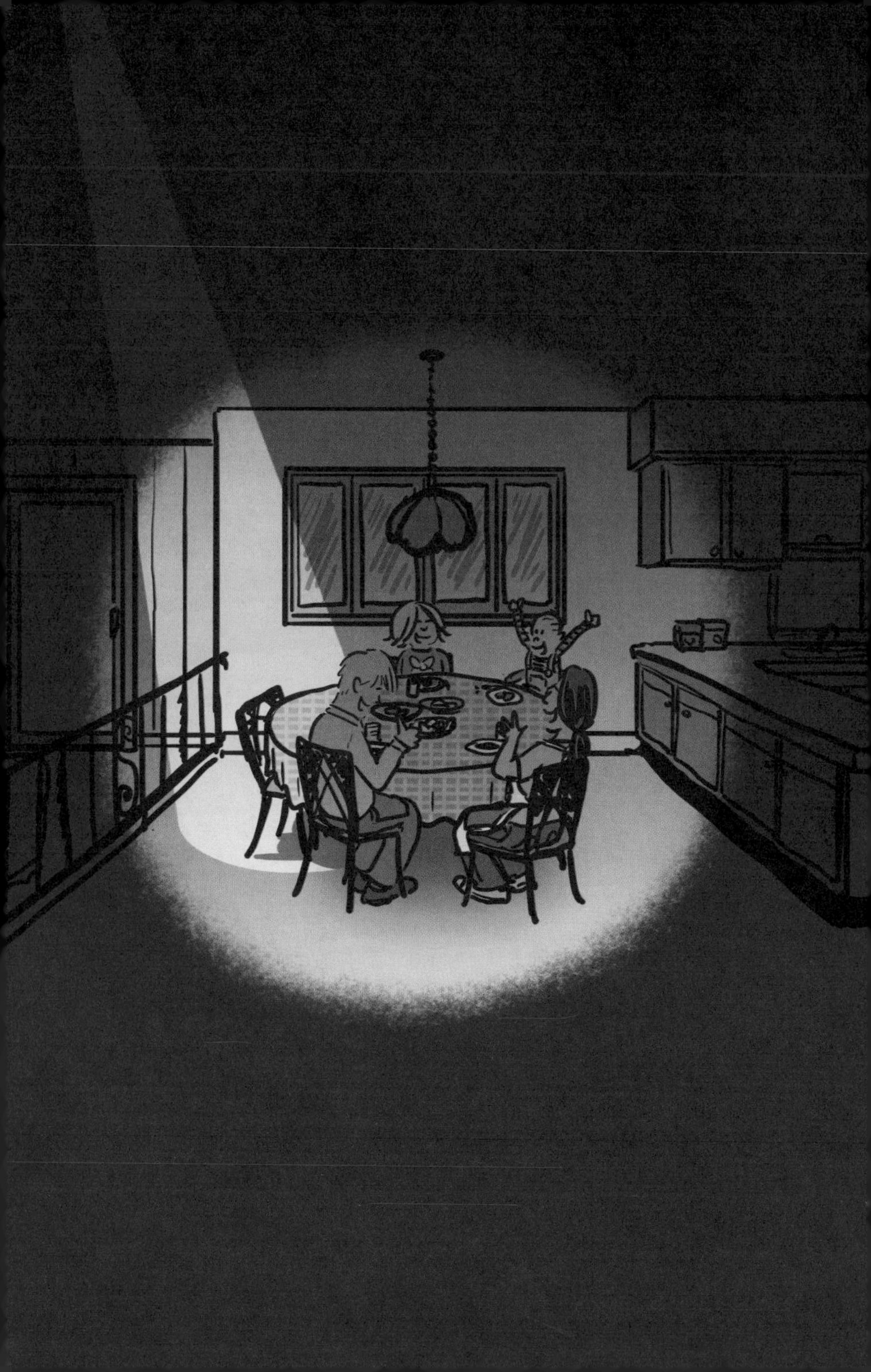

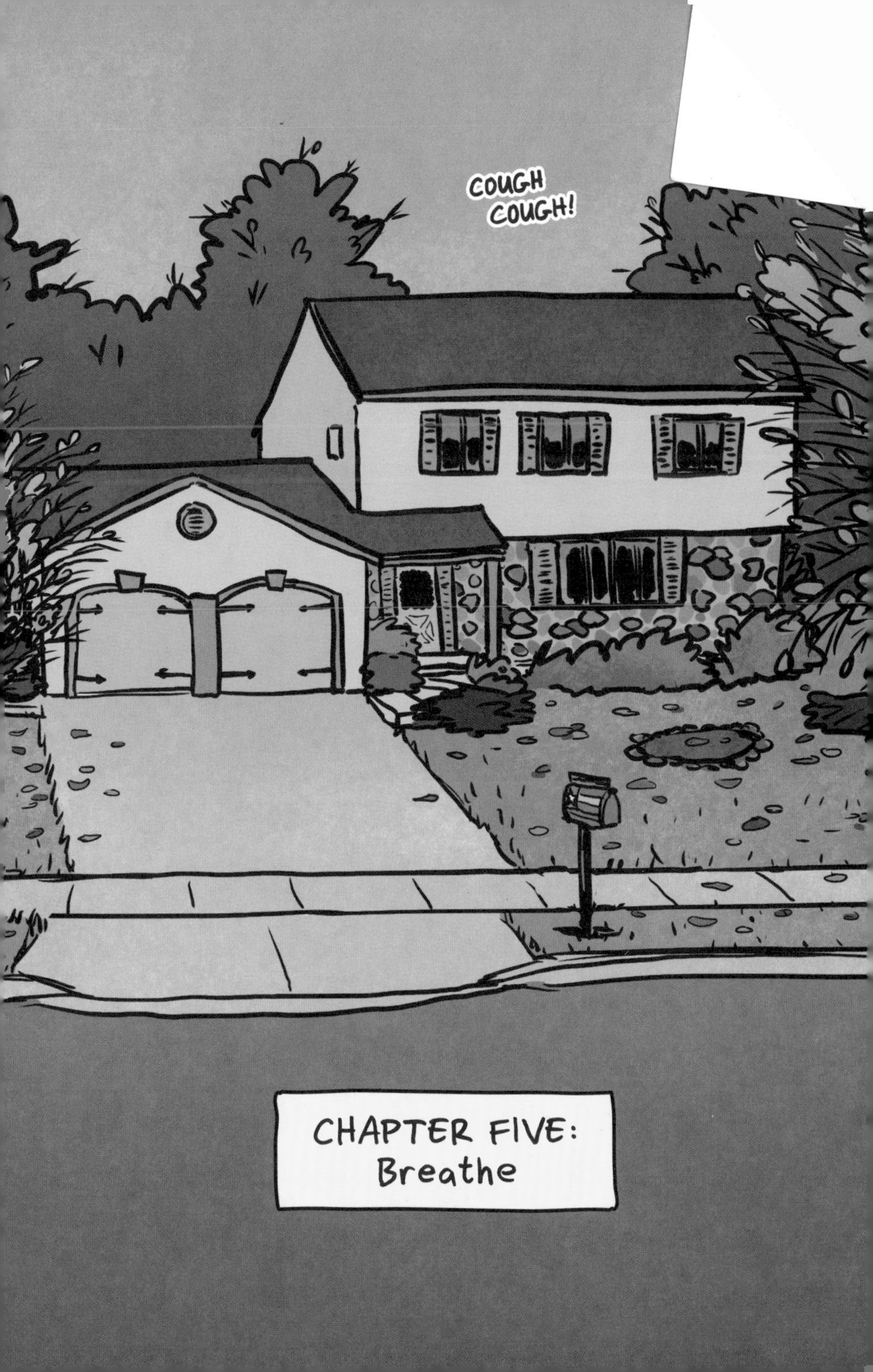
COUGH COUGH!
CHAPTER FIVE:
Breathe

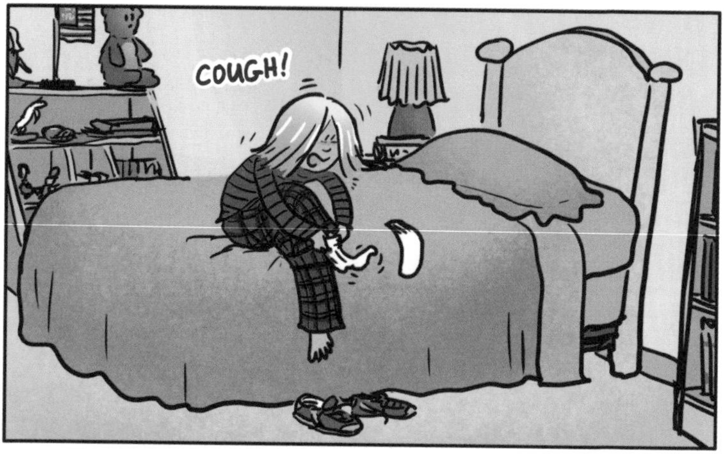
COUGH!

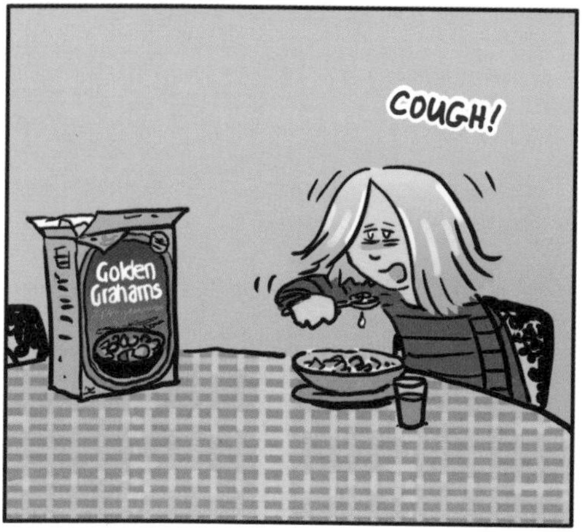
COUGH!
Golden Grahams

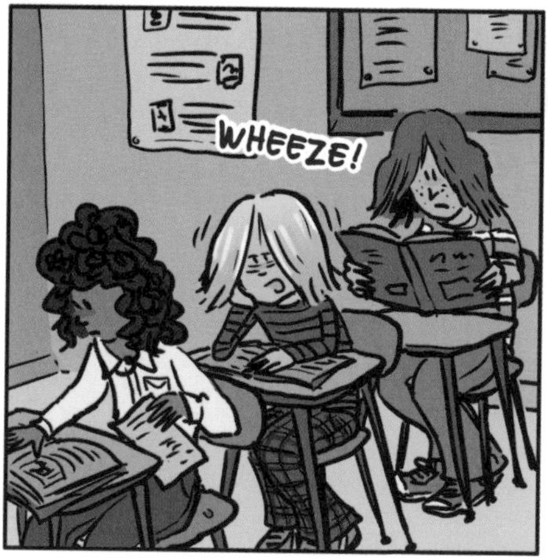
WHEEZE!

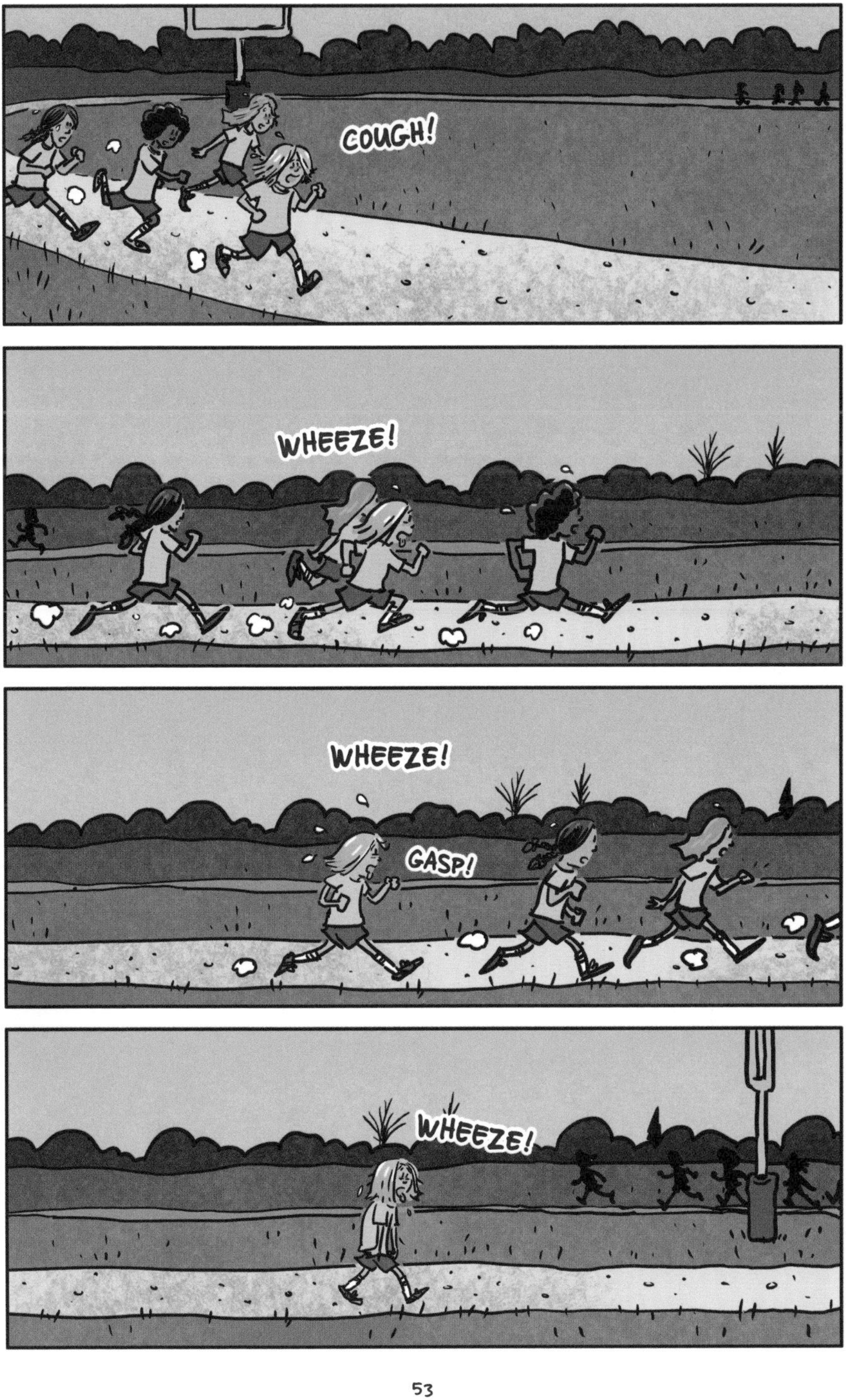
COUGH!
WHEEZE!
WHEEZE!
GASP!
WHEEZE!

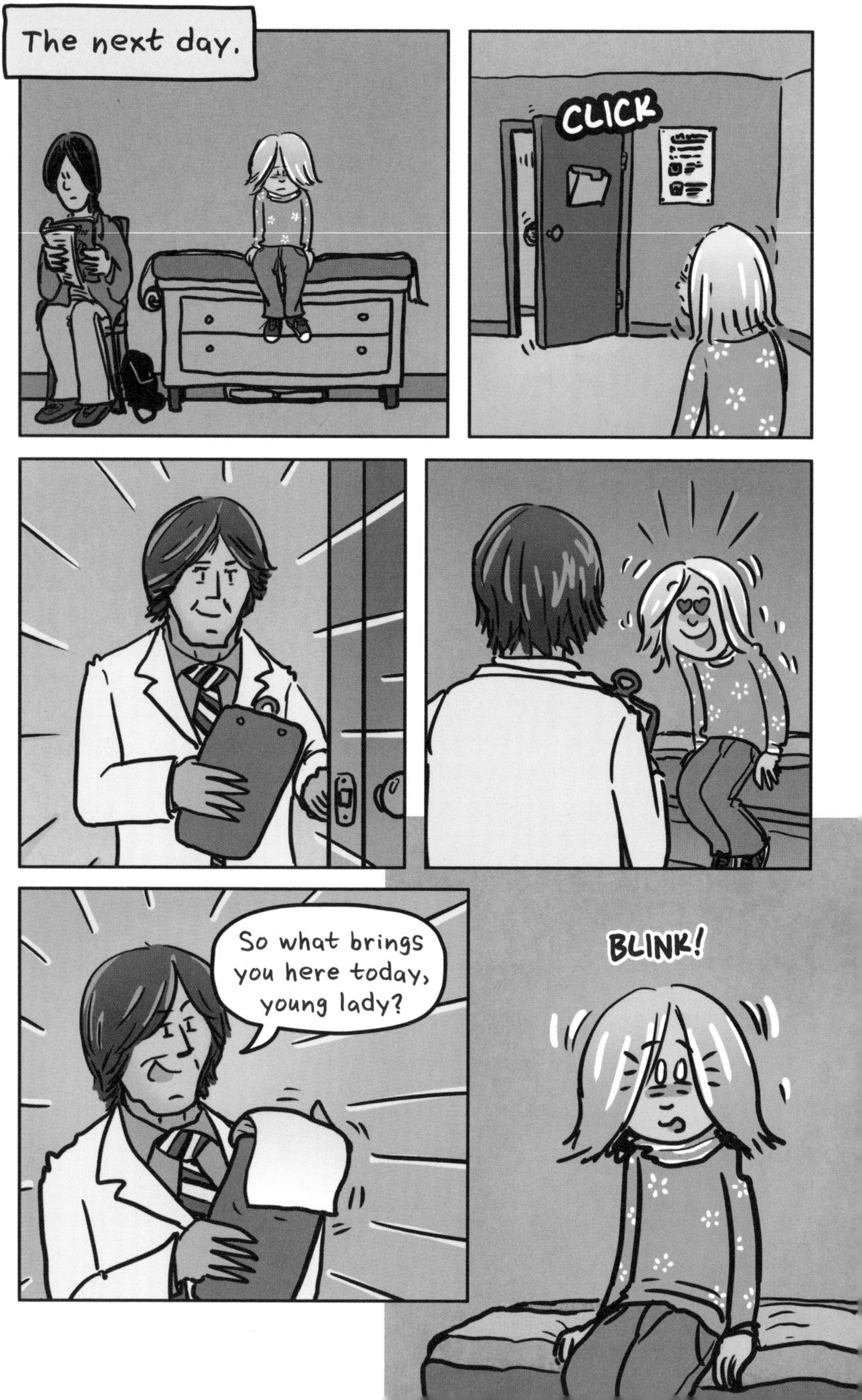
The next day.
CLICK
So what brings you here today, young lady?
BLINK!

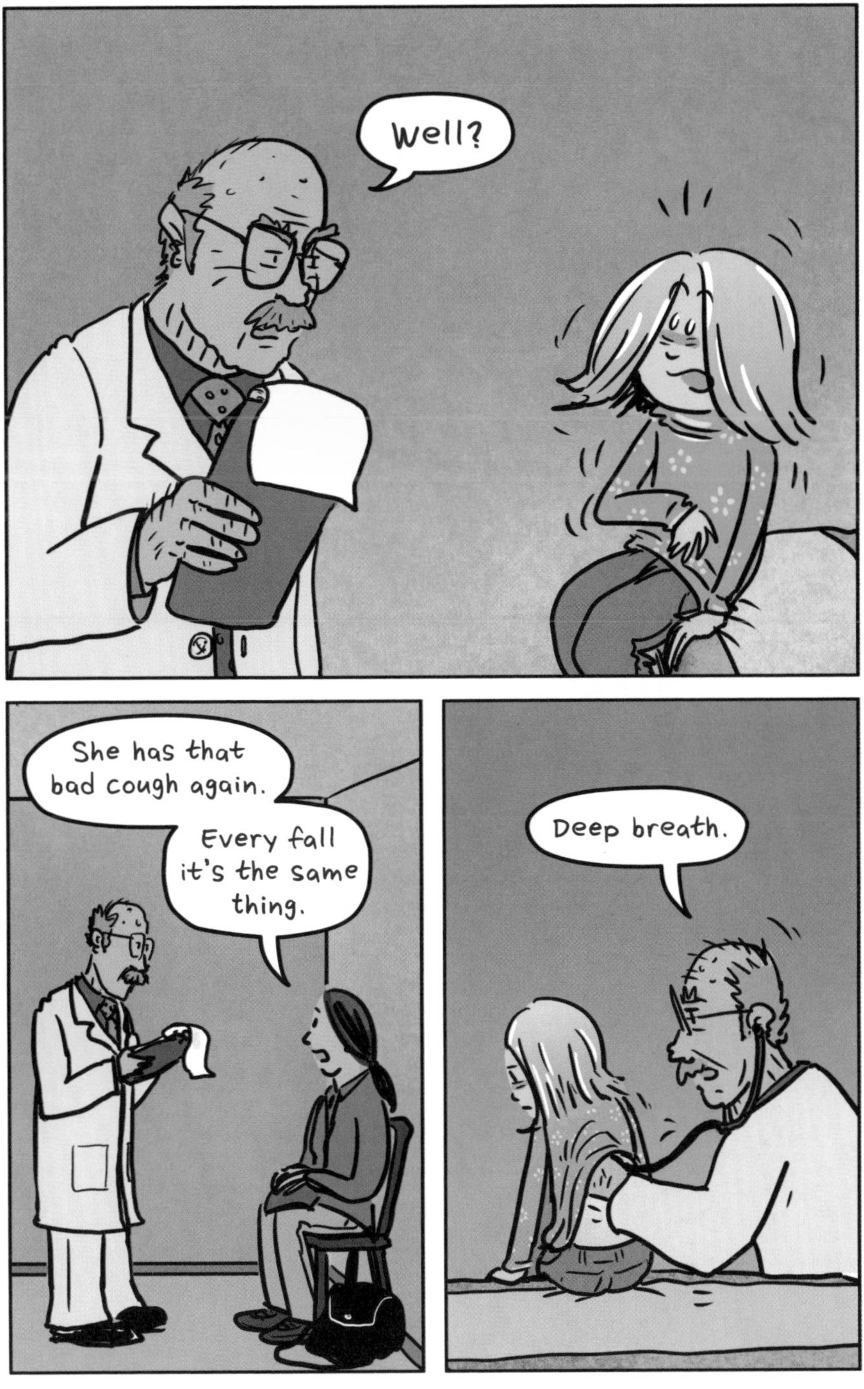
Well?
She has that bad cough again.
Every fall it's the same thing.
Deep breath.

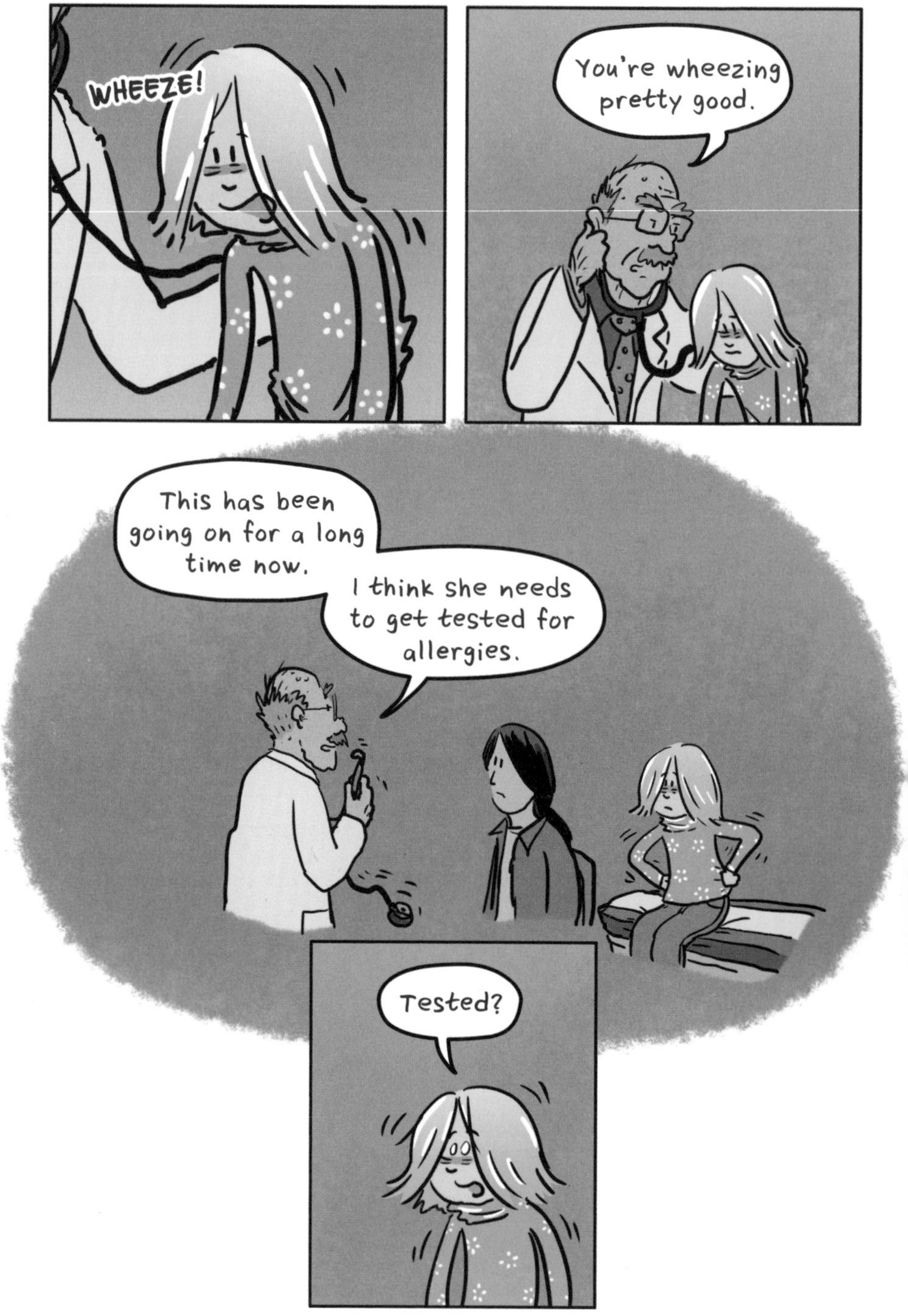
WHEEZE!
You're wheezing pretty good.
This has been going on for a long time now.
I think she needs to get tested for allergies.
Tested?

Later that week.

Valley Allergy Associates, P.C.

Craig Jacobson, M.D.
Jeffrey DiDario, M.D.

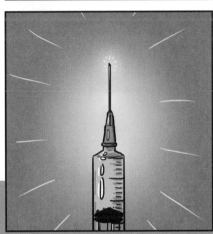

I'm putting an allergen under your skin to see if you are allergic.

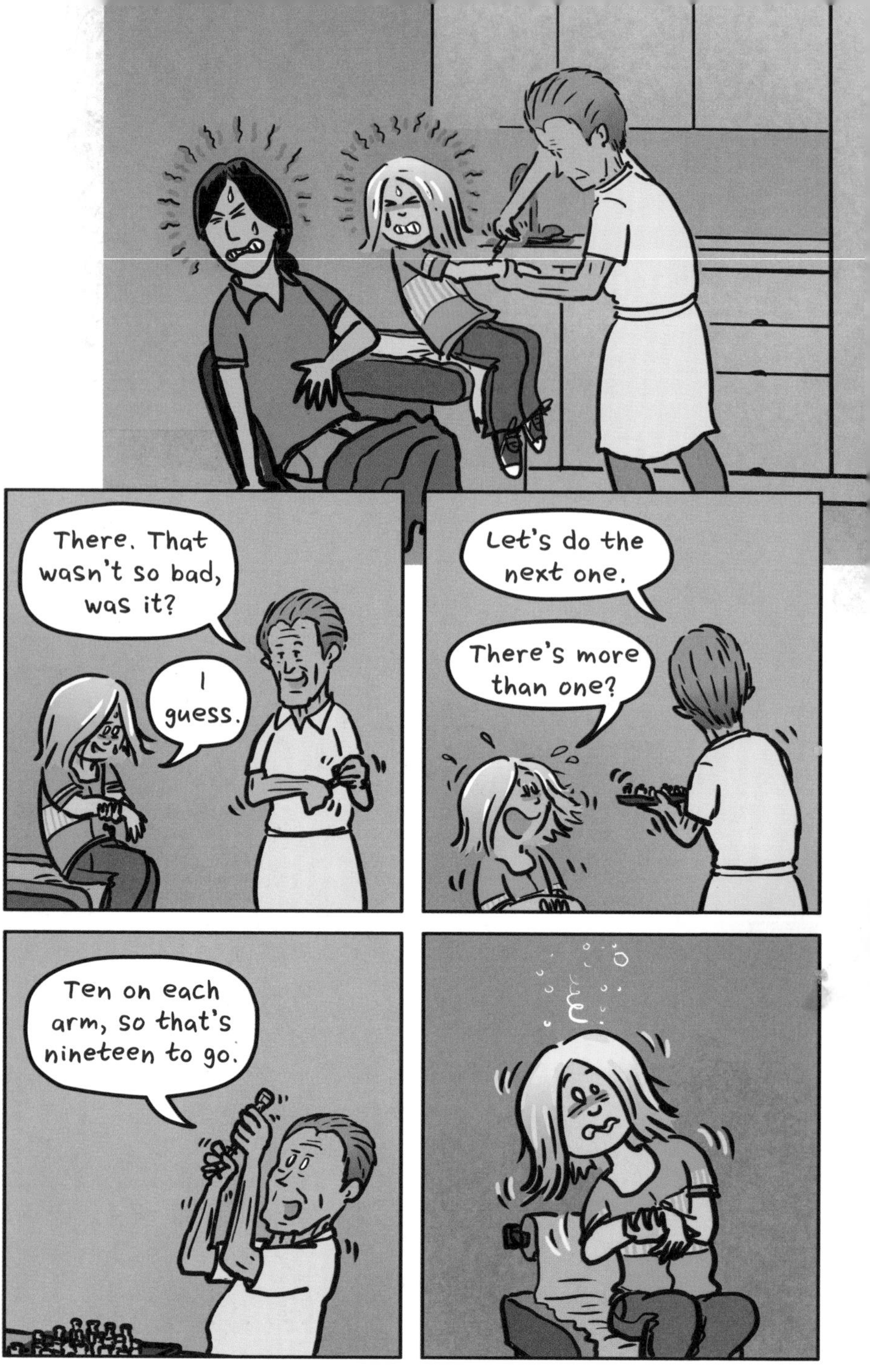
There. That wasn't so bad, was it?
I guess.
Let's do the next one.
There's more than one?
Ten on each arm, so that's nineteen to go.

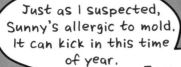

Just as I suspected, Sunny's allergic to mold. It can kick in this time of year.

Everything's damp and wet. Some people are really susceptible to it.

Is there medicine?

We can give her allergy shots once a week.

ONCE A WEEK?!?!?!?

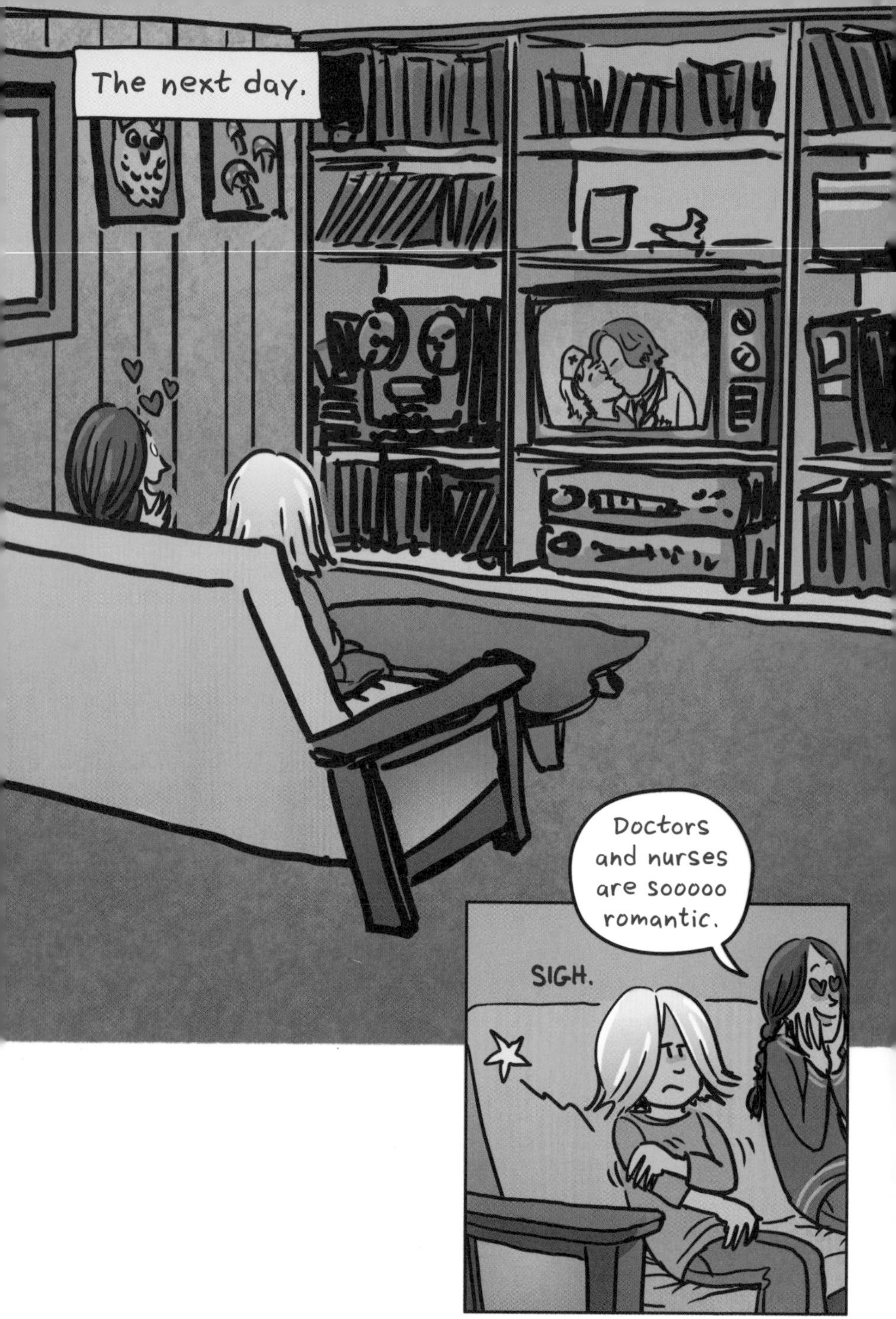
The next day.
Doctors and nurses are sooooo romantic.
SIGH.

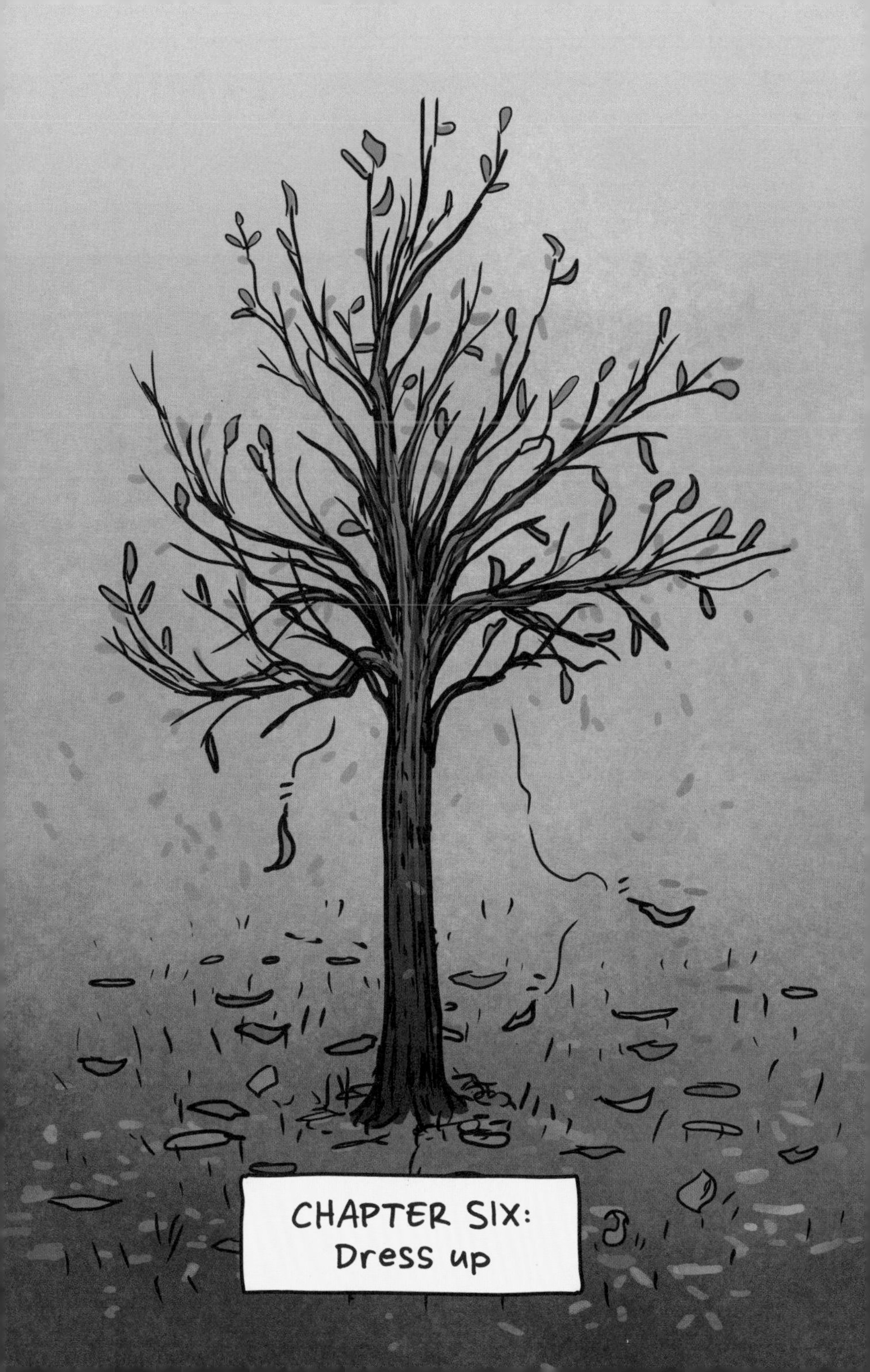
CHAPTER SIX:
Dress up

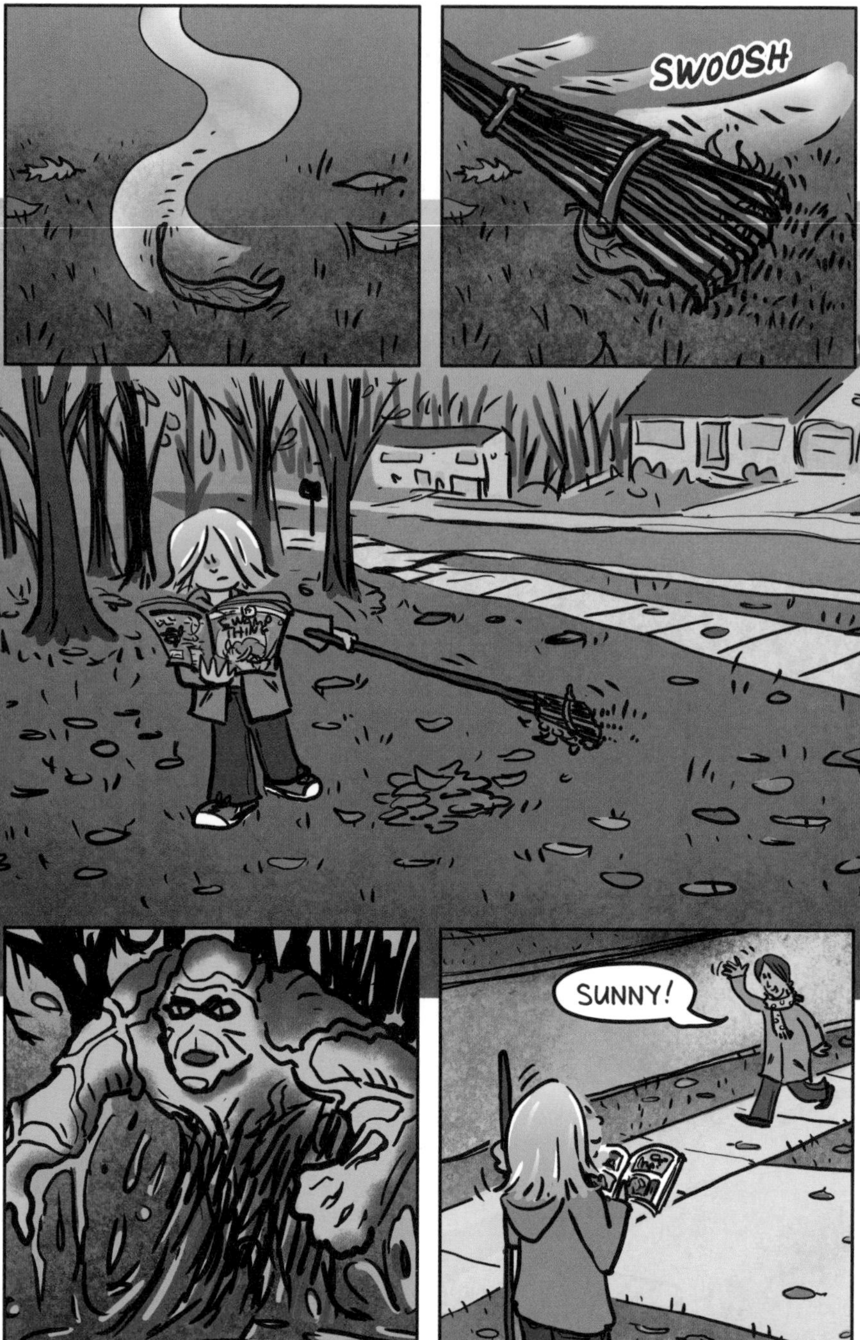
SWOOSH
SUNNY!

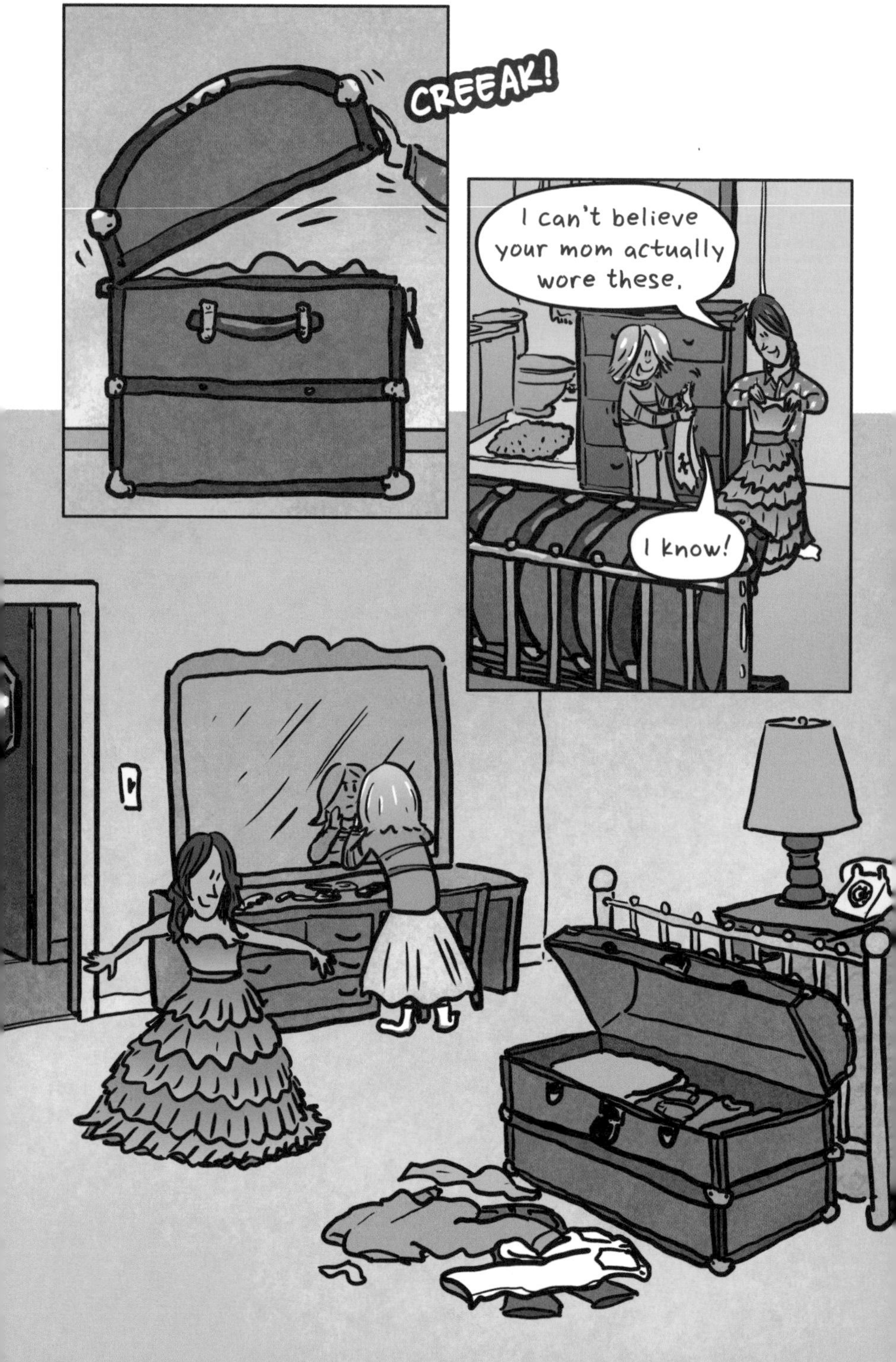
CREEAK!
I can't believe your mom actually wore these.
I know!

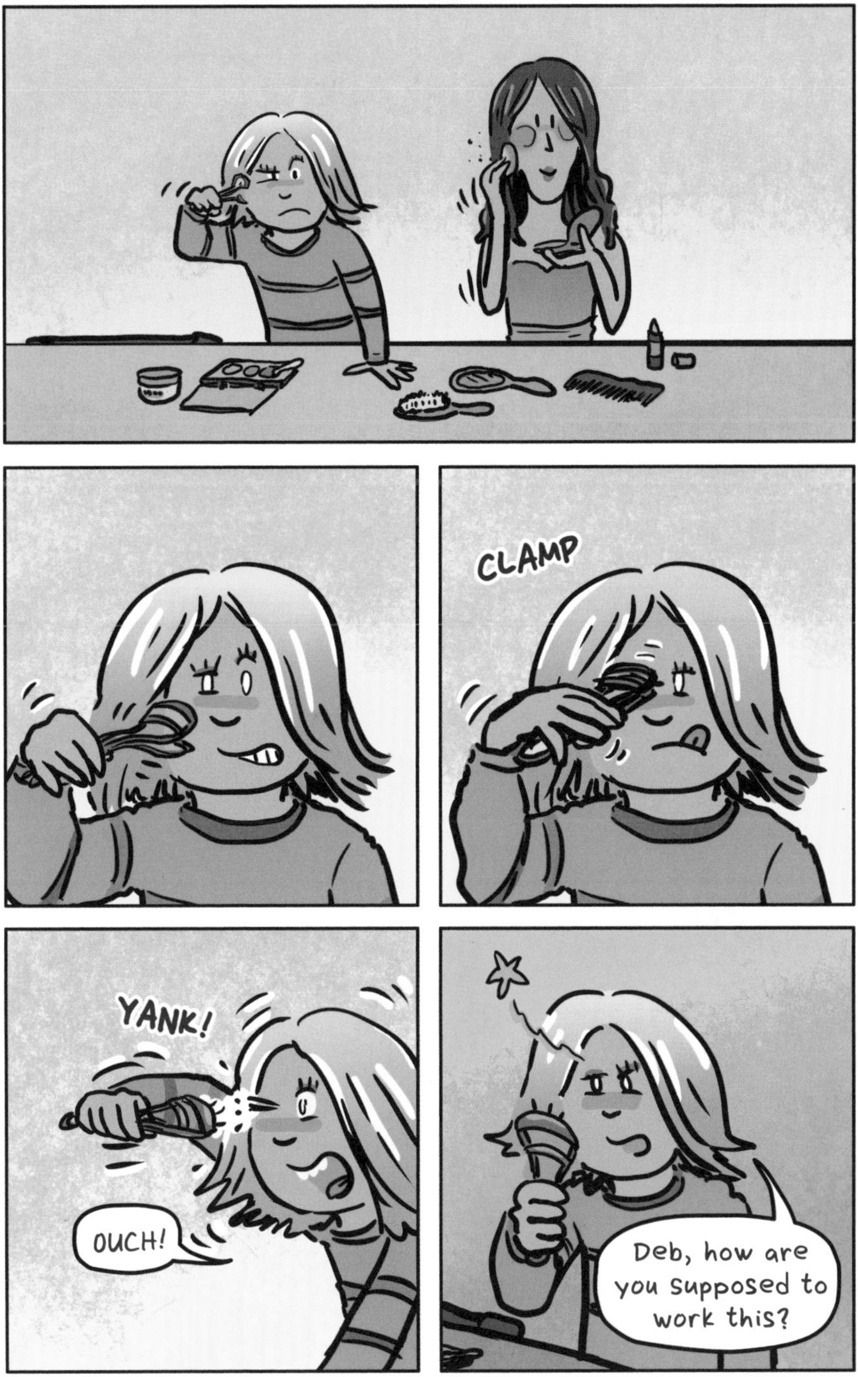
CLAMP
YANK!
OUCH!
Deb, how are you supposed to work this?

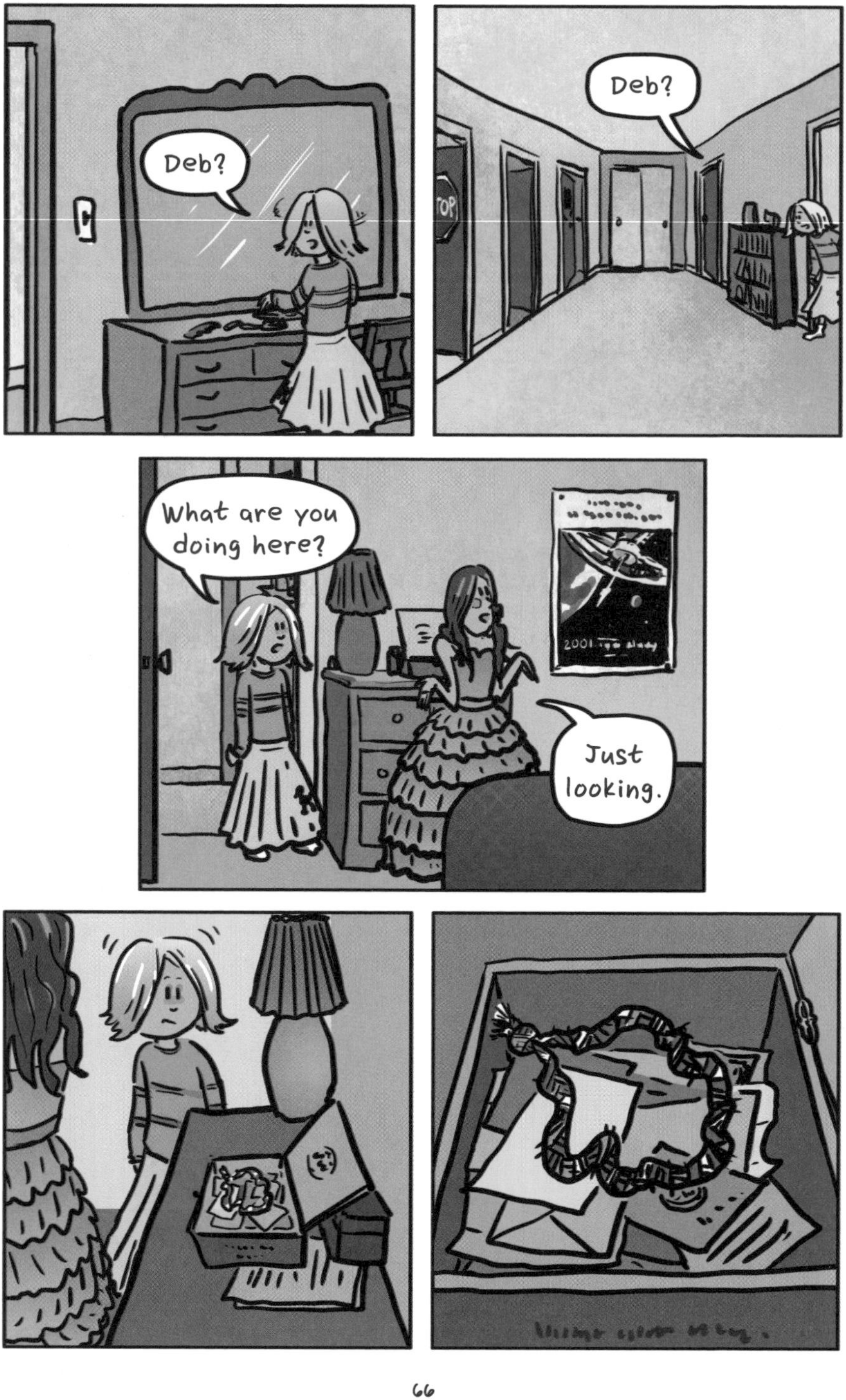
Deb?
Deb?
What are you doing here?
Just looking.

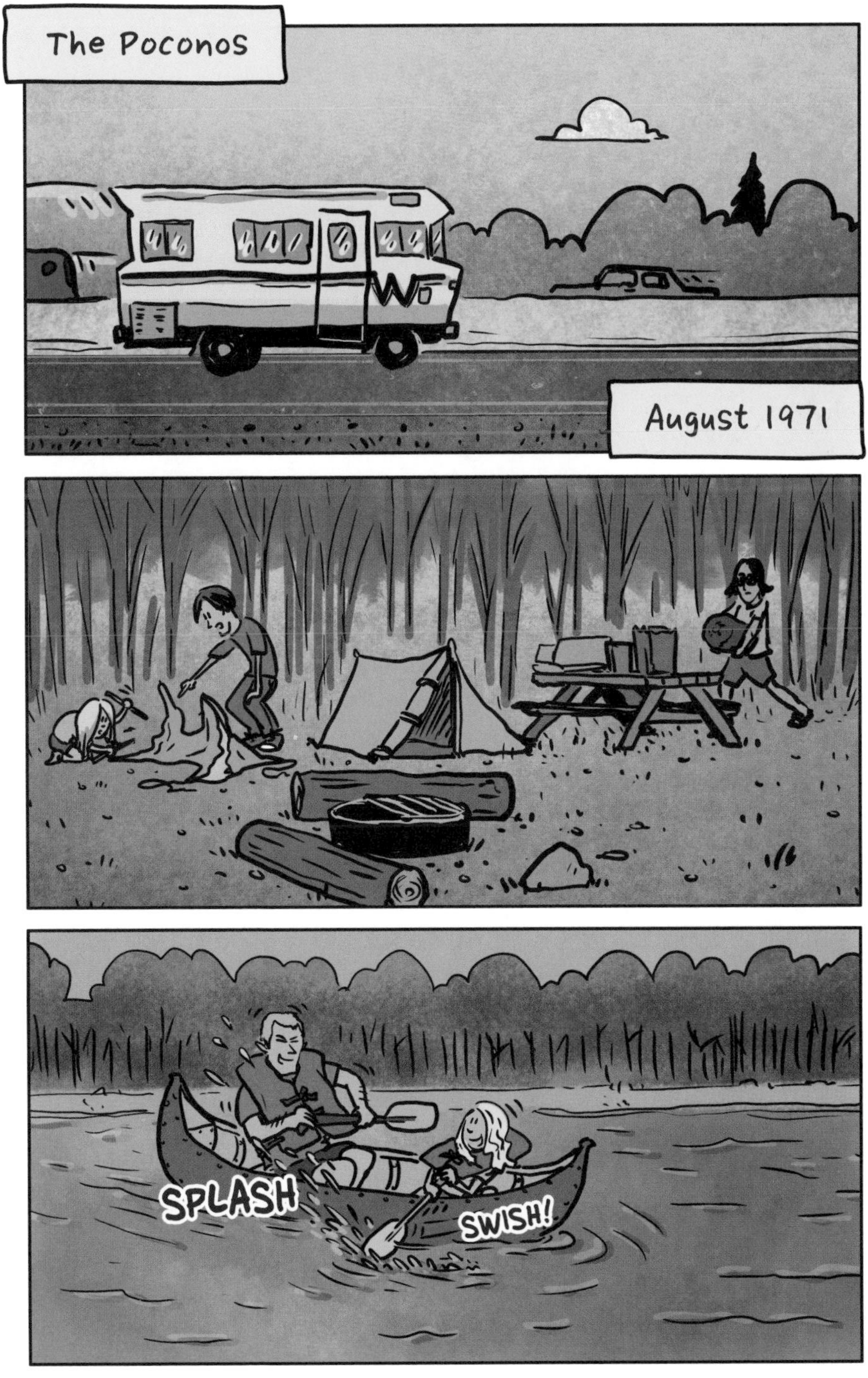
The Poconos
August 1971
SPLASH
SWISH!

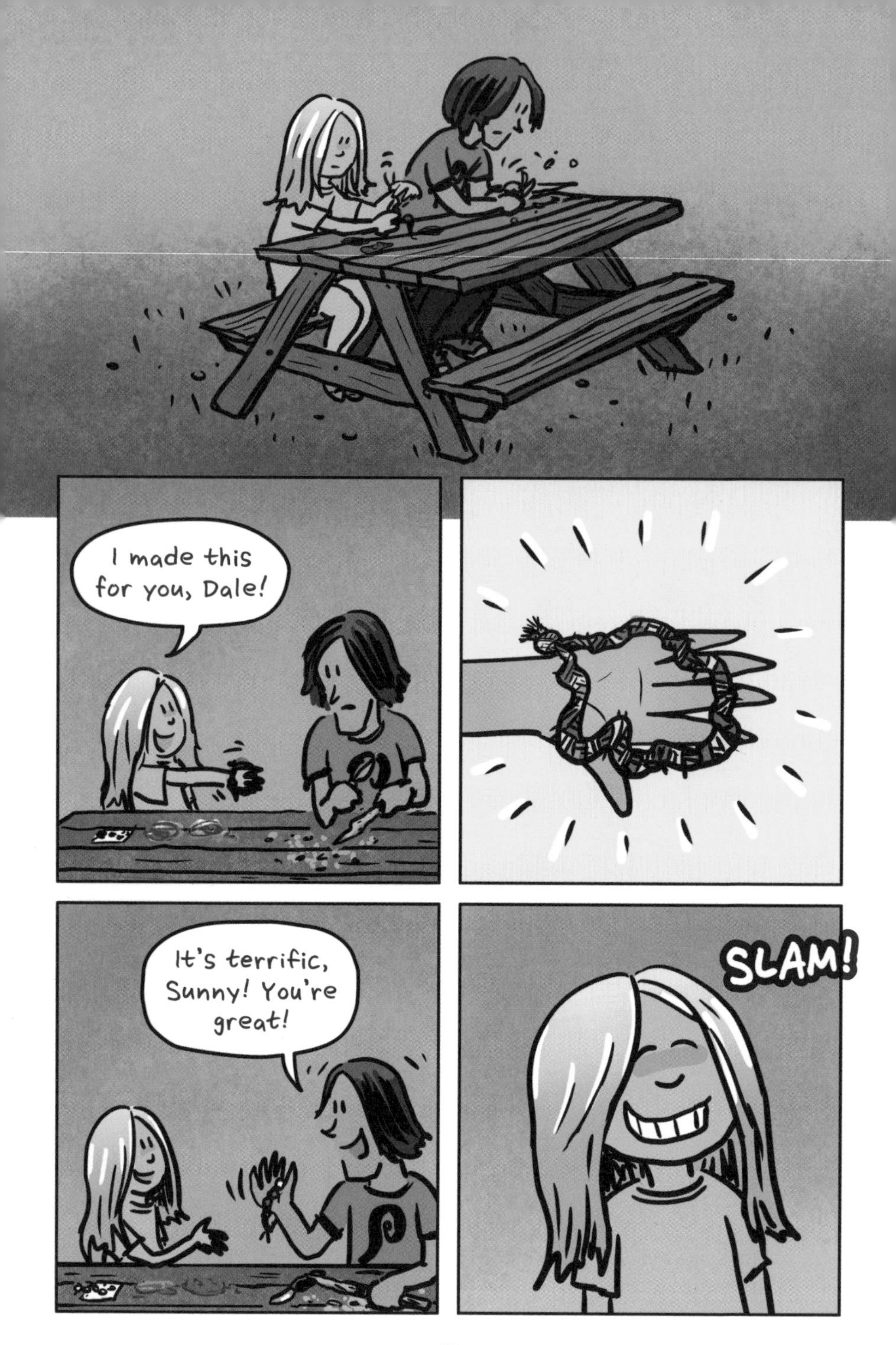
I made this for you, Dale!
It's terrific, Sunny! You're great!
SLAM!

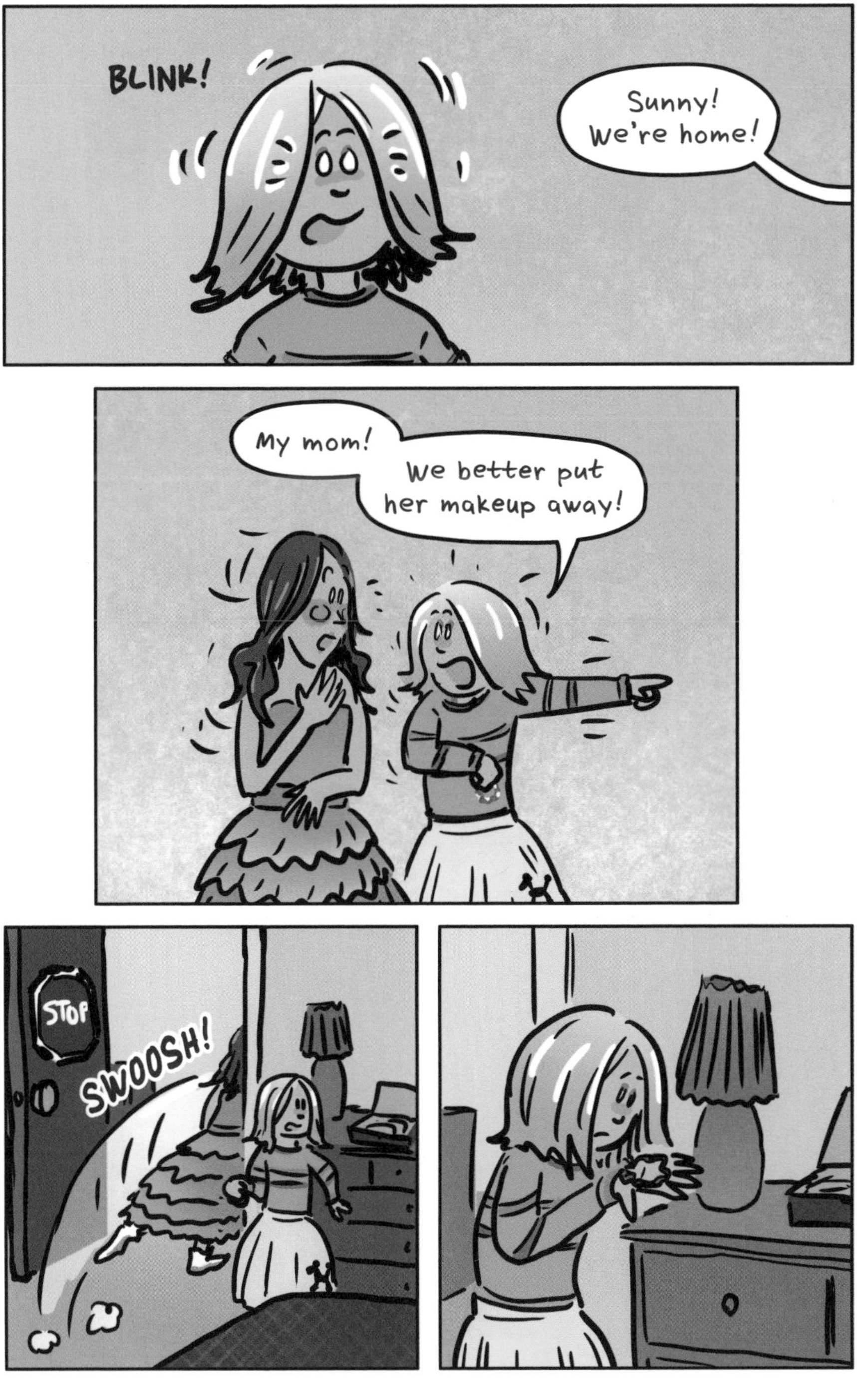
BLINK!
Sunny! We're home!
My mom!
We better put her makeup away!
STOP
SWOOSH!

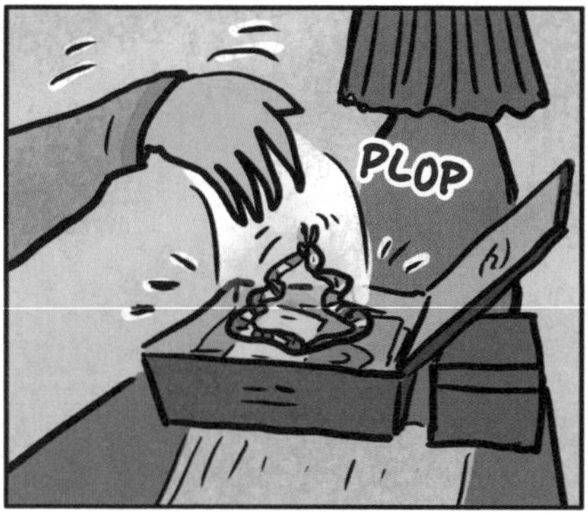
PLOP

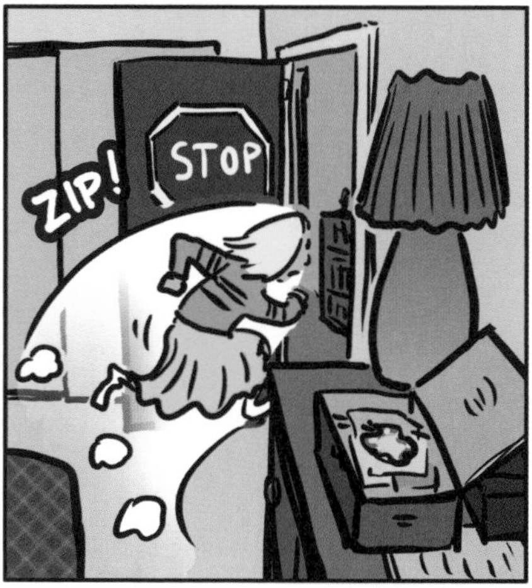
STOP
ZIP!

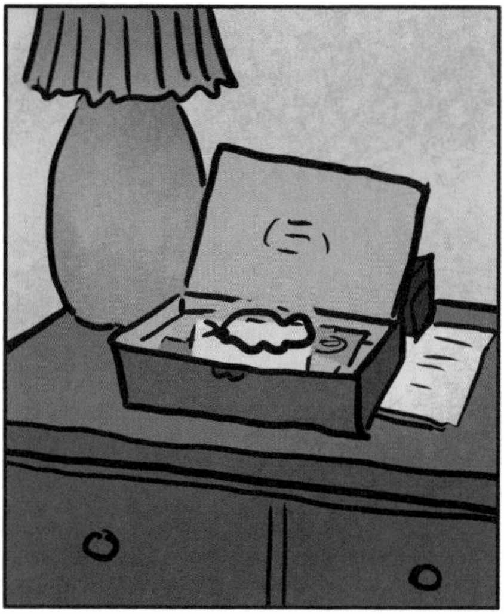

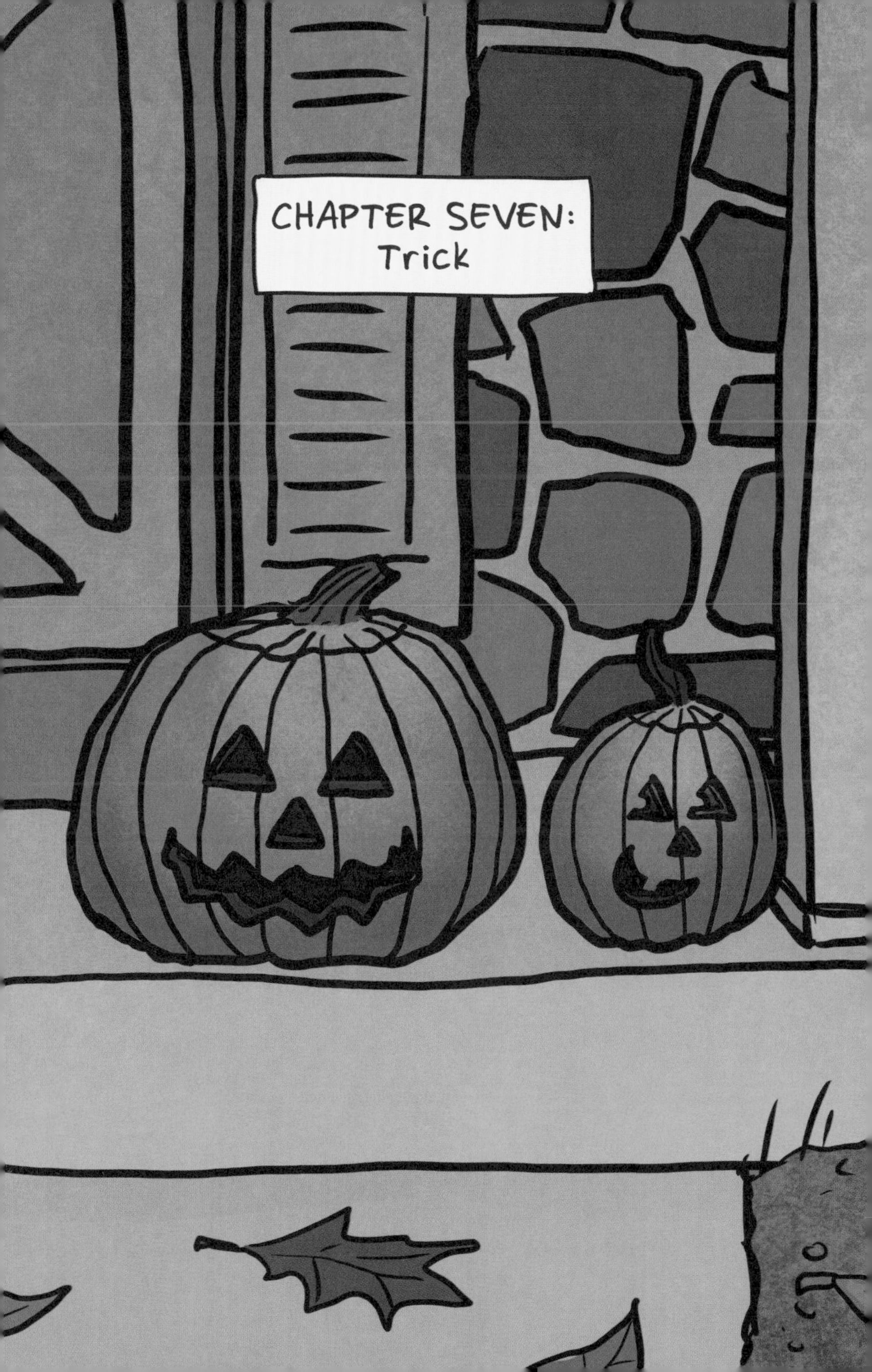
CHAPTER SEVEN:
Trick

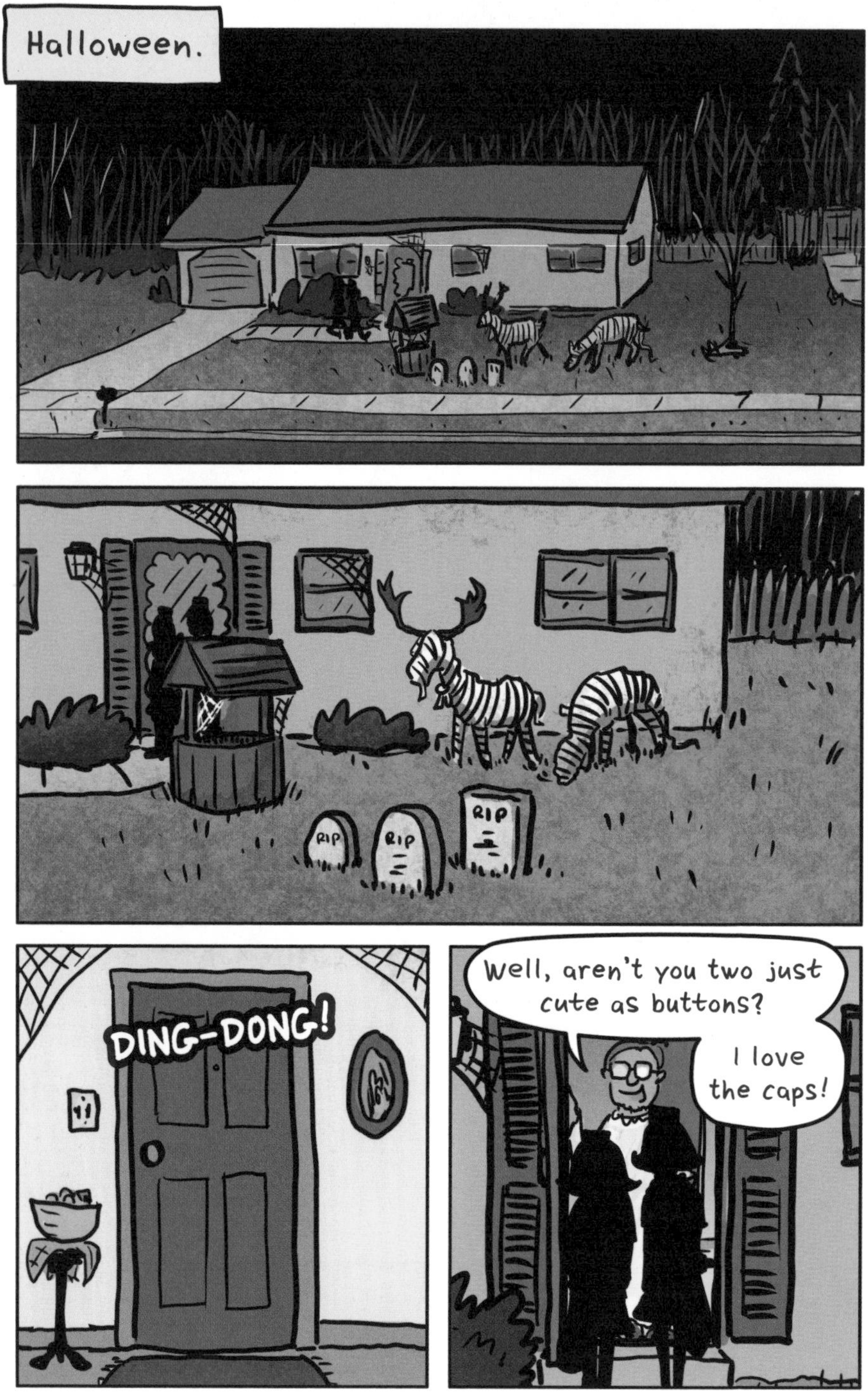
Halloween.
DING-DONG!
Well, aren't you two just cute as buttons?
I love the caps!

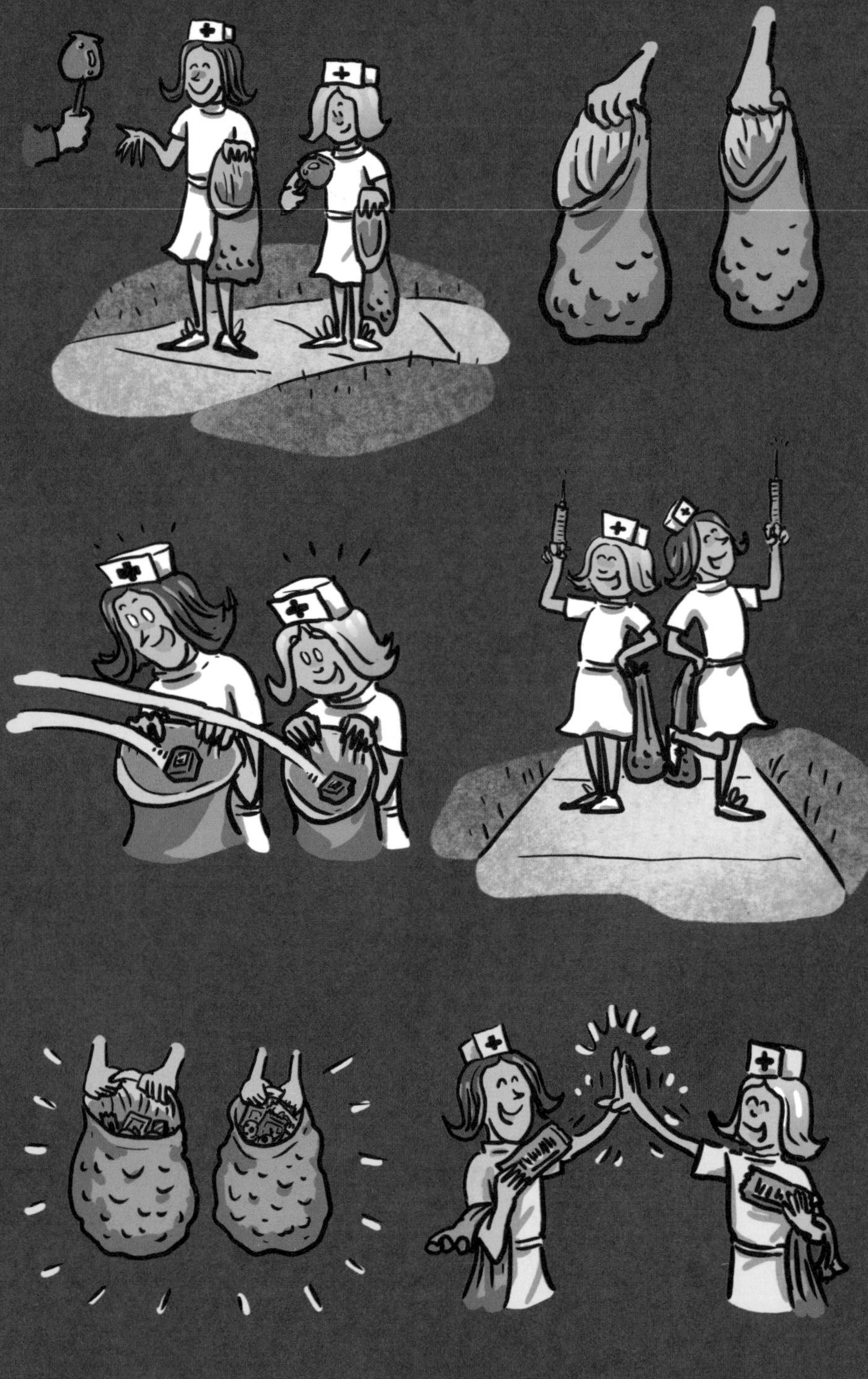

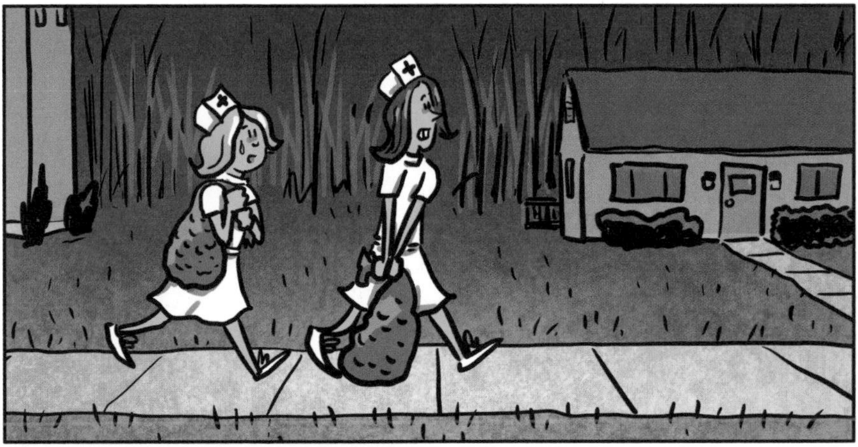

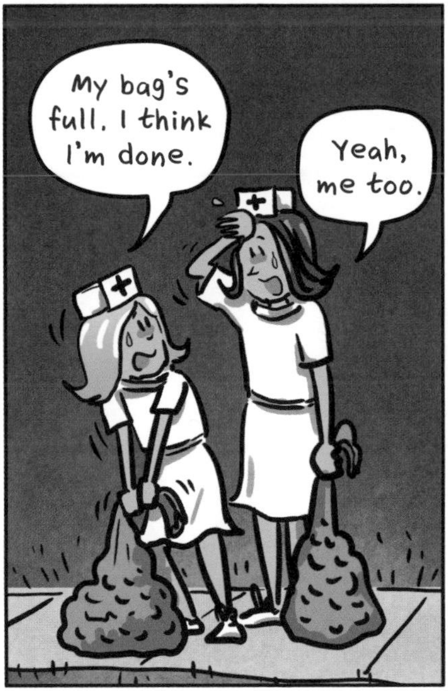
My bag's full. I think I'm done.
Yeah, me too.

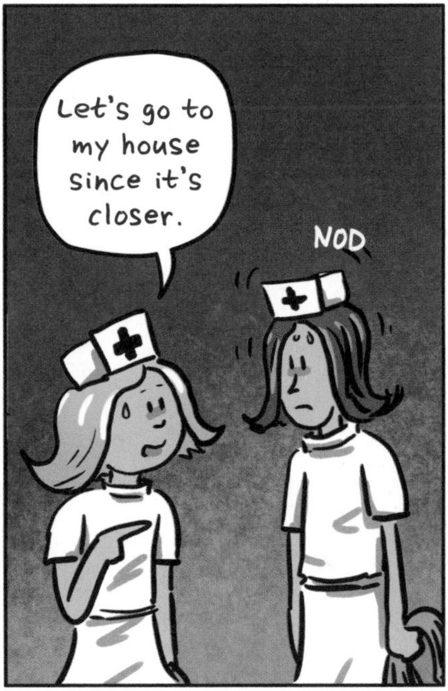
Let's go to my house since it's closer.
NOD

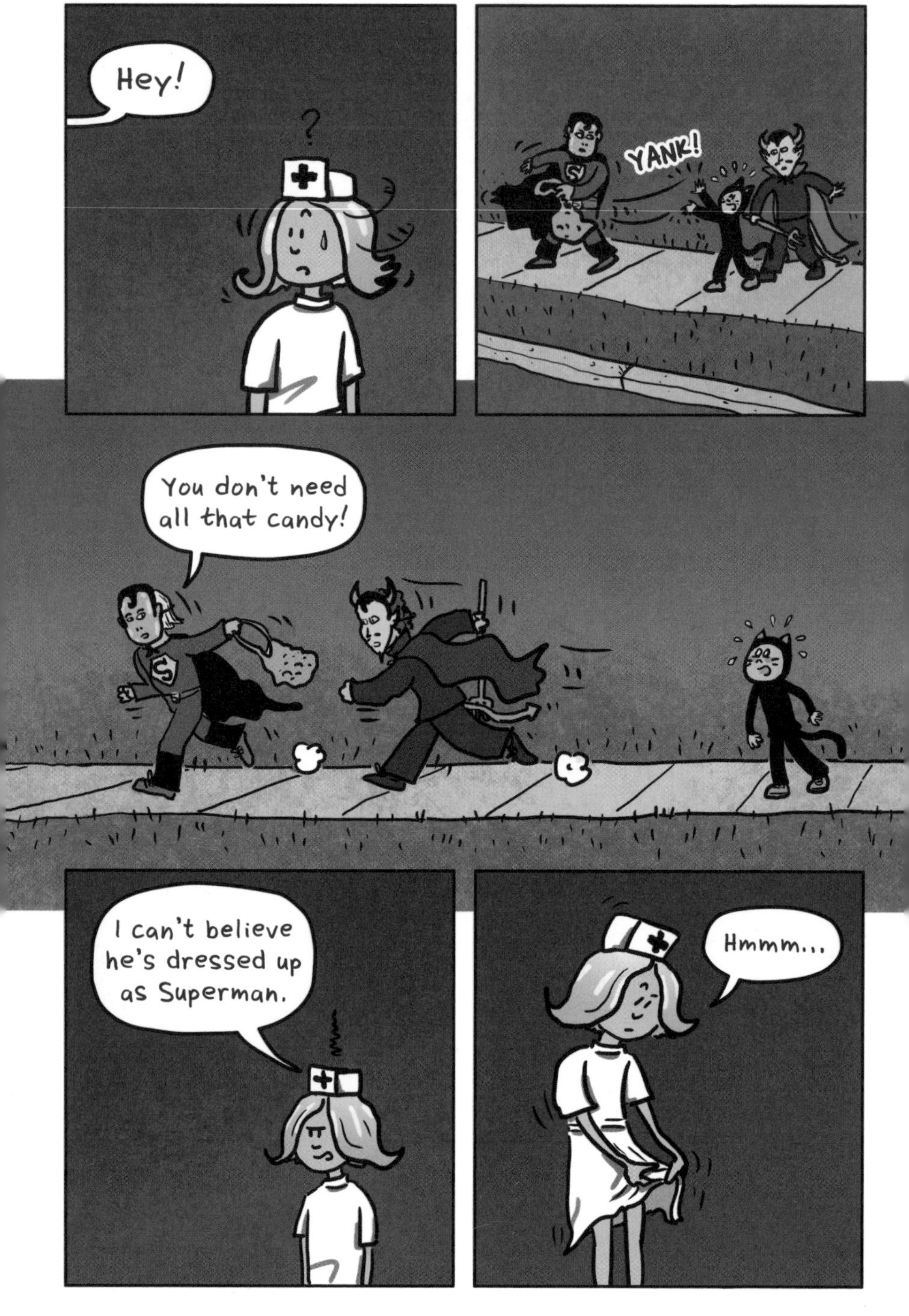
Hey!
?
YANK!
You don't need all that candy!
I can't believe he's dressed up as Superman.
Hmmm...

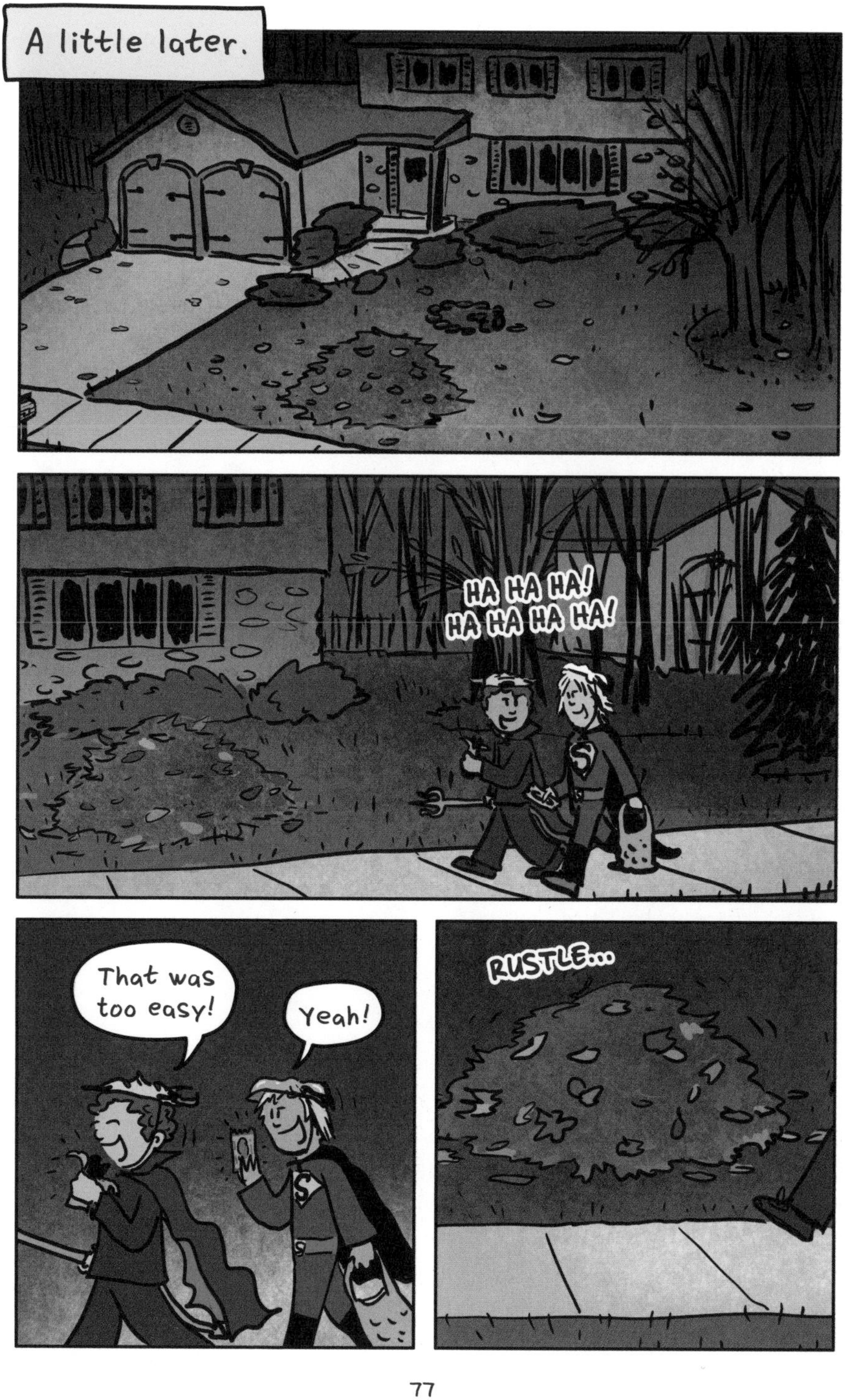
A little later.
HA HA HA!
HA HA HA HA!
That was too easy!
Yeah!
RUSTLE...

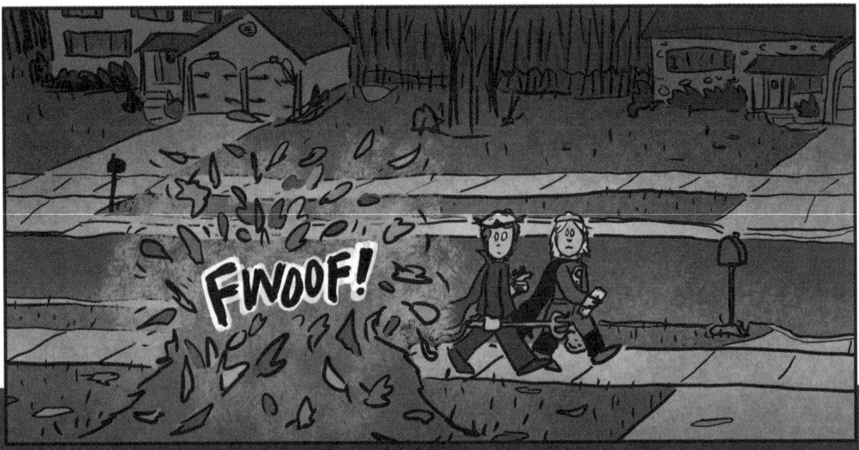
FWOOF!

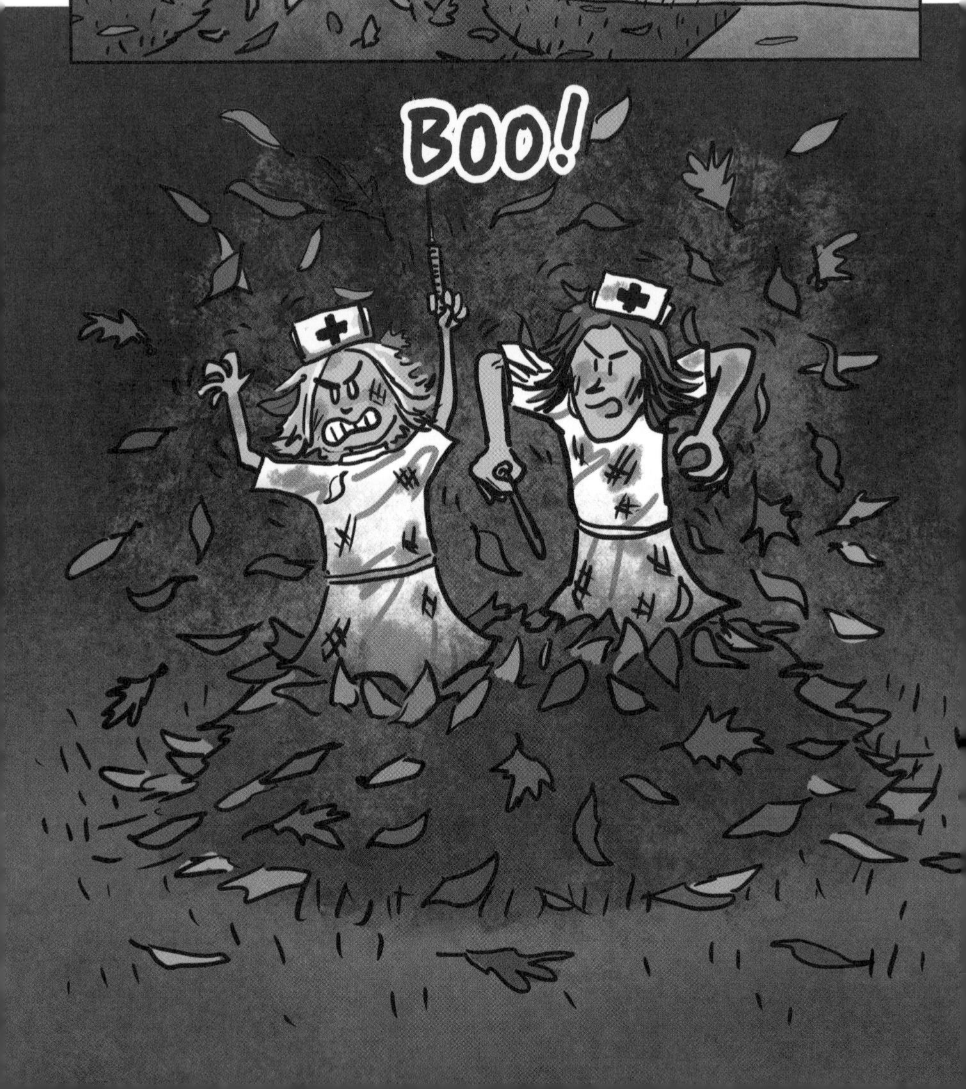
BOO!

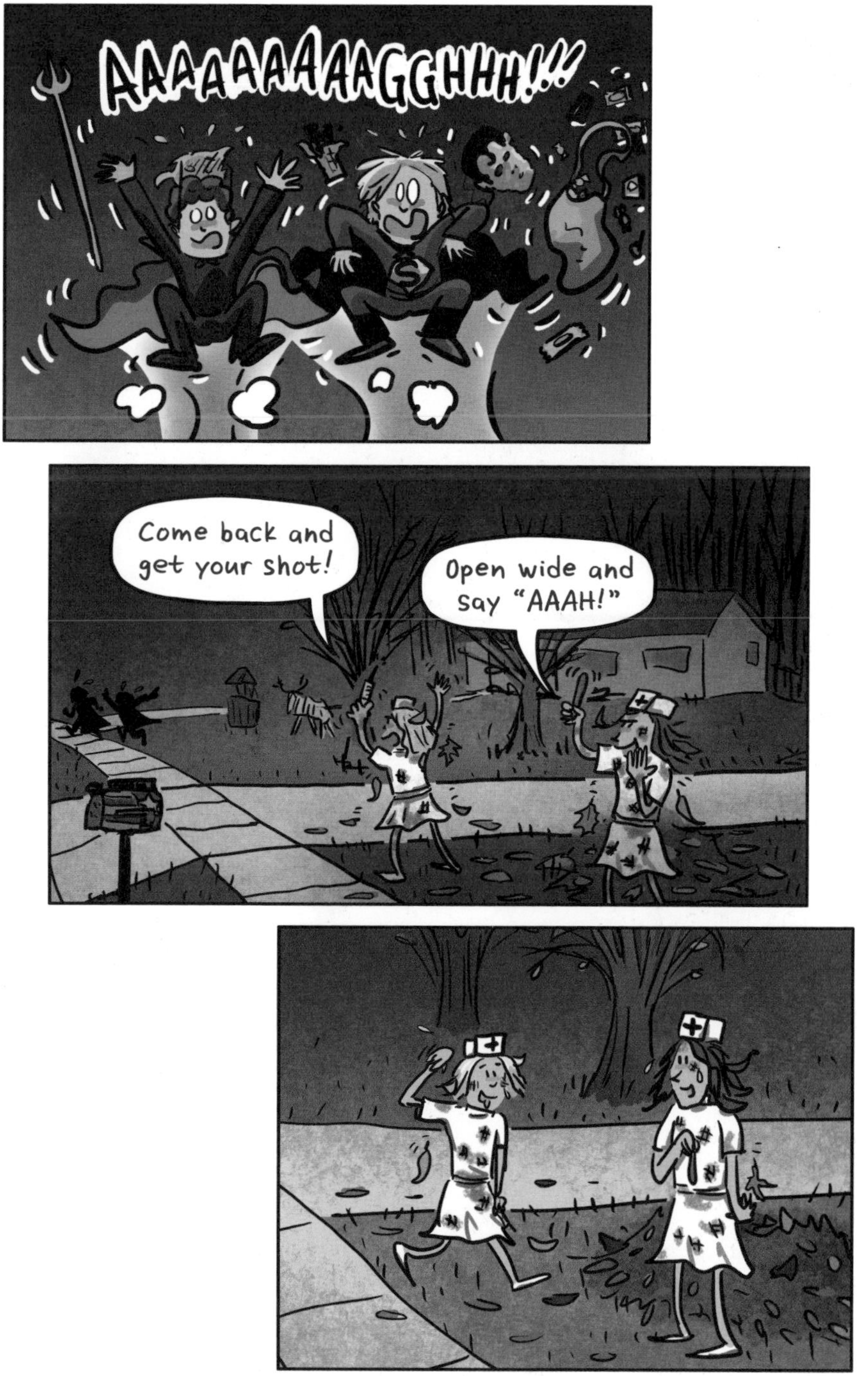
AAAAAAAAAGGHHH!!!
Come back and get your shot!
Open wide and say "AAAH!"

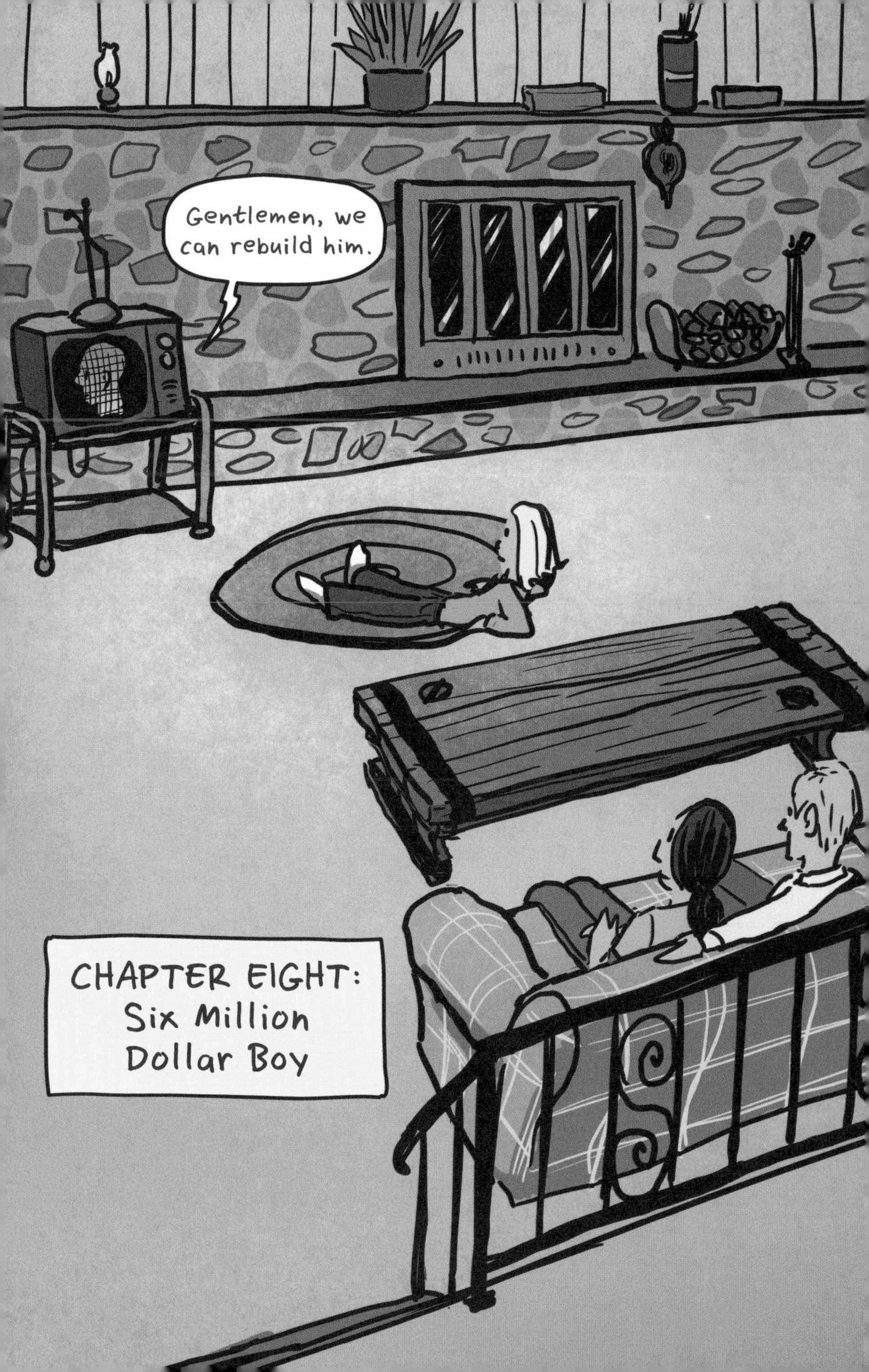
Gentlemen, we can rebuild him.
CHAPTER EIGHT: Six Million Dollar Boy

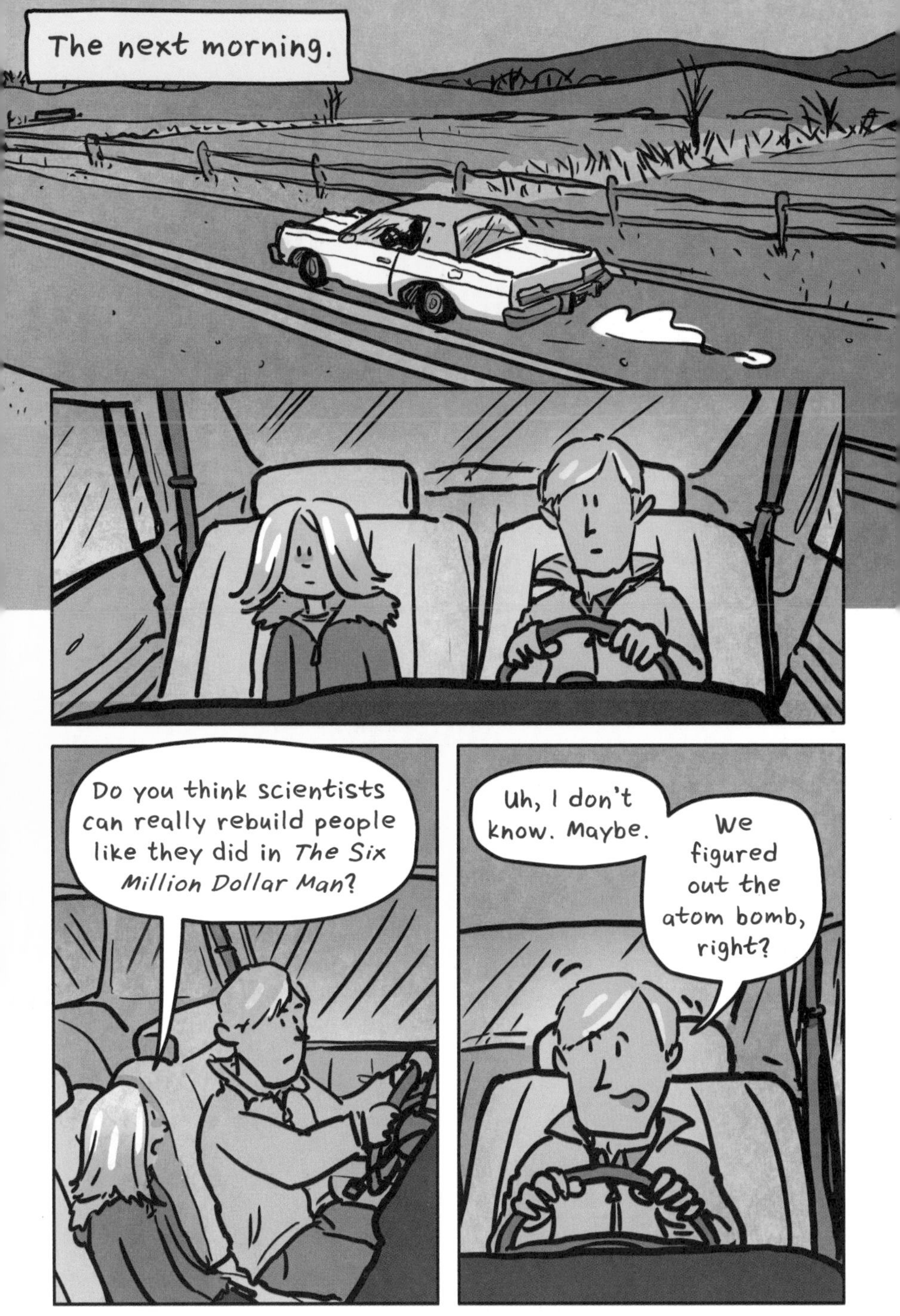
The next morning.
Do you think scientists can really rebuild people like they did in *The Six Million Dollar Man*?
Uh, I don't know. Maybe.
We figured out the atom bomb, right?

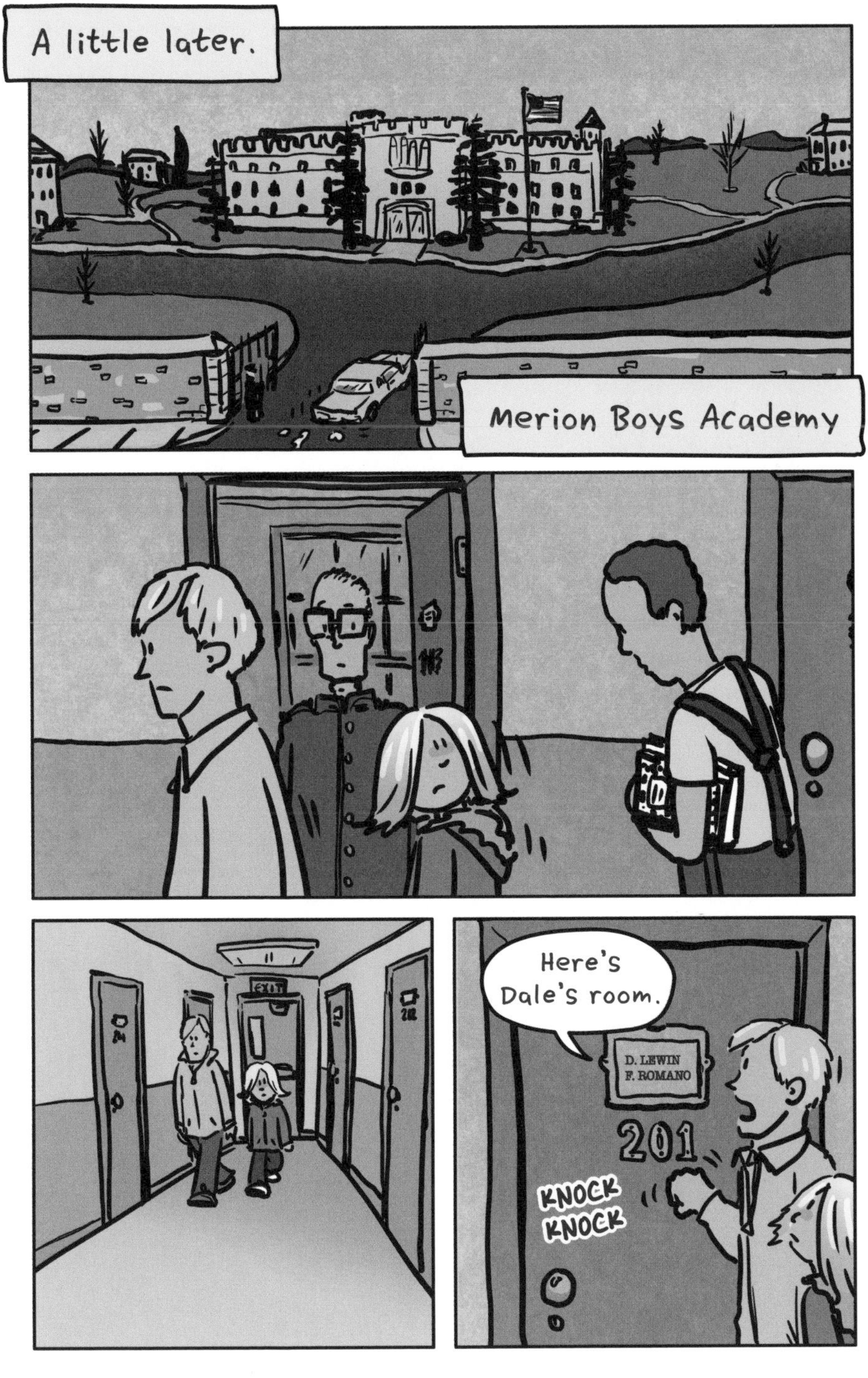
A little later.
Merion Boys Academy
Here's Dale's room.
D. LEWIN
F. ROMANO
201
KNOCK KNOCK

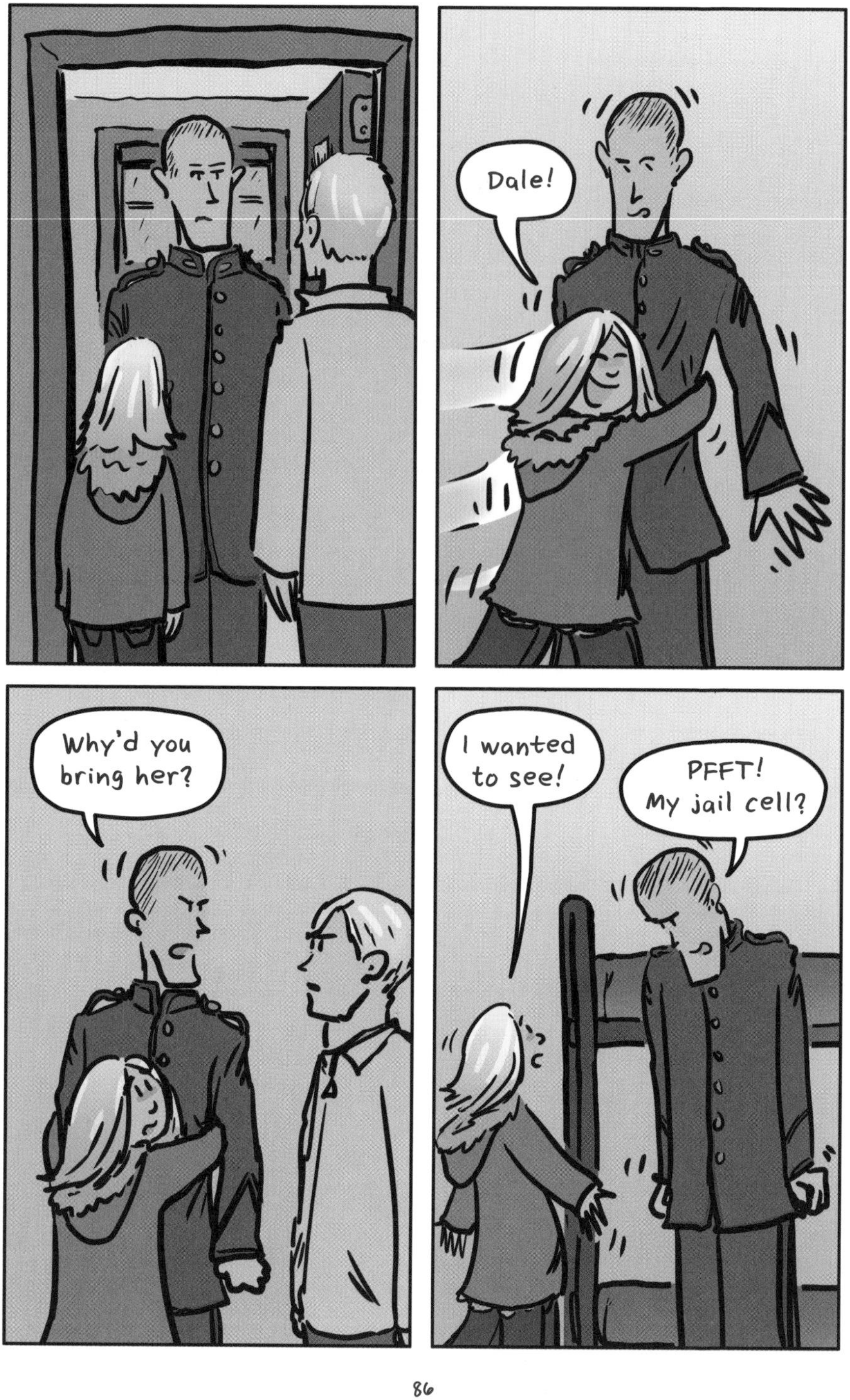
Dale!
Why'd you bring her?
I wanted to see!
PFFT! My jail cell?

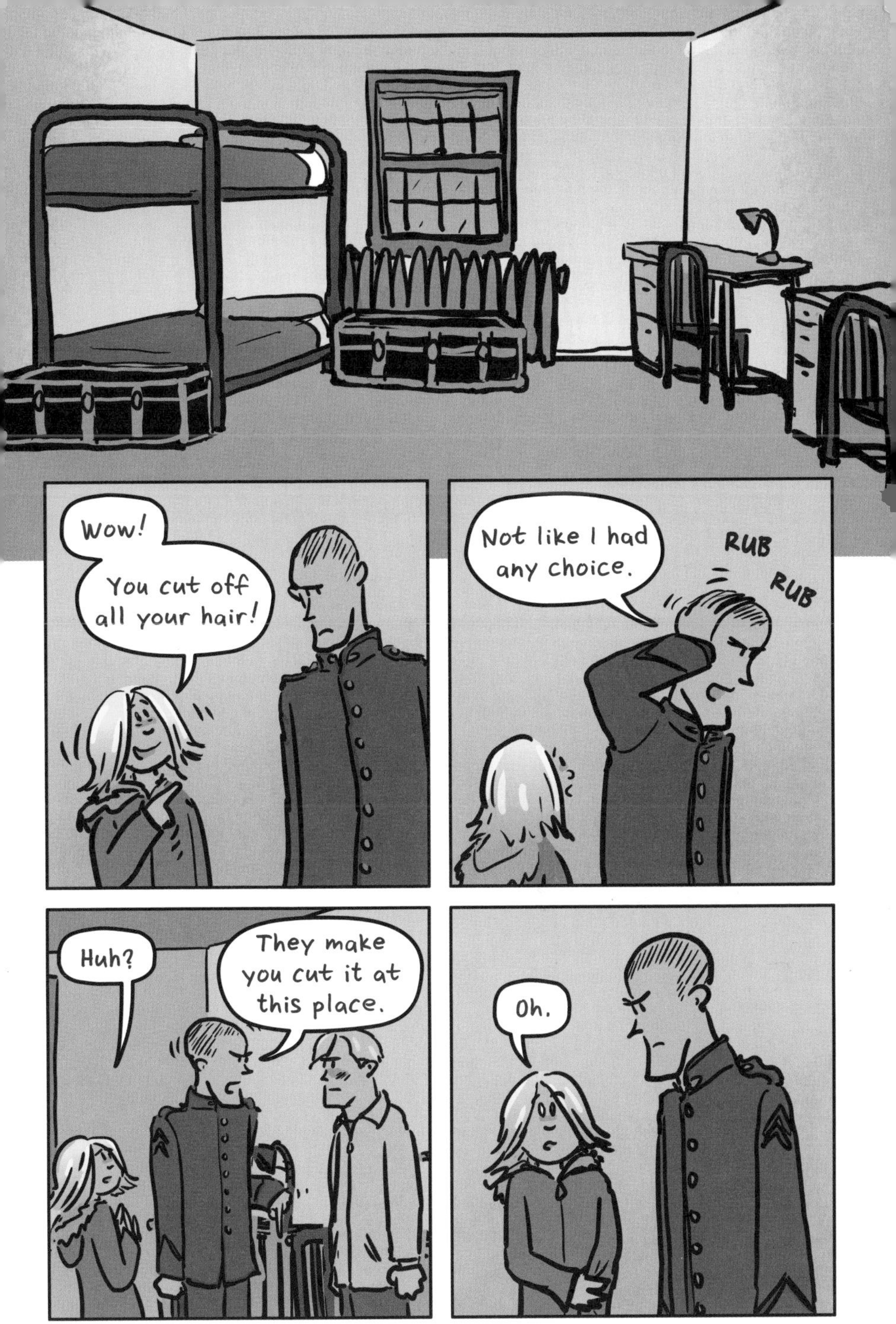
Wow!
You cut off all your hair!
Not like I had any choice.
RUB
RUB
Huh?
They make you cut it at this place.
Oh.

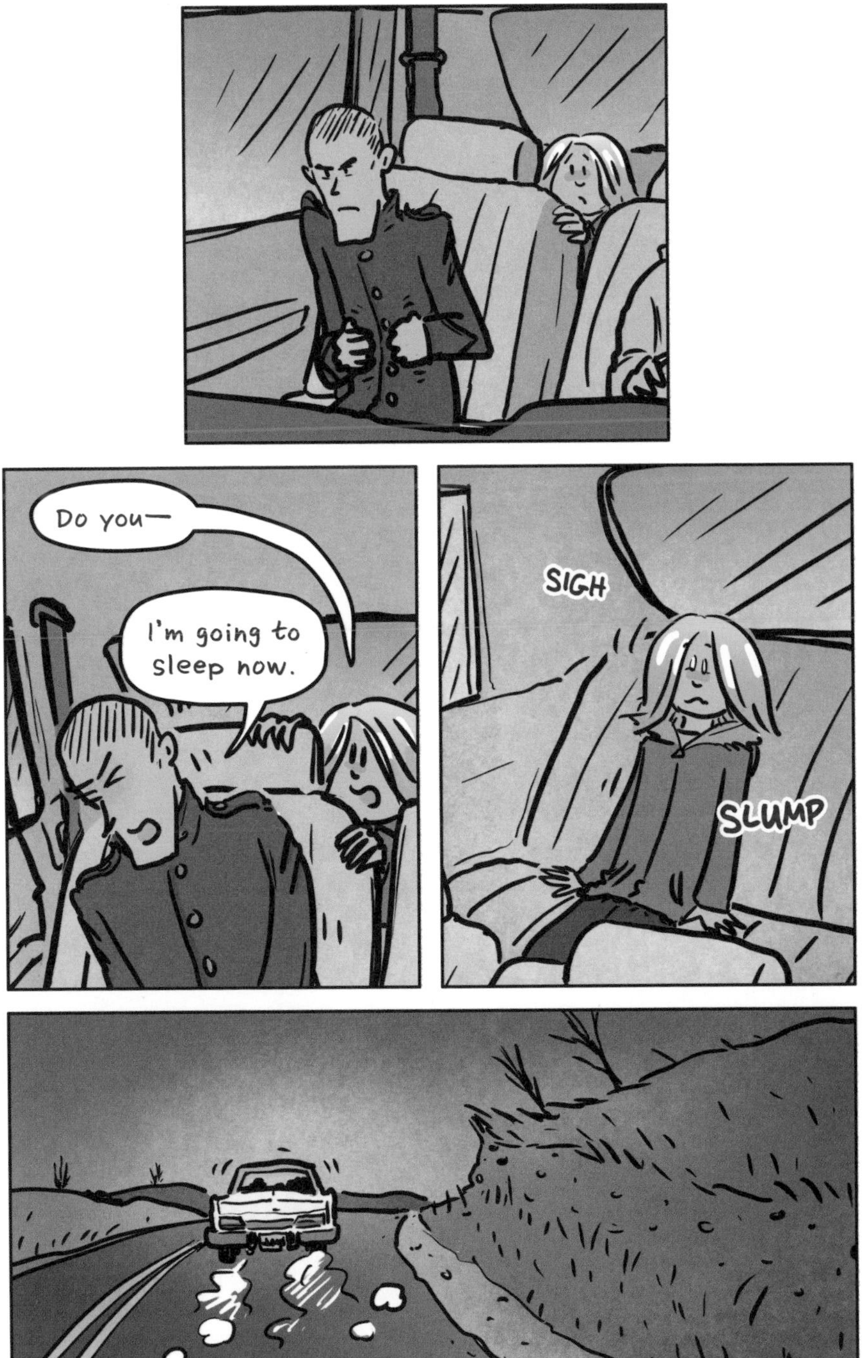
Do you—
I'm going to sleep now.
SIGH
SLUMP

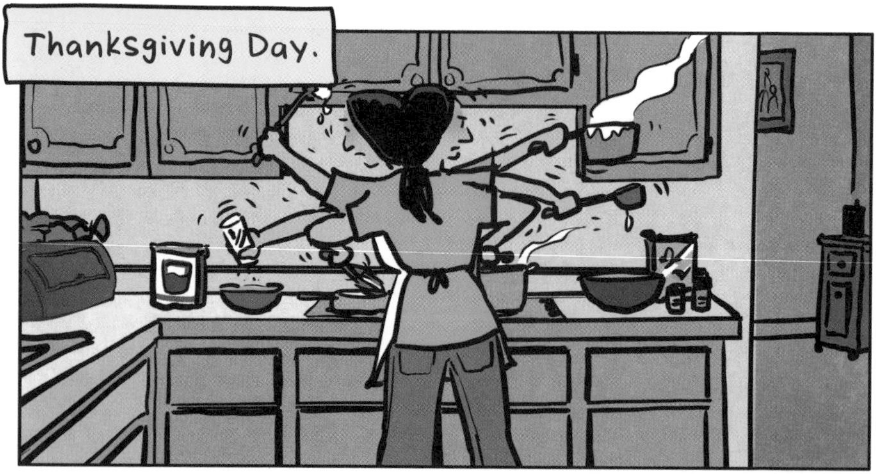
Thanksgiving Day.

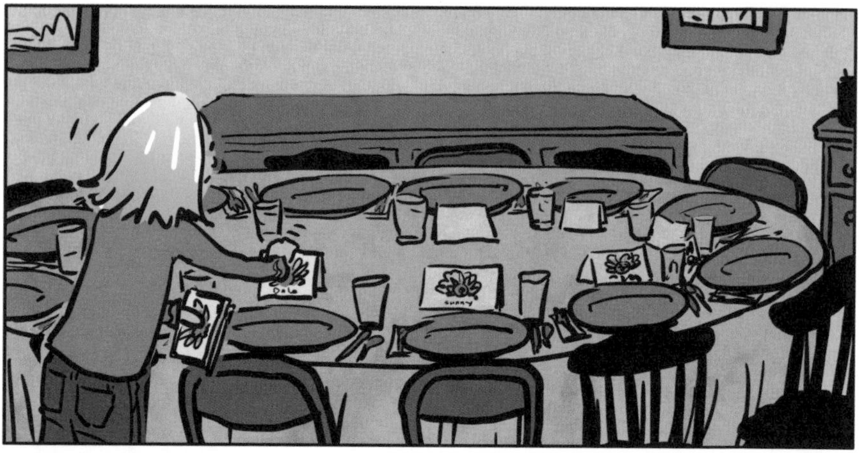
Dale
Sunny

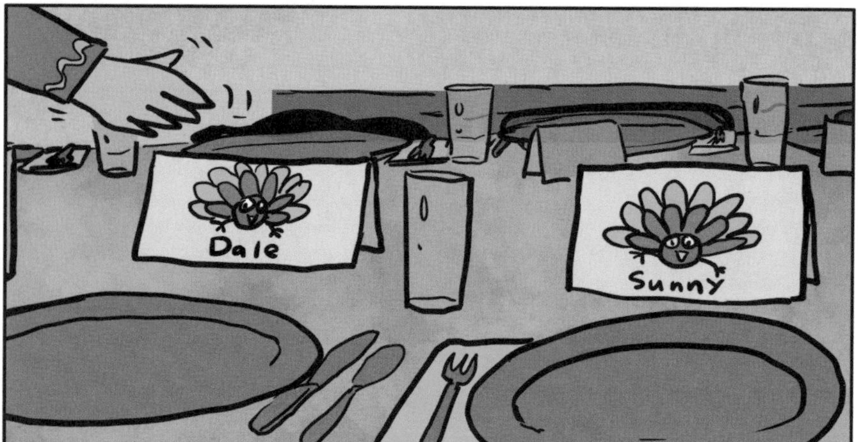
Dale
Sunny

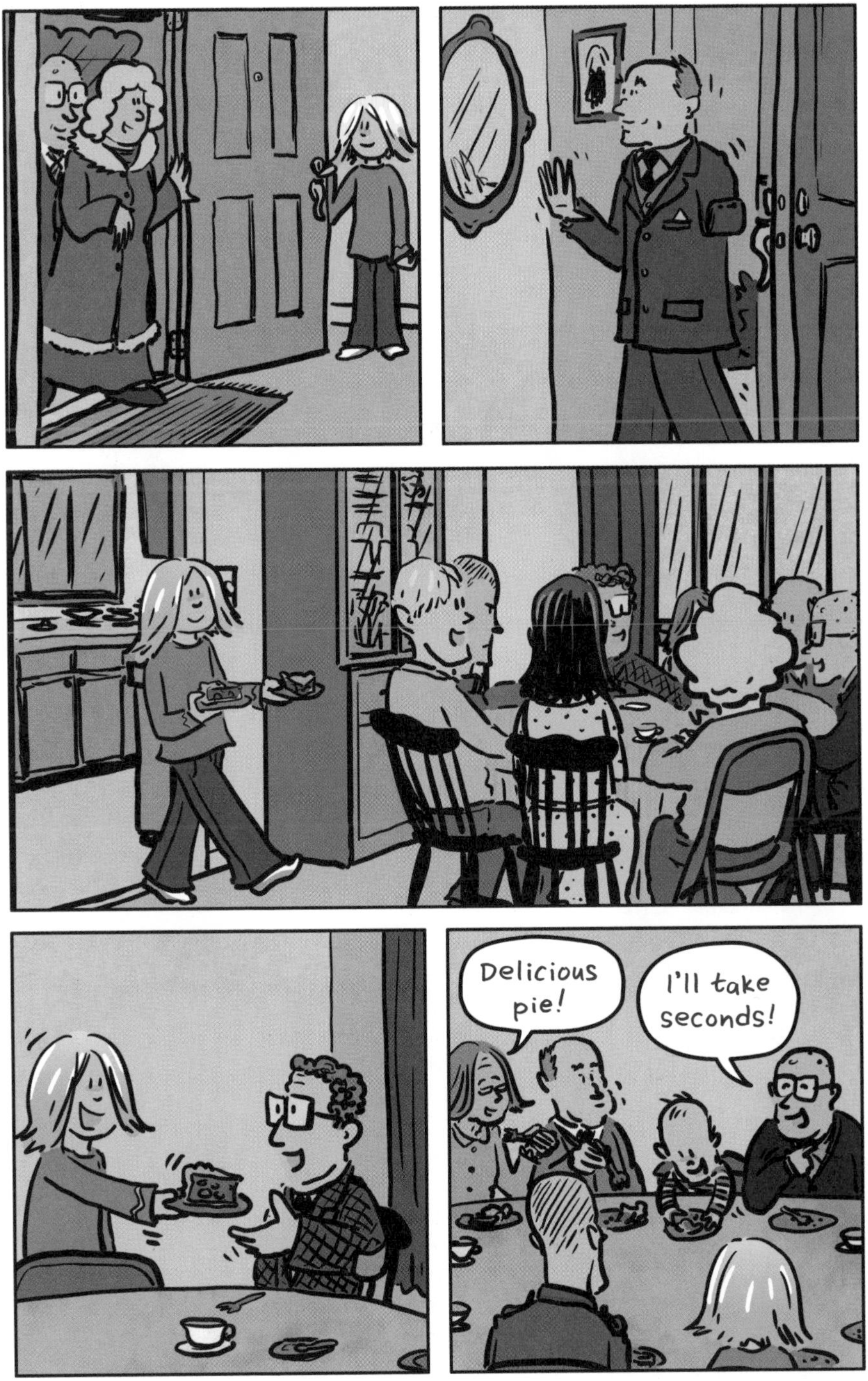
Delicious pie!
I'll take seconds!

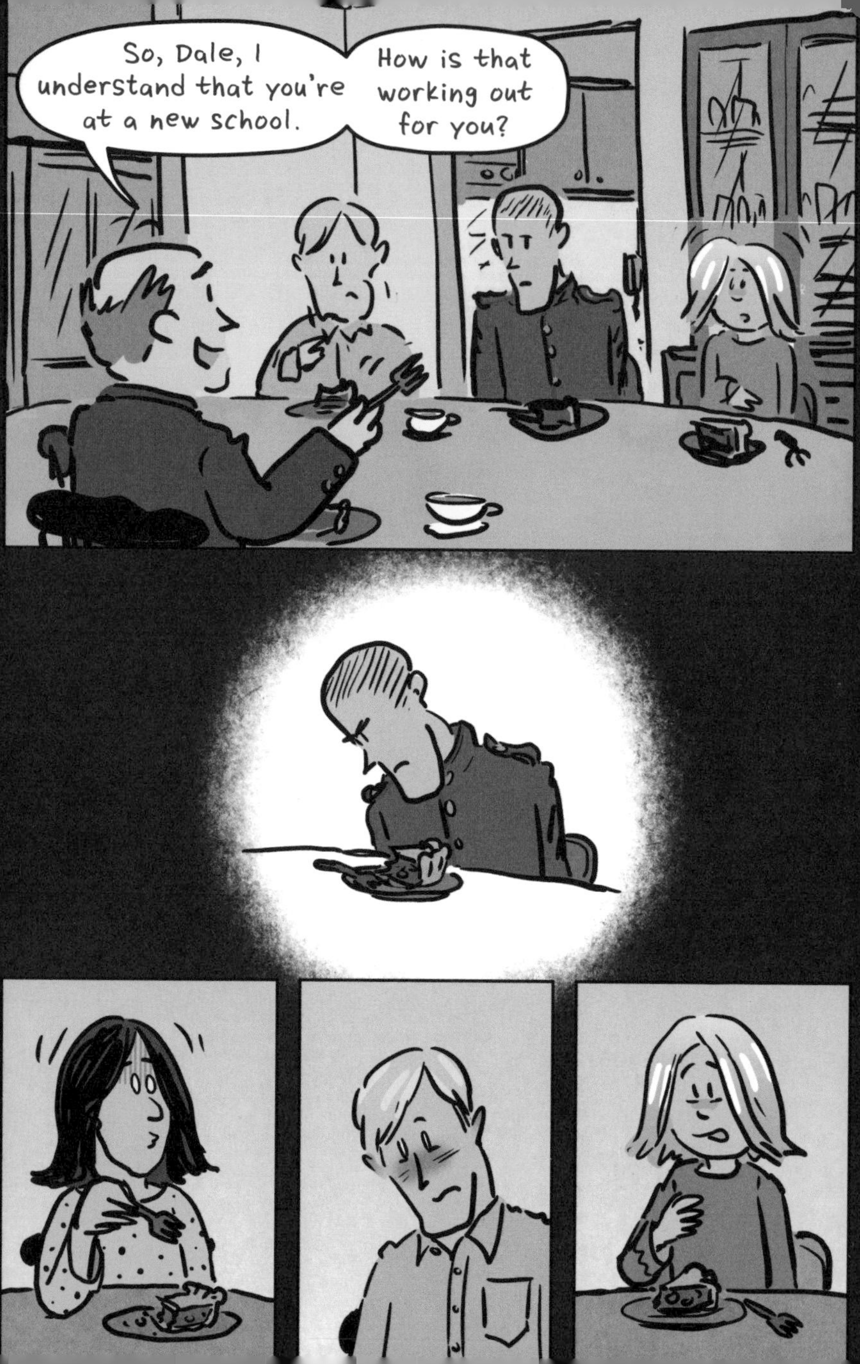
So, Dale, I understand that you're at a new school.
How is that working out for you?

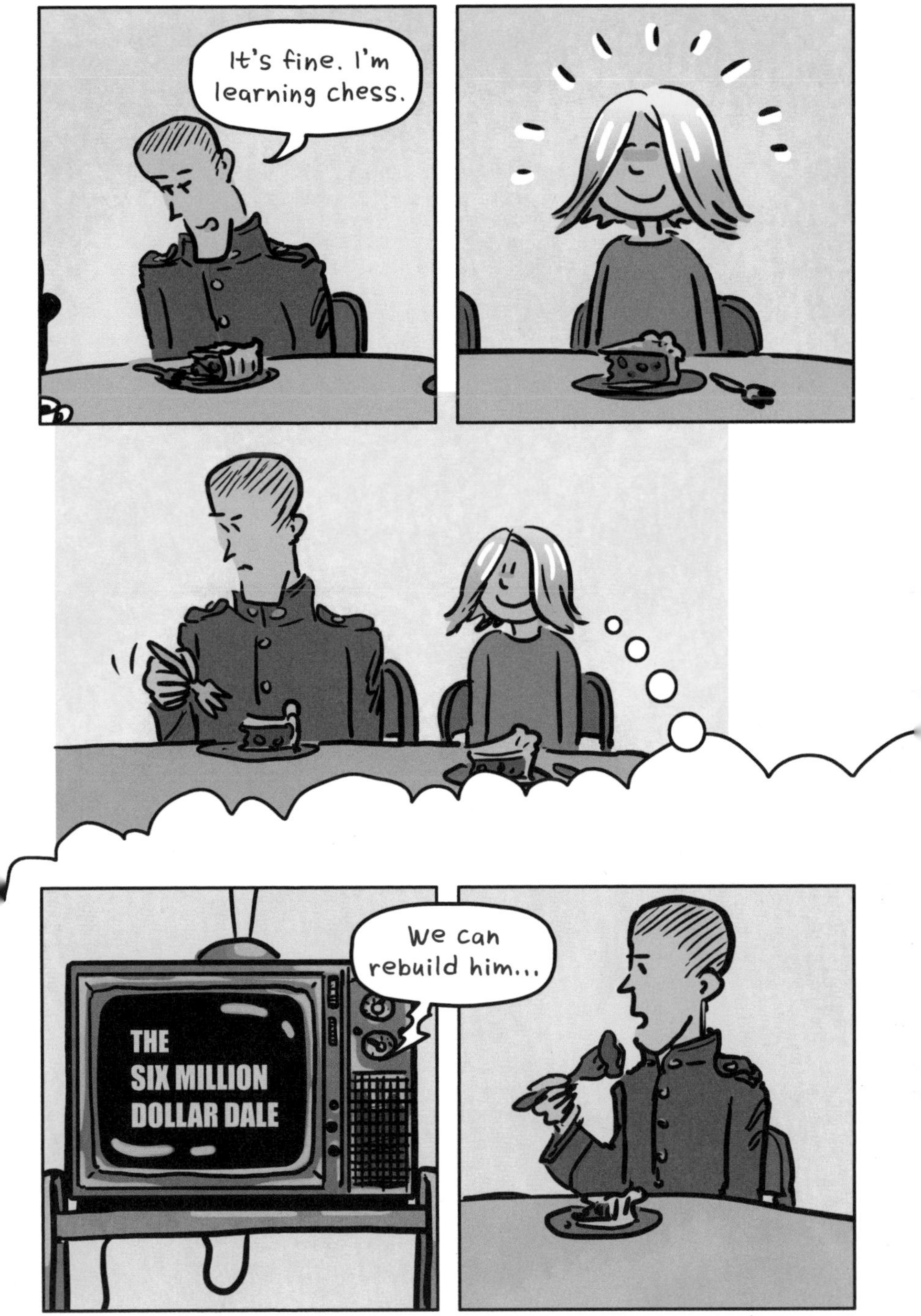
It's fine. I'm learning chess.
THE SIX MILLION DOLLAR DALE
We can rebuild him...

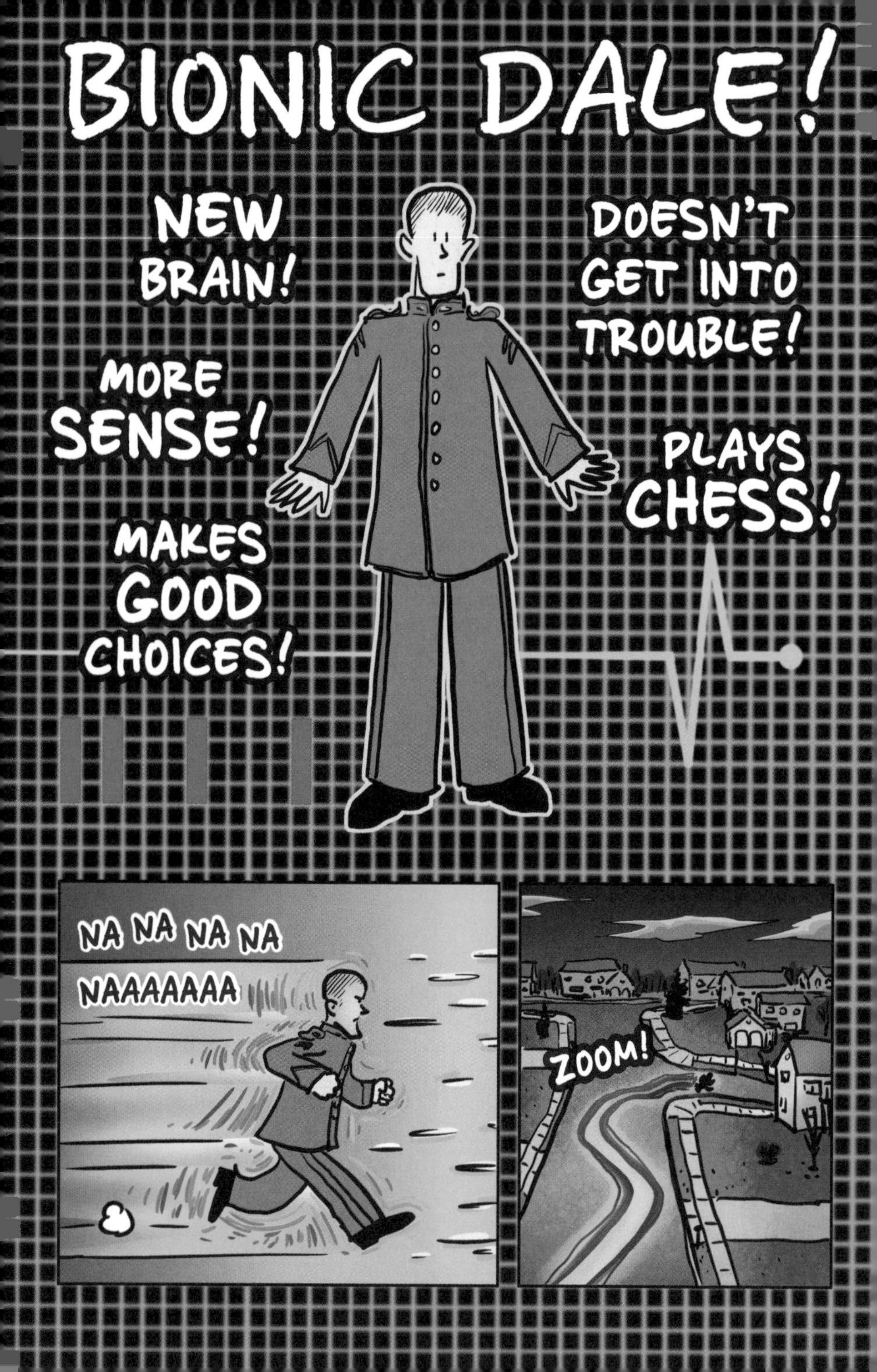
BIONIC DALE!
NEW BRAIN!
DOESN'T GET INTO TROUBLE!
MORE SENSE!
PLAYS CHESS!
MAKES GOOD CHOICES!
NA NA NA NA
NAAAAAAA
ZOOM!

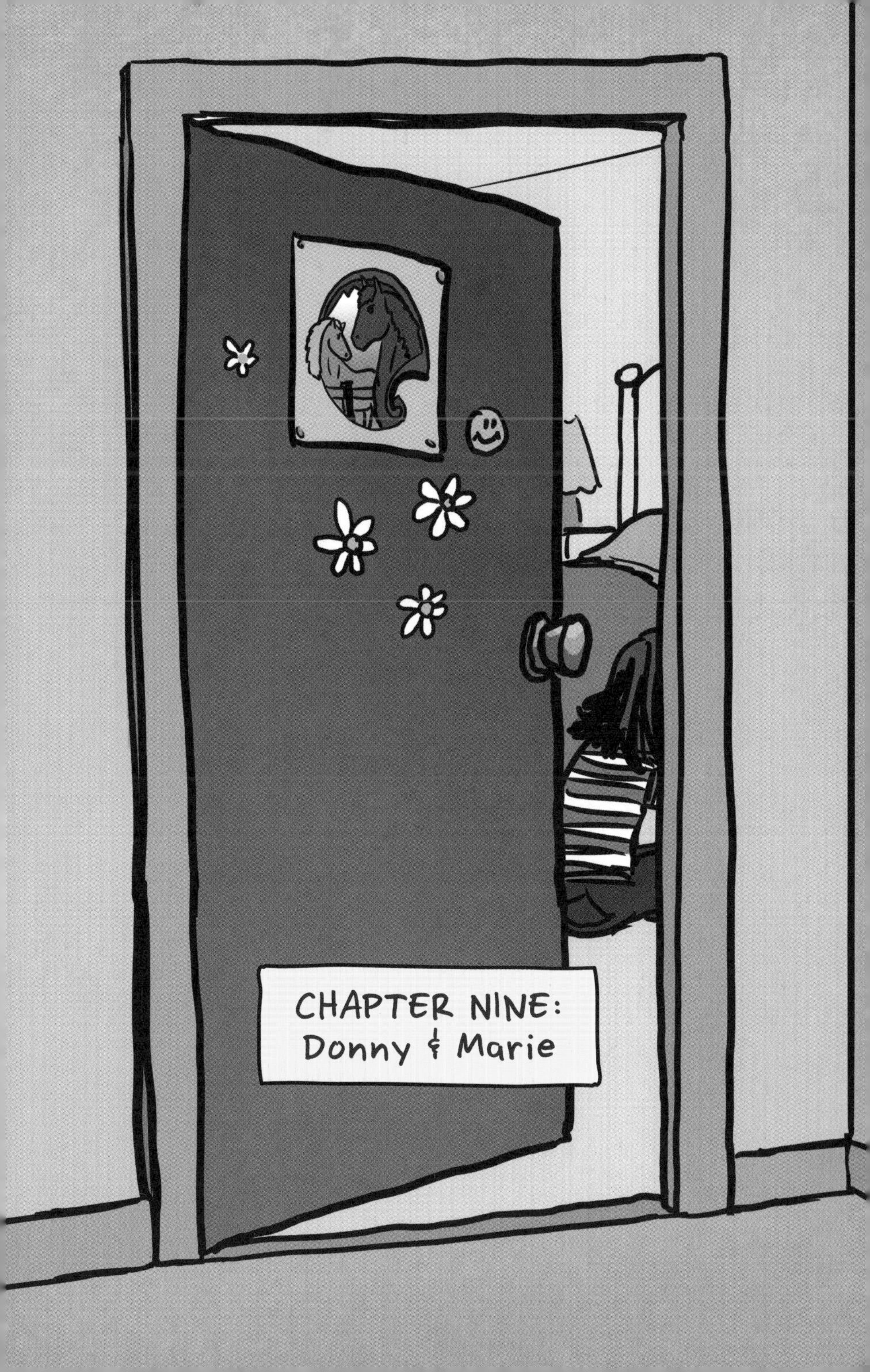
CHAPTER NINE:
Donny & Marie

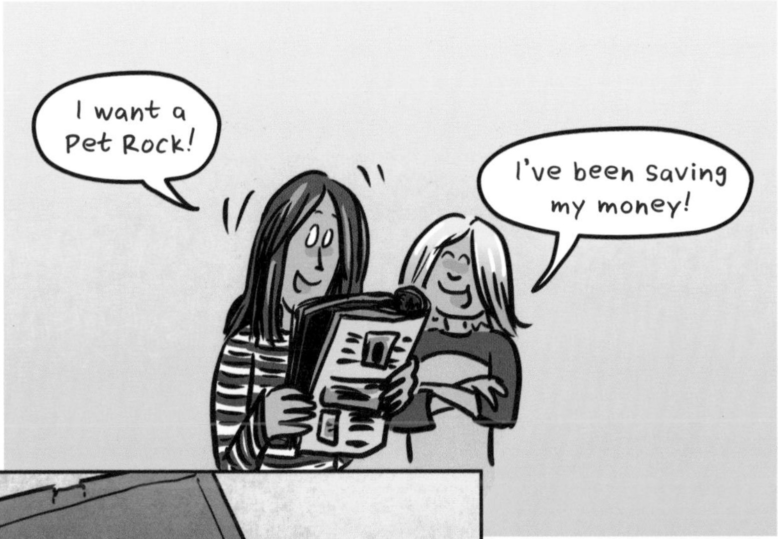
I want a Pet Rock!
I've been saving my money!

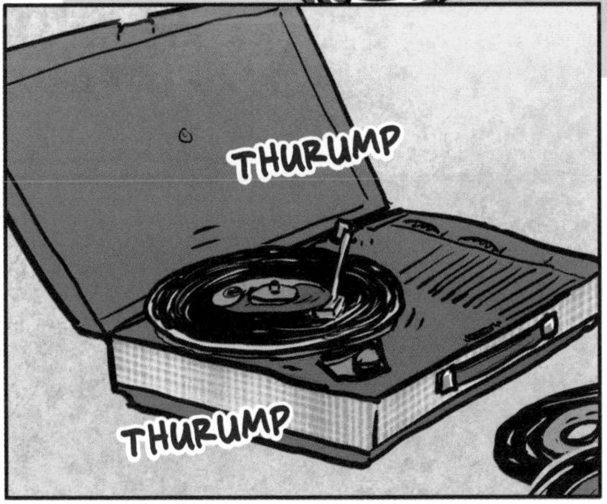
THURUMP
THURUMP

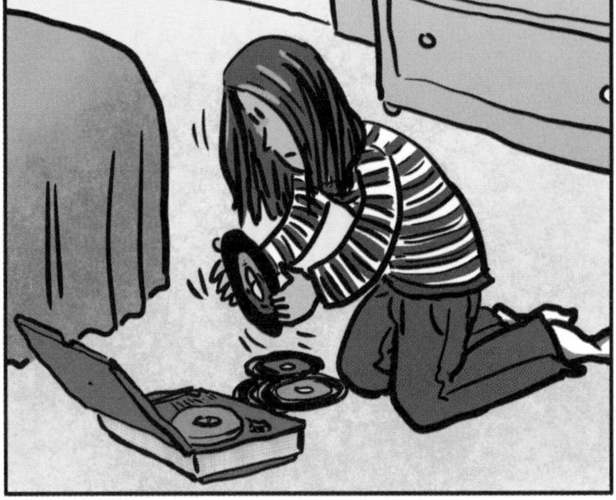

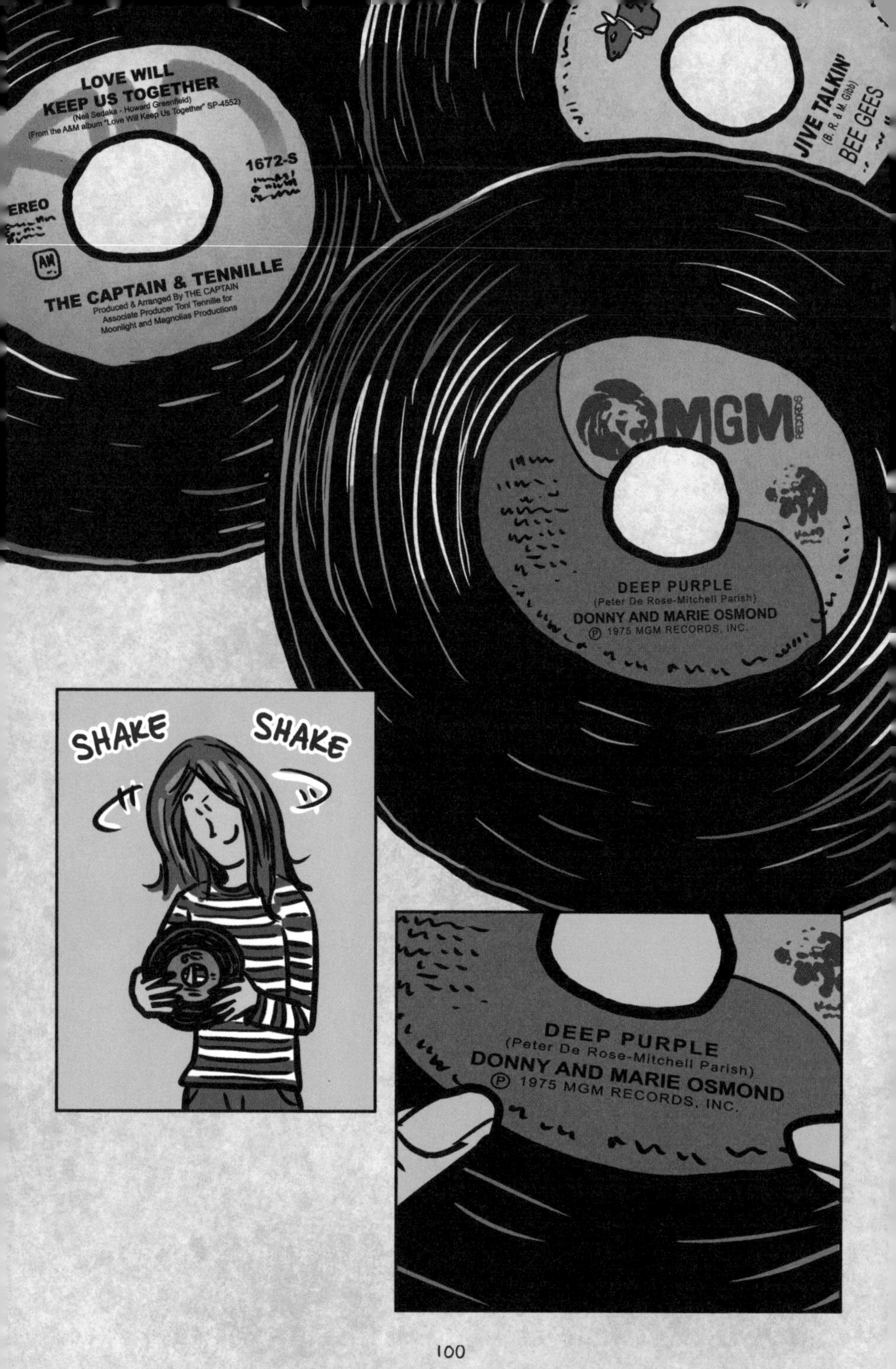
LOVE WILL KEEP US TOGETHER
(Neil Sedaka - Howard Greenfield)
(From the A&M album "Love Will Keep Us Together" SP-4552)
1672-S
THE CAPTAIN & TENNILLE
Produced & Arranged By THE CAPTAIN
Associate Producer Toni Tennille for
Moonlight and Magnolias Productions
JIVE TALKIN'
(B. R. & M. Gibb)
BEE GEES
MGM RECORDS
DEEP PURPLE
(Peter De Rose-Mitchell Parish)
DONNY AND MARIE OSMOND
℗ 1975 MGM RECORDS, INC.
SHAKE
SHAKE
DEEP PURPLE
(Peter De Rose-Mitchell Parish)
DONNY AND MARIE OSMOND
℗ 1975 MGM RECORDS, INC.

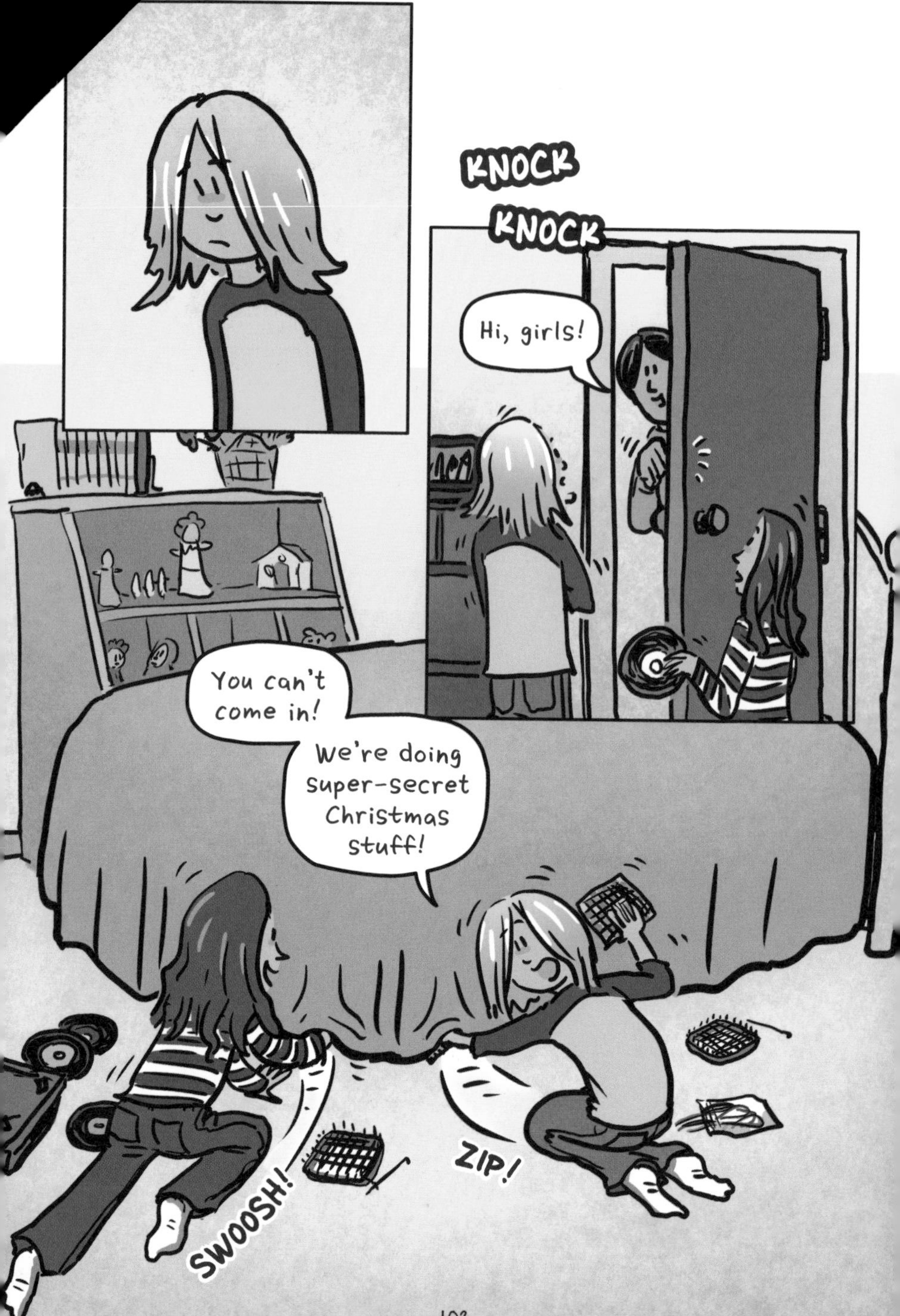
KNOCK
KNOCK
Hi, girls!
You can't come in!
We're doing super-secret Christmas stuff!
SWOOSH!
ZIP!

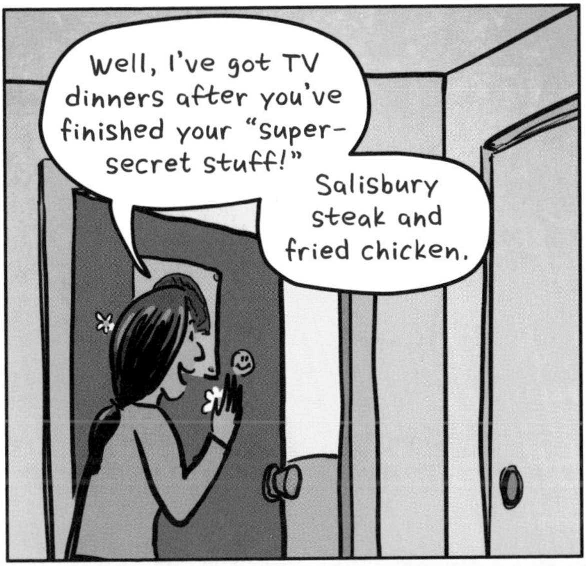
Well, I've got TV dinners after you've finished your "super-secret stuff!"
Salisbury steak and fried chicken.

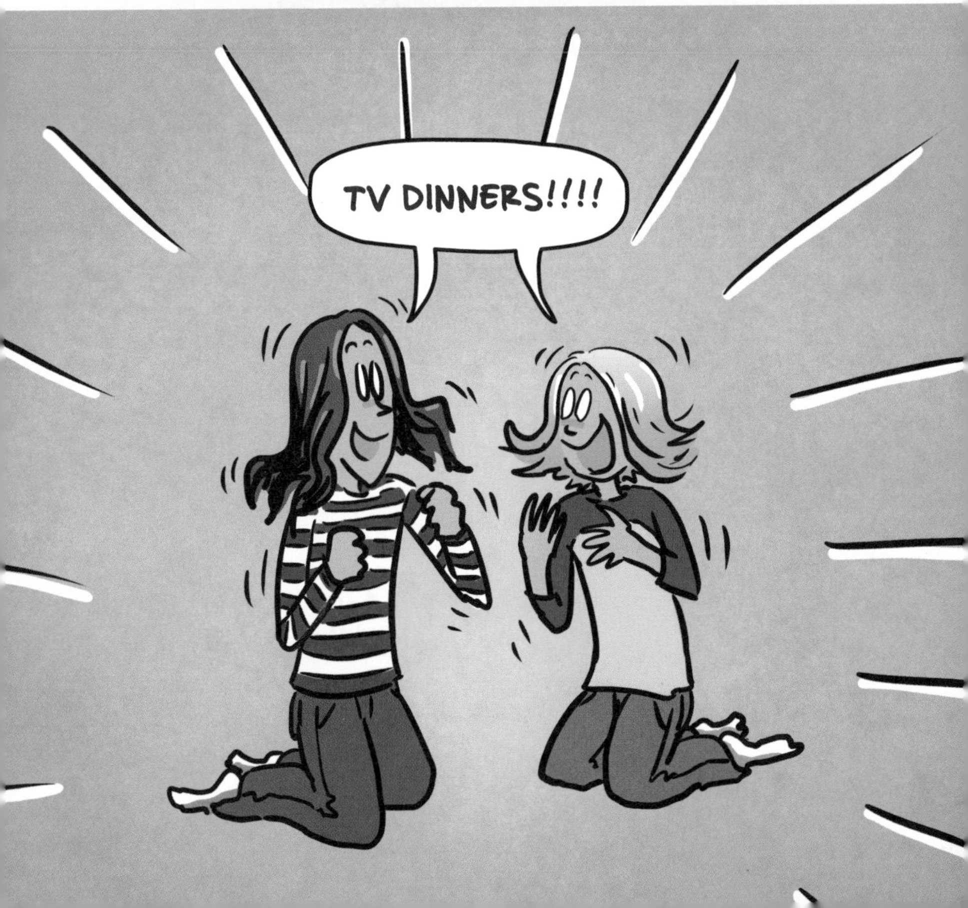
TV DINNERS!!!!

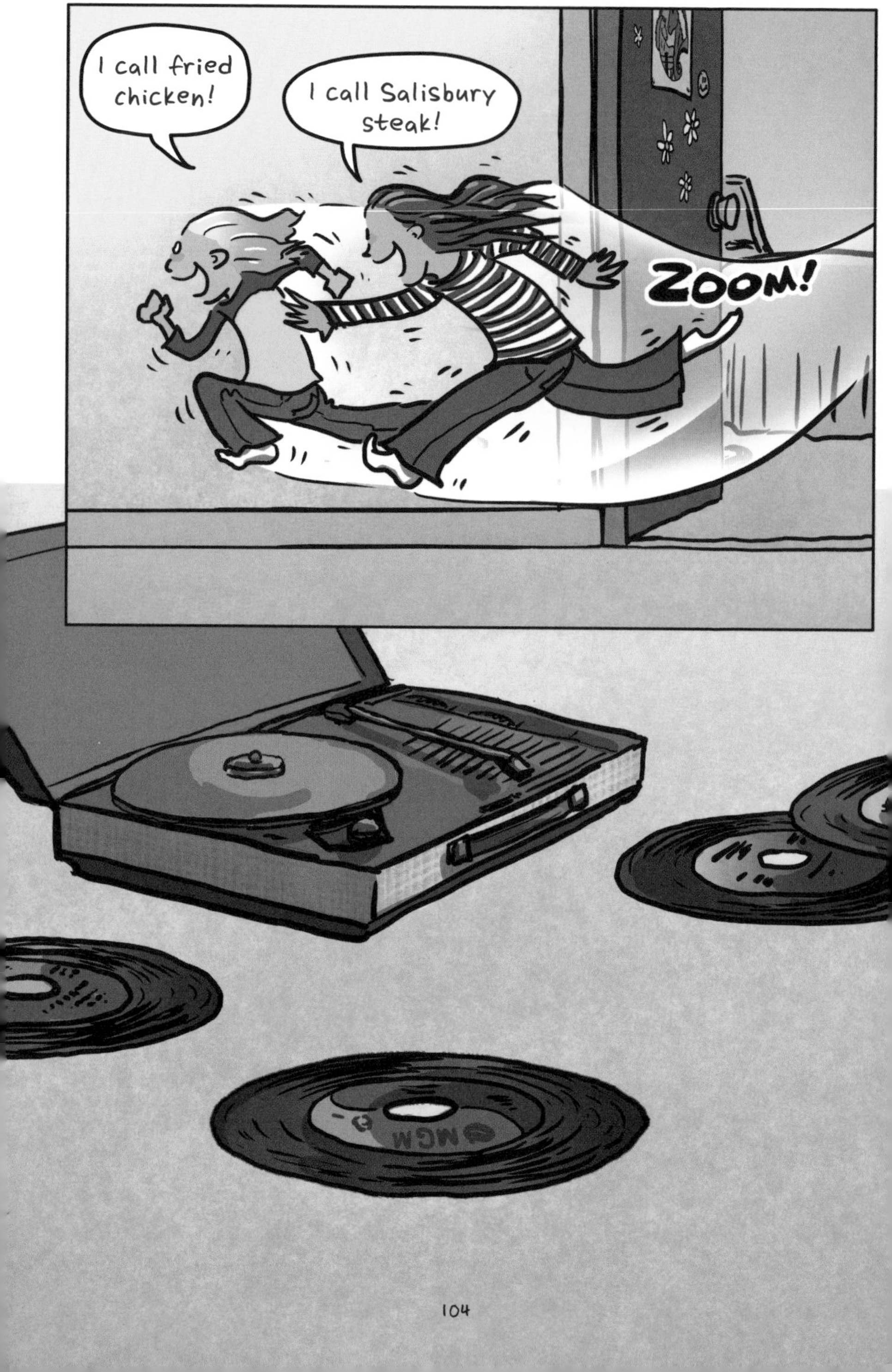
I call fried chicken!
I call Salisbury steak!
ZOOM!
MGM

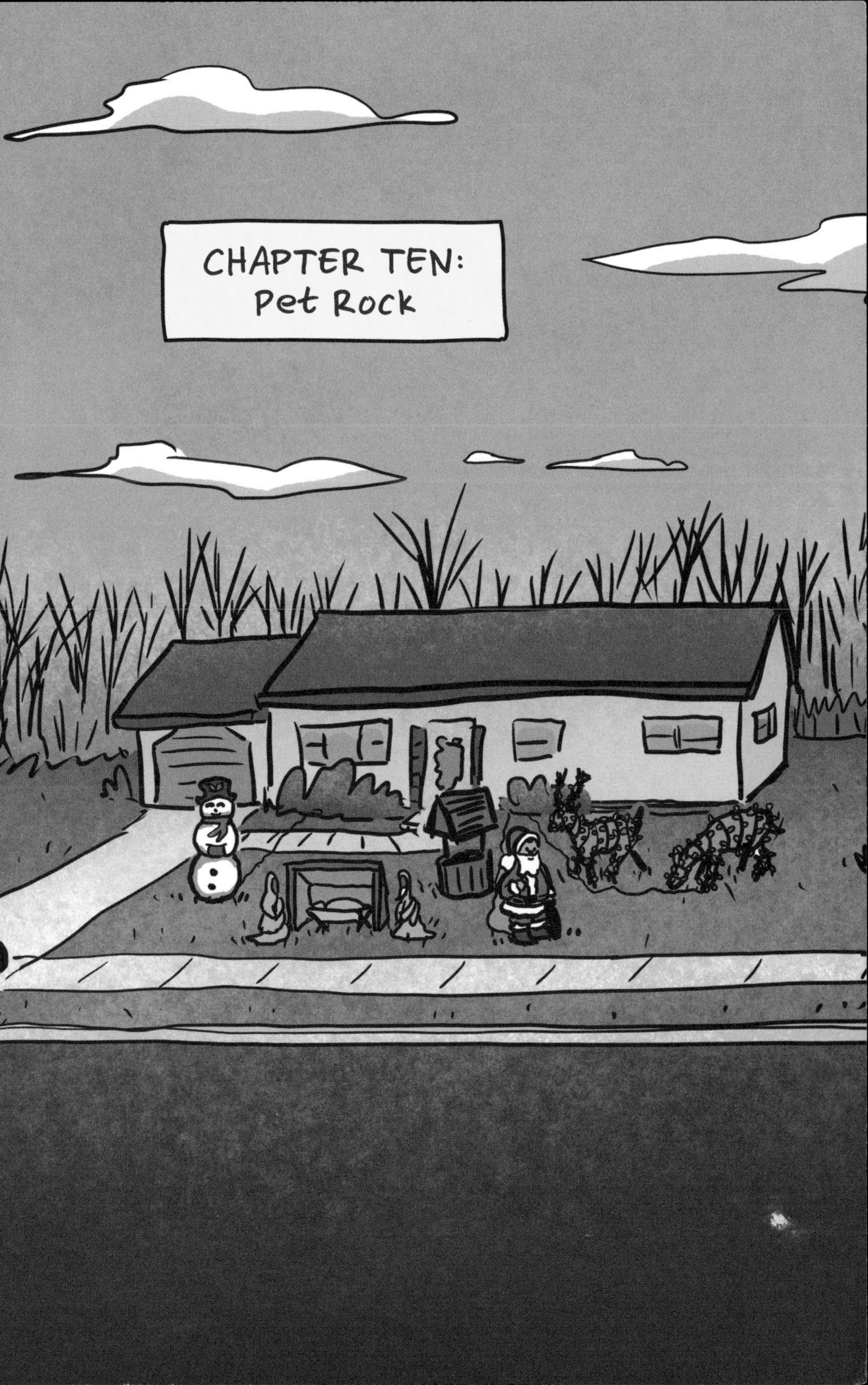
CHAPTER TEN:
Pet Rock

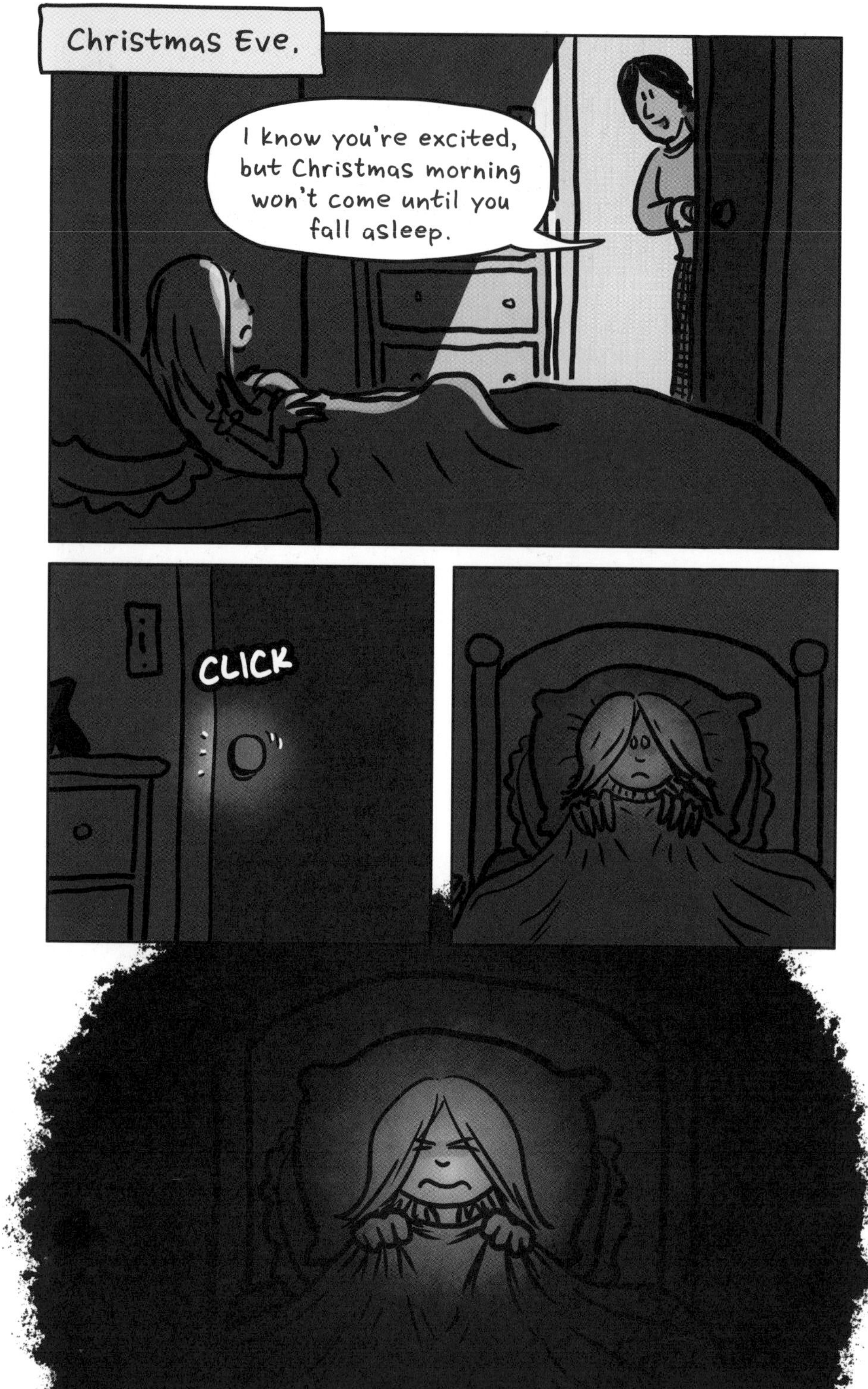
Christmas Eve.
I know you're excited, but Christmas morning won't come until you fall asleep.
CLICK

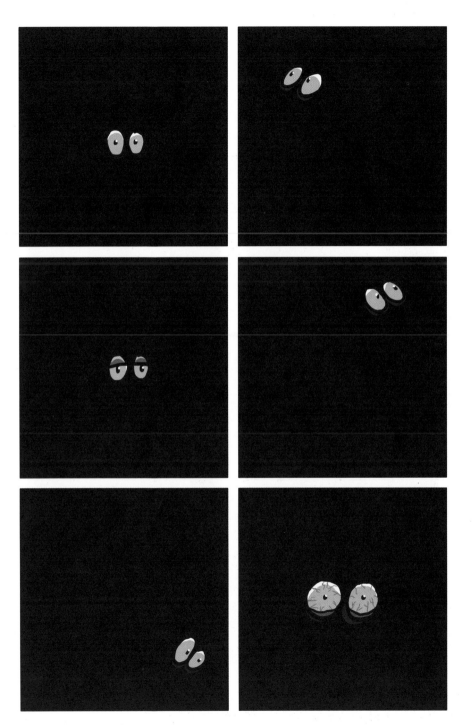

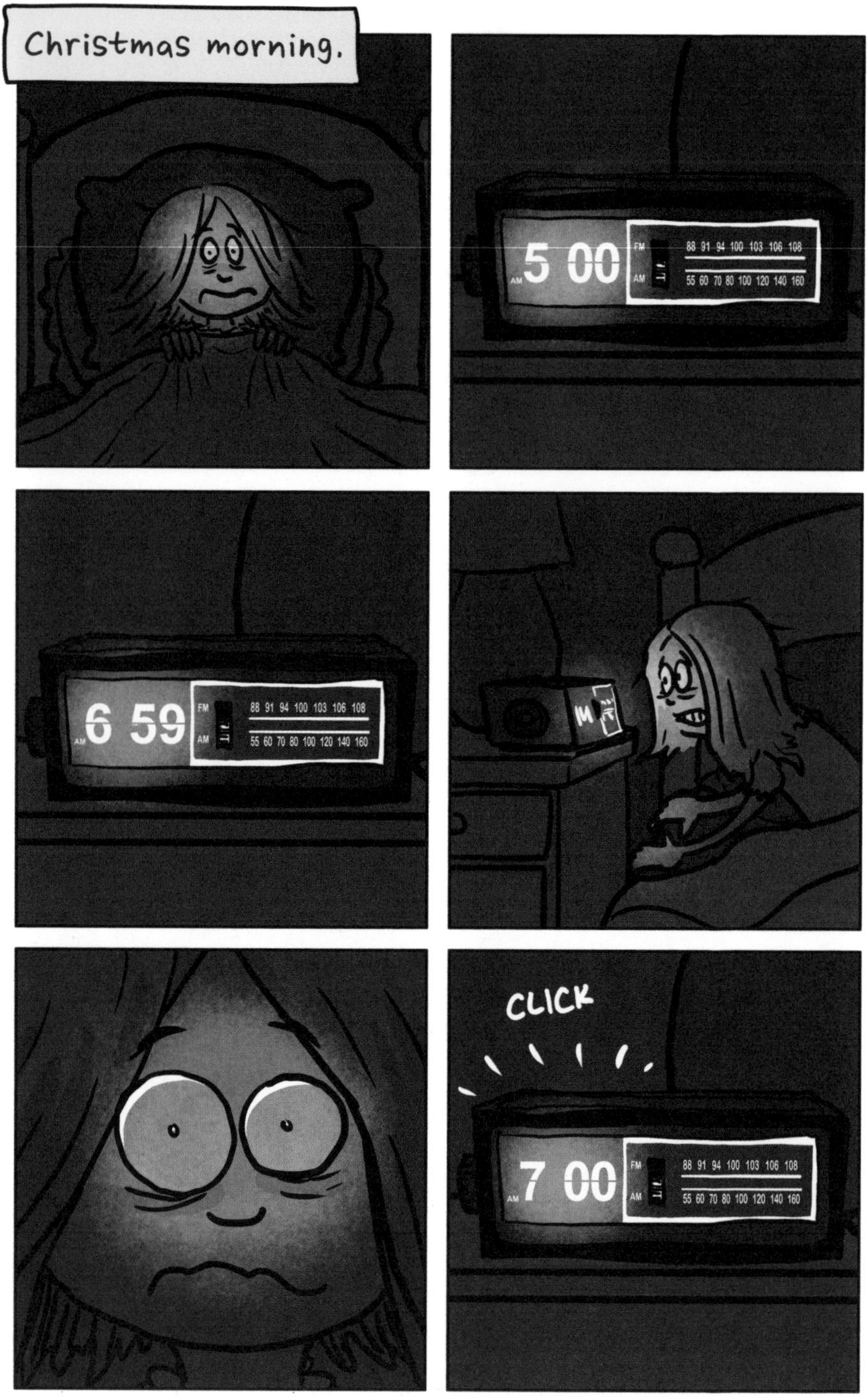
Christmas morning.
5 00
6 59
CLICK
7 00

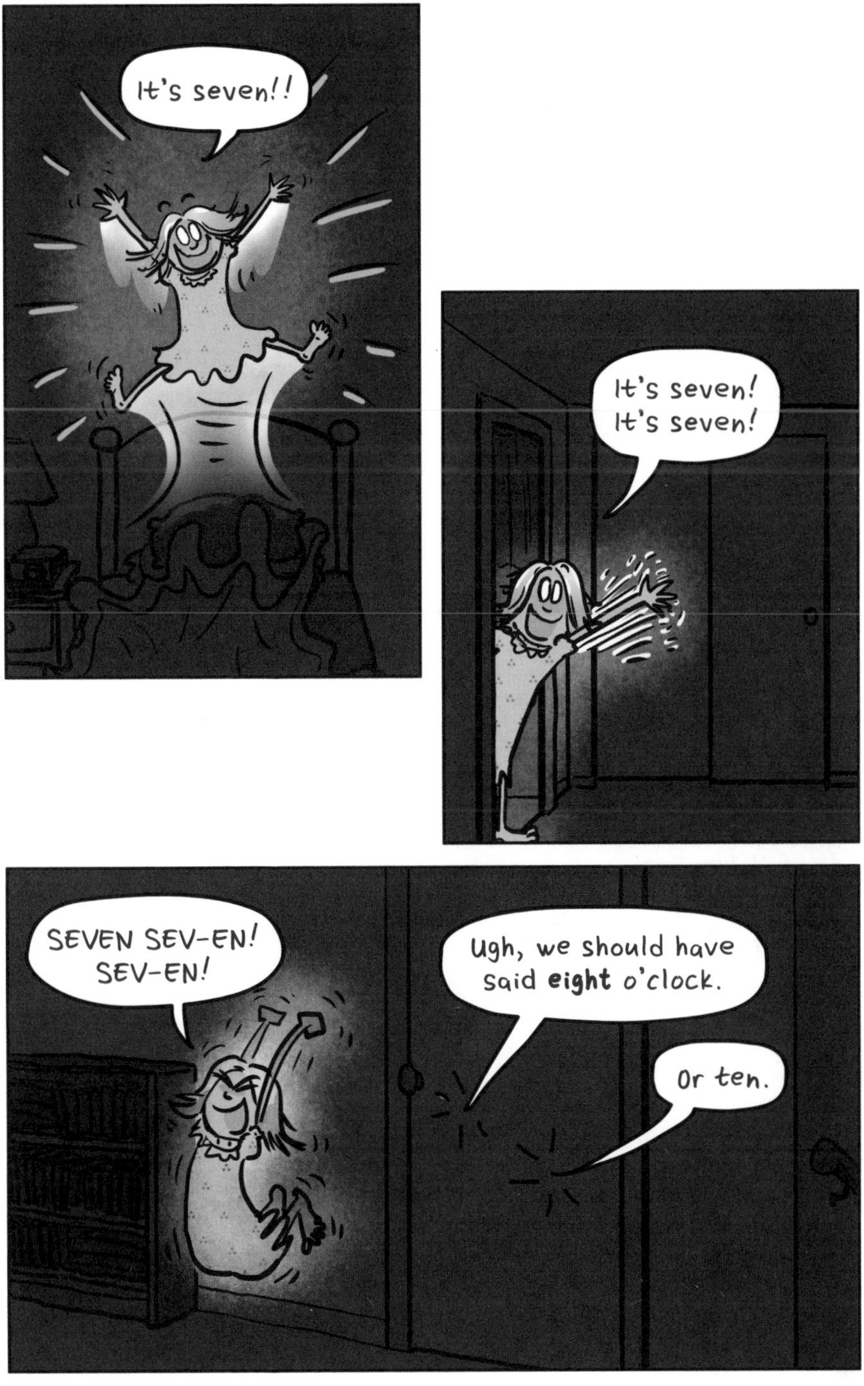
It's seven!!
It's seven! It's seven!
SEVEN SEV-EN! SEV-EN!
Ugh, we should have said **eight** o'clock.
Or ten.

A few minutes later.

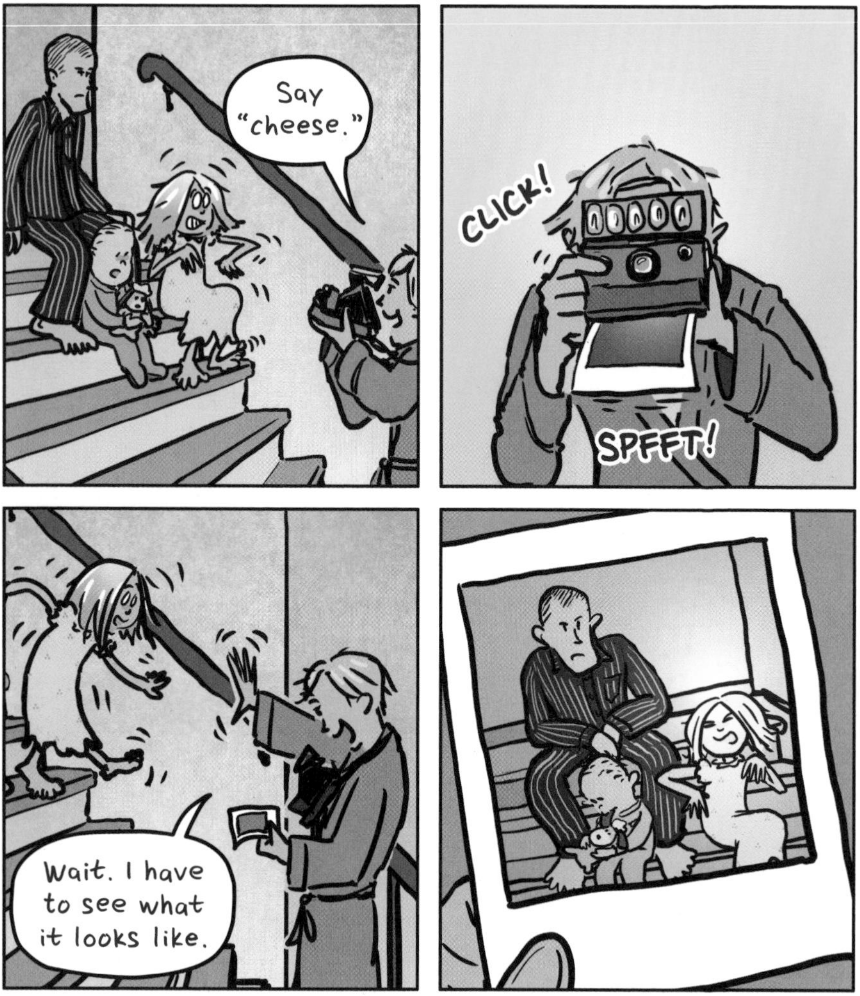
Say "cheese."
CLICK!
SPFFT!
Wait. I have to see what it looks like.

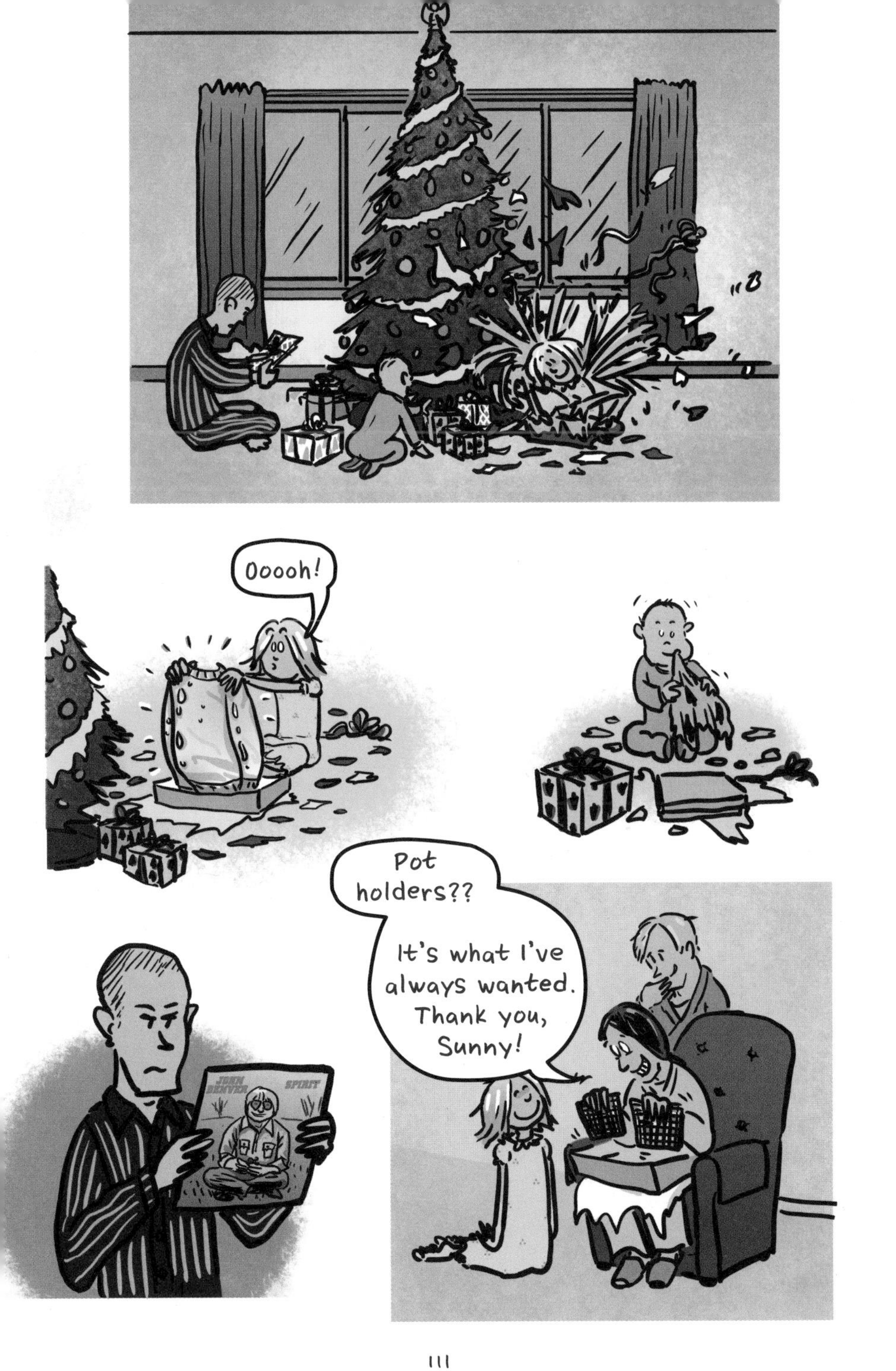
Ooooh!
JOHN DENVER
SPIRIT
Pot holders??
It's what I've always wanted. Thank you, Sunny!

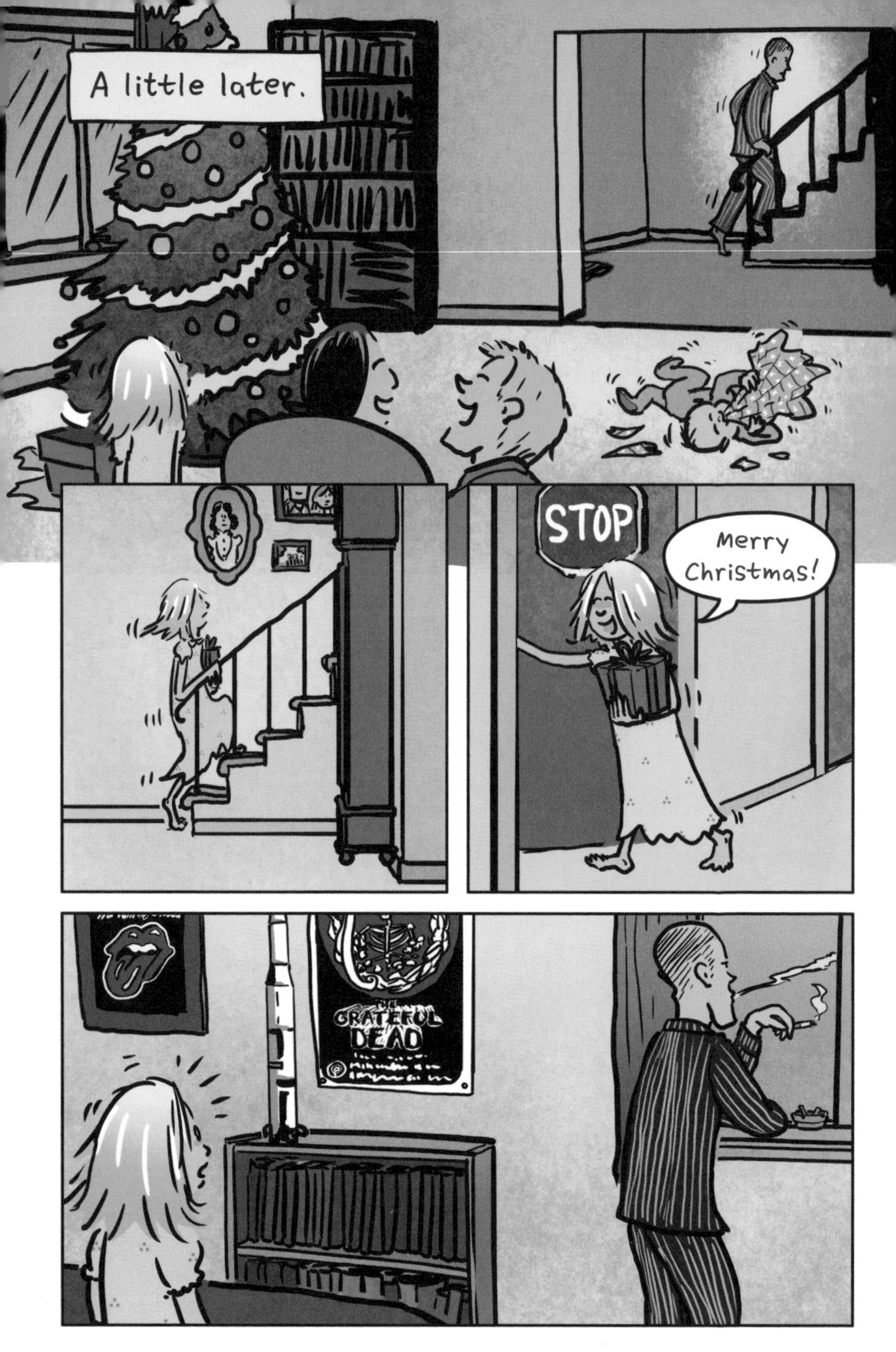
A little later.
STOP
Merry Christmas!
GRATEFUL DEAD

CHAPTER ELEVEN:
Ball Drop

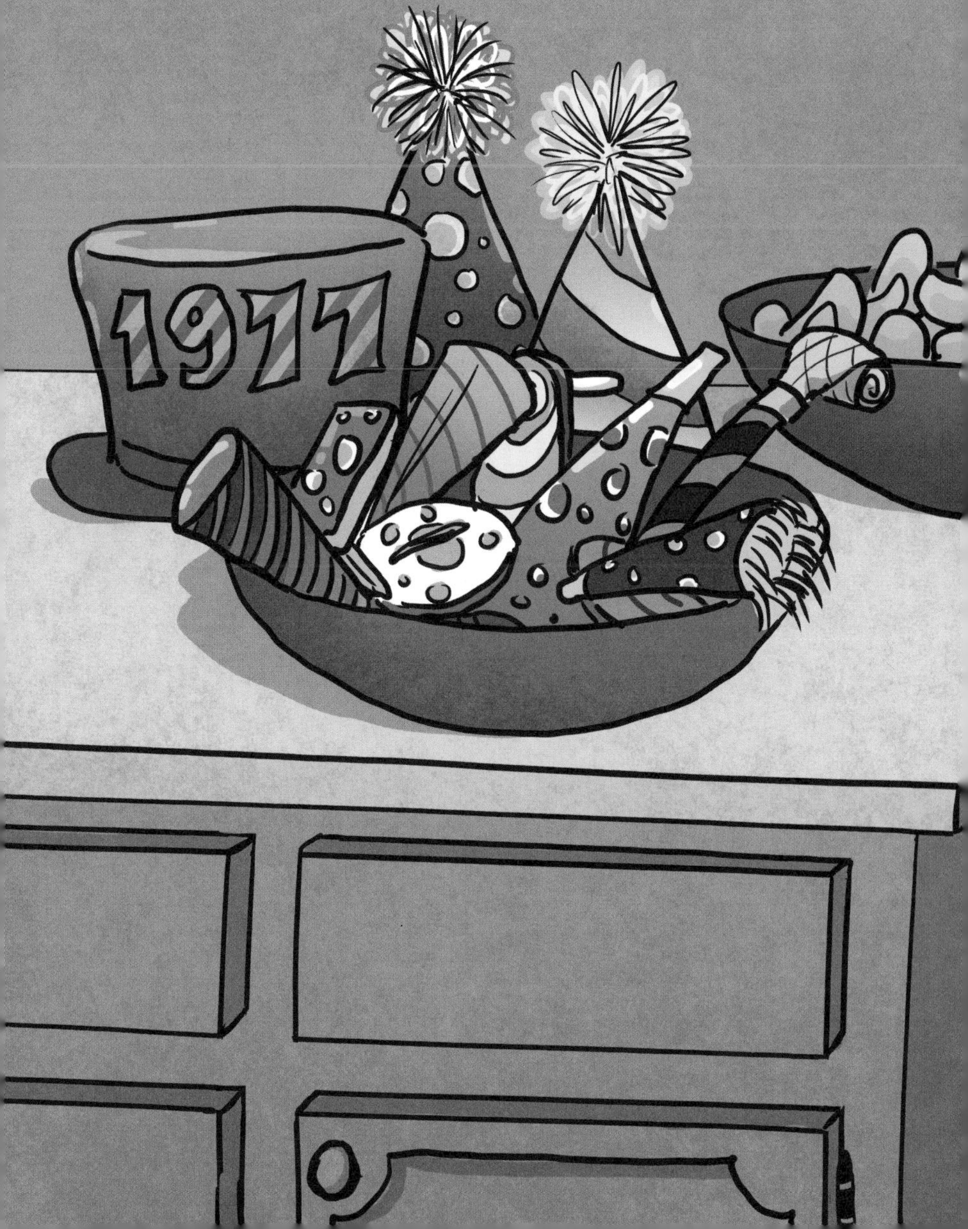
1977

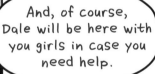

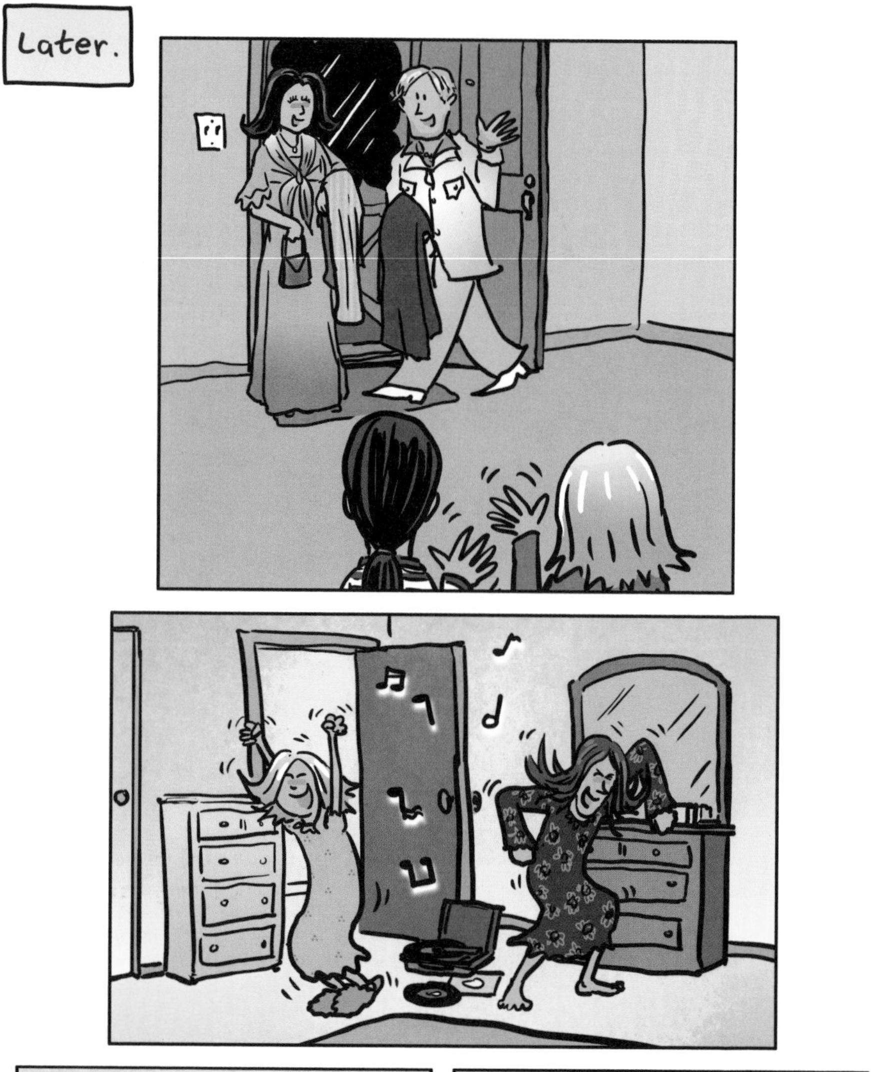
Later.
12
9
3
6

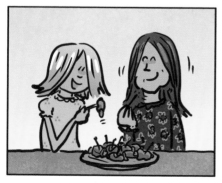

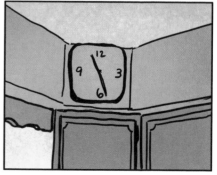

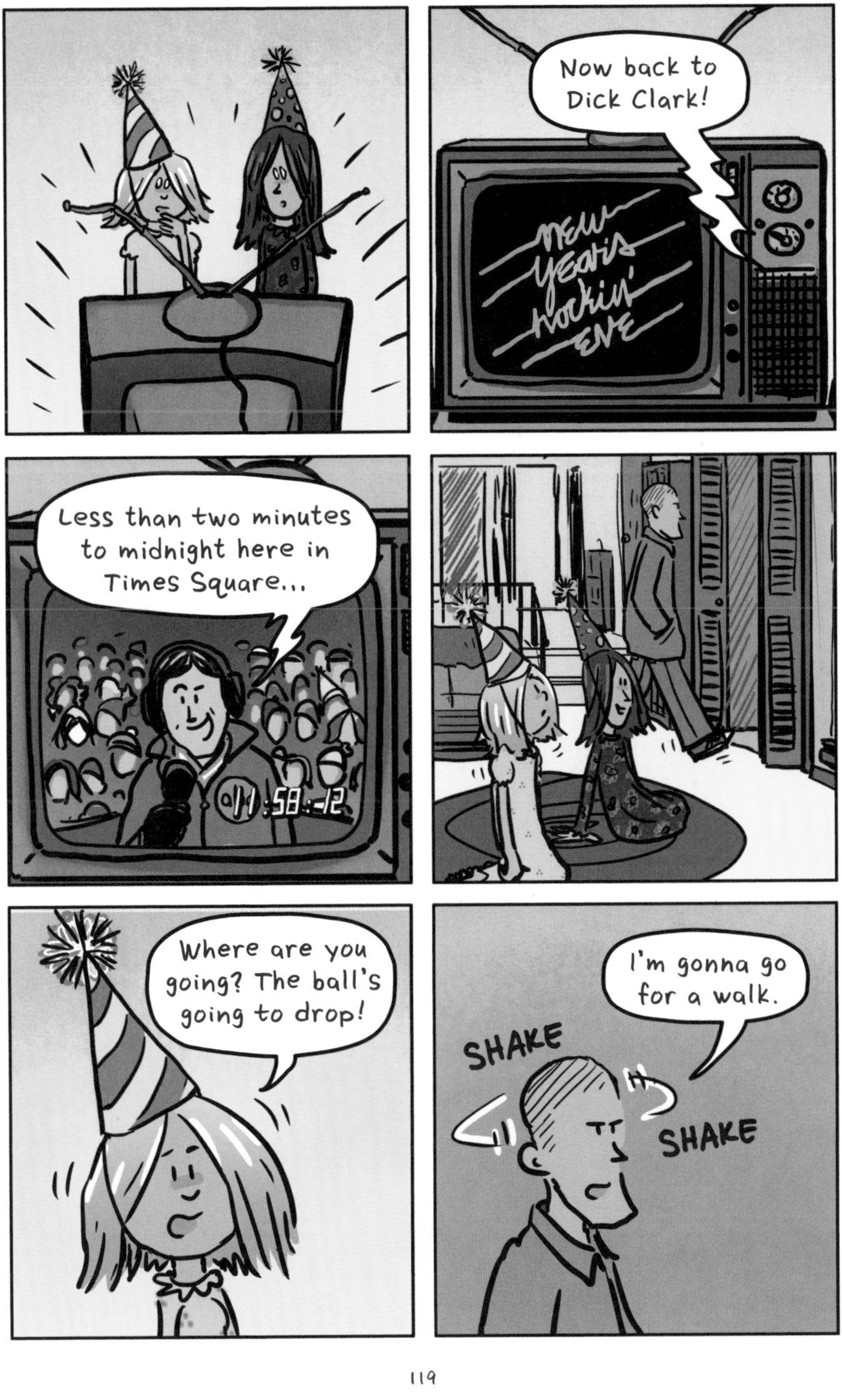
Now back to Dick Clark!
NEW YEAR'S ROCKIN' EVE
Less than two minutes to midnight here in Times Square...
11:58:12
Where are you going? The ball's going to drop!
I'm gonna go for a walk.
SHAKE
SHAKE

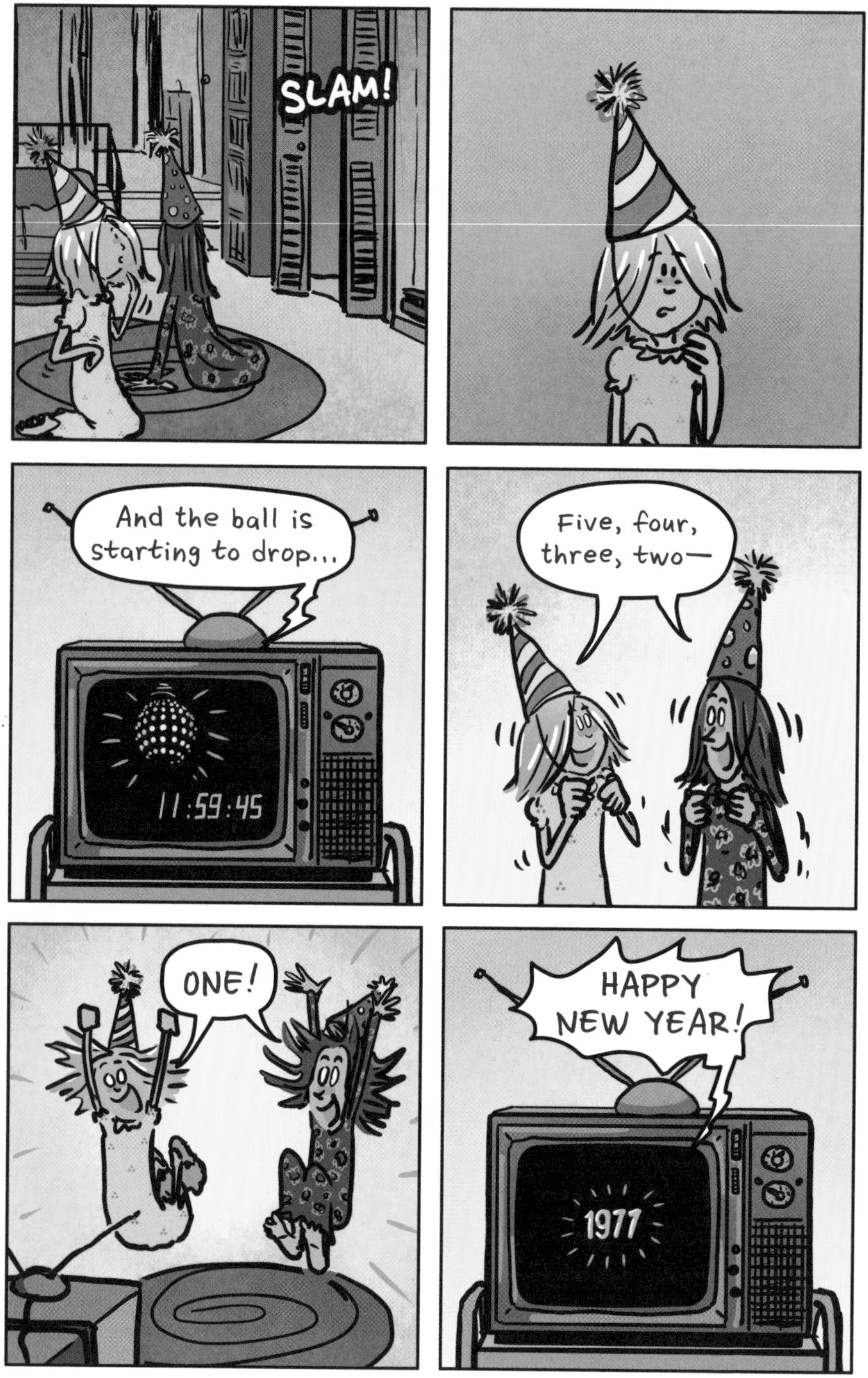
SLAM!
And the ball is starting to drop...
11:59:45
Five, four, three, two—
ONE!
HAPPY NEW YEAR!
1977

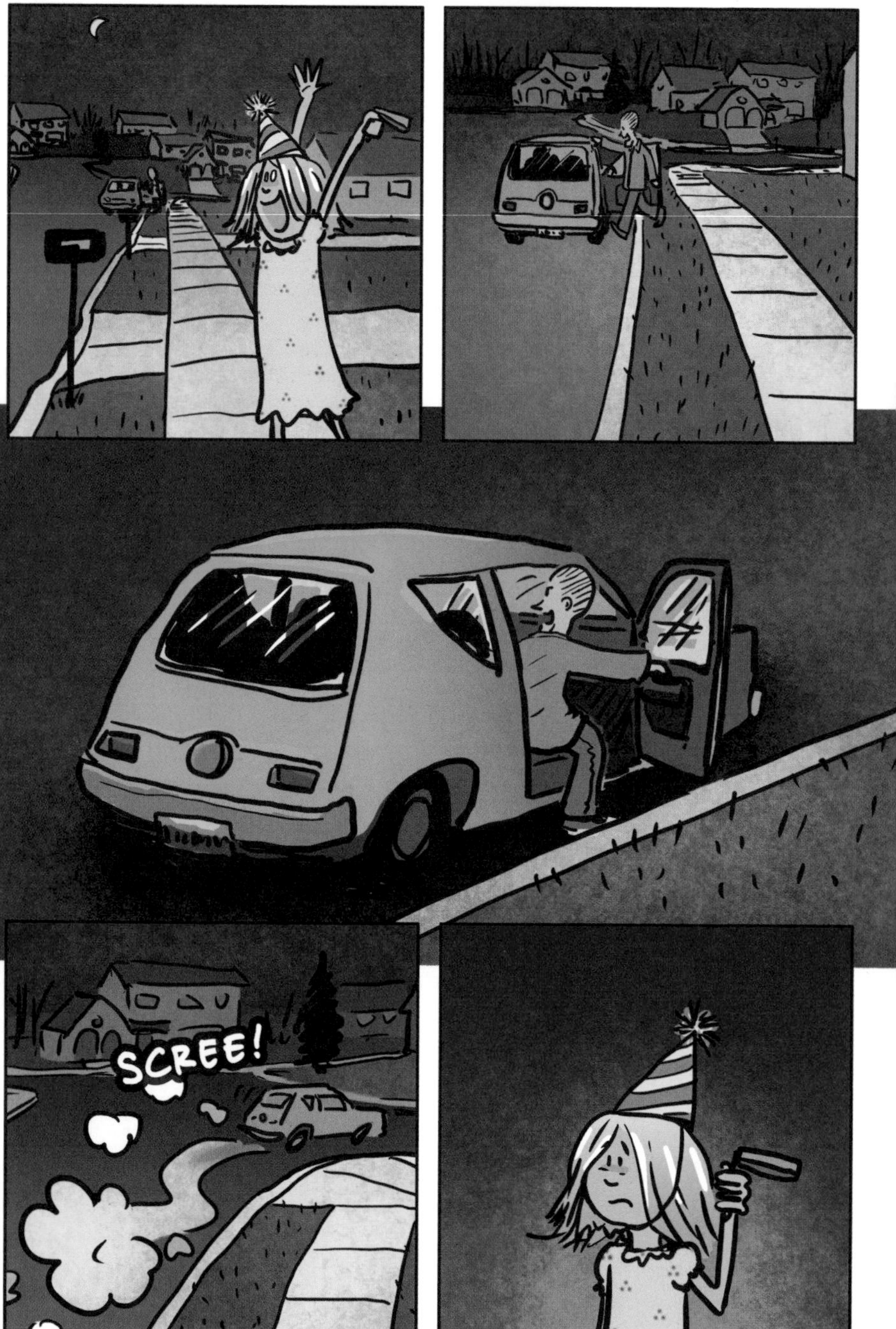
SCREE!

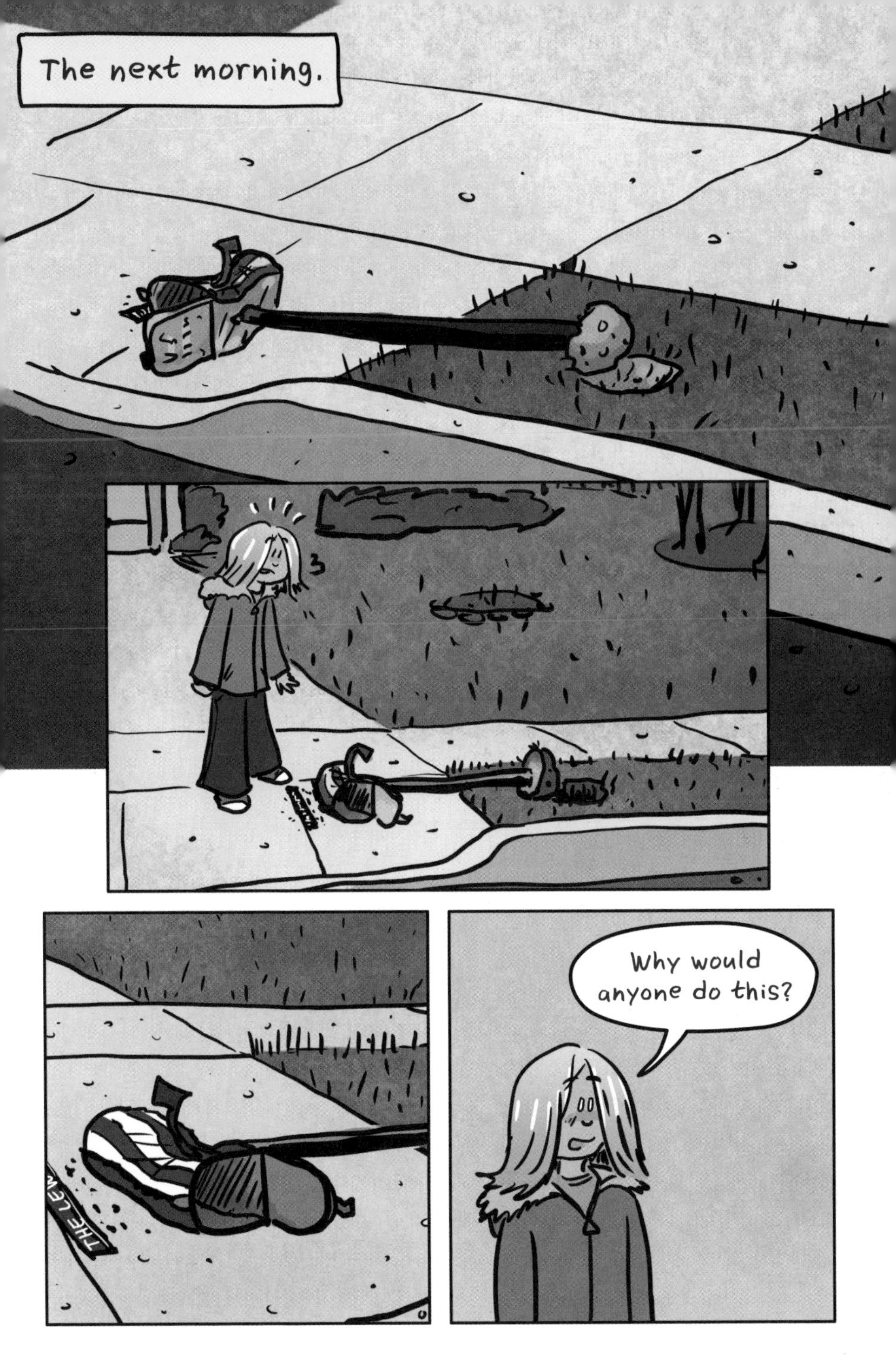

The next morning.
THE LEW
Why would anyone do this?

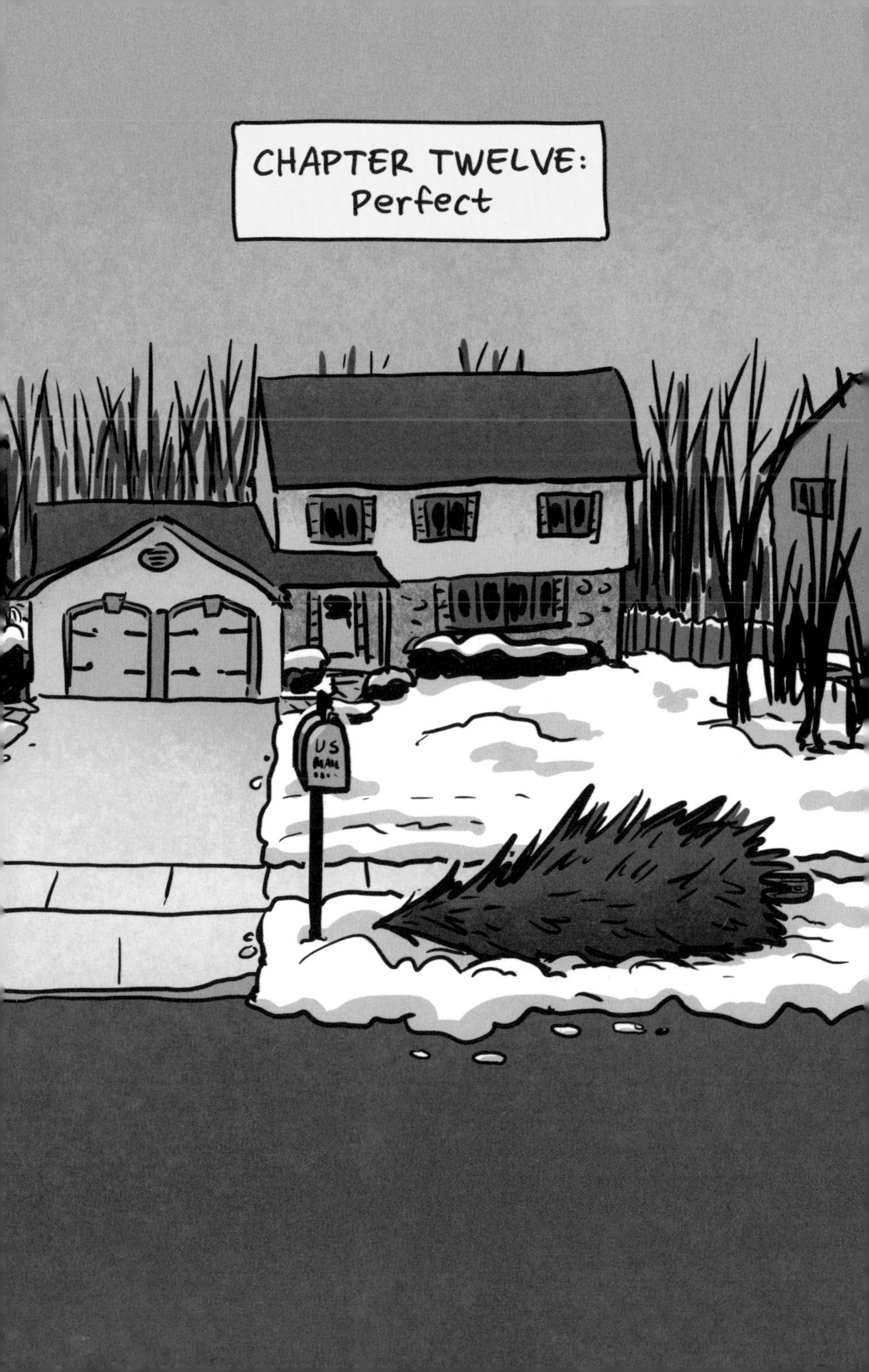
CHAPTER TWELVE:
Perfect
US

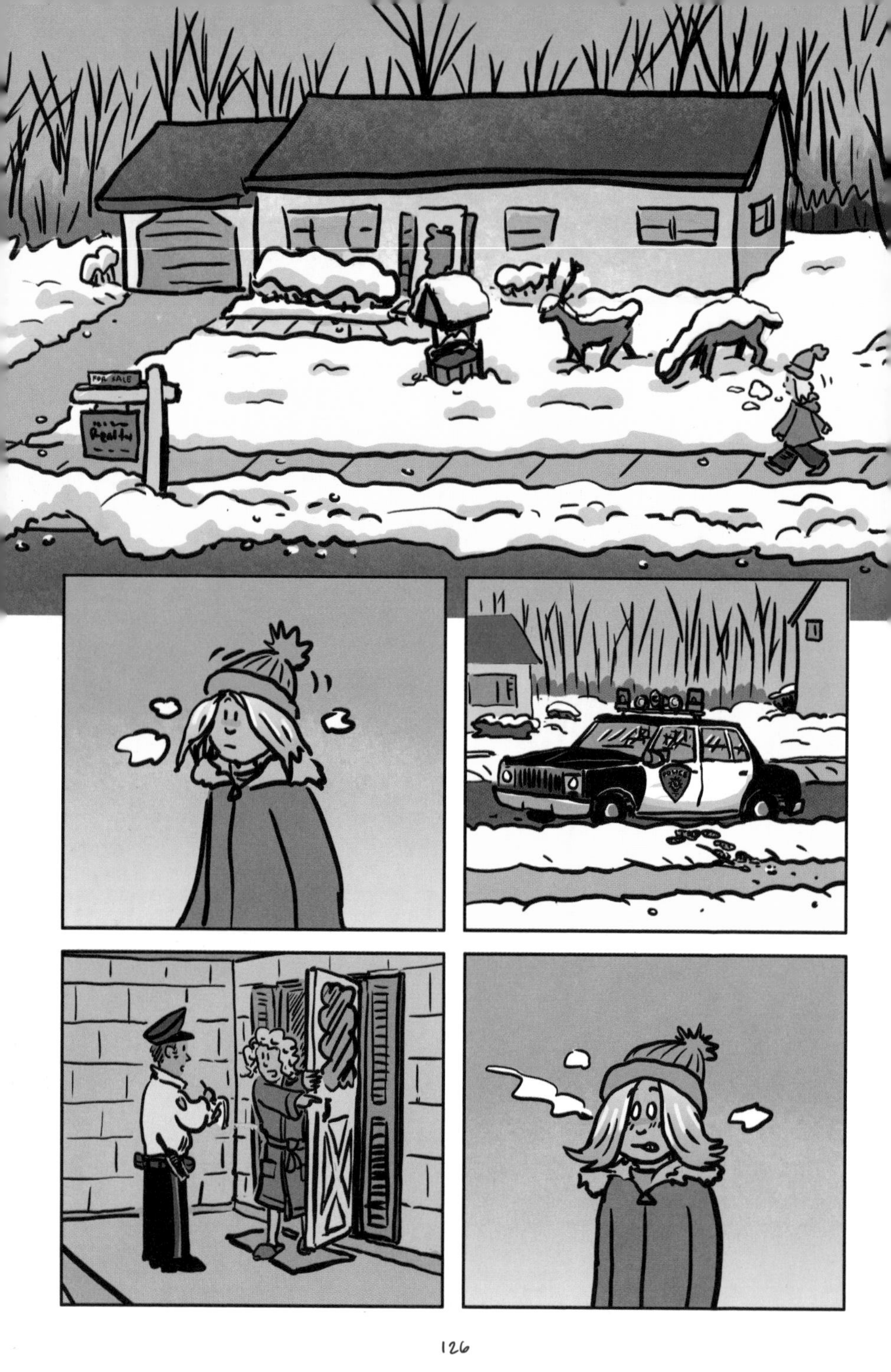
FOR SALE
POLICE

BRADY BUNCH!

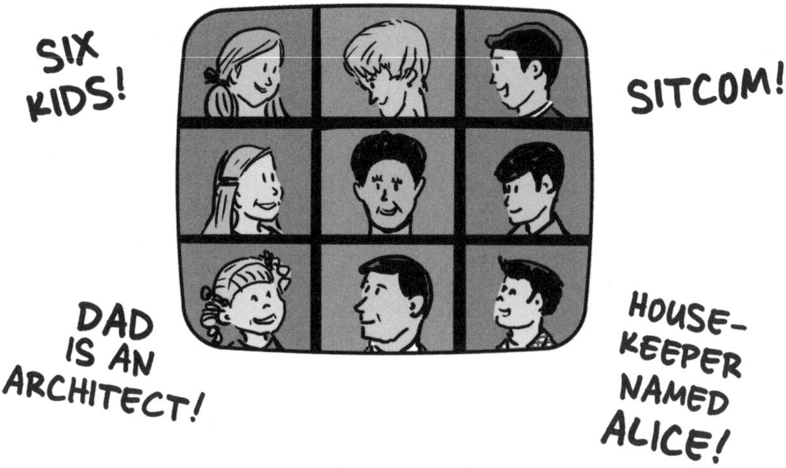
SIX KIDS!
SITCOM!
DAD IS AN ARCHITECT!
HOUSE-KEEPER NAMED ALICE!

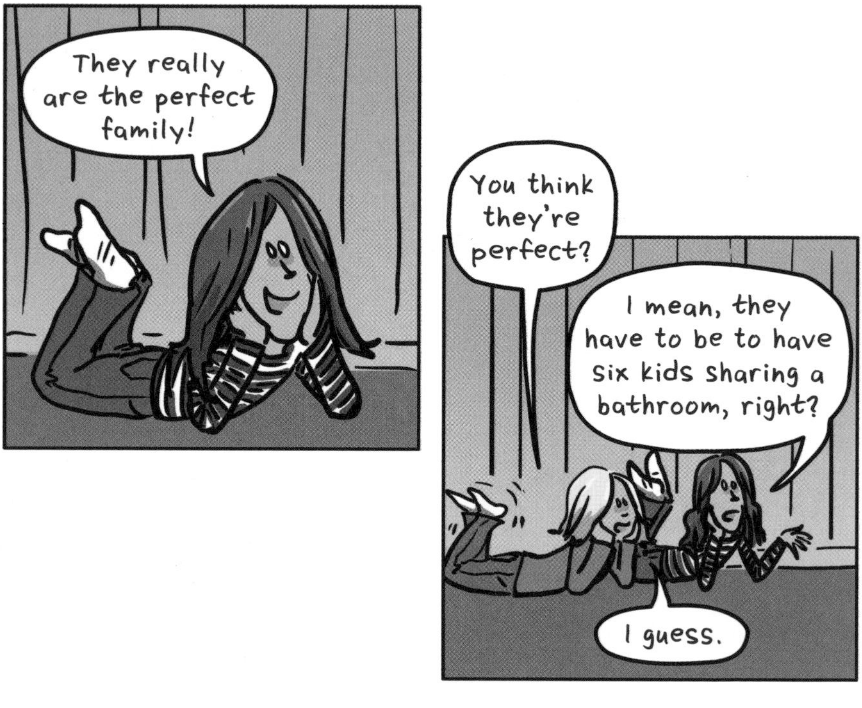
They really are the perfect family!
You think they're perfect?
I mean, they have to be to have six kids sharing a bathroom, right?
I guess.

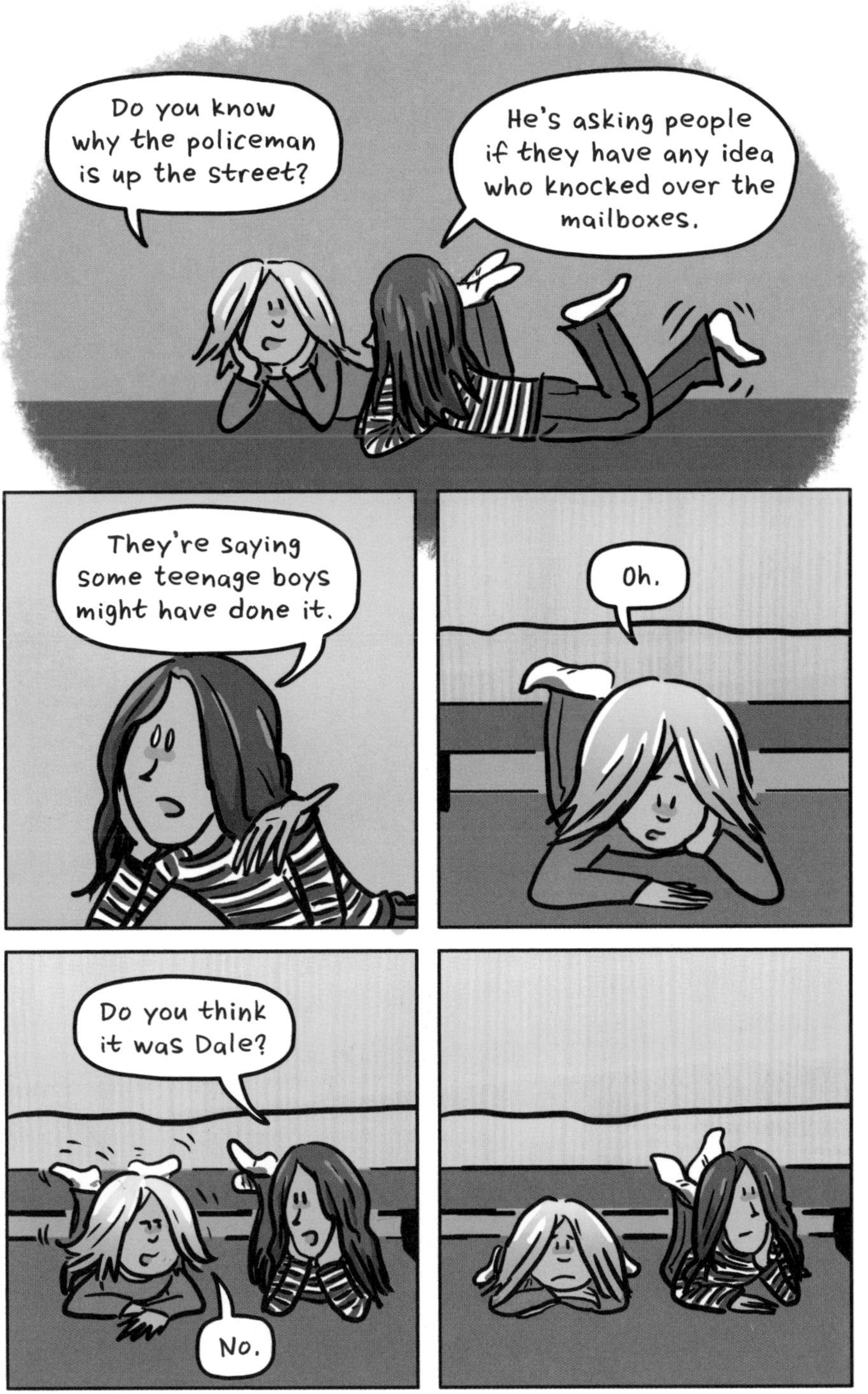

Do you know why the policeman is up the street?
He's asking people if they have any idea who knocked over the mailboxes.
They're saying some teenage boys might have done it.
Oh.
Do you think it was Dale?
No.

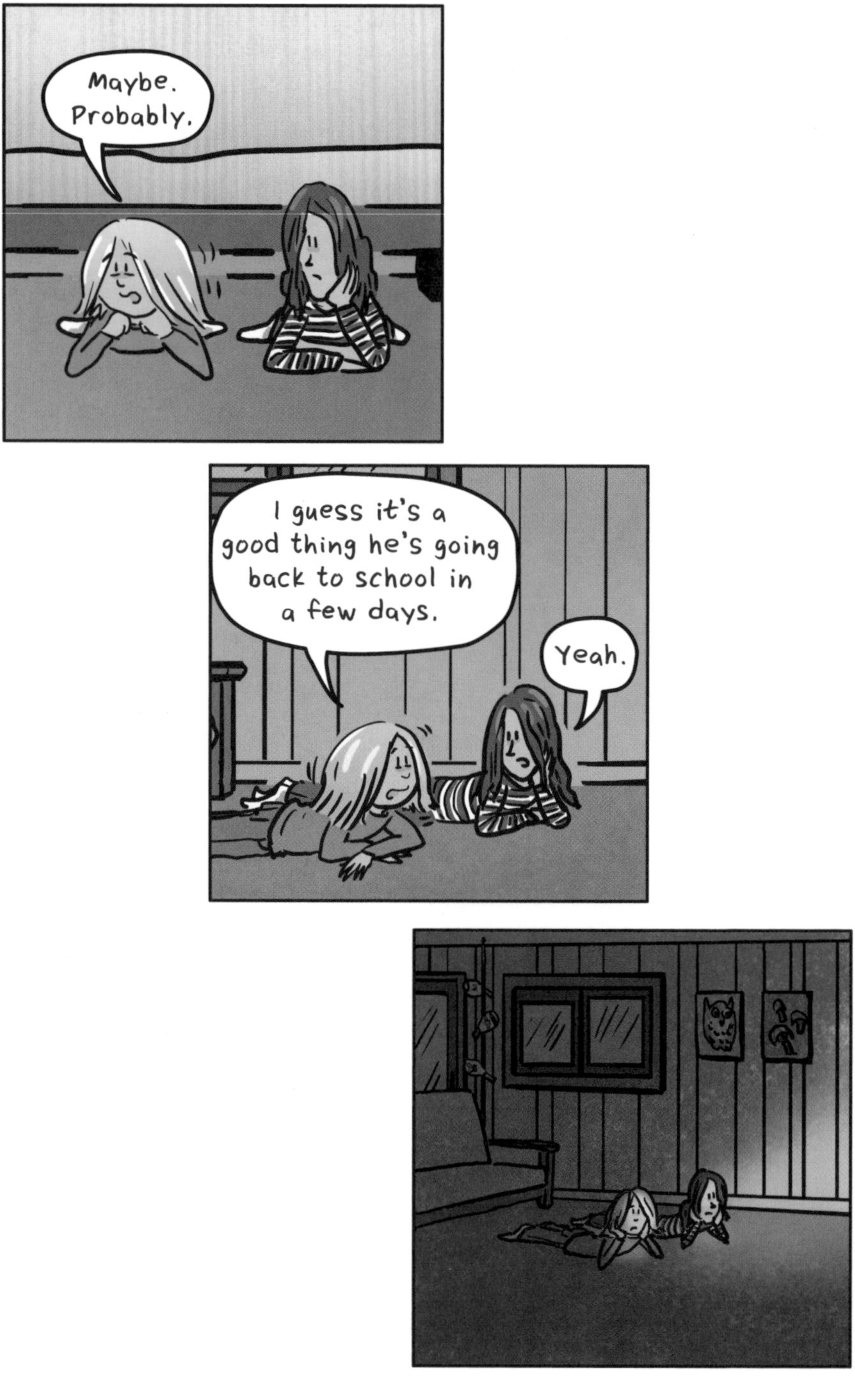
Maybe. Probably.
I guess it's a good thing he's going back to school in a few days.
Yeah.

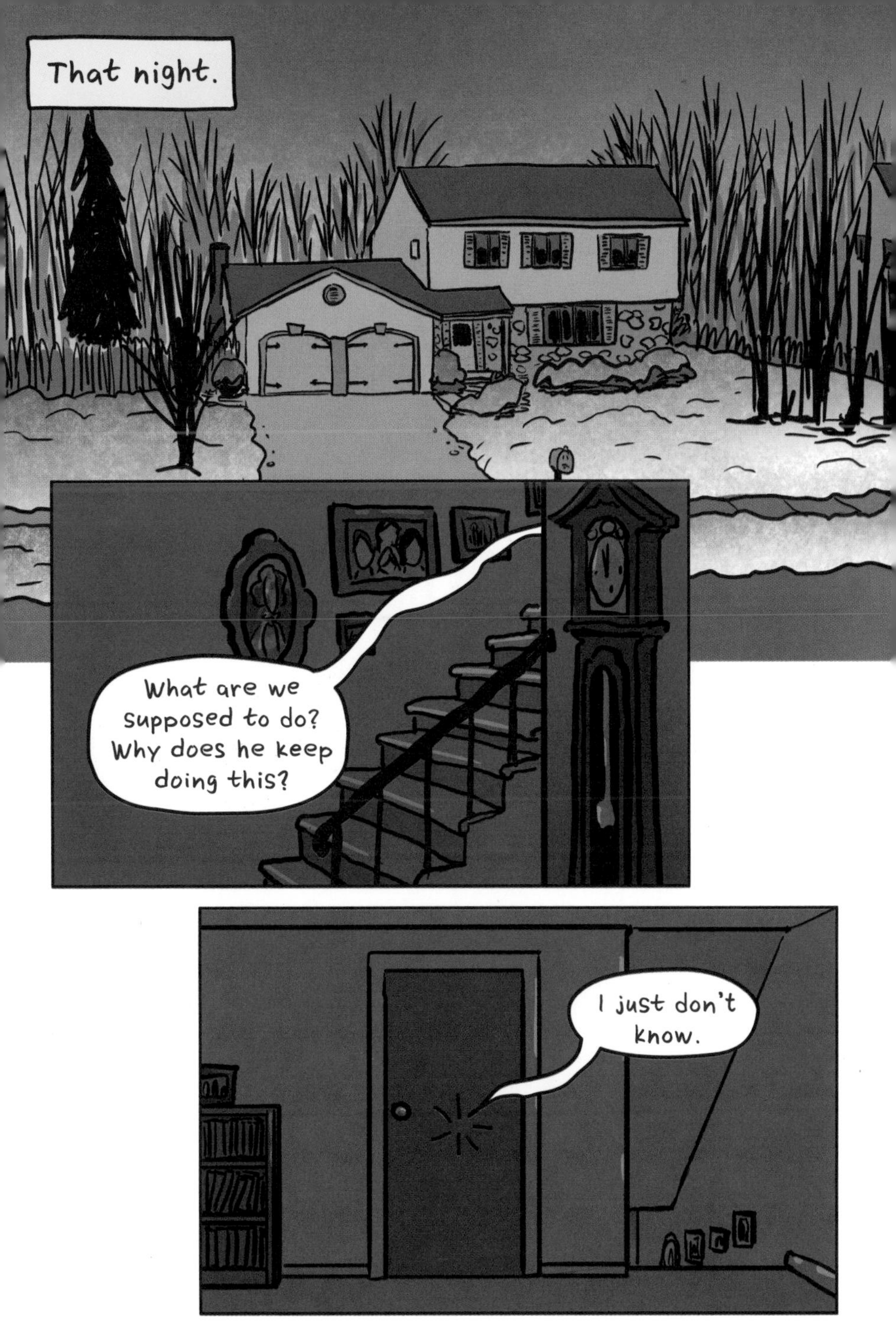
That night.
What are we supposed to do? Why does he keep doing this?
I just don't know.

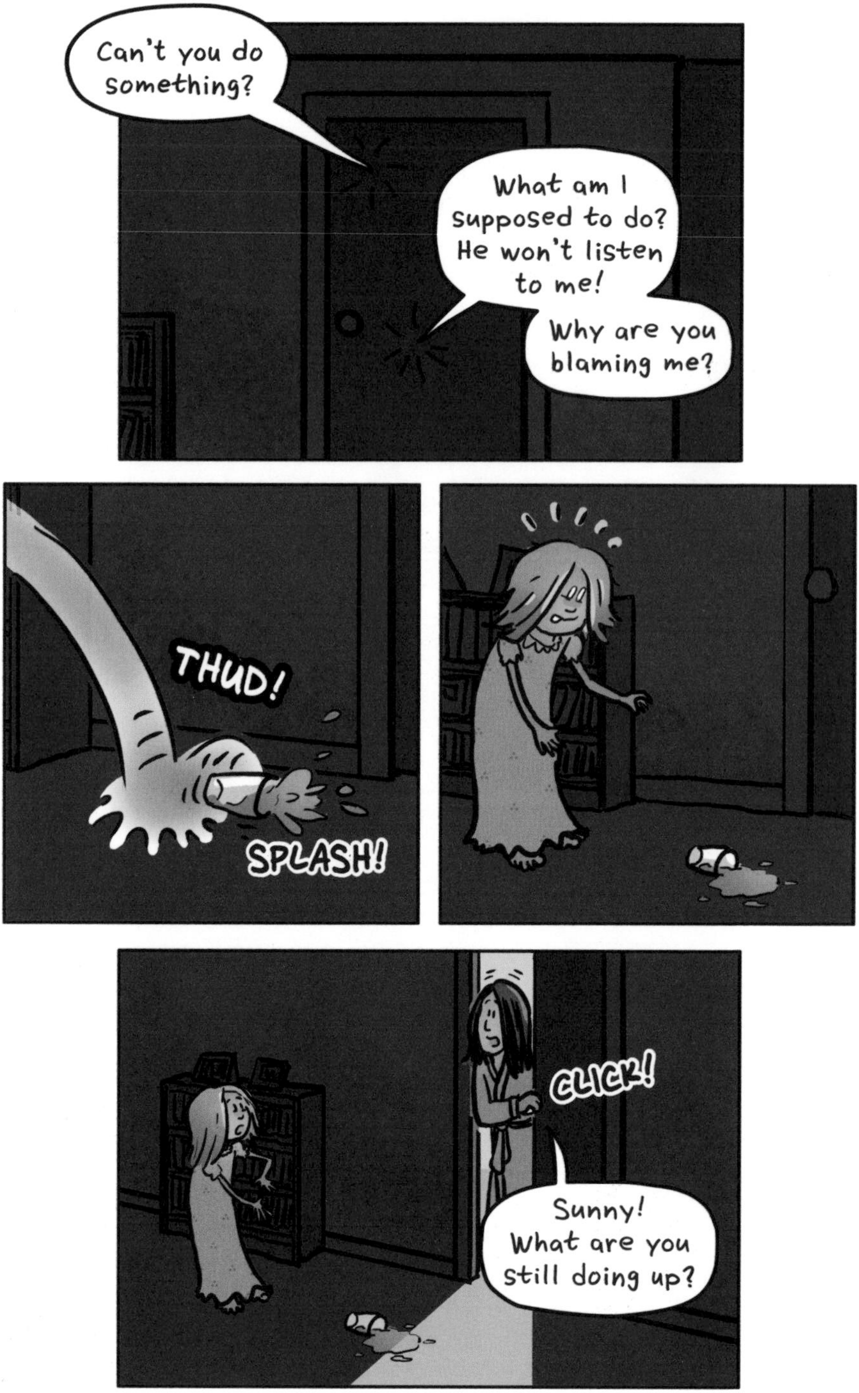
Can't you do something?
What am I supposed to do? He won't listen to me!
Why are you blaming me?
THUD!
SPLASH!
CLICK!
Sunny! What are you still doing up?

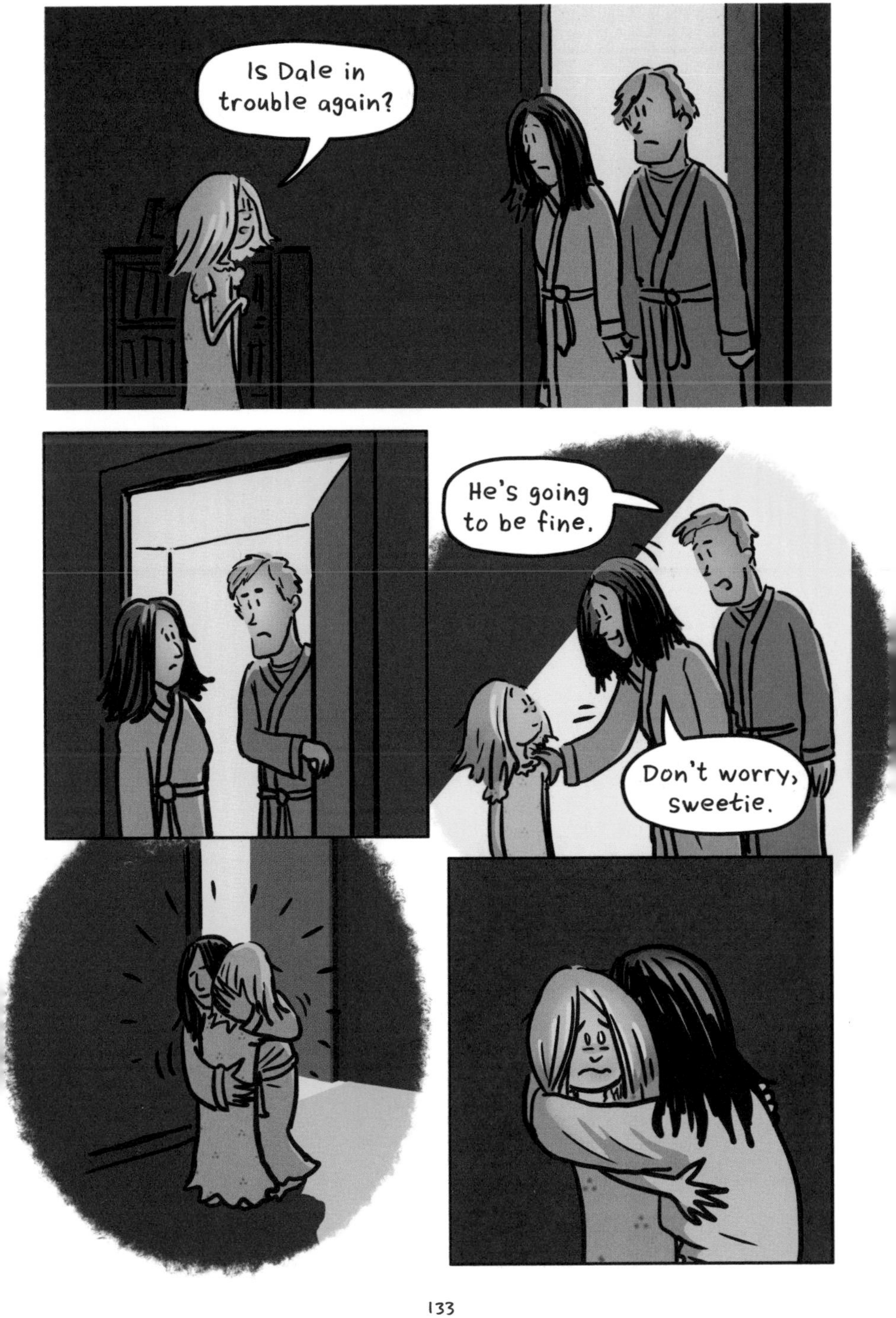
Is Dale in trouble again?
He's going to be fine.
Don't worry, sweetie.

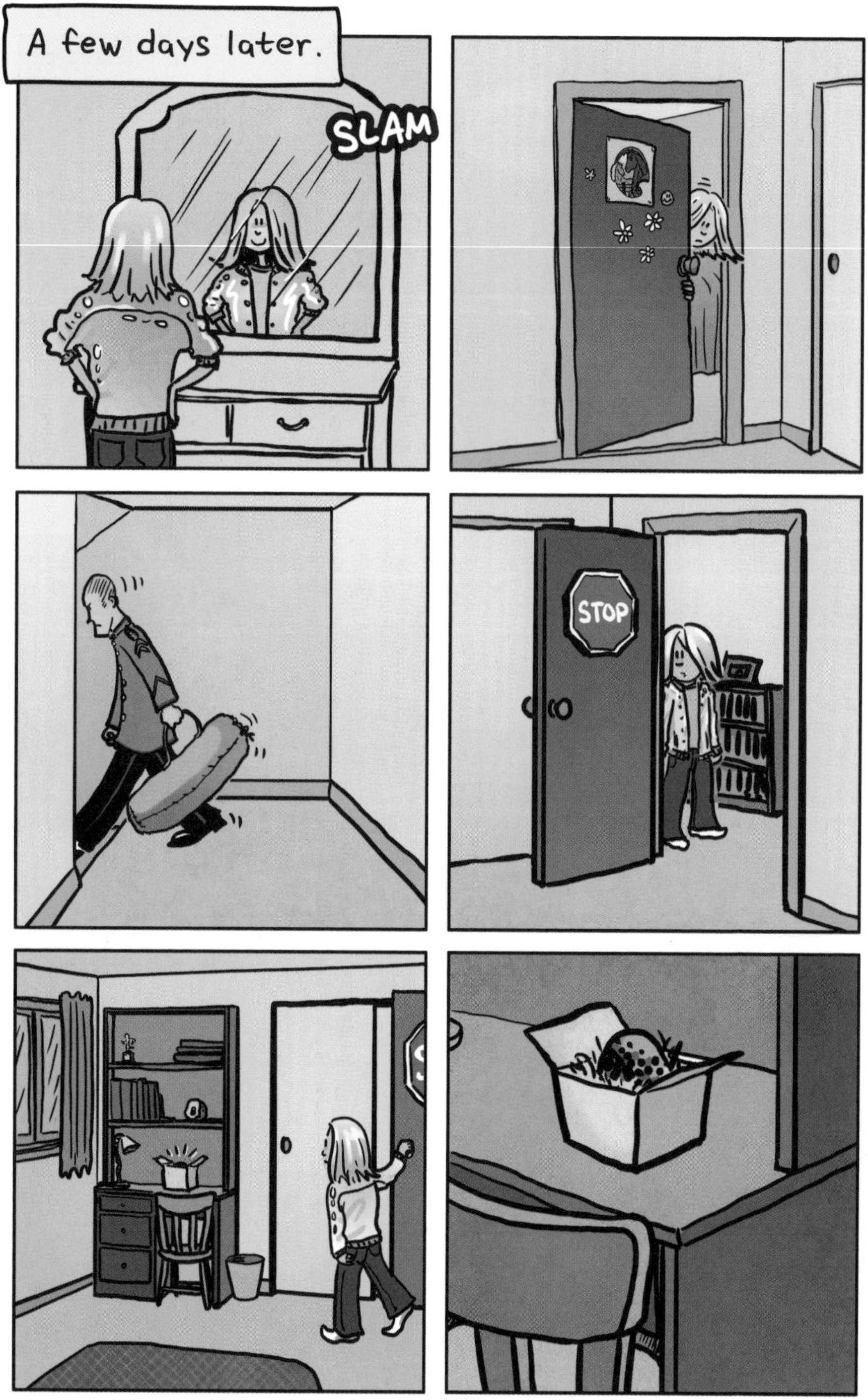
A few days later.
SLAM
STOP

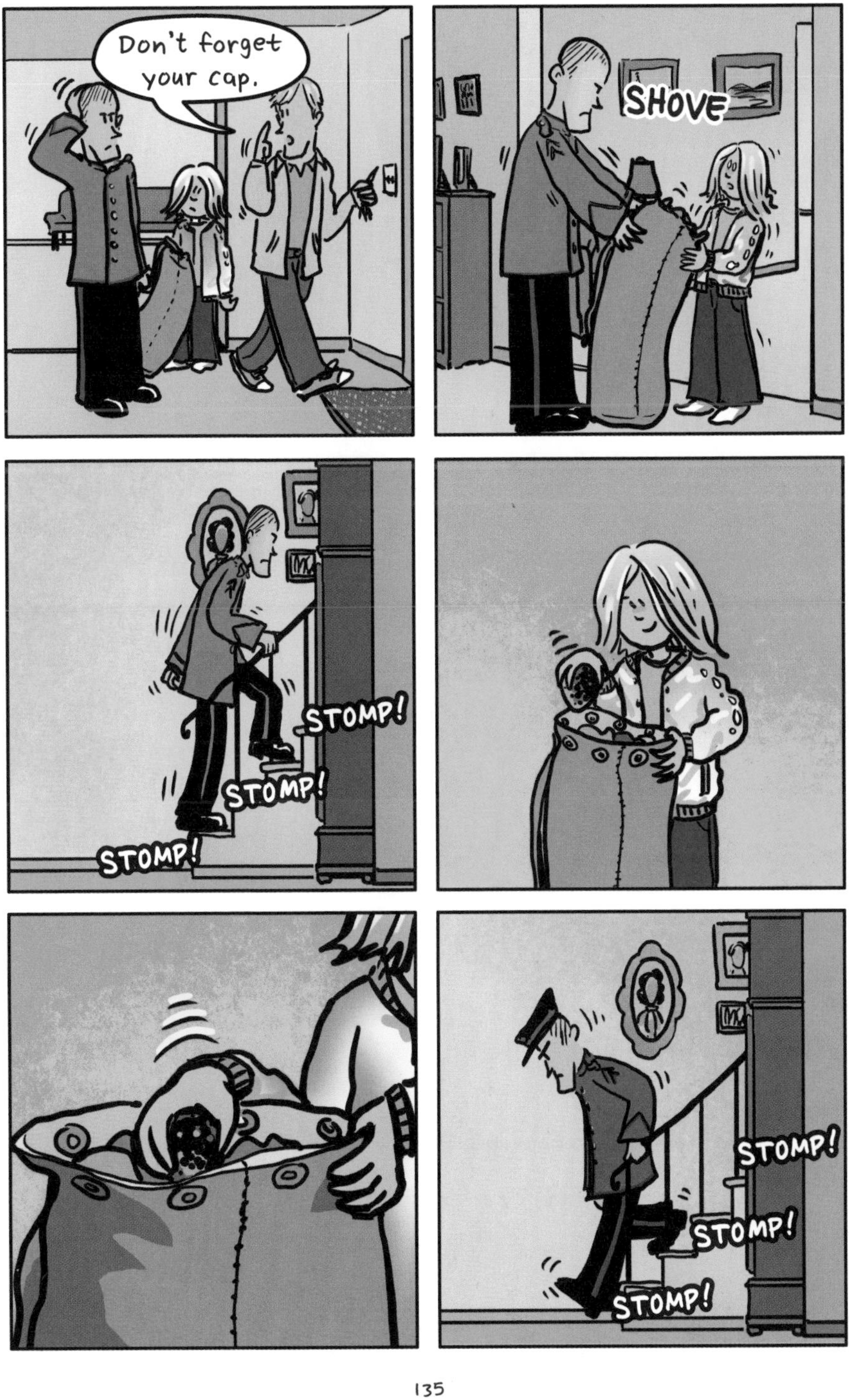
Don't forget your cap.
SHOVE
STOMP!
STOMP!
STOMP!
STOMP!
STOMP!
STOMP!

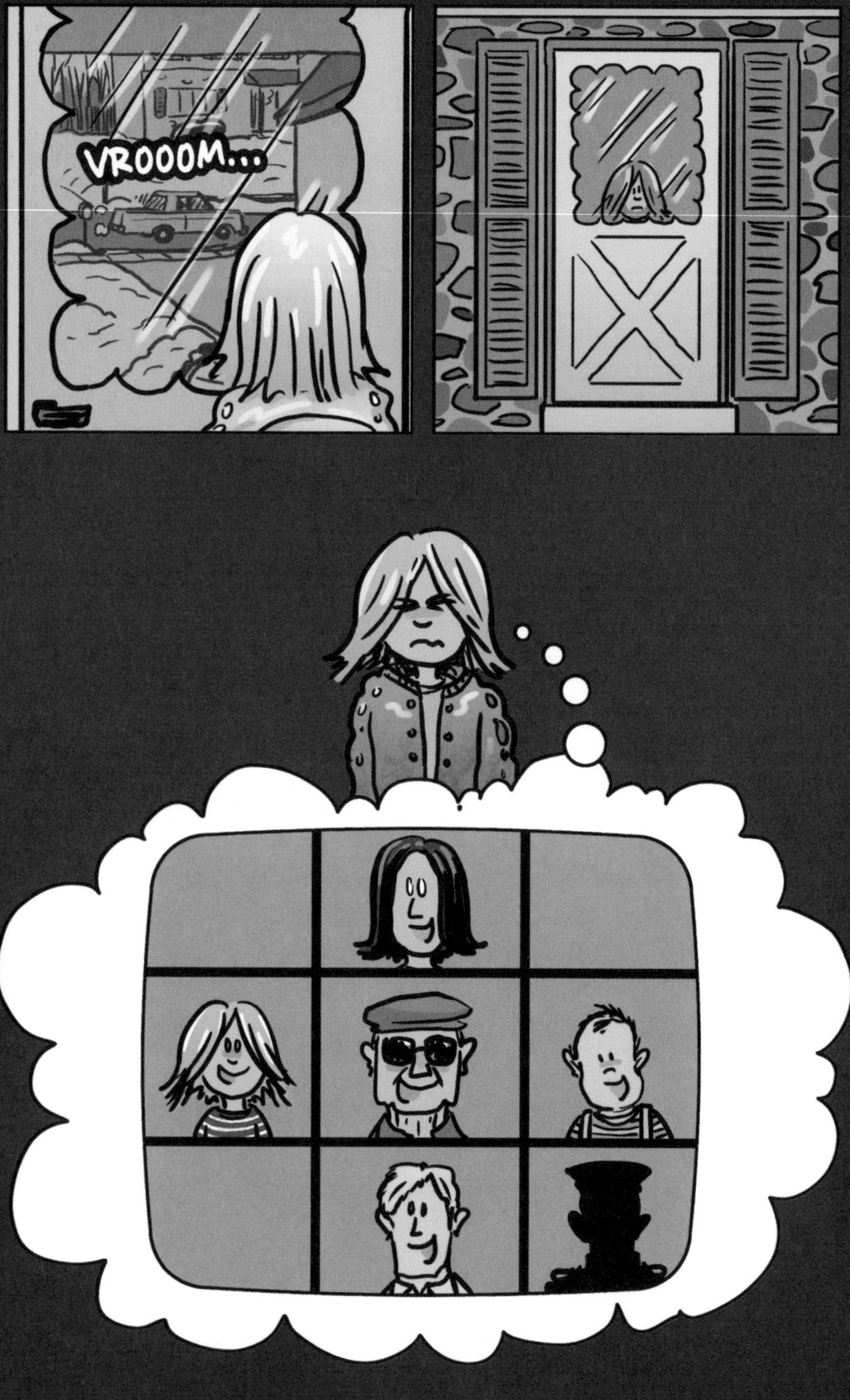
VROOOM...

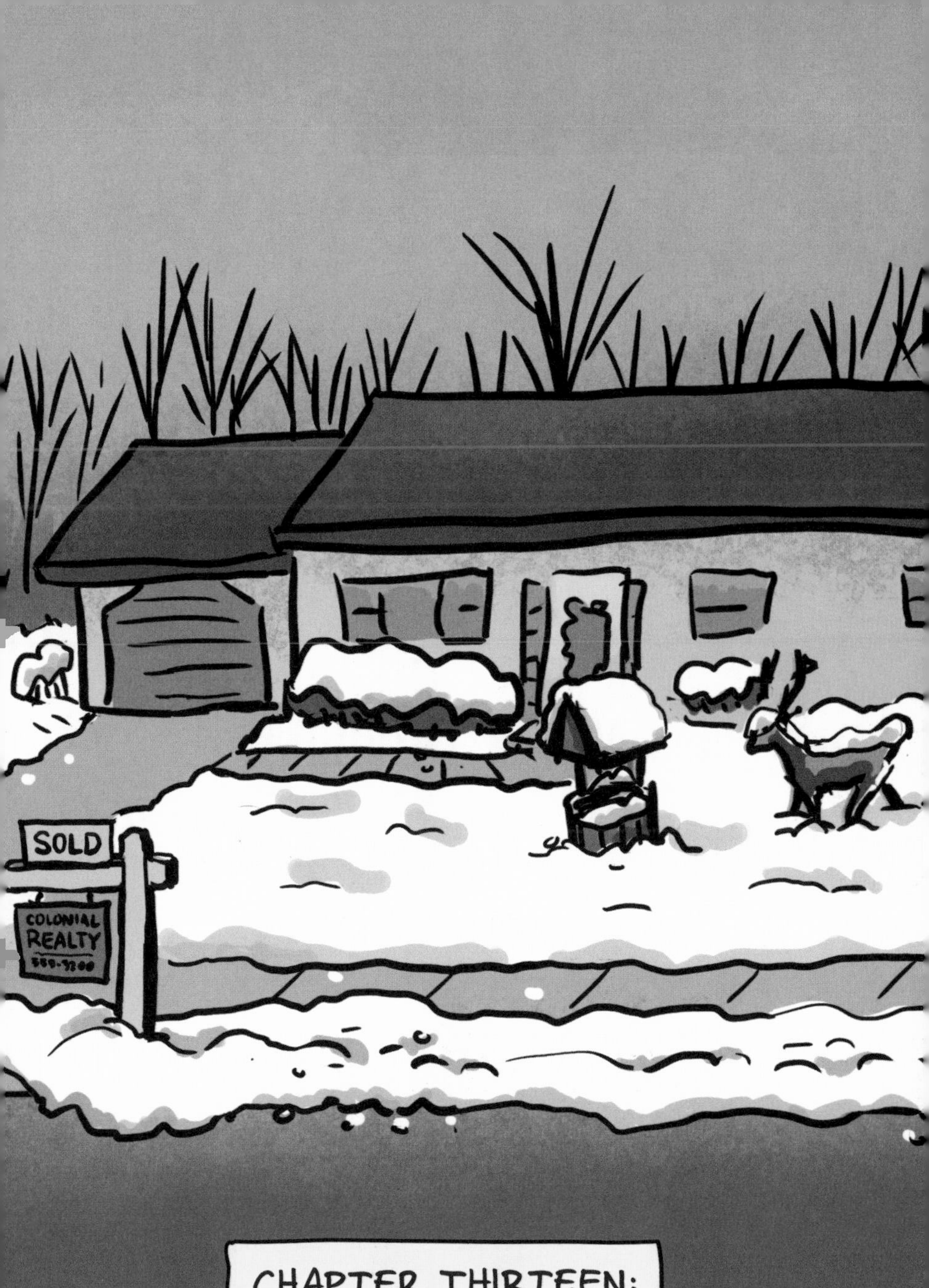
SOLD
COLONIAL
REALTY

CHAPTER THIRTEEN: Snowbird

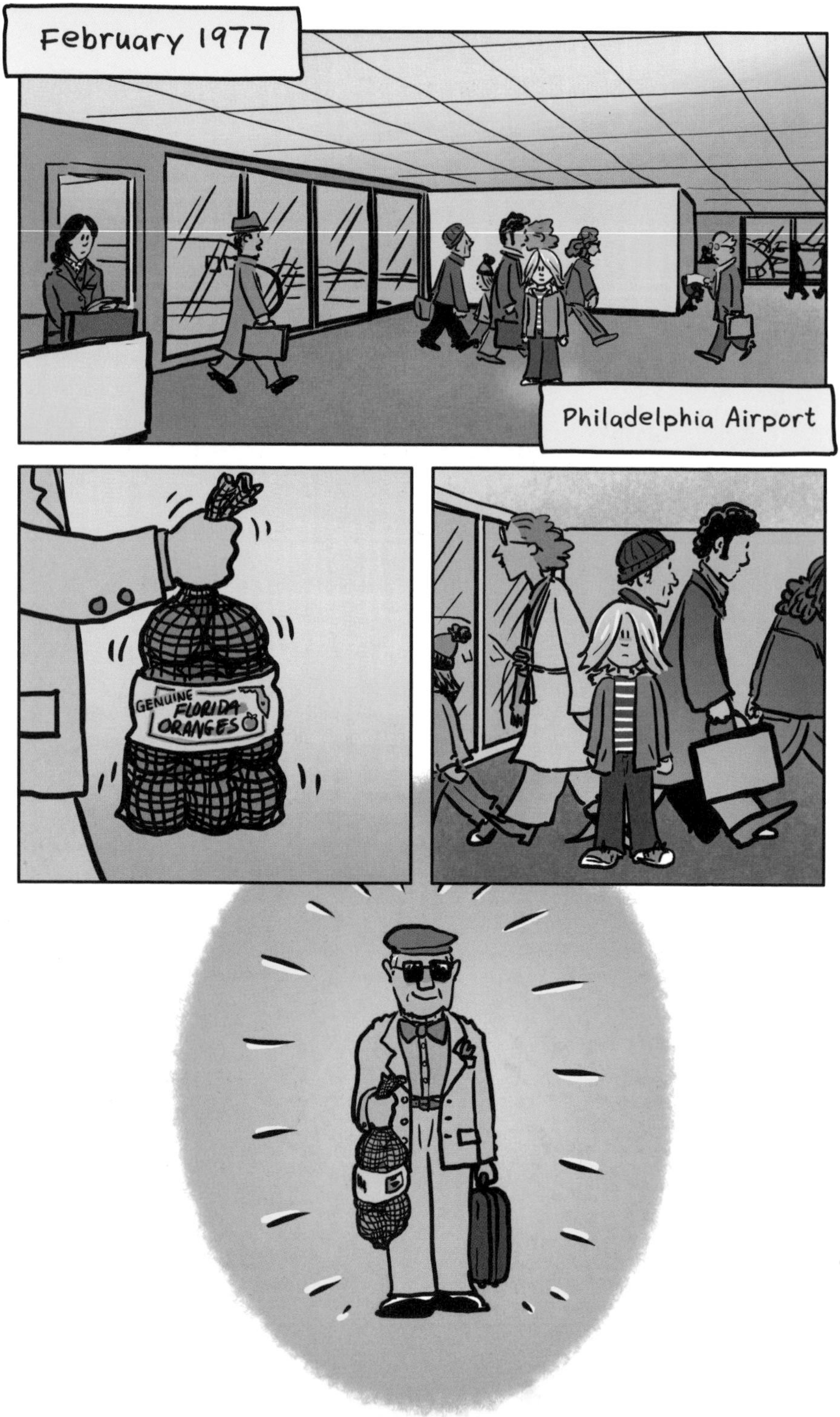
February 1977
Philadelphia Airport
GENUINE FLORIDA ORANGES

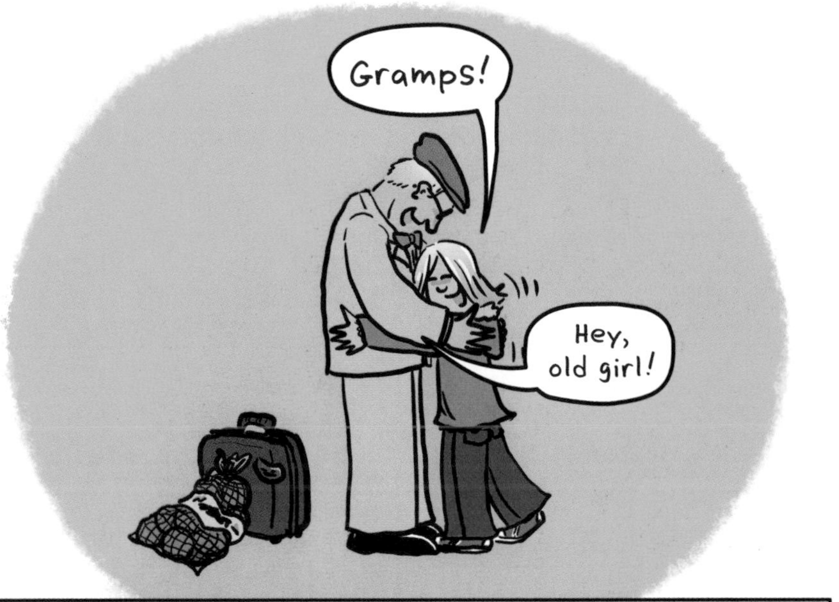
Gramps!
Hey, old girl!

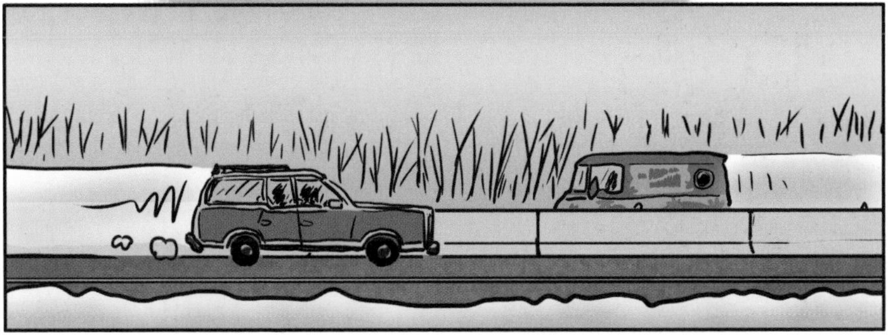

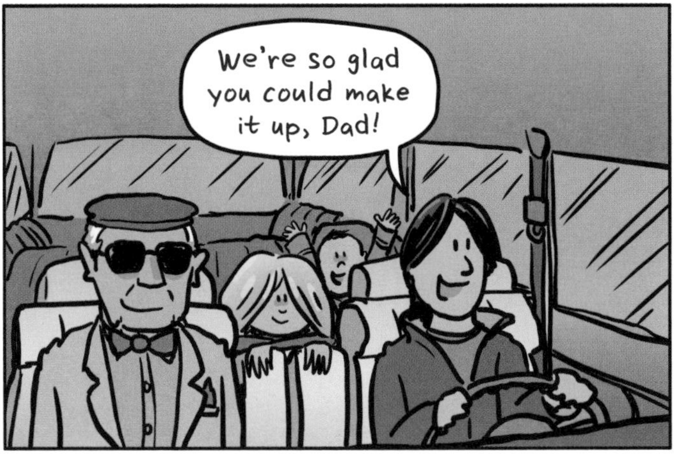
We're so glad you could make it up, Dad!

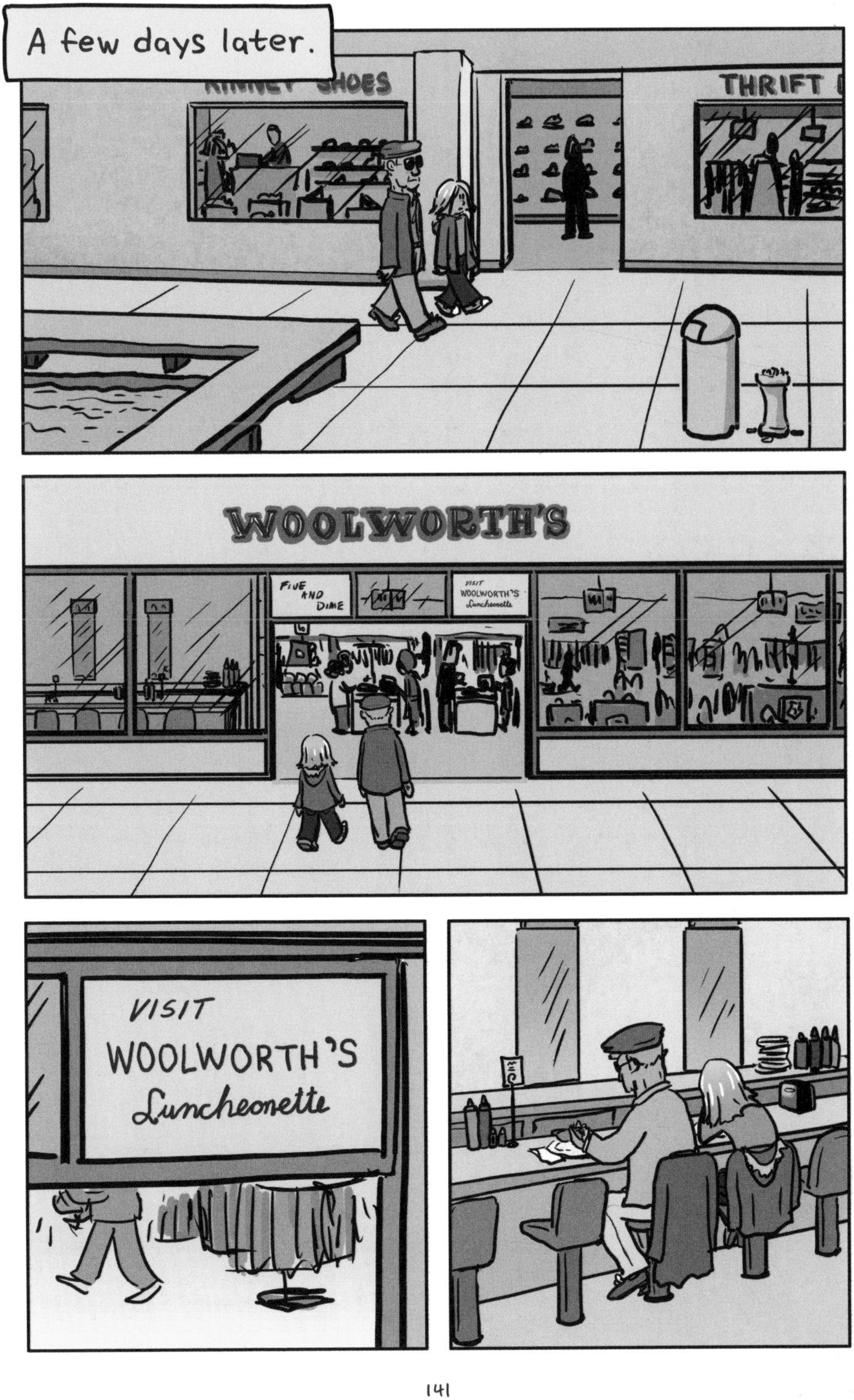
A few days later.
SHOES
THRIFT
WOOLWORTH'S
FIVE AND DIME
VISIT WOOLWORTH'S Luncheonette
VISIT
WOOLWORTH'S
Luncheonette

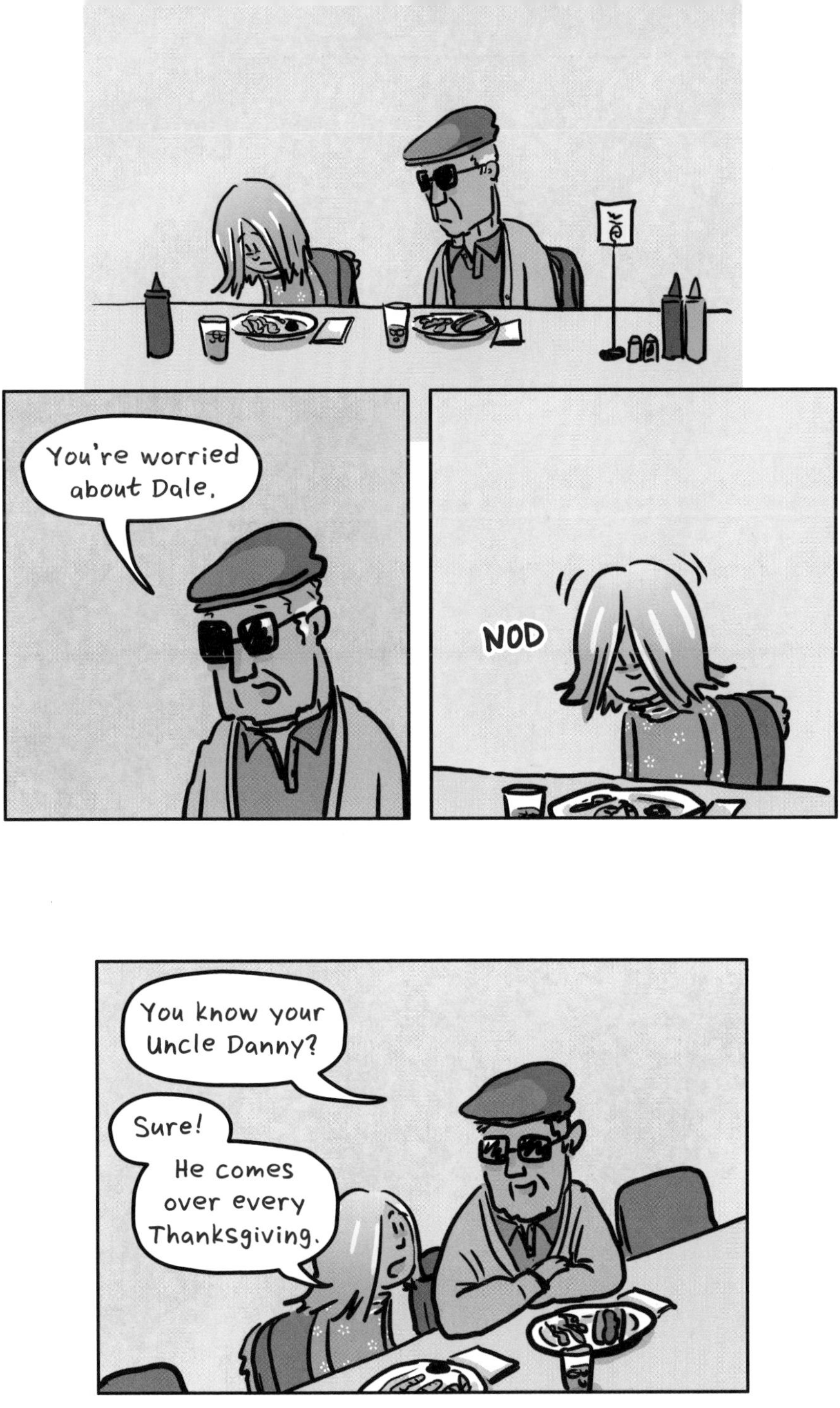
You're worried about Dale.
NOD
You know your Uncle Danny?
Sure!
He comes over every Thanksgiving.

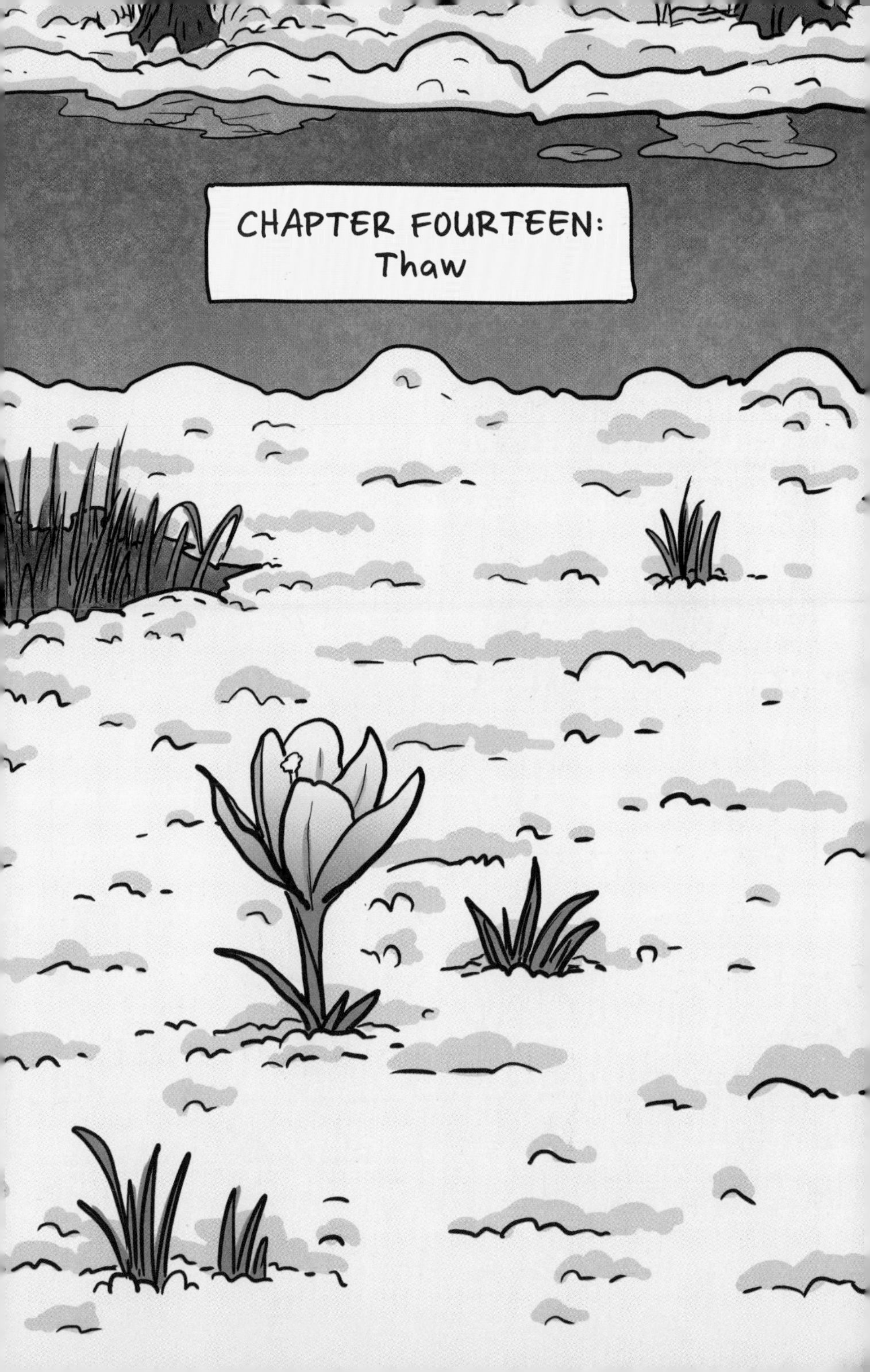
CHAPTER FOURTEEN:
Thaw

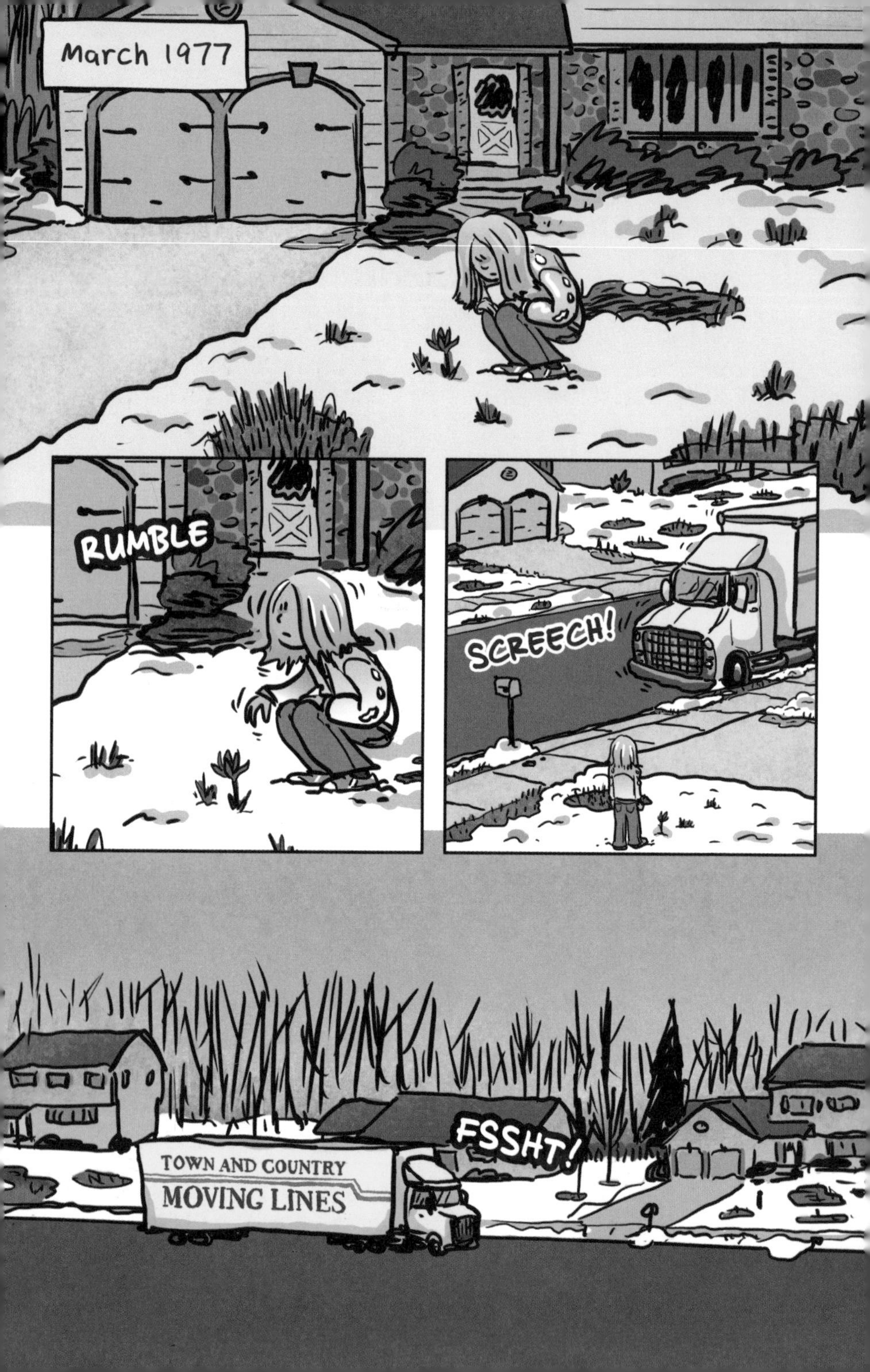
March 1977
RUMBLE
SCREECH!
TOWN AND COUNTRY
MOVING LINES
FSSHT!

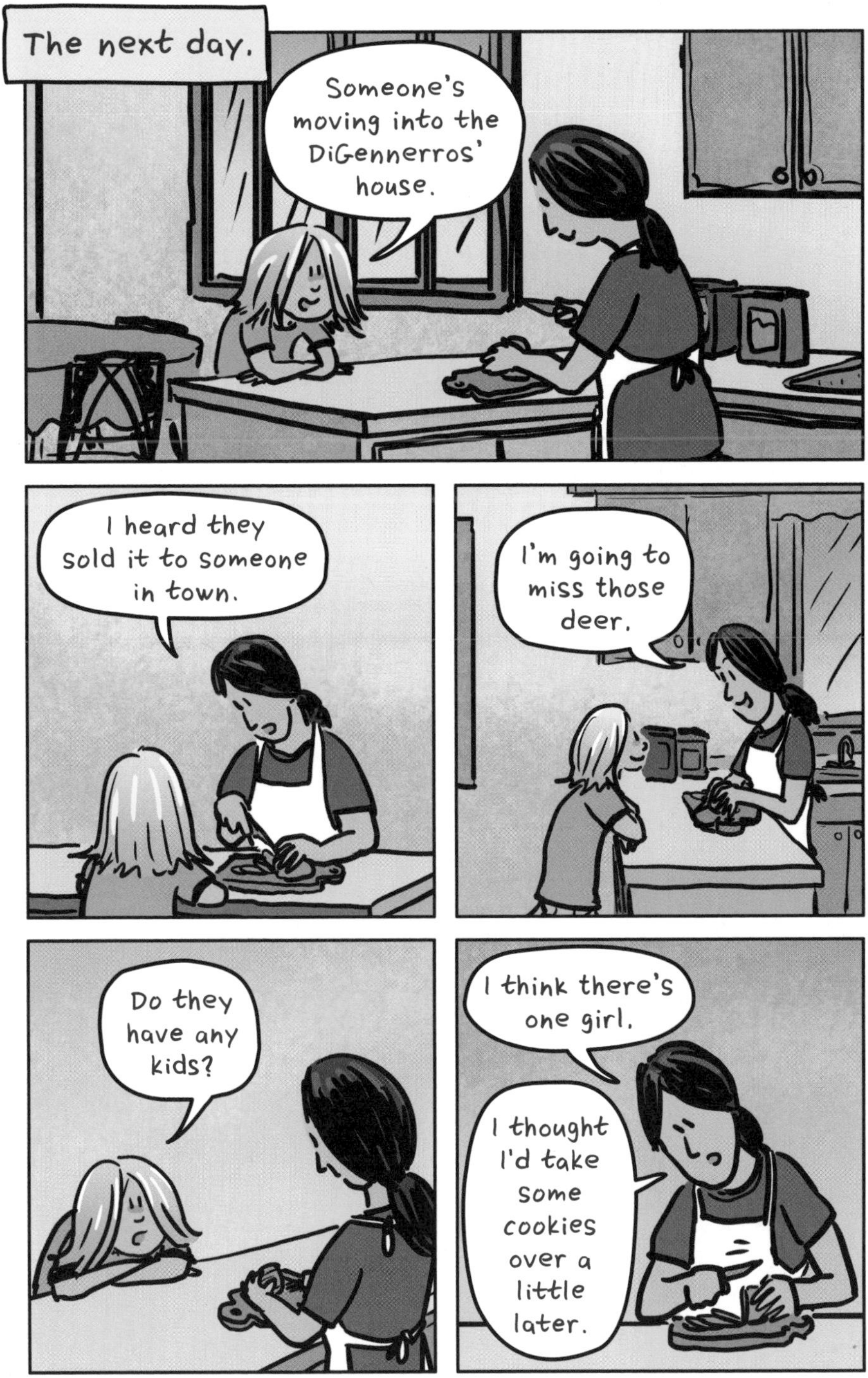
The next day.
Someone's moving into the DiGennerros' house.
I heard they sold it to someone in town.
I'm going to miss those deer.
Do they have any kids?
I think there's one girl.
I thought I'd take some cookies over a little later.

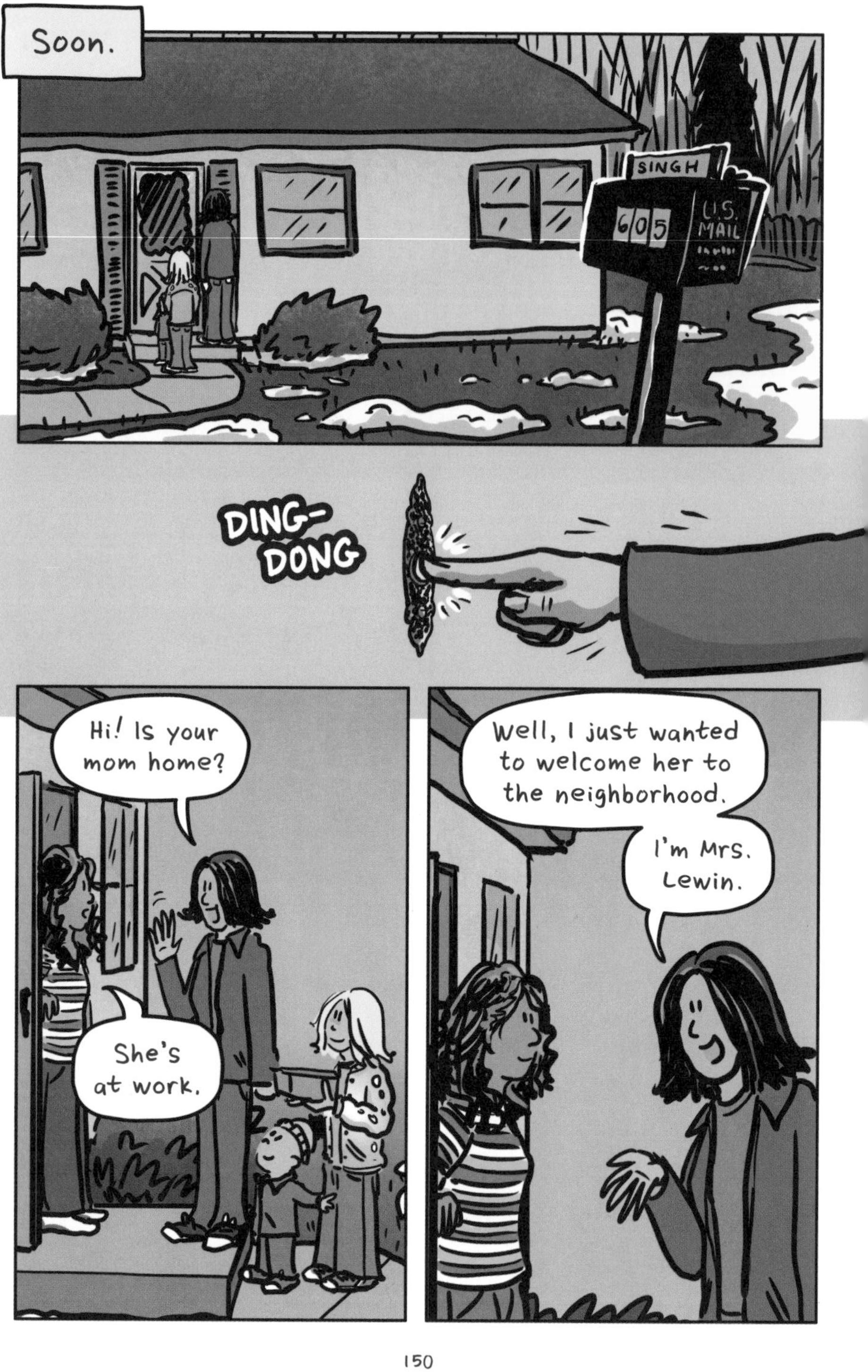
Soon.
SINGH
605
U.S. MAIL
DING-DONG
Hi! Is your mom home?
She's at work.
Well, I just wanted to welcome her to the neighborhood.
I'm Mrs. Lewin.

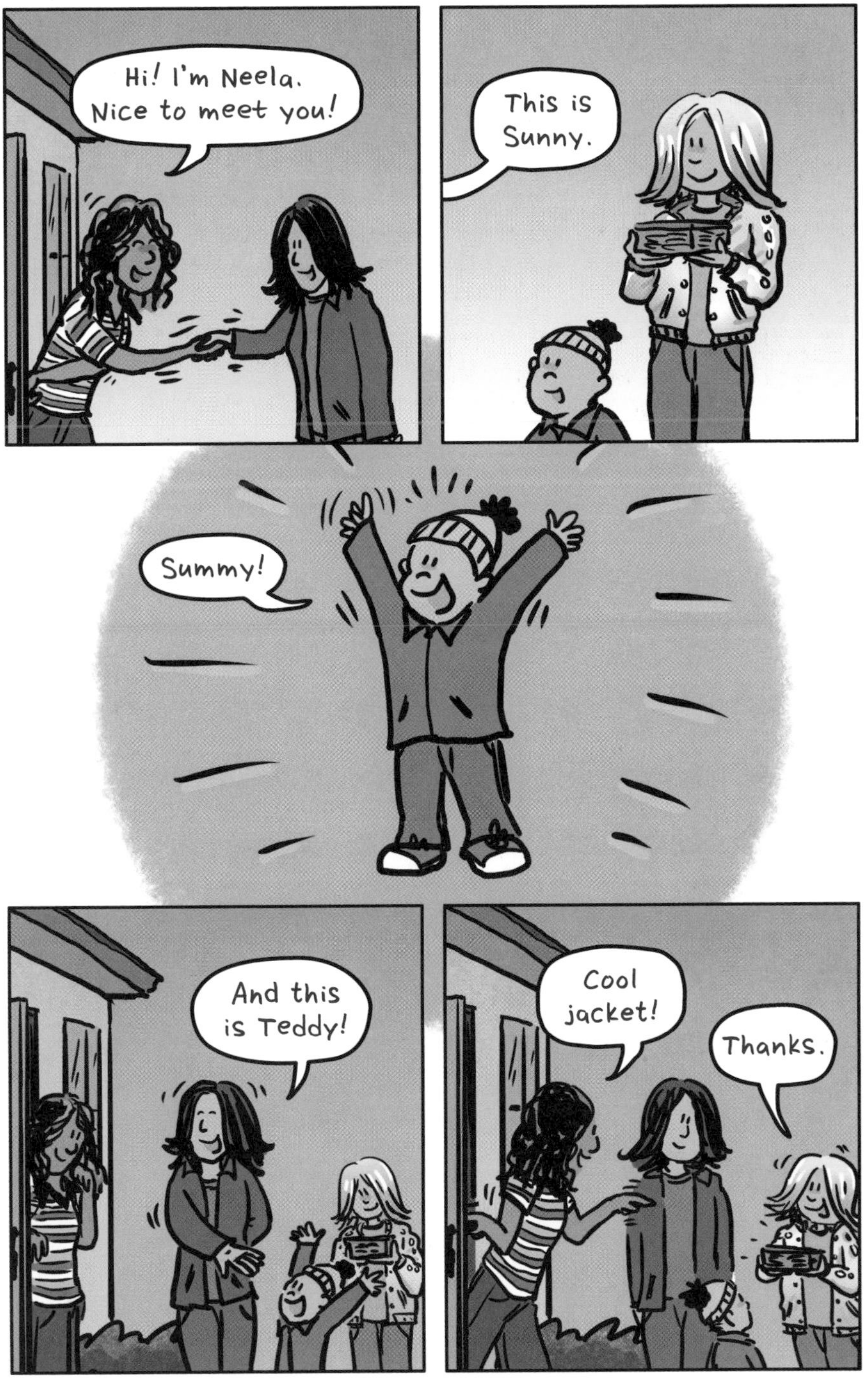
Hi! I'm Neela. Nice to meet you!
This is Sunny.
Summy!
And this is Teddy!
Cool jacket!
Thanks.

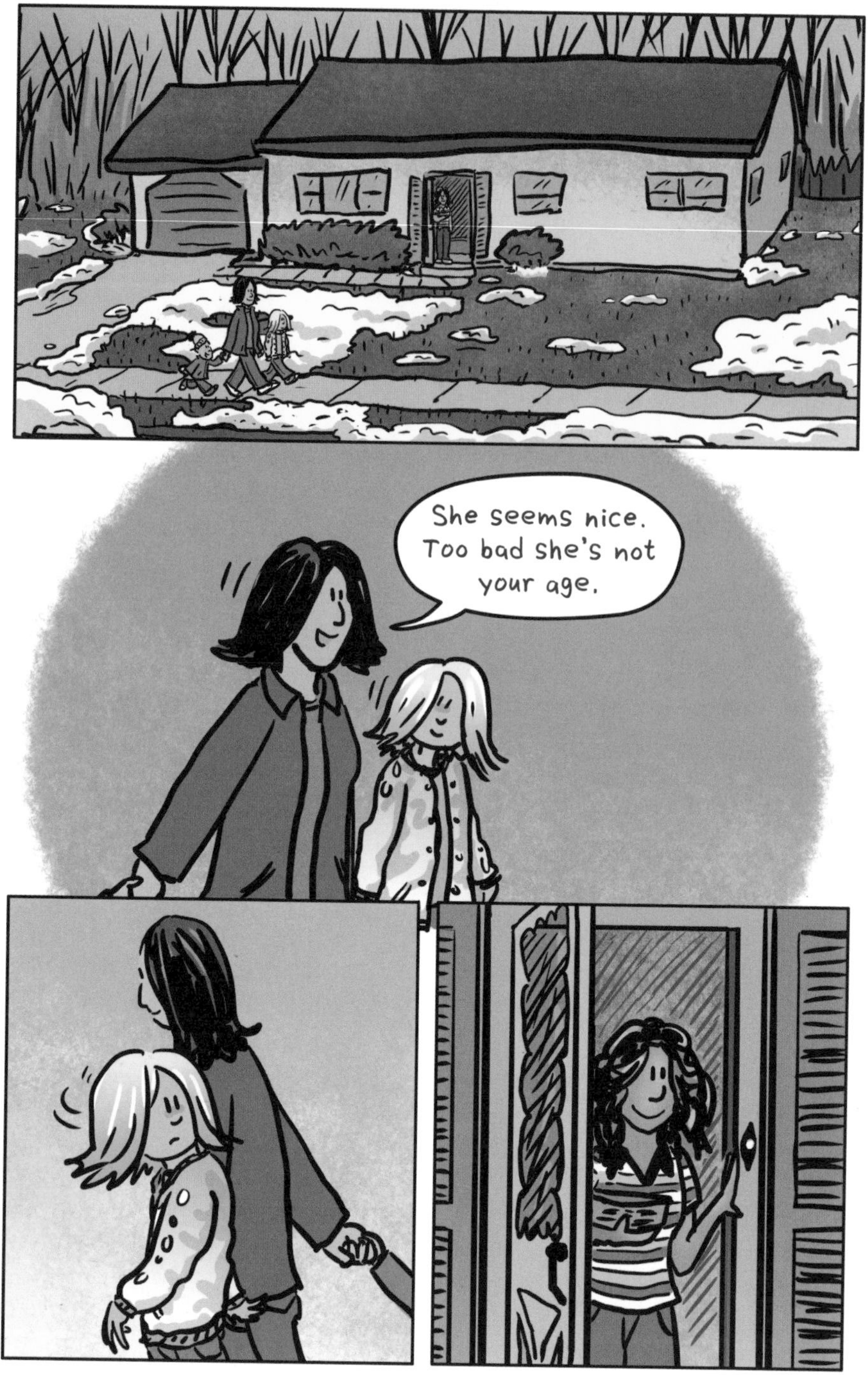
She seems nice. Too bad she's not your age.

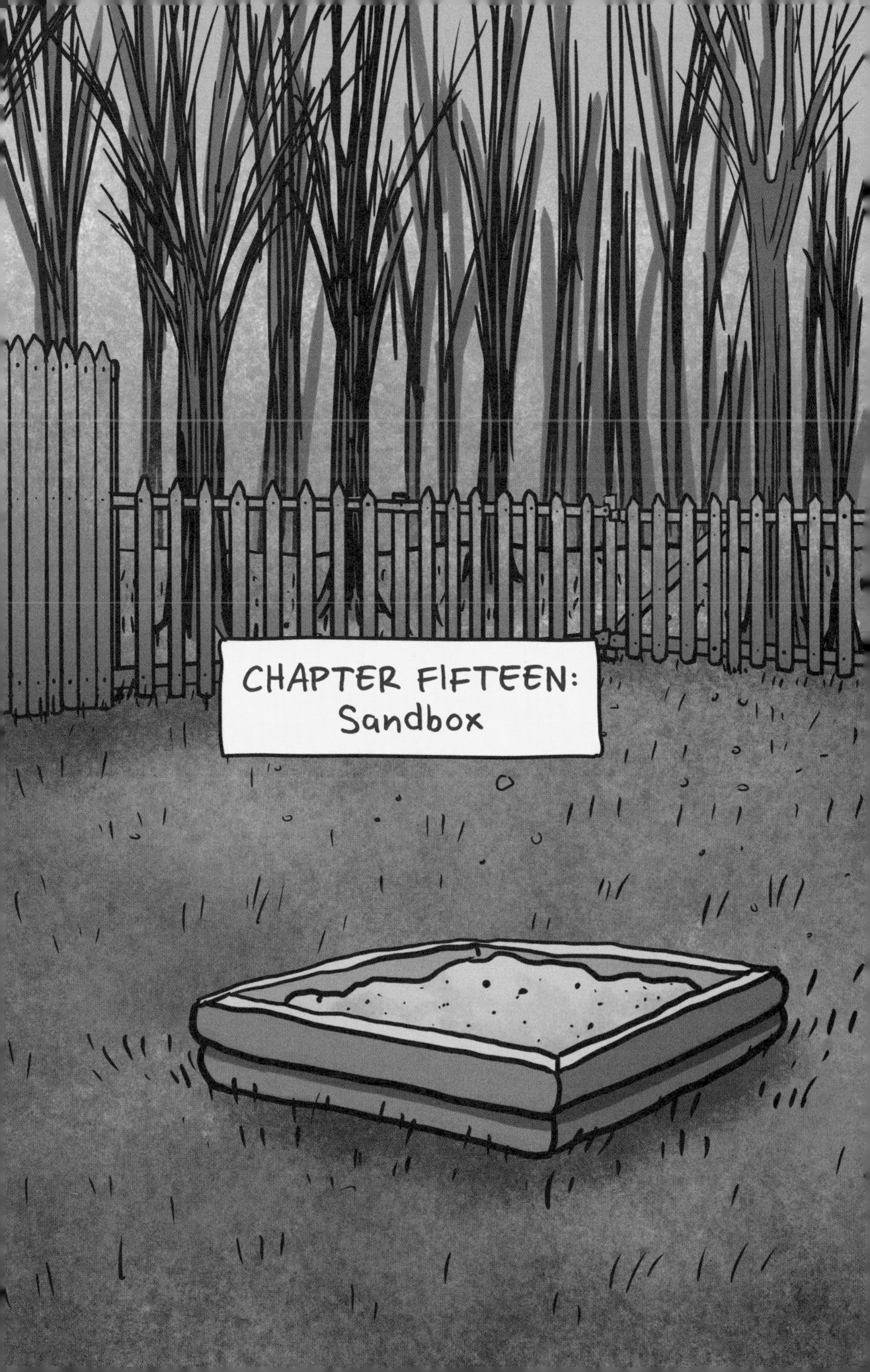
CHAPTER FIFTEEN:
Sandbox

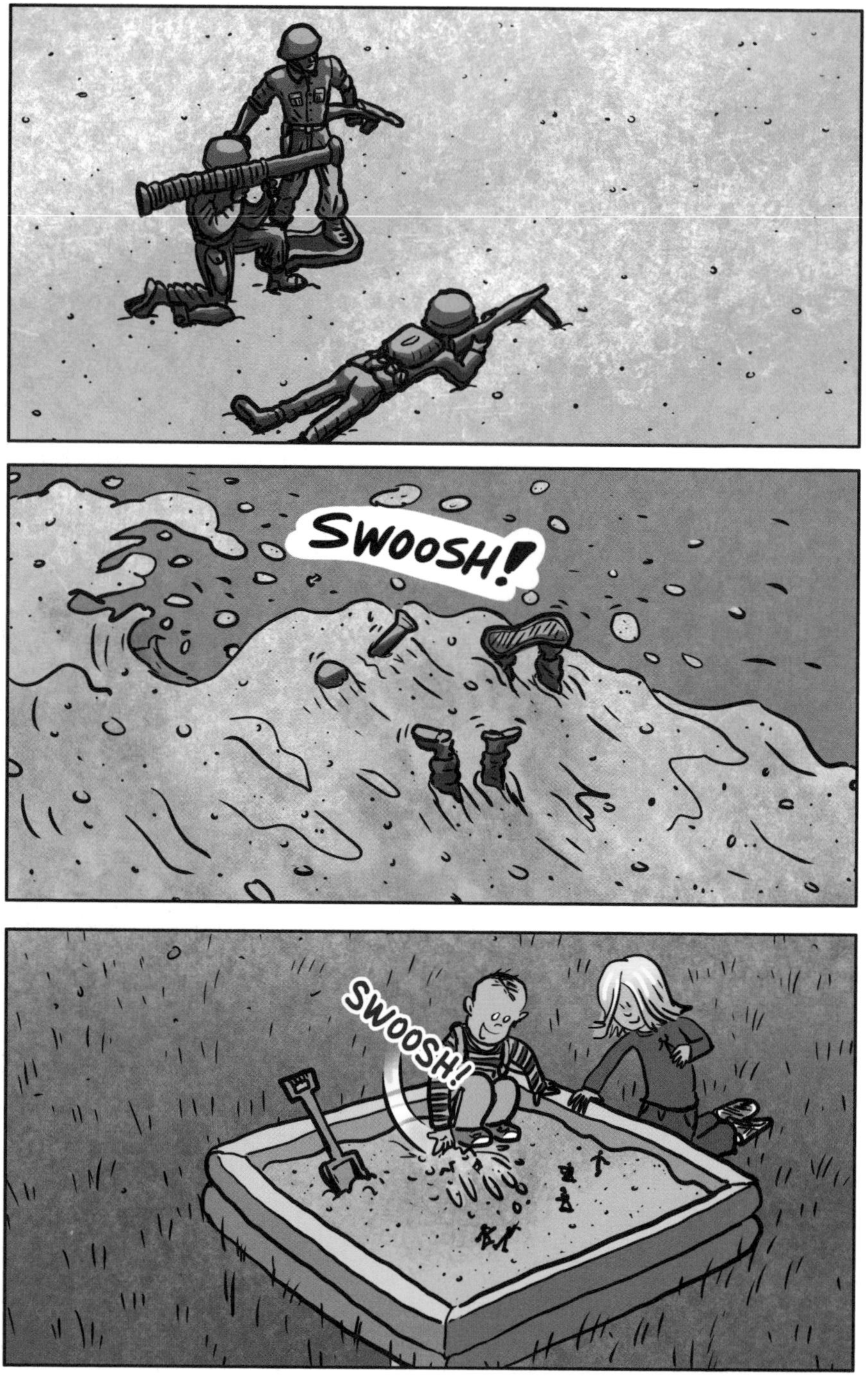
SWOOSH!
SWOOSH!

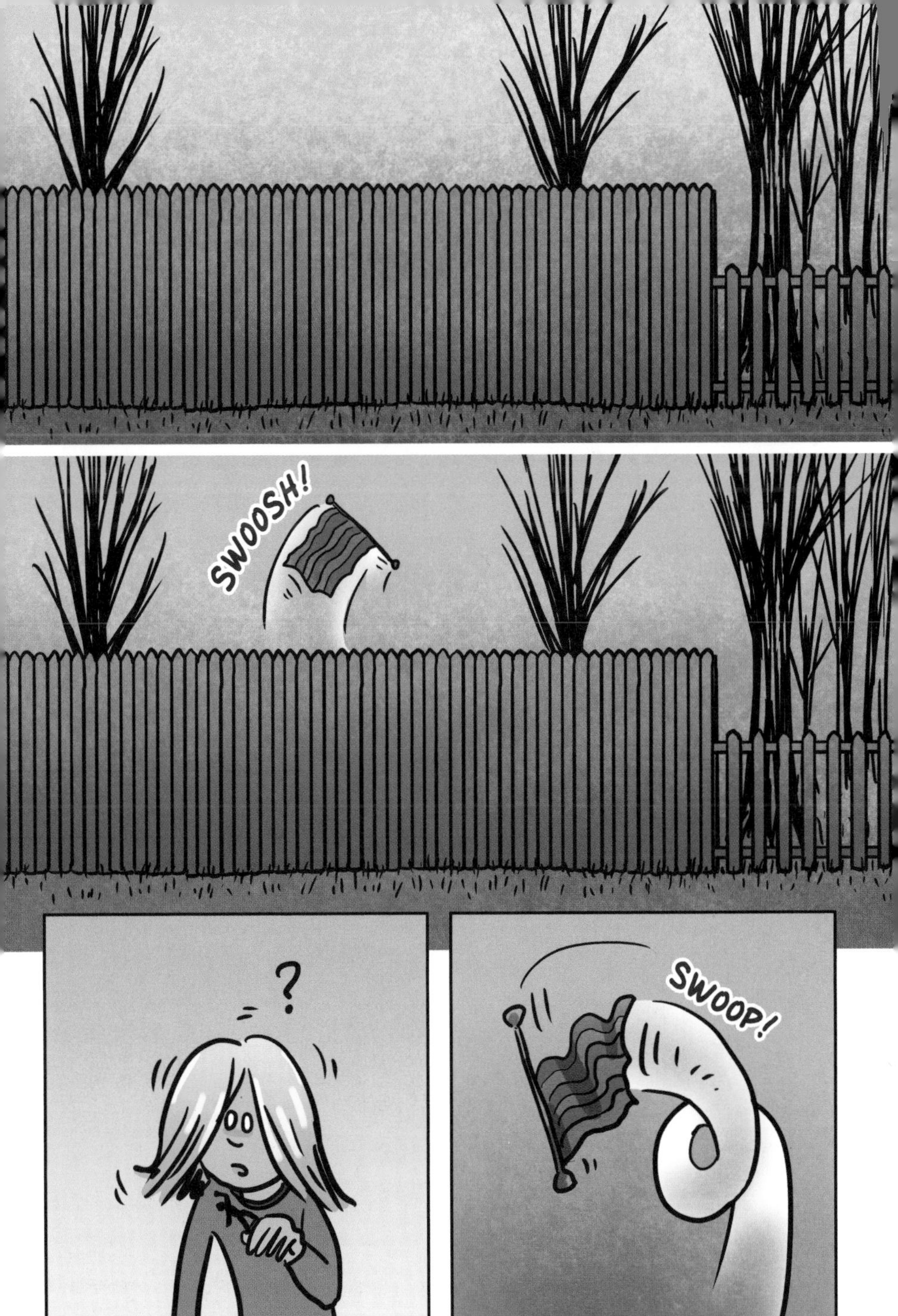
SWOOSH!
?
SWOOP!

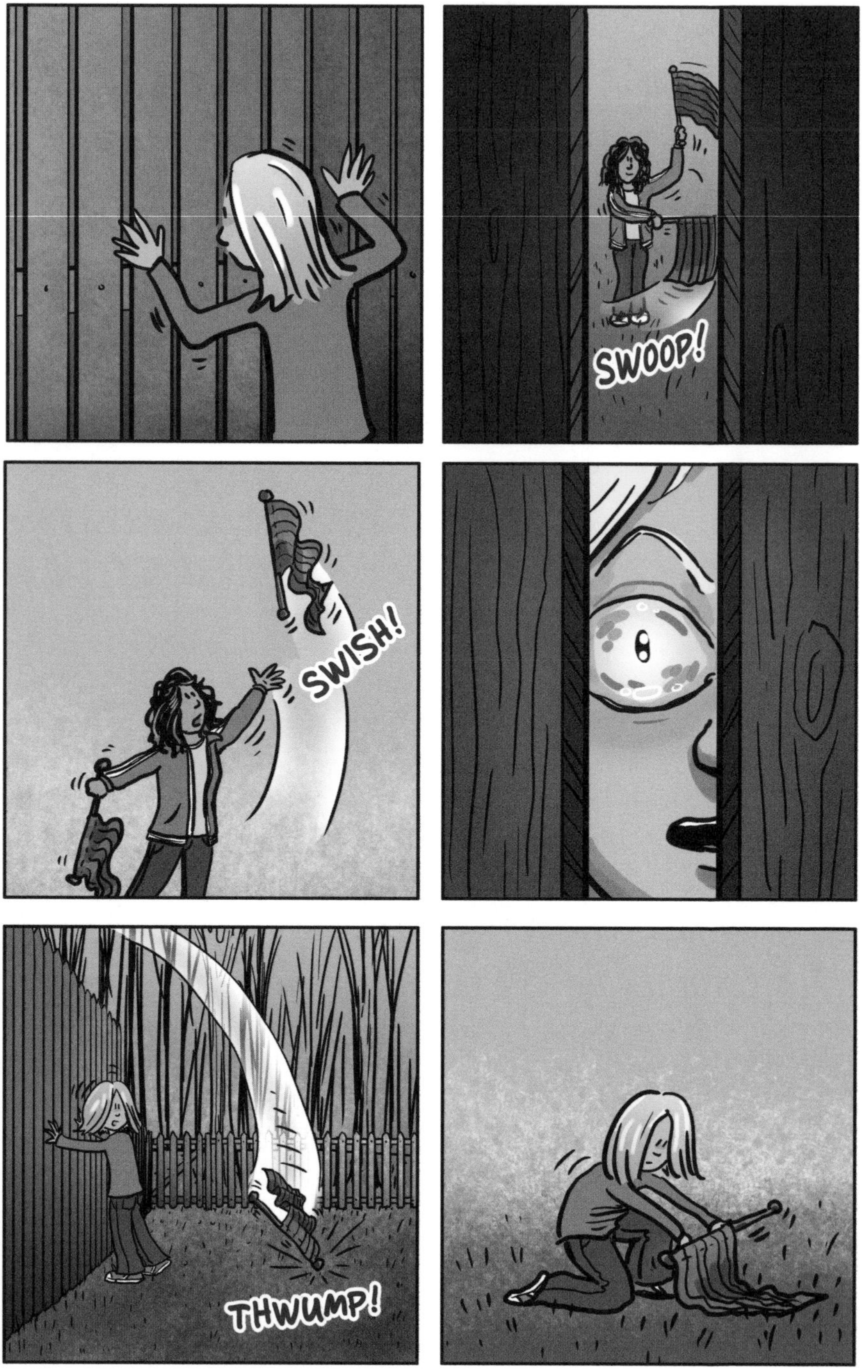
SWOOP!
SWISH!
THWUMP!

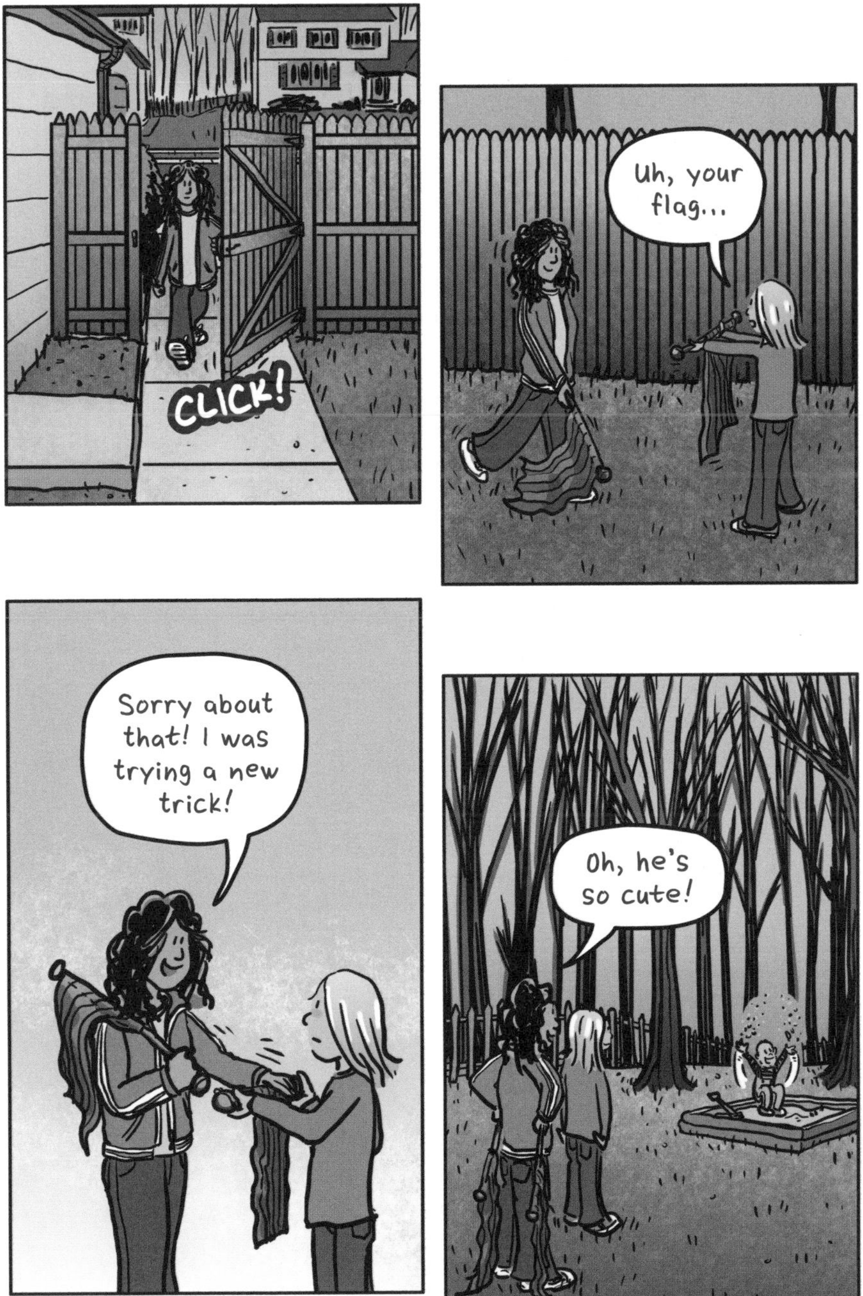
CLICK!
Uh, your flag...
Sorry about that! I was trying a new trick!
Oh, he's so cute!

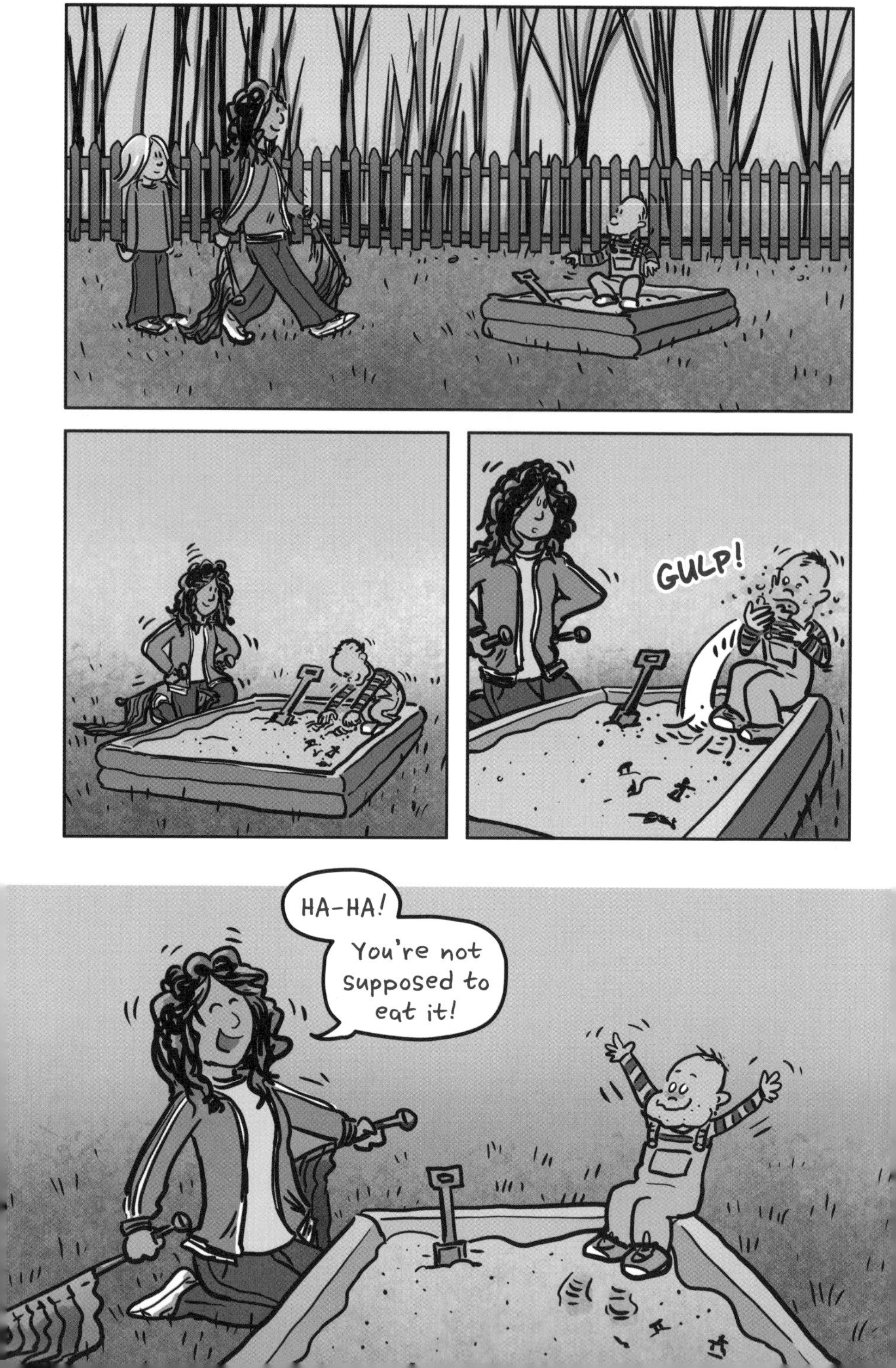
GULP!
HA-HA!
You're not supposed to eat it!

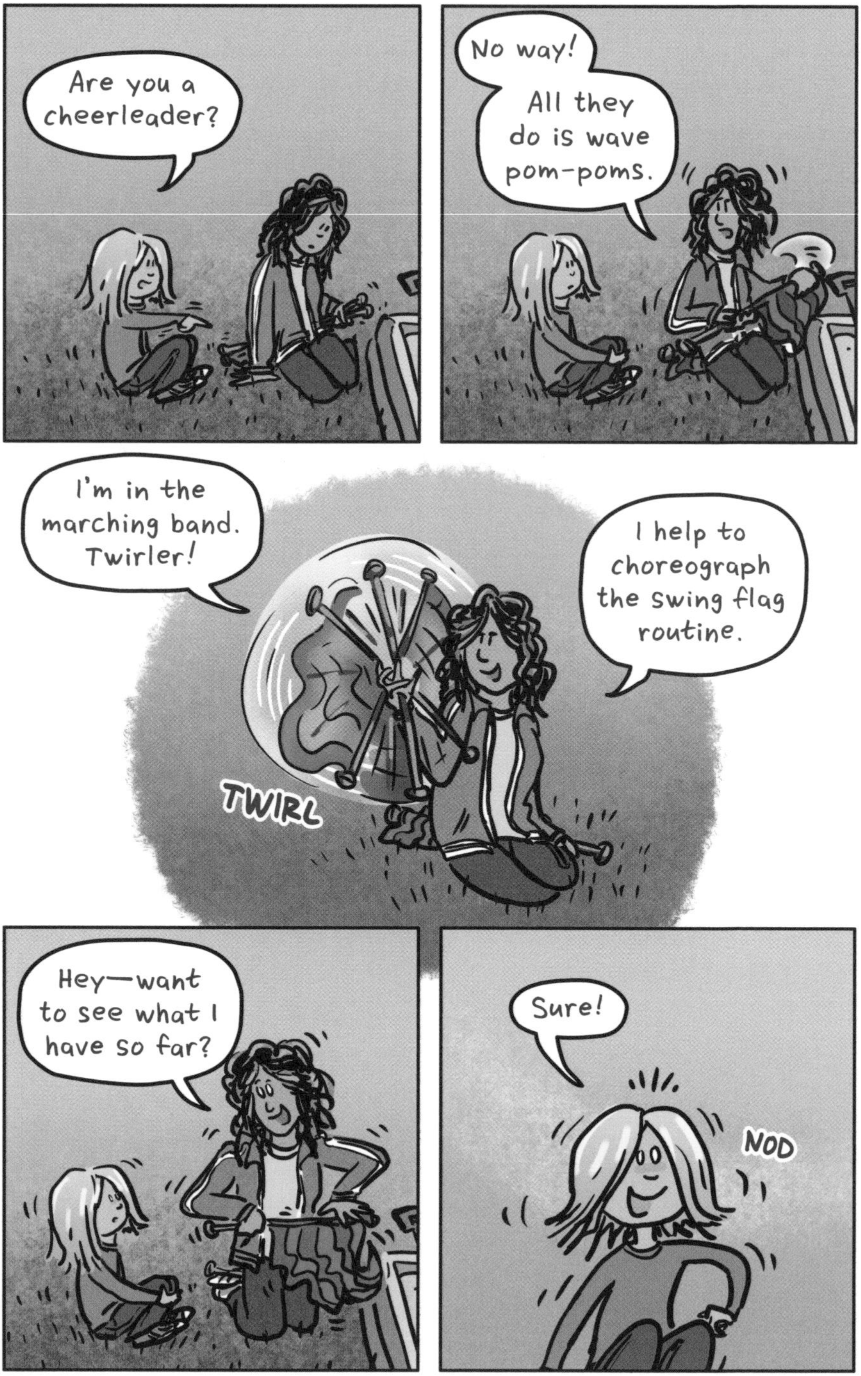
Are you a cheerleader?
No way!
All they do is wave pom-poms.
I'm in the marching band. Twirler!
I help to choreograph the swing flag routine.
TWIRL
Hey—want to see what I have so far?
Sure!
NOD

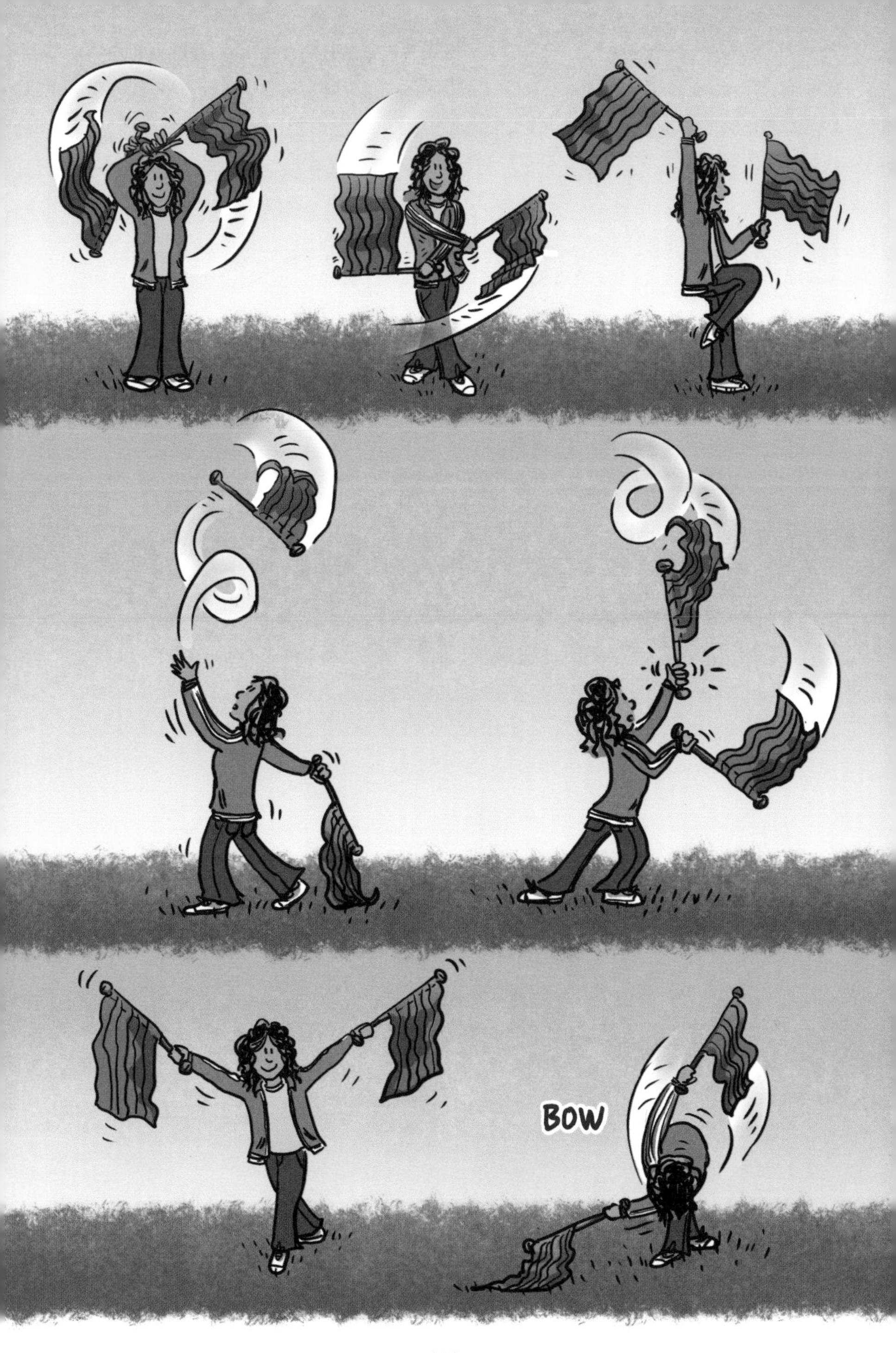
BOW

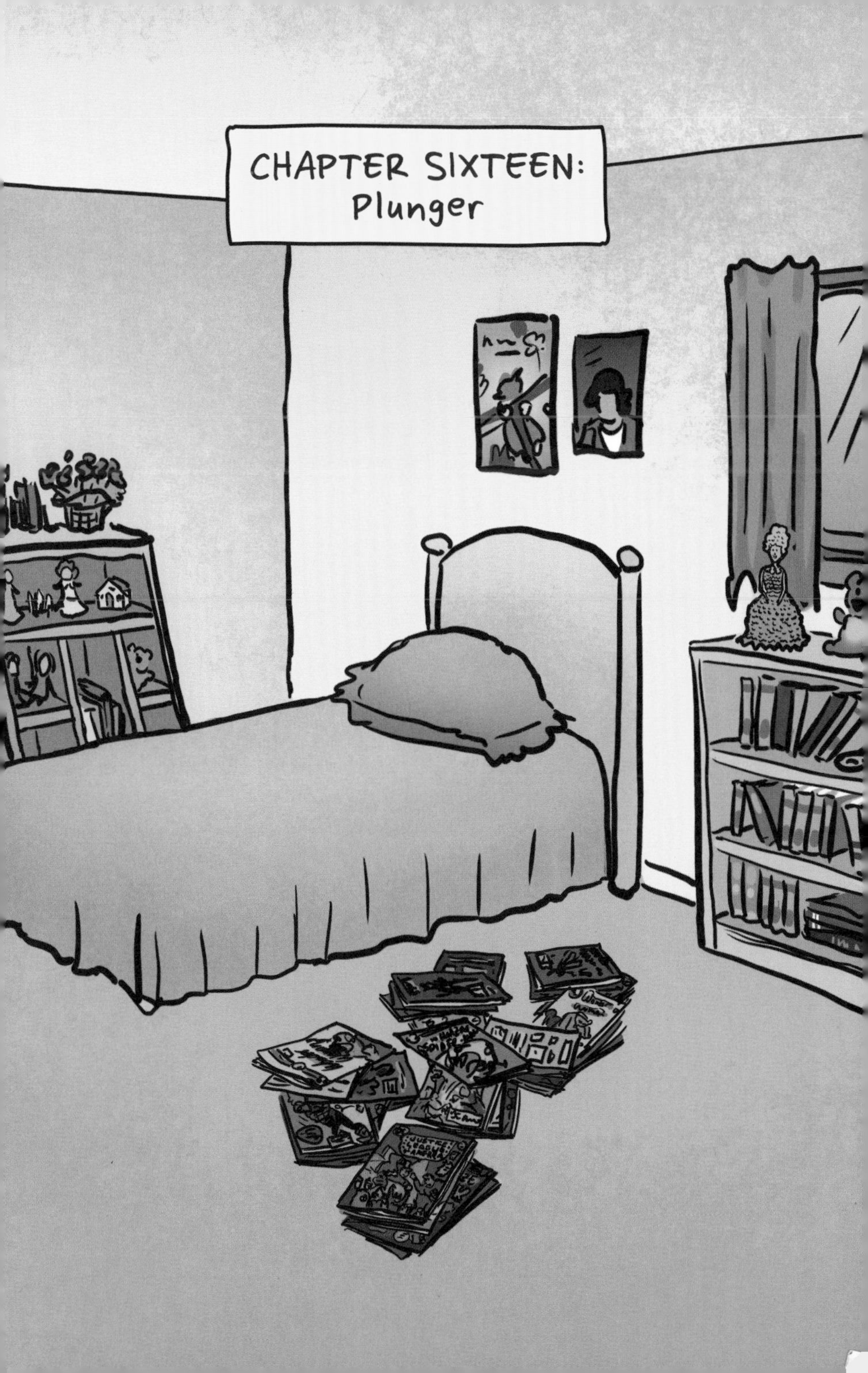
CHAPTER SIXTEEN:
Plunger

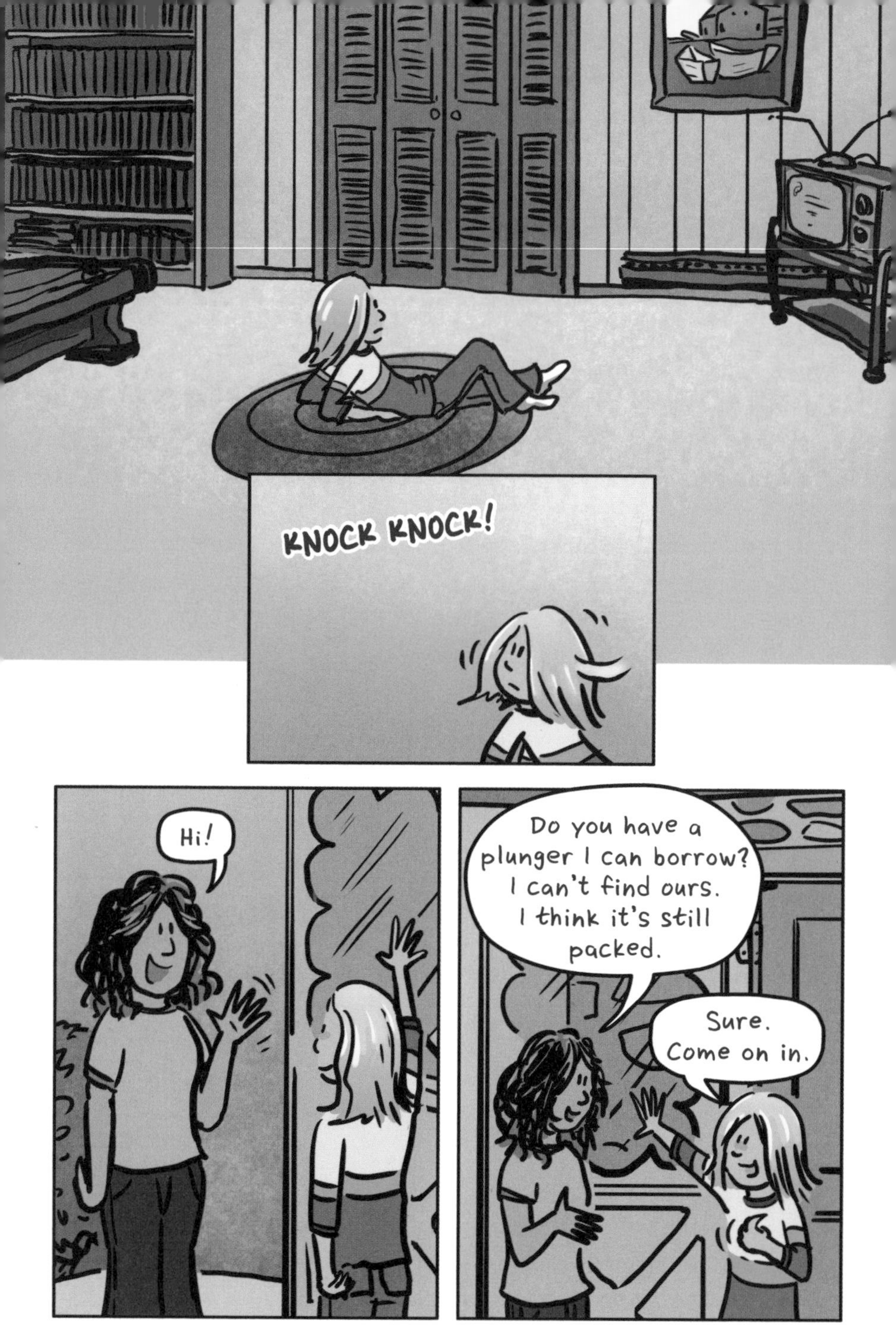
KNOCK KNOCK!
Hi!
Do you have a plunger I can borrow? I can't find ours. I think it's still packed.
Sure. Come on in.

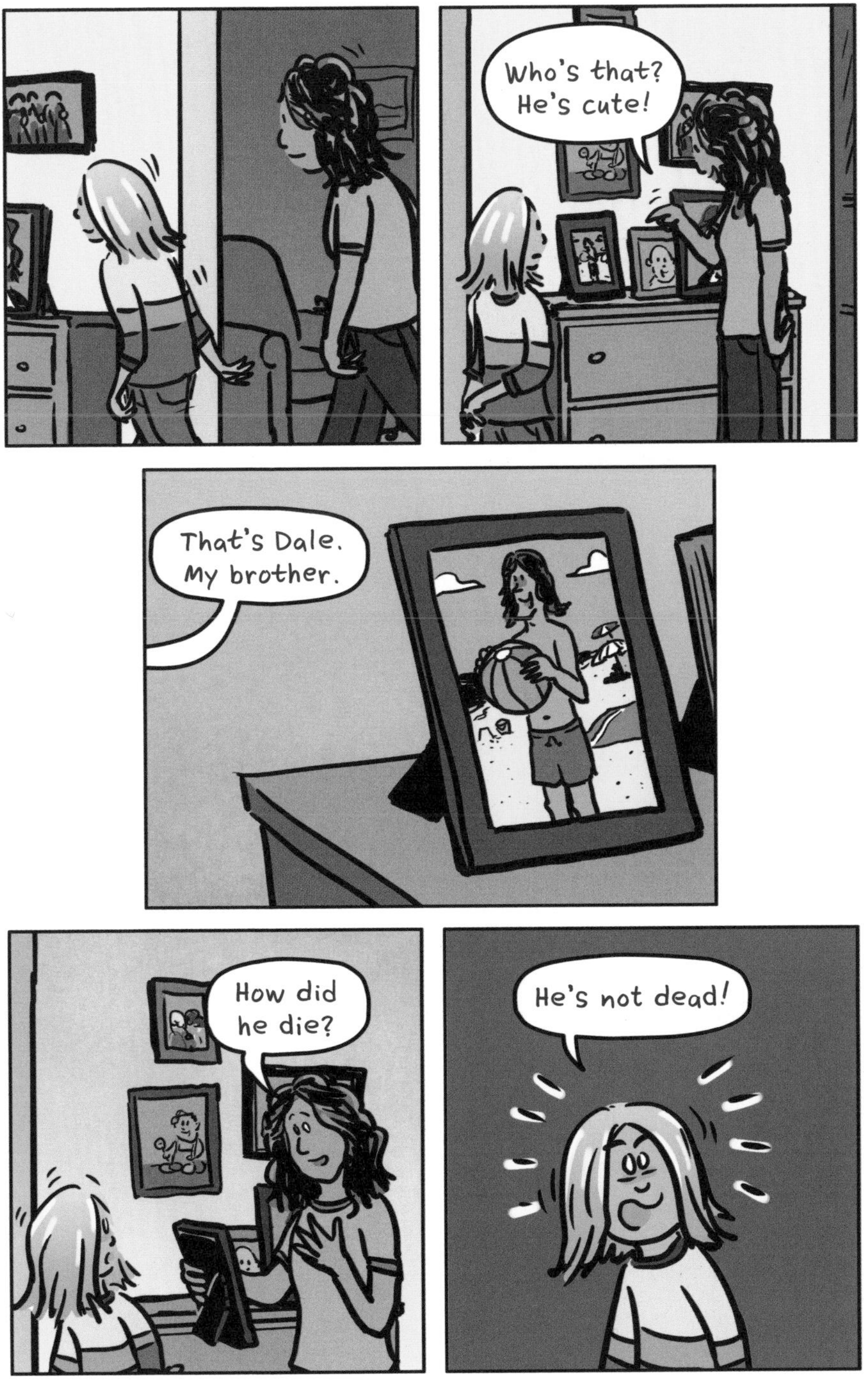
Who's that? He's cute!
That's Dale. My brother.
How did he die?
He's not dead!

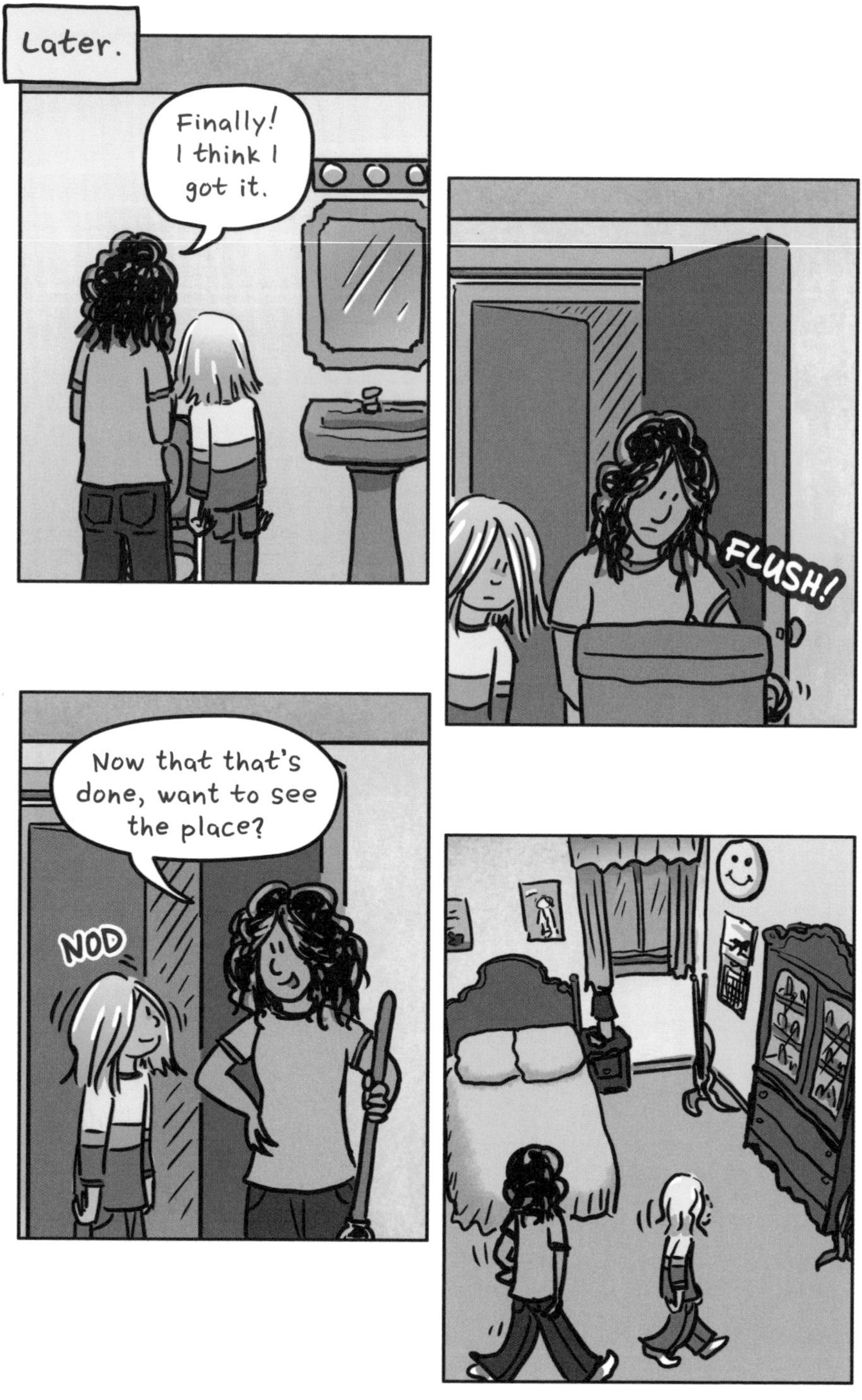
Later.
Finally! I think I got it.
FLUSH!
Now that that's done, want to see the place?
NOD

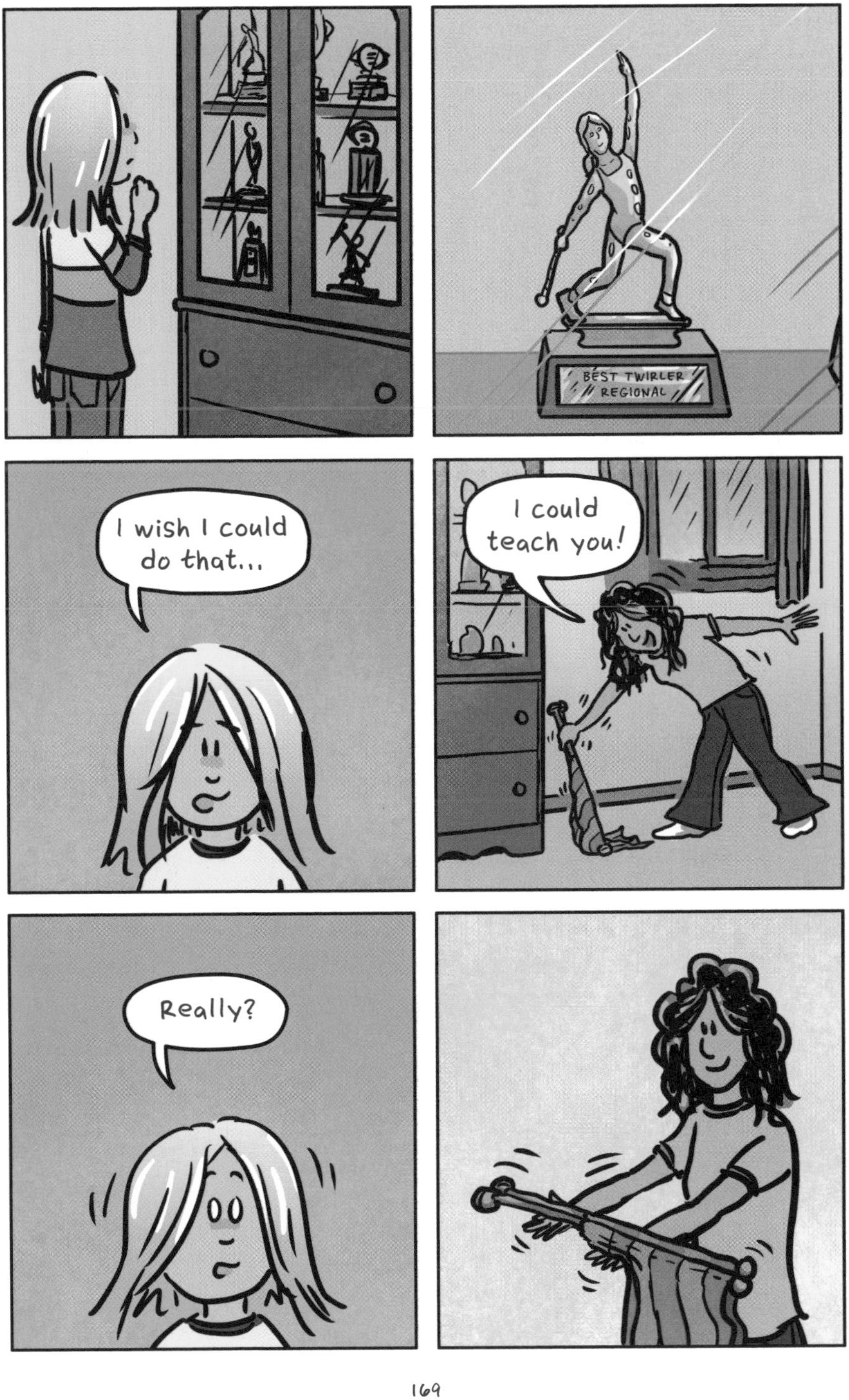
BEST TWIRLER
REGIONAL
I wish I could do that...
I could teach you!
Really?

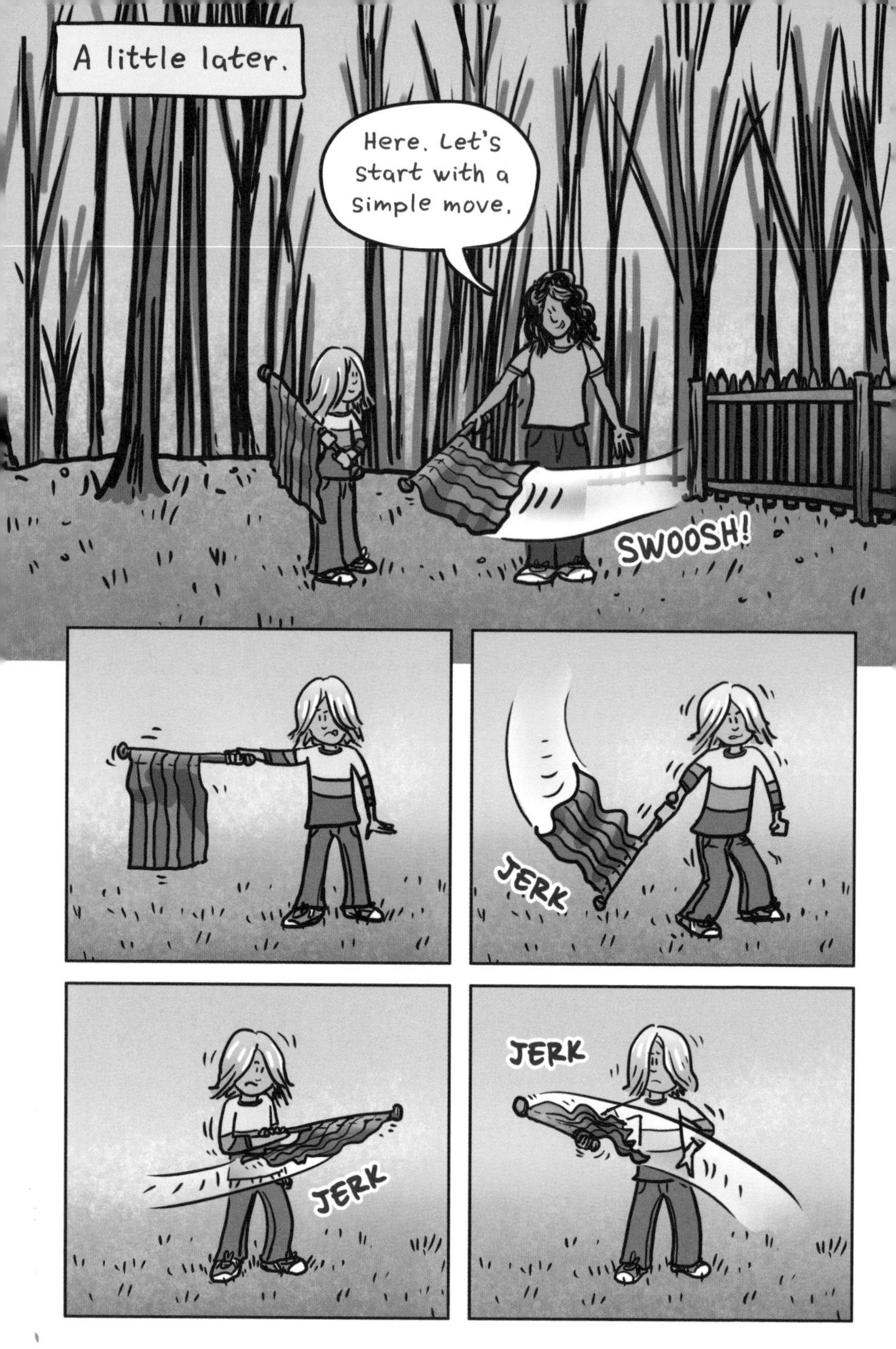
A little later.
Here. Let's start with a simple move.
SWOOSH!
JERK
JERK
JERK

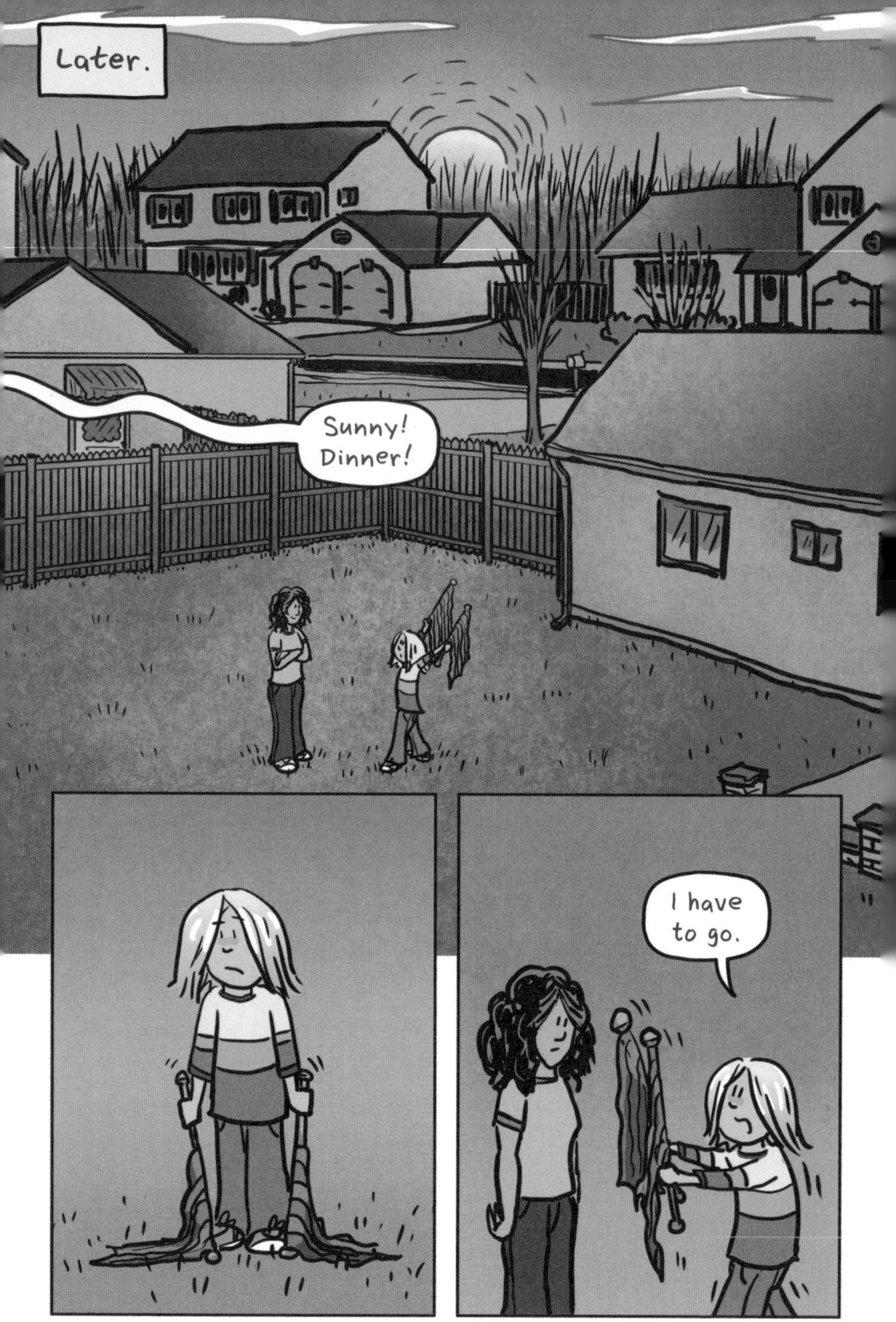
Later.
Sunny! Dinner!
I have to go.

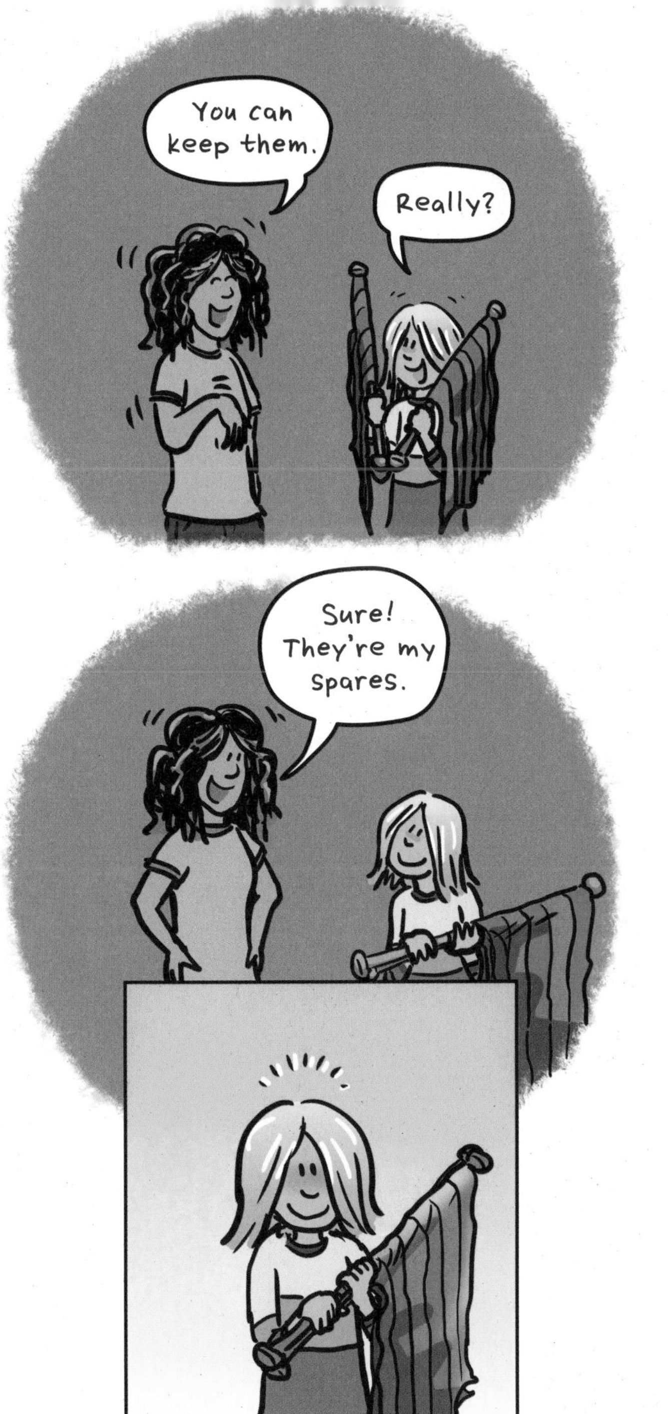
You can keep them.
Really?
Sure! They're my spares.

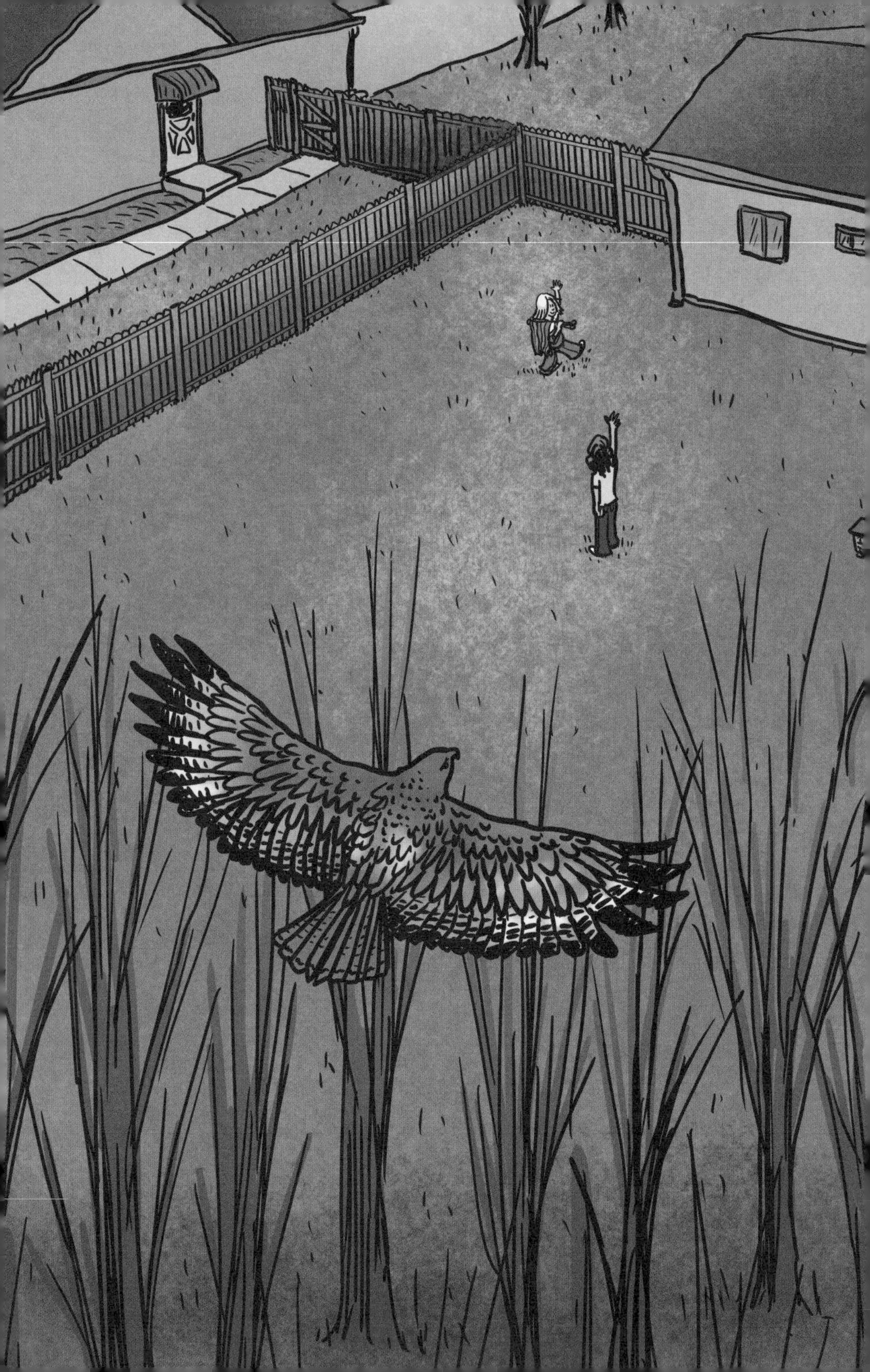

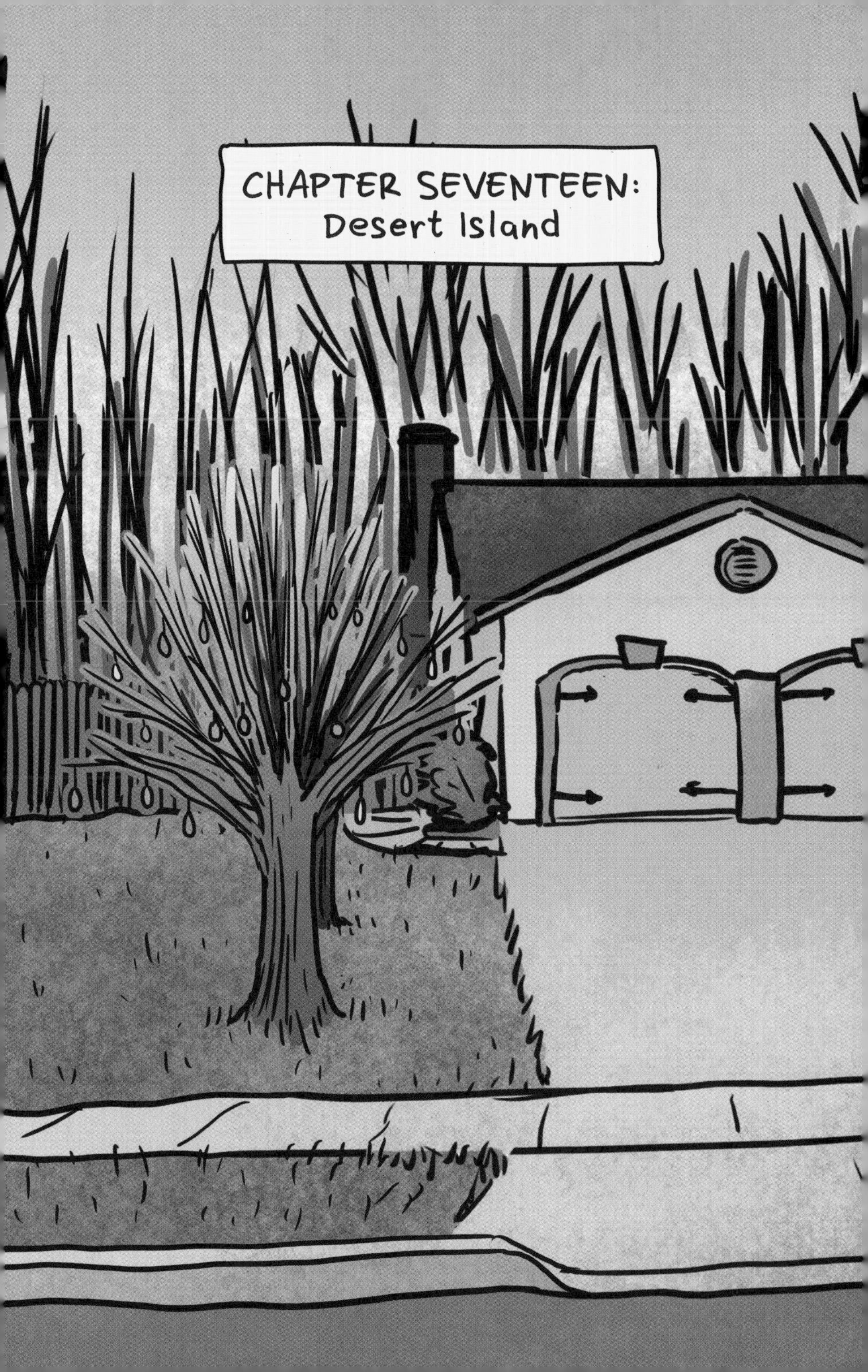
CHAPTER SEVENTEEN:
Desert Island

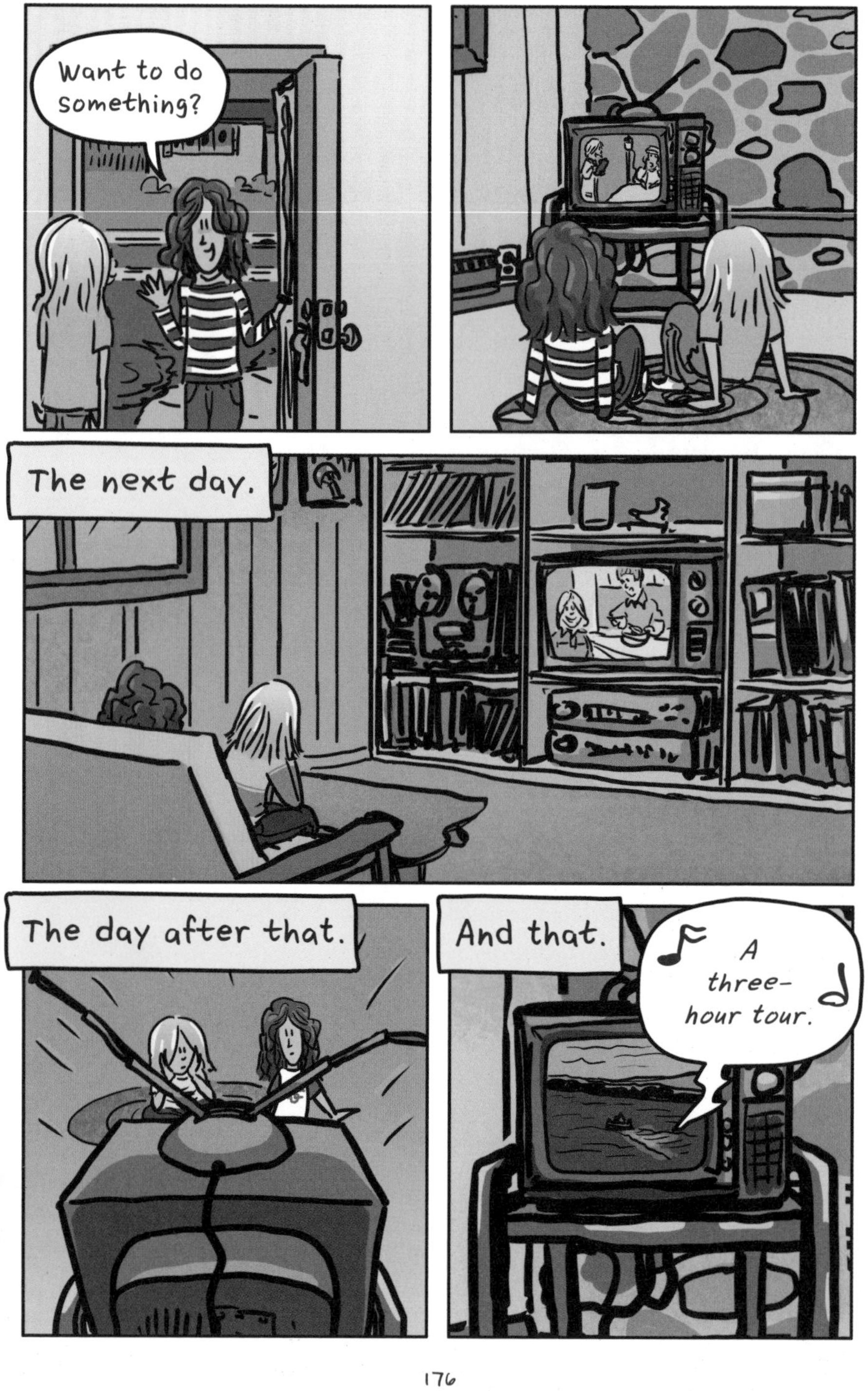
Want to do something?
The next day.
The day after that.
And that.
A three-hour tour.

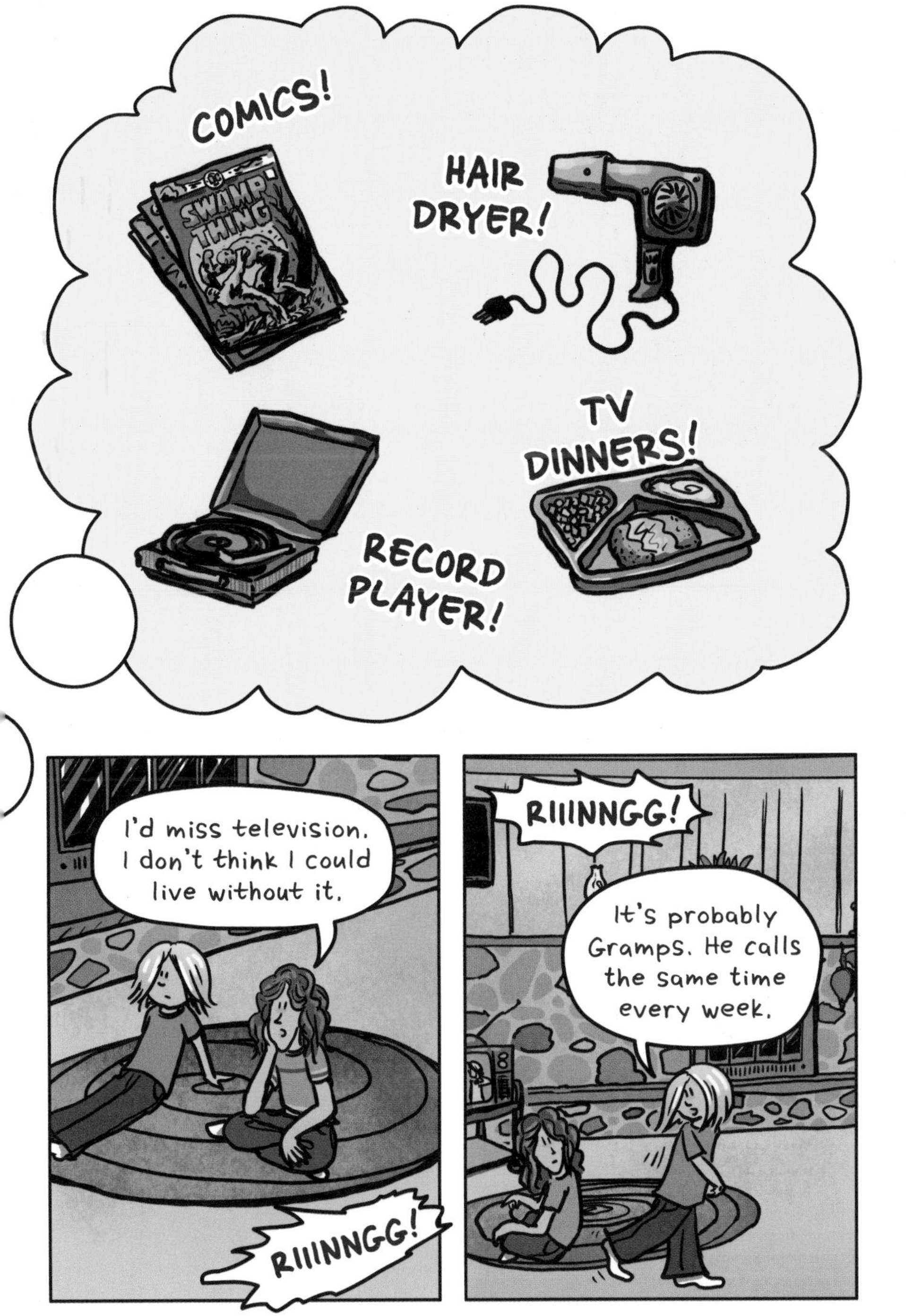
COMICS!
SWAMP THING
HAIR DRYER!
RECORD PLAYER!
TV DINNERS!
I'd miss television. I don't think I could live without it.
RIIINNGG!
RIIINNGG!
It's probably Gramps. He calls the same time every week.

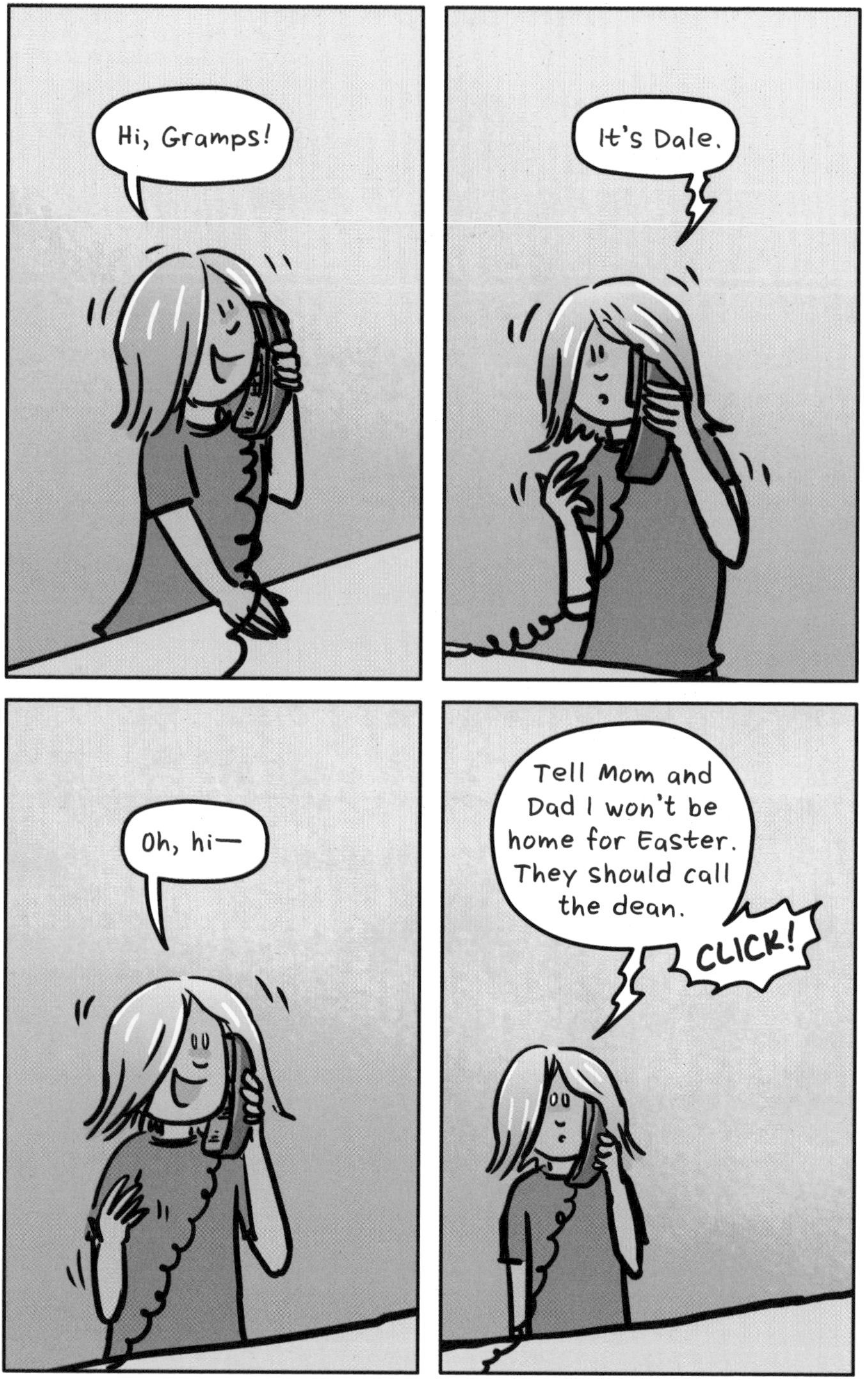
Hi, Gramps!
It's Dale.
Oh, hi—
Tell Mom and Dad I won't be home for Easter. They should call the dean.
CLICK!

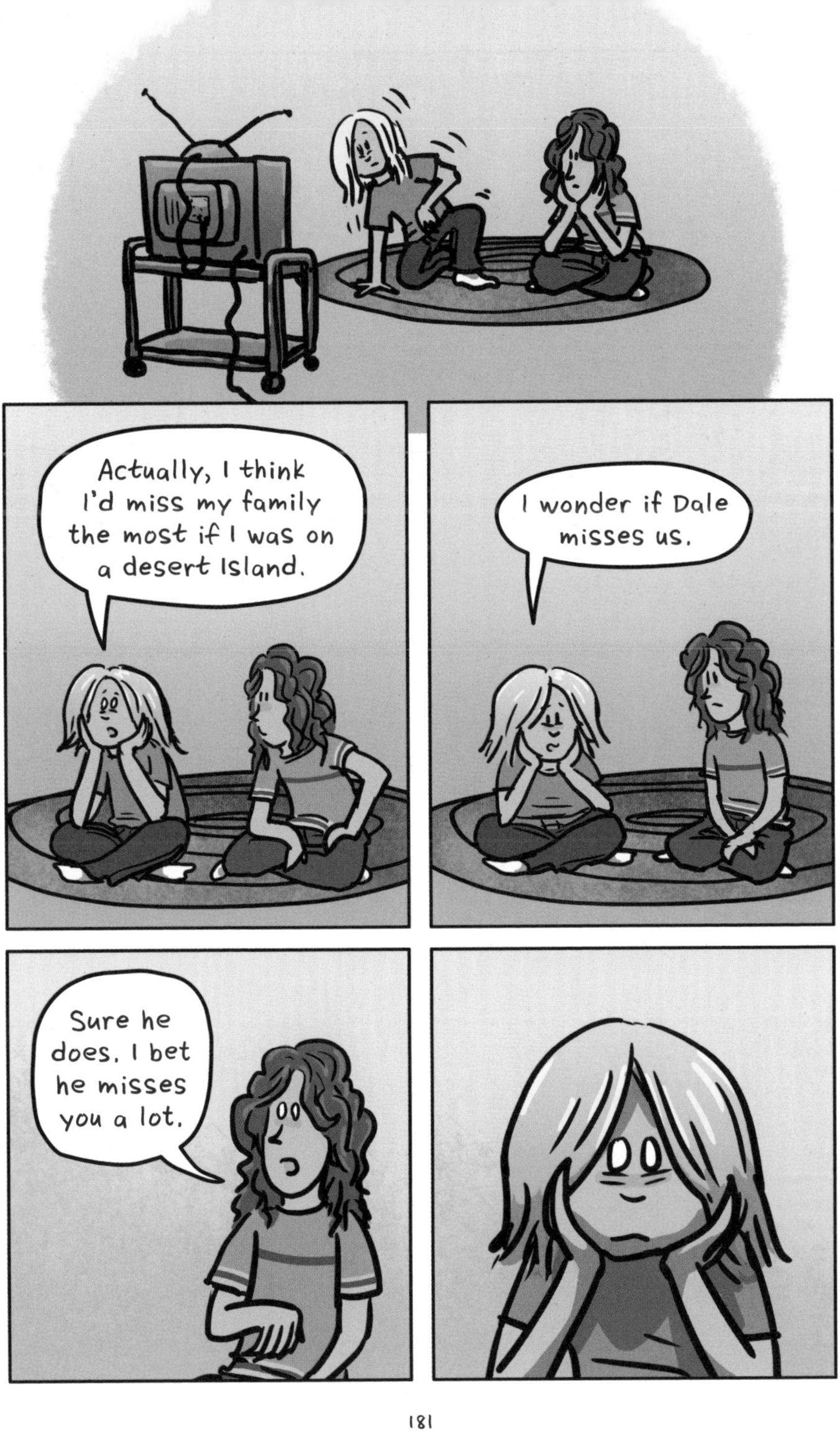
Actually, I think I'd miss my family the most if I was on a desert Island.
I wonder if Dale misses us.
Sure he does. I bet he misses you a lot.

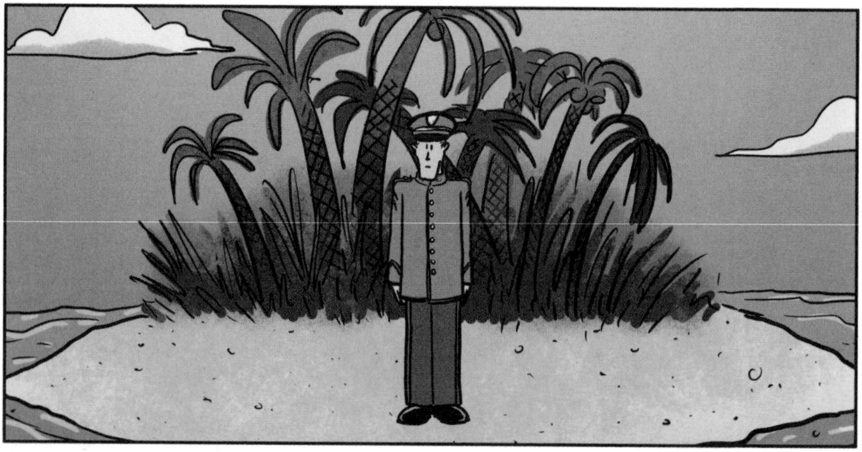

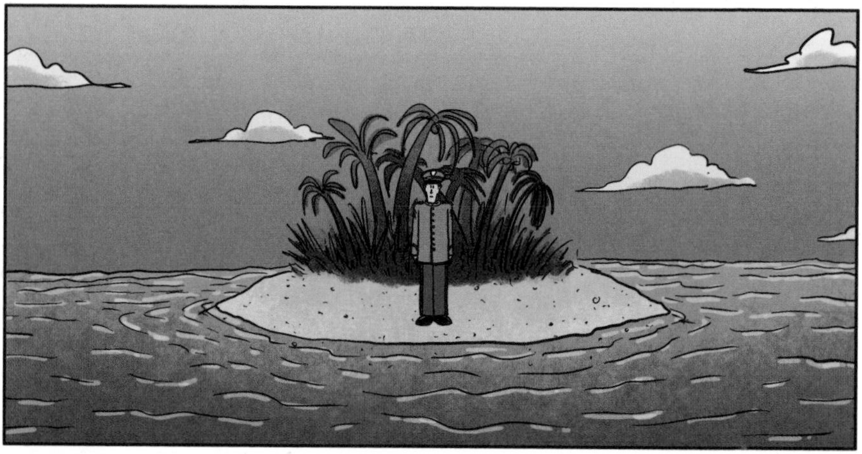

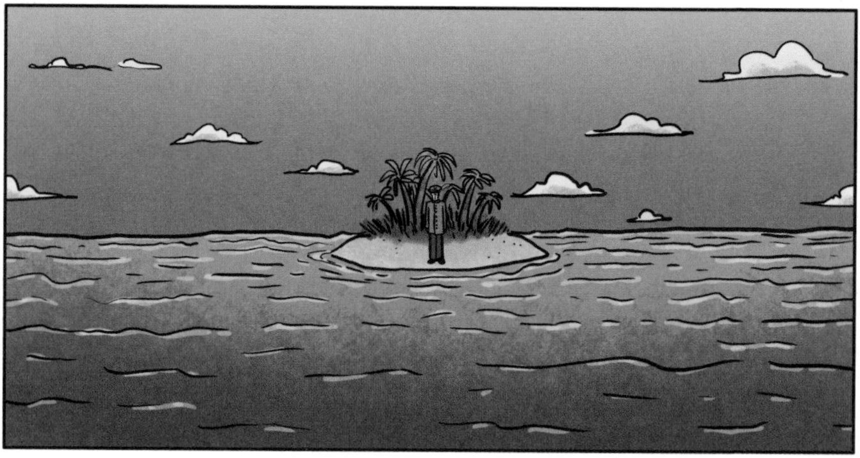

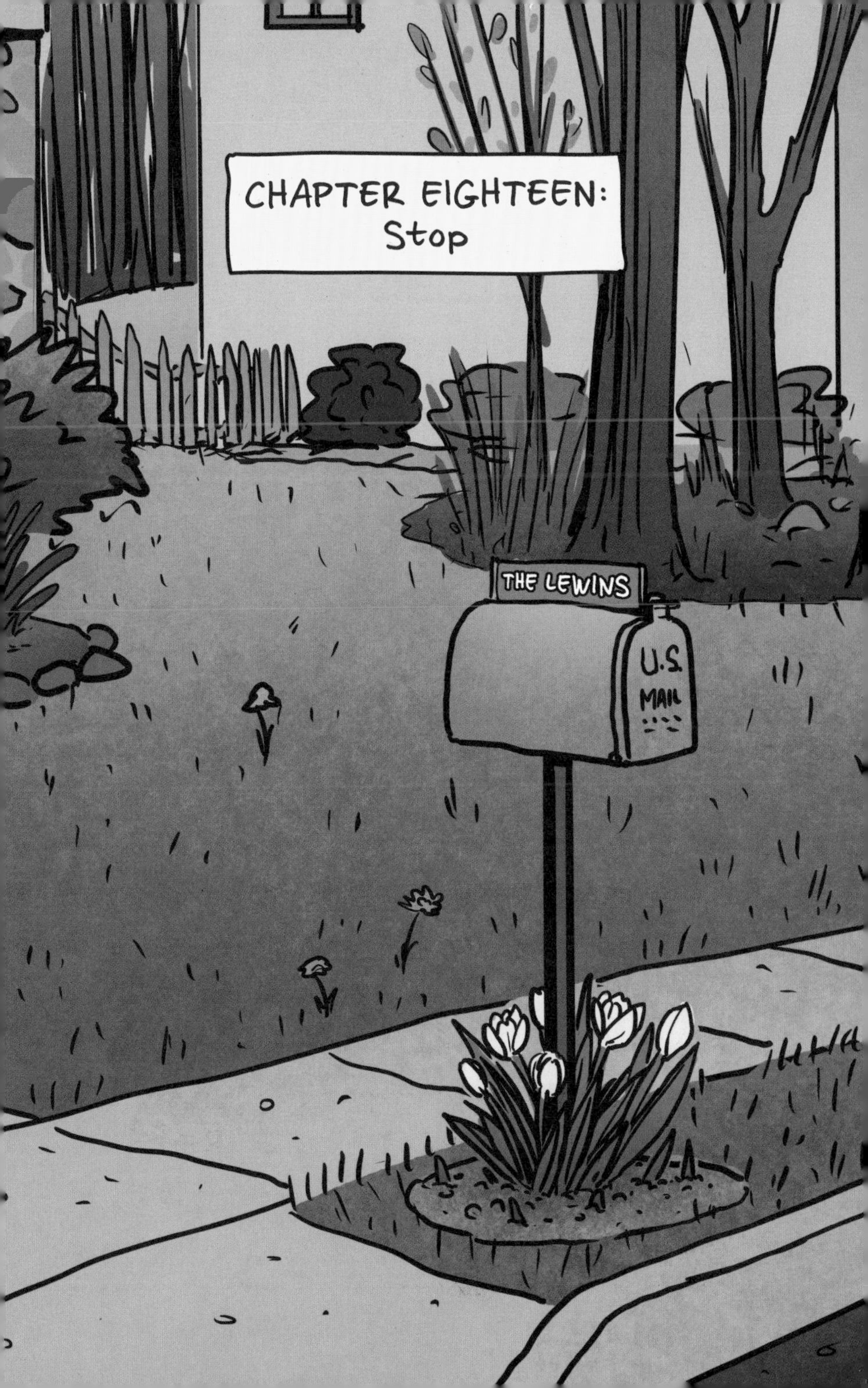
CHAPTER EIGHTEEN:
Stop
THE LEWINS
U.S.
MAIL

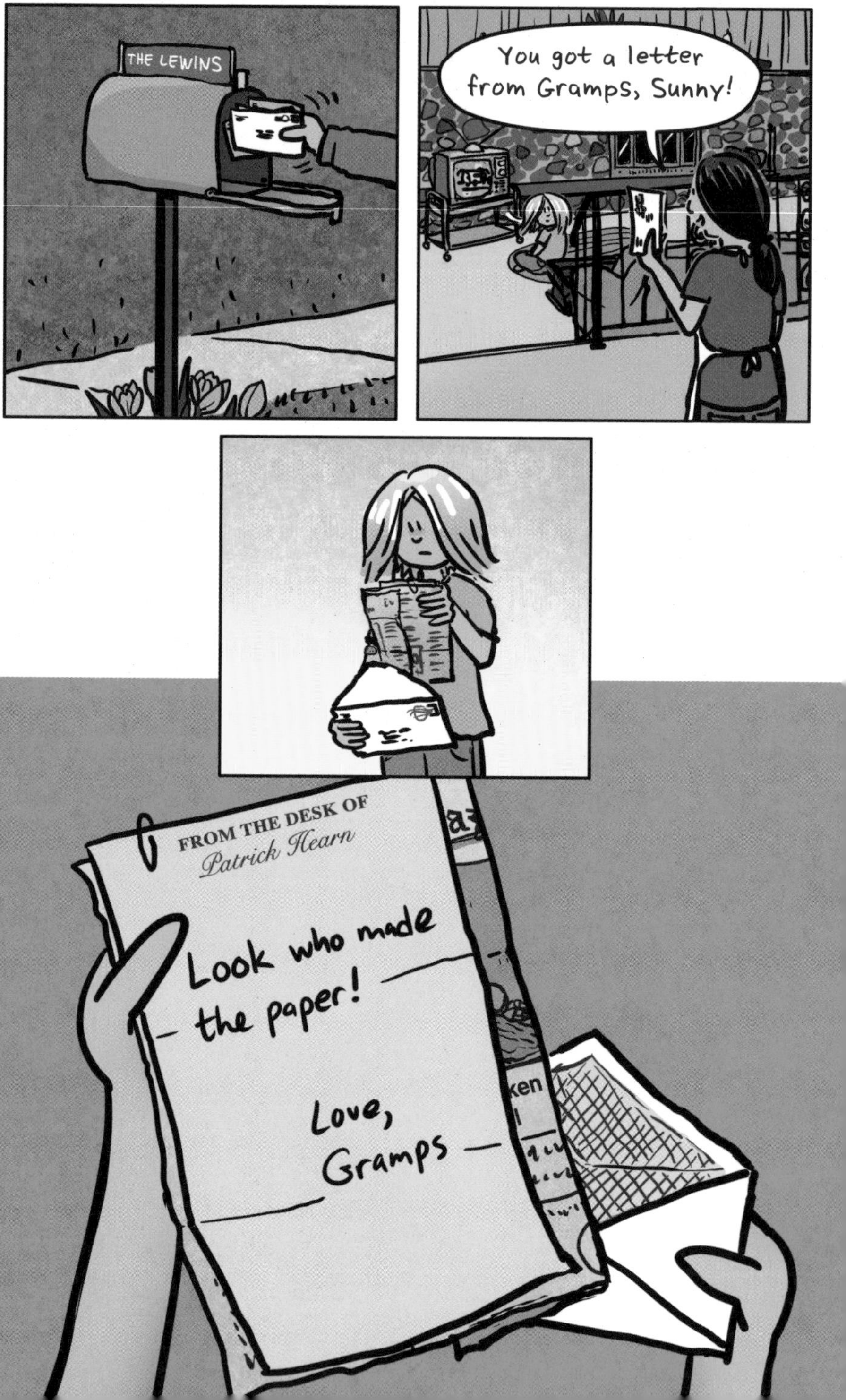
THE LEWINS
You got a letter from Gramps, Sunny!
FROM THE DESK OF
Patrick Hearn
Look who made the paper!
Love,
Gramps

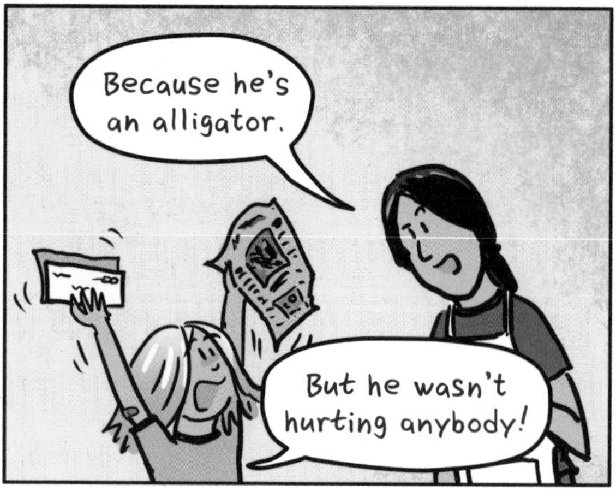
Because he's an alligator.
But he wasn't hurting anybody!

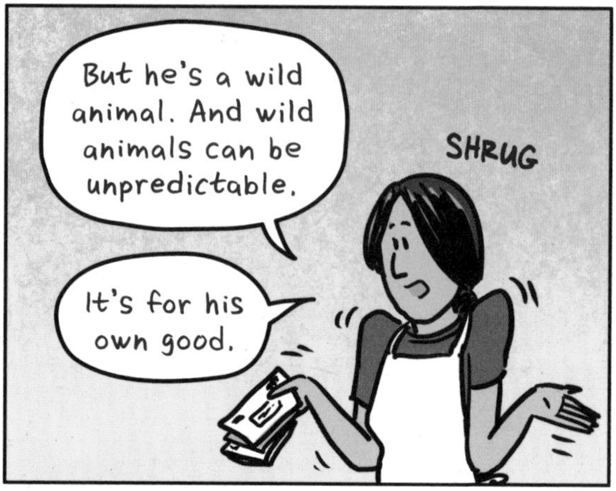
But he's a wild animal. And wild animals can be unpredictable.
SHRUG
It's for his own good.

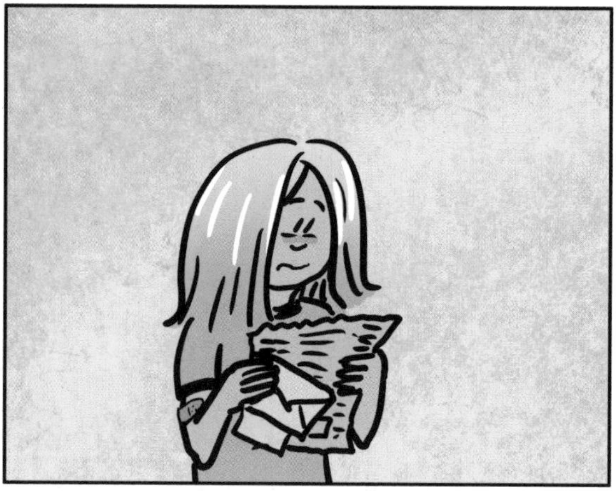

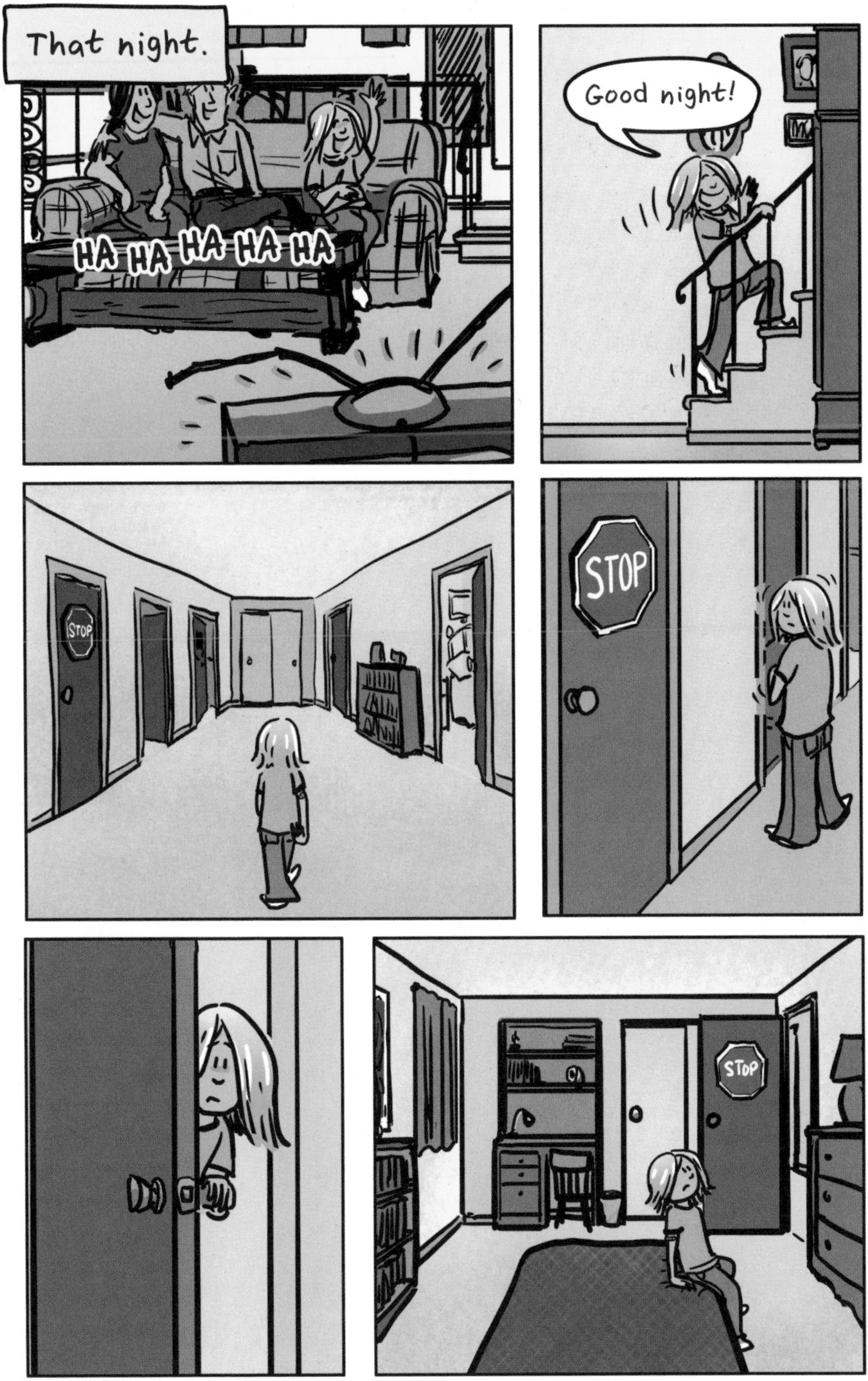
That night.
HA HA HA HA HA
Good night!
STOP
STOP
STOP

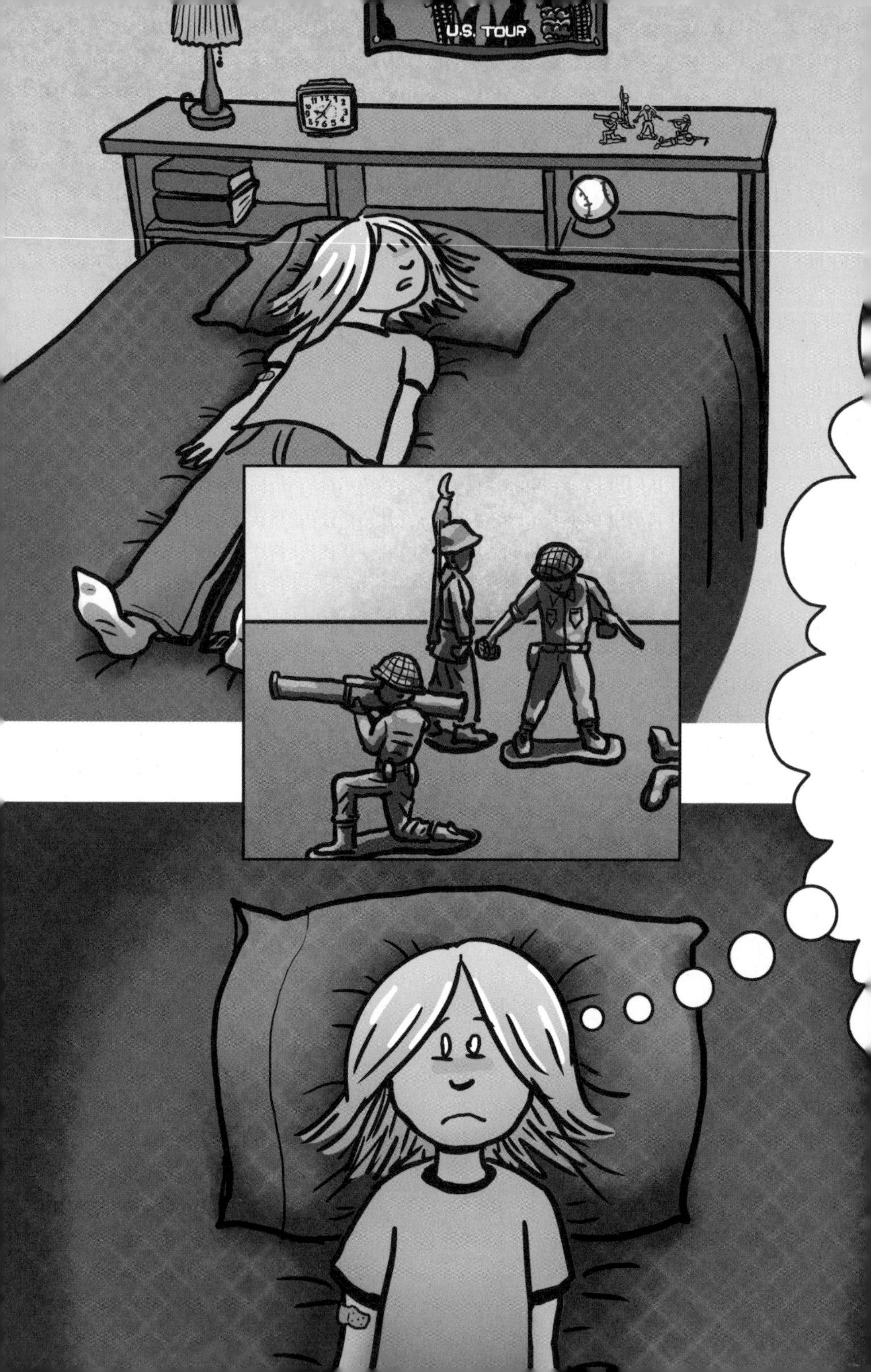
U.S. TOUR

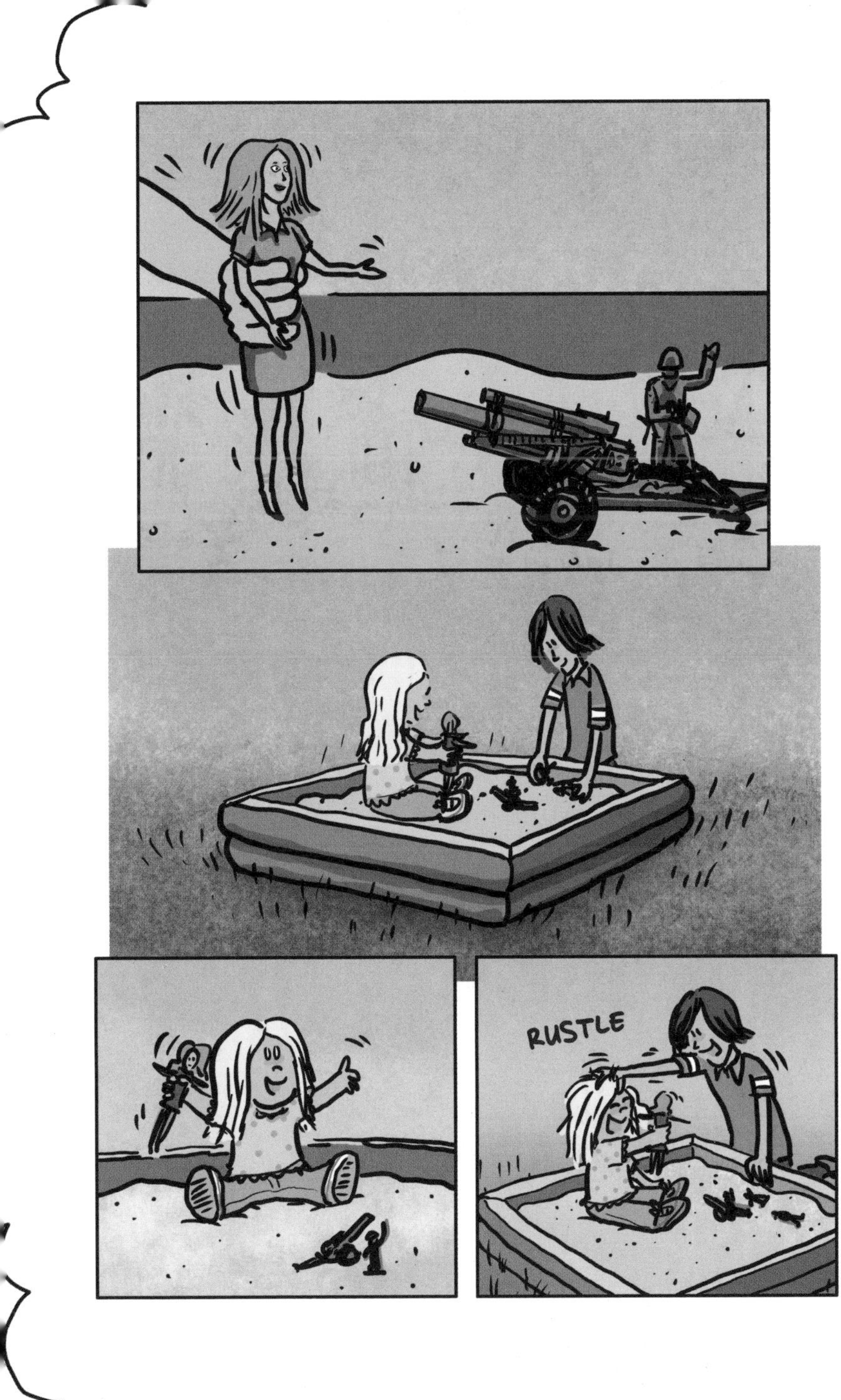
RUSTLE

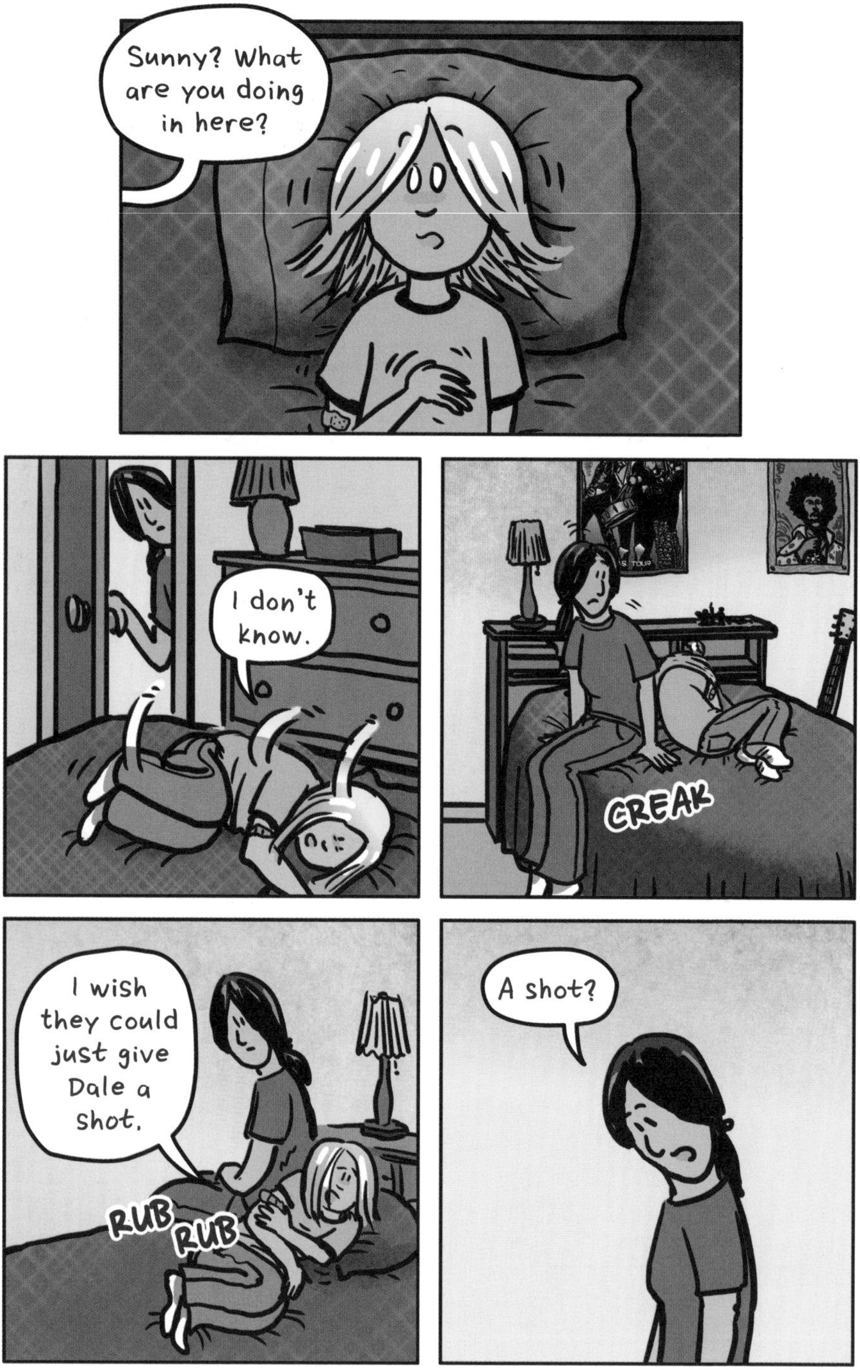

Sunny? What are you doing in here?
I don't know.
CREAK
I wish they could just give Dale a shot.
RUB
RUB
A shot?

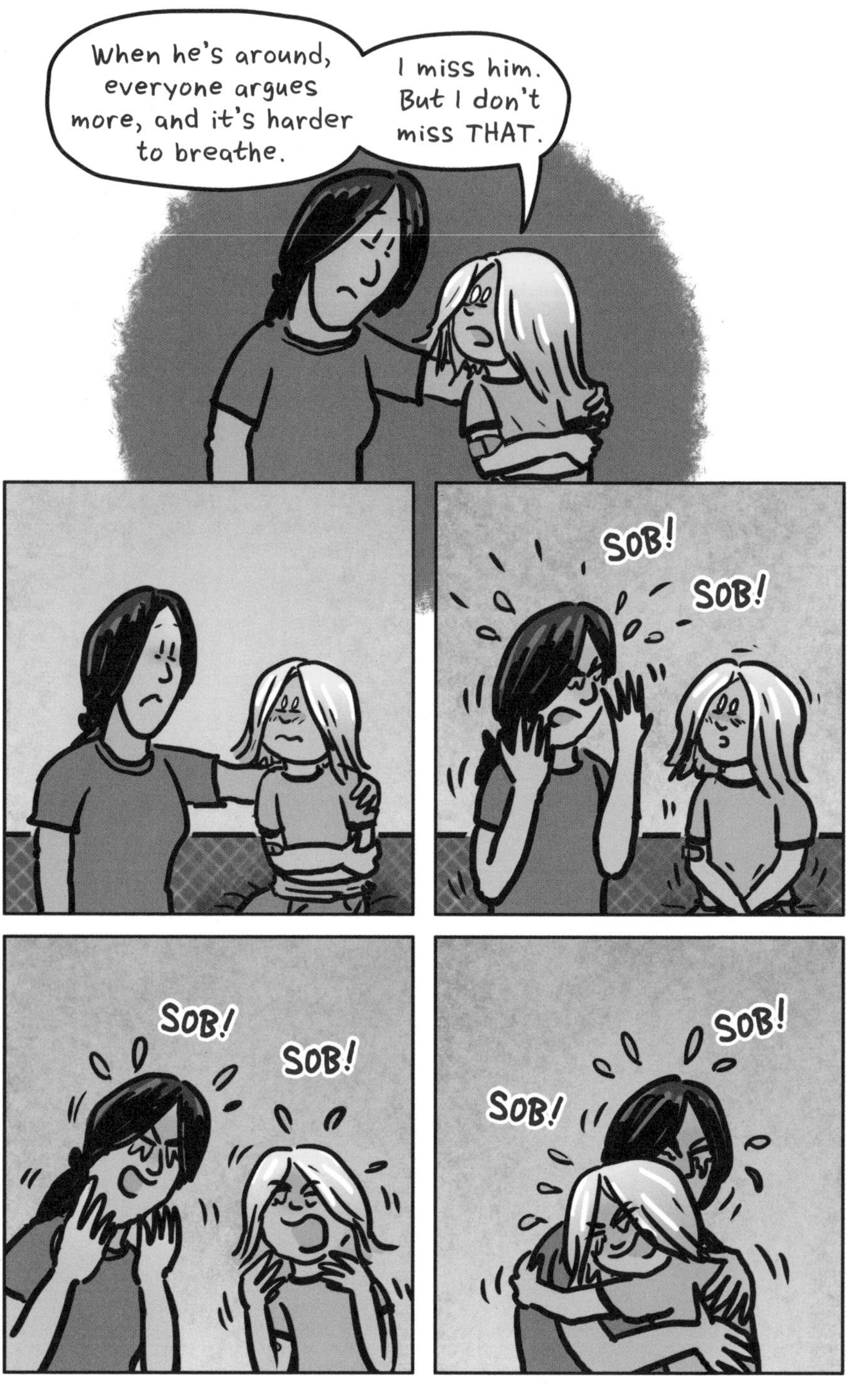
When he's around, everyone argues more, and it's harder to breathe.
I miss him. But I don't miss THAT.
SOB!
SOB!
SOB!
SOB!
SOB!
SOB!

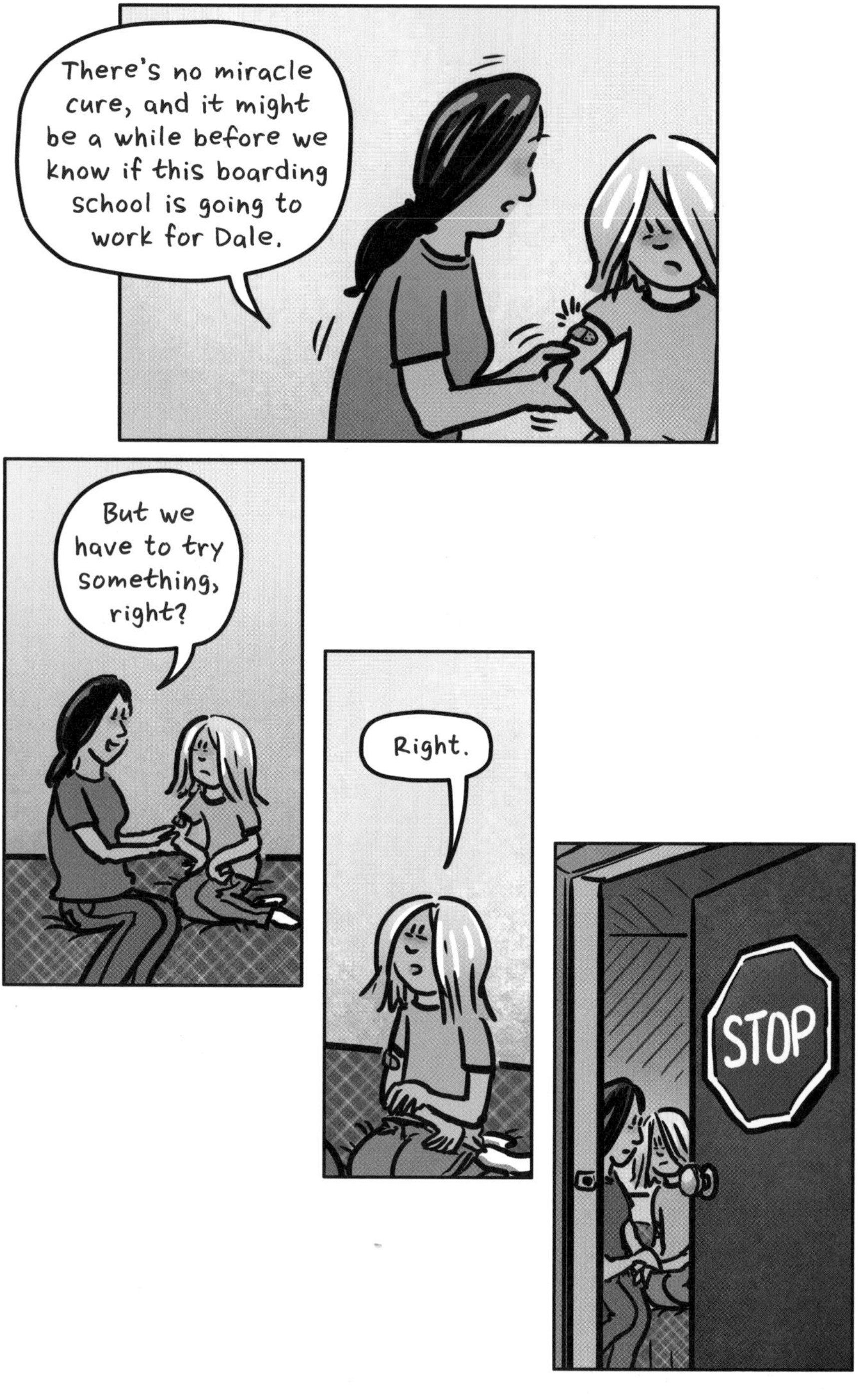
There's no miracle cure, and it might be a while before we know if this boarding school is going to work for Dale.
But we have to try something, right?
Right.
STOP

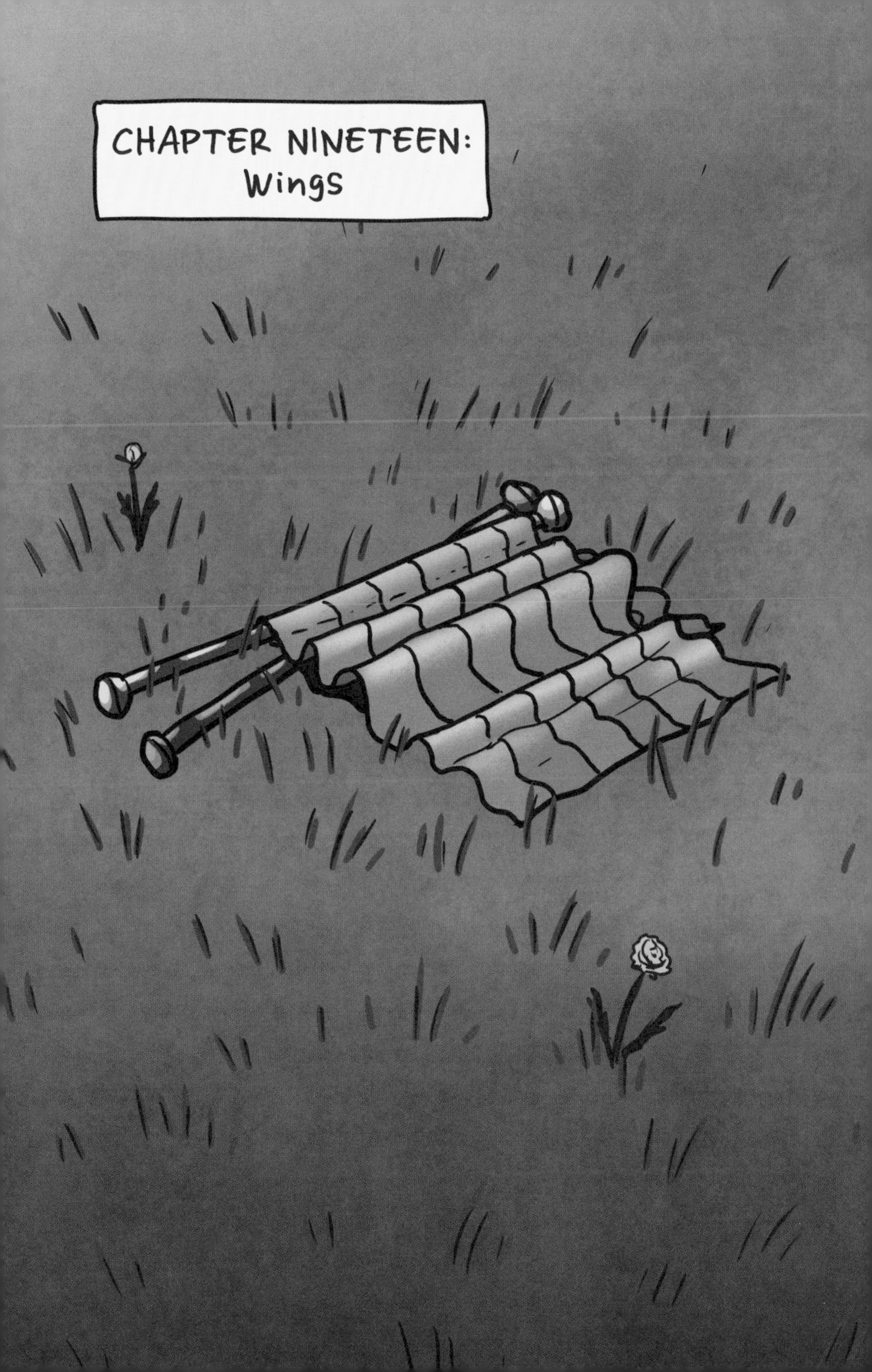
CHAPTER NINETEEN:
Wings

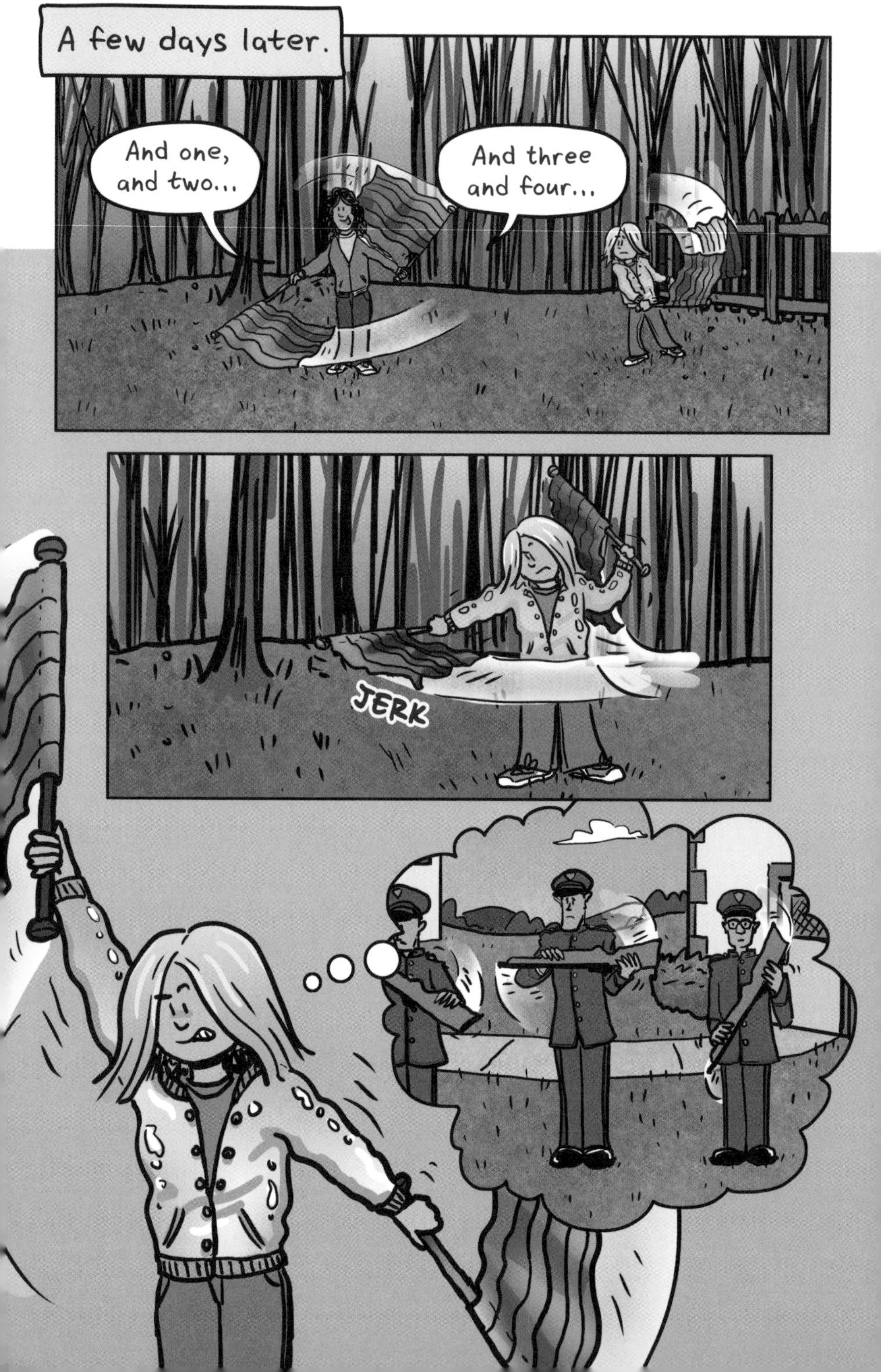
A few days later.
And one, and two...
And three and four...
JERK

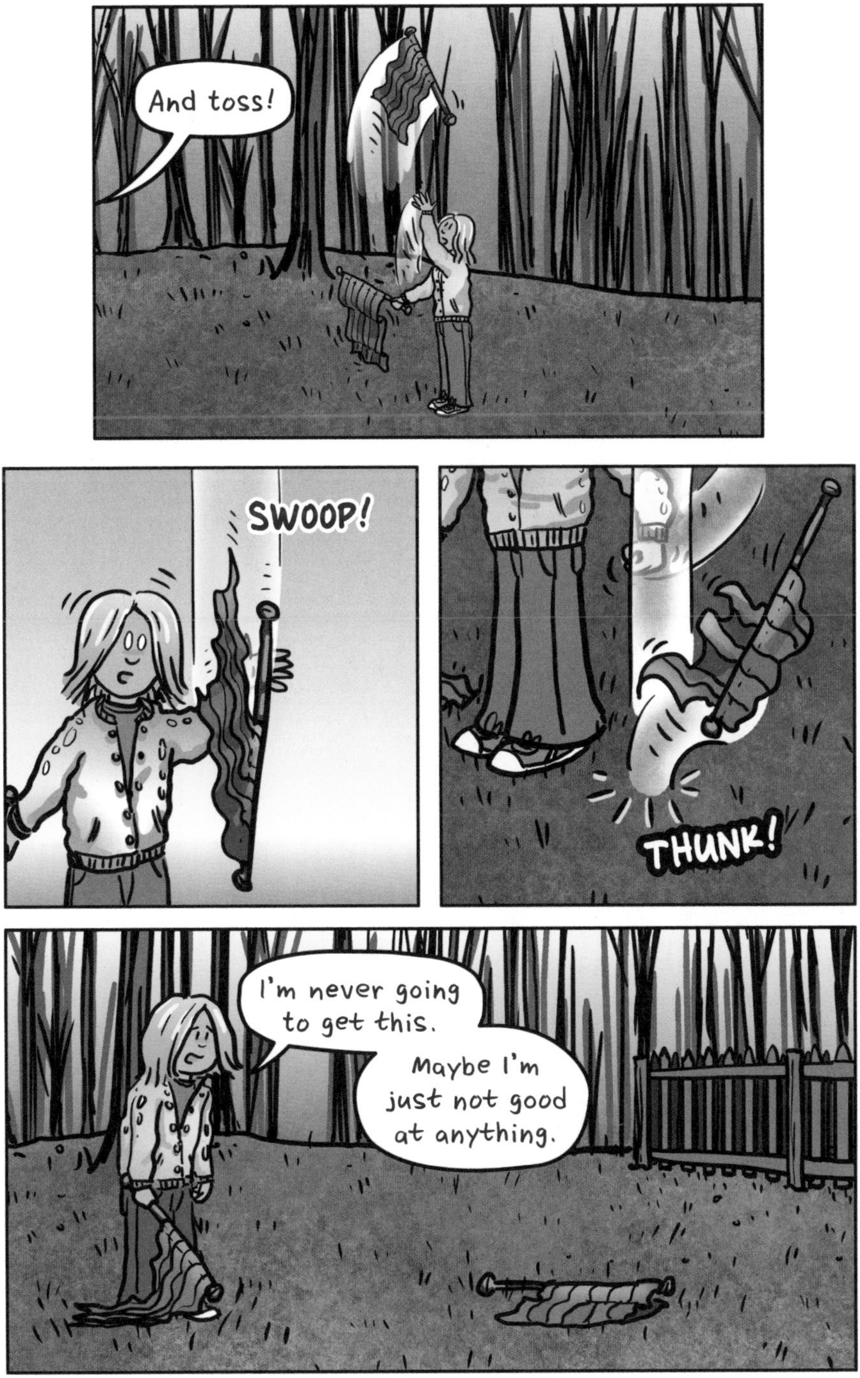
And toss!
SWOOP!
THUNK!
I'm never going to get this.
Maybe I'm just not good at anything.

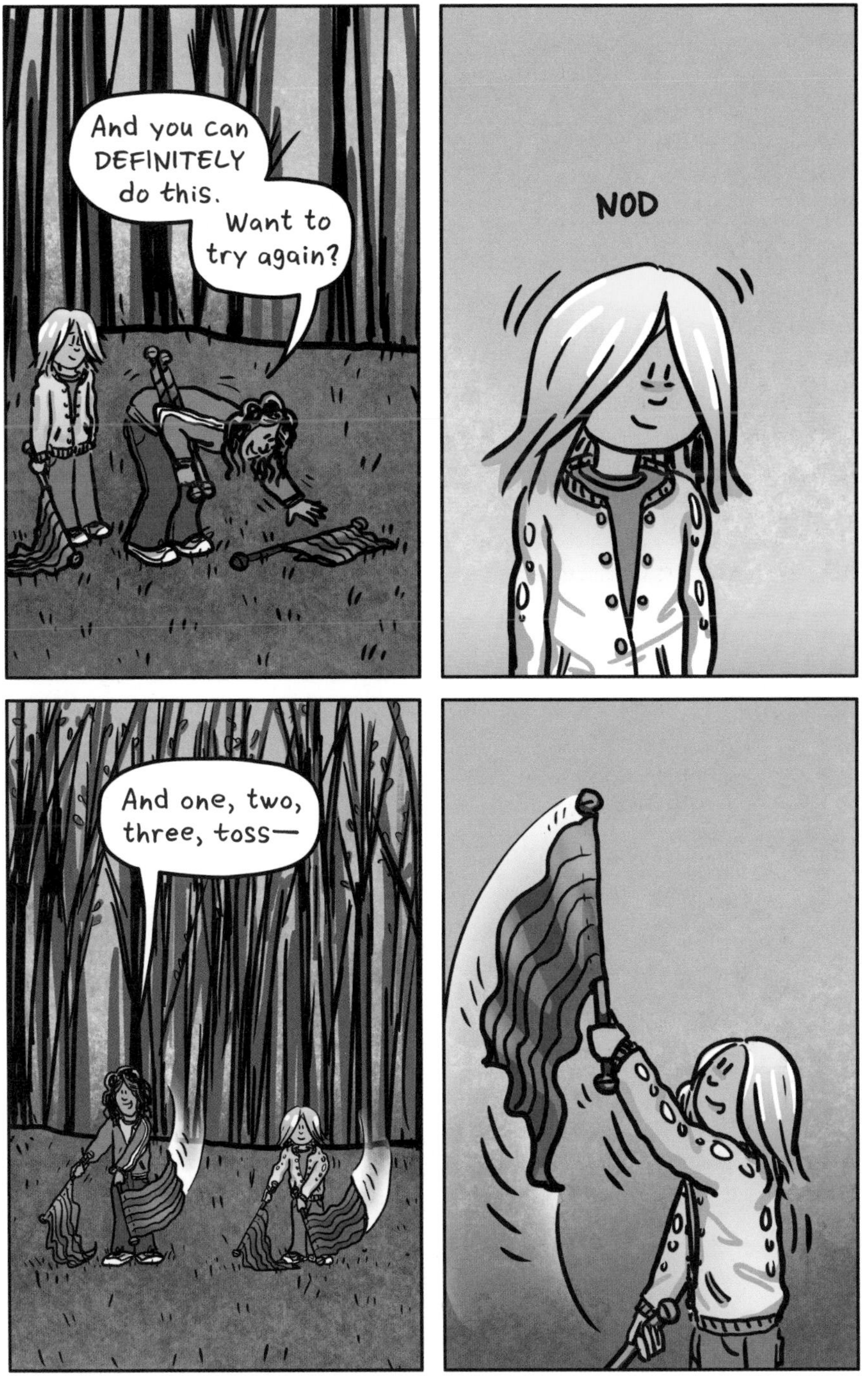
And you can DEFINITELY do this.
Want to try again?
NOD
And one, two, three, toss—

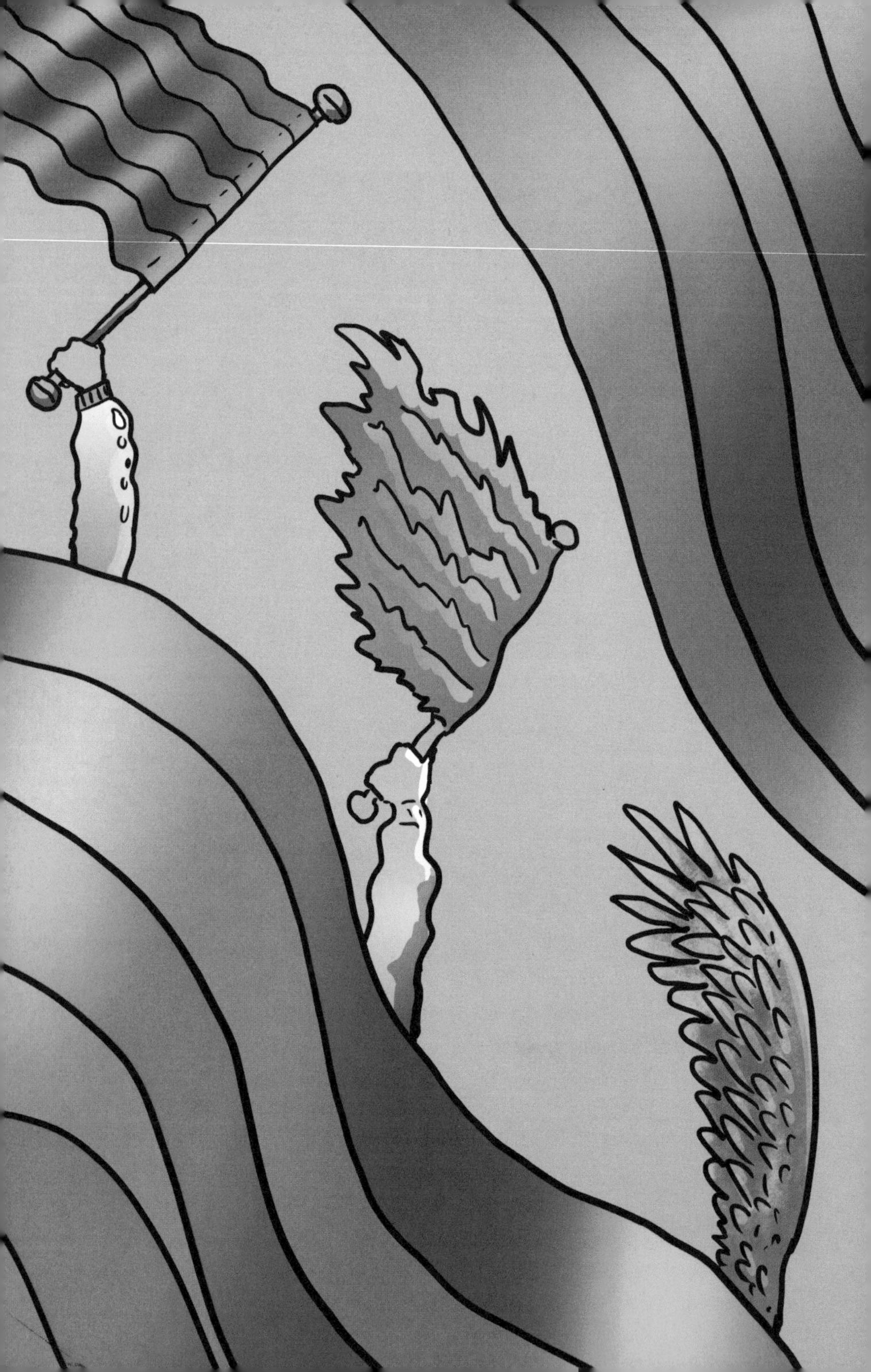

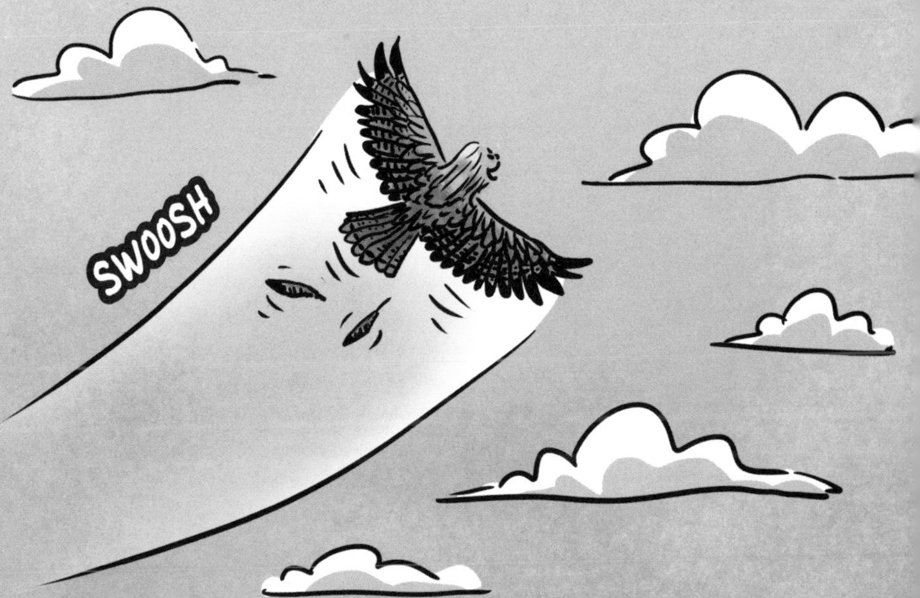
SWOOSH

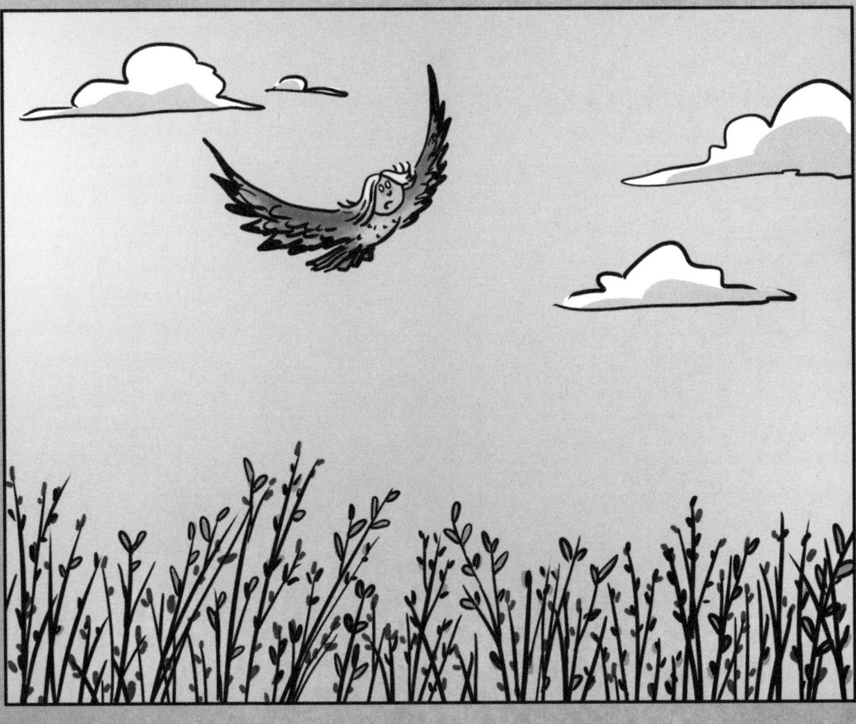

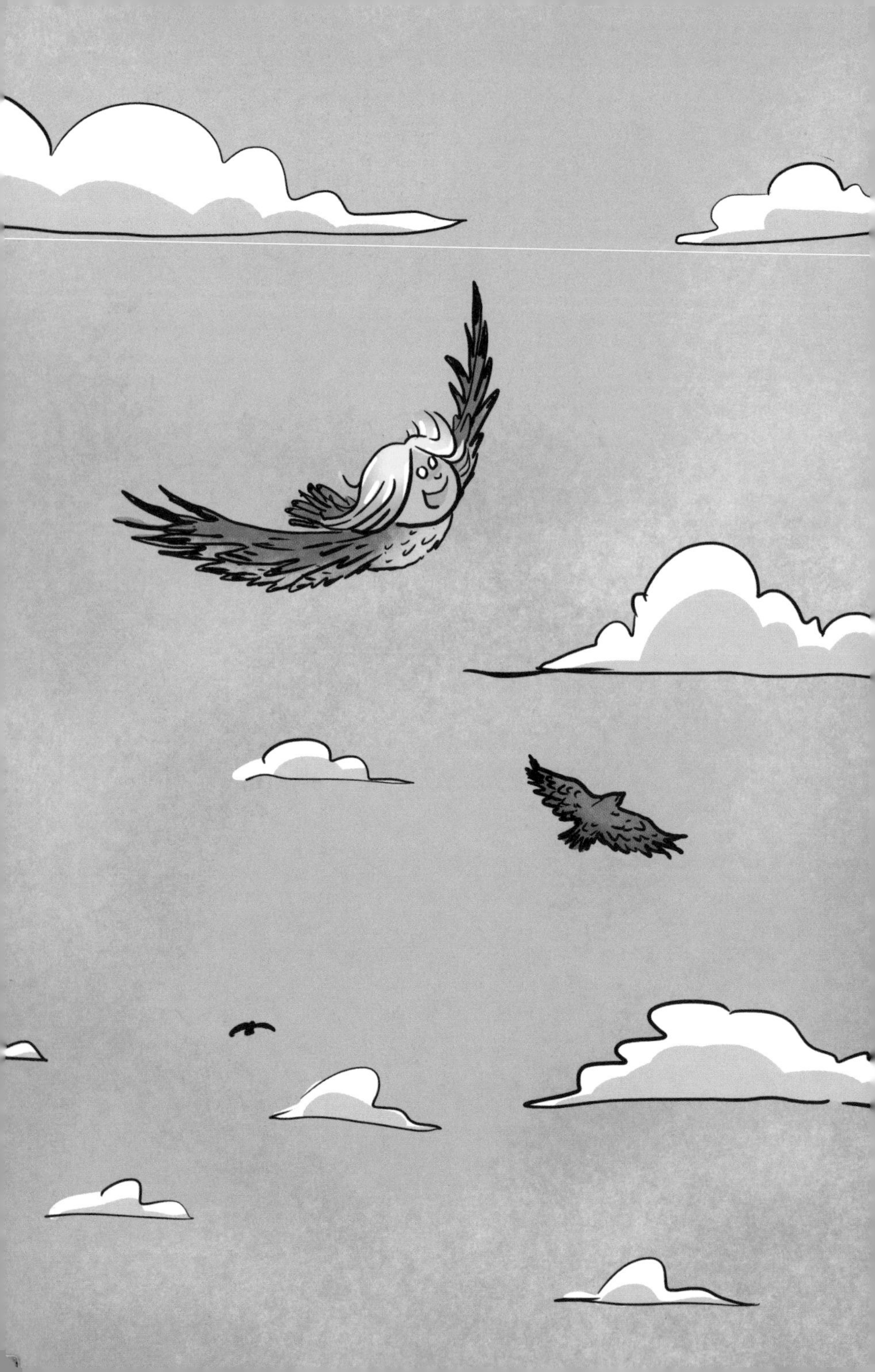

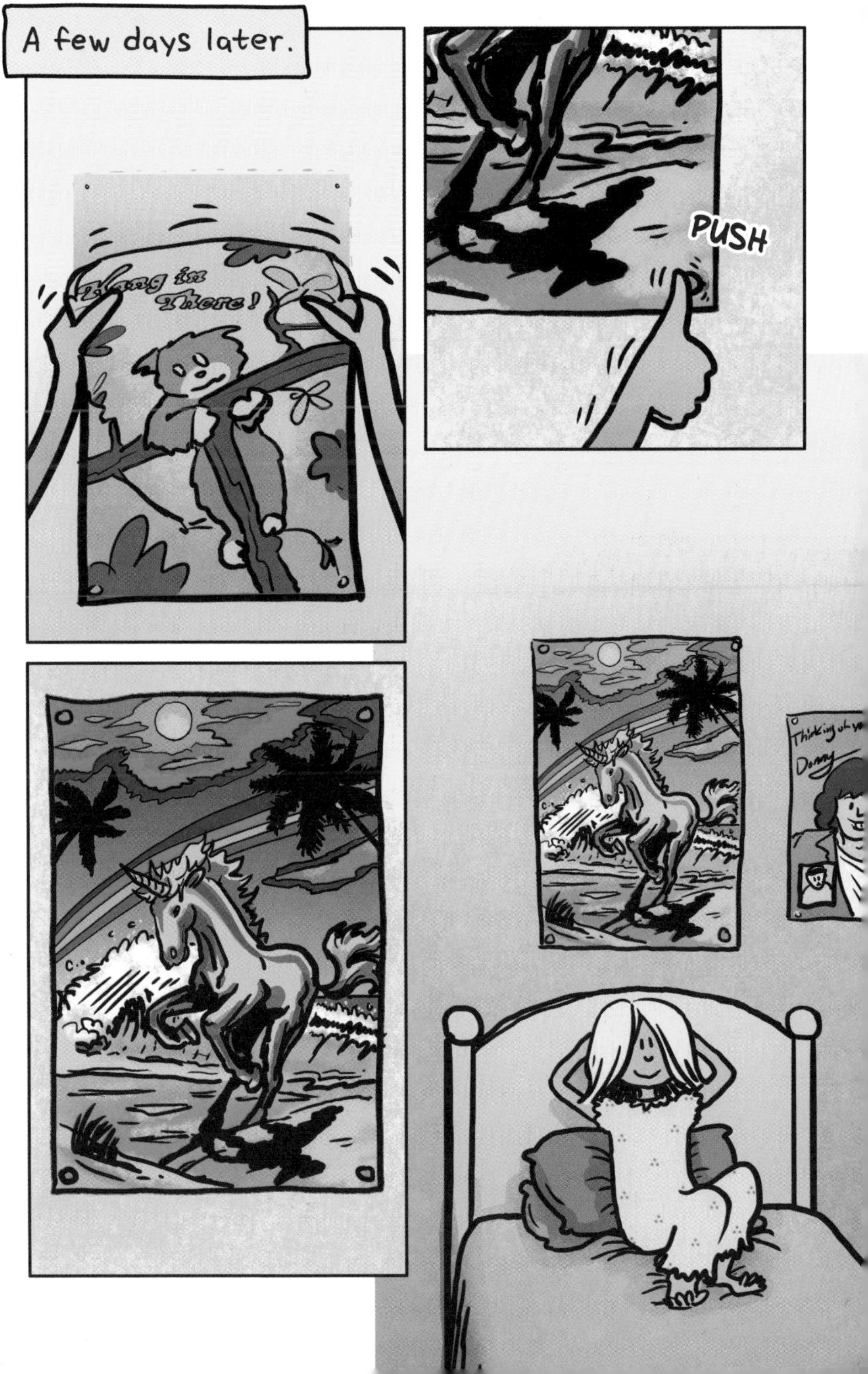

A few days later.
Hang in There!
PUSH

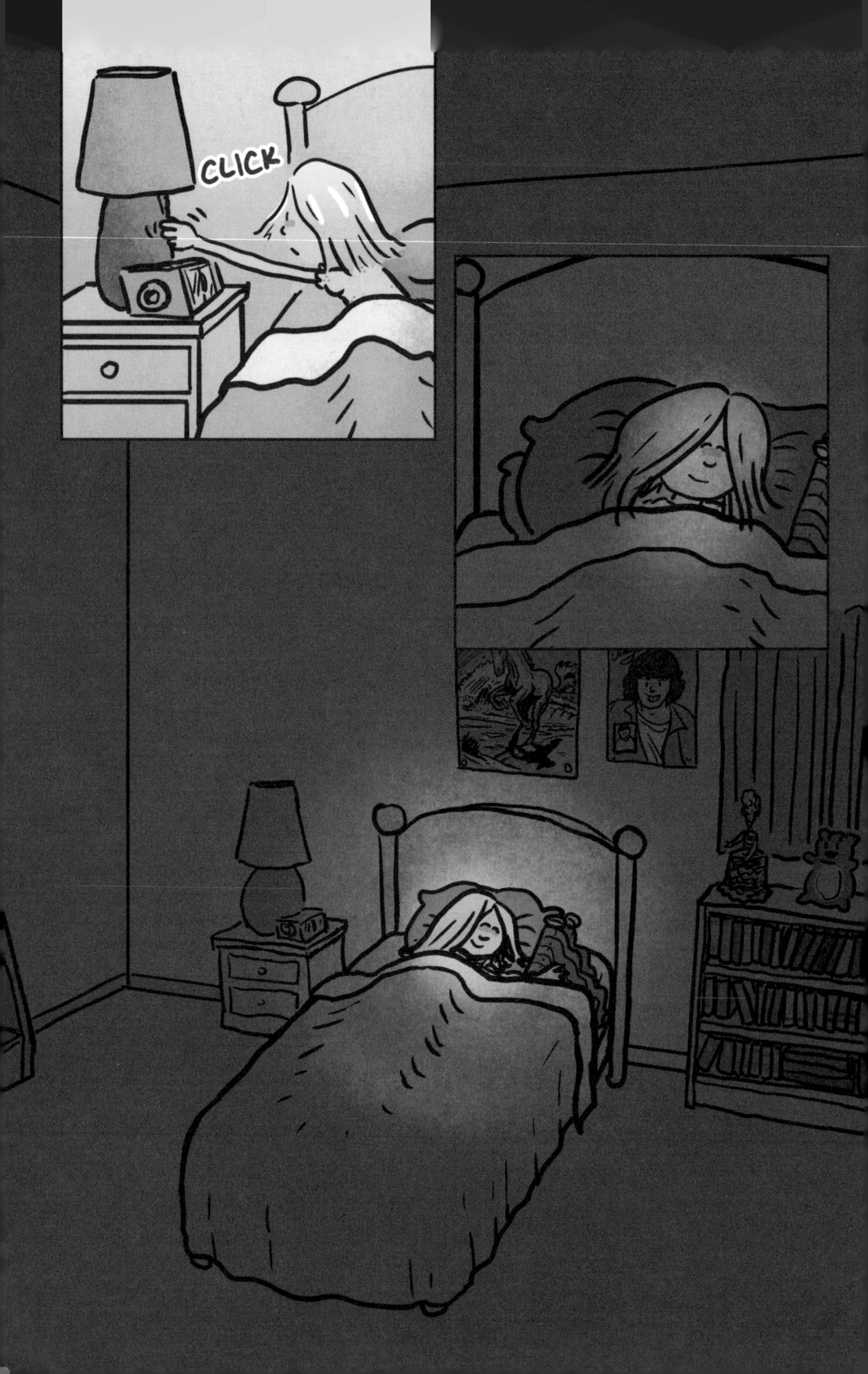
CLICK

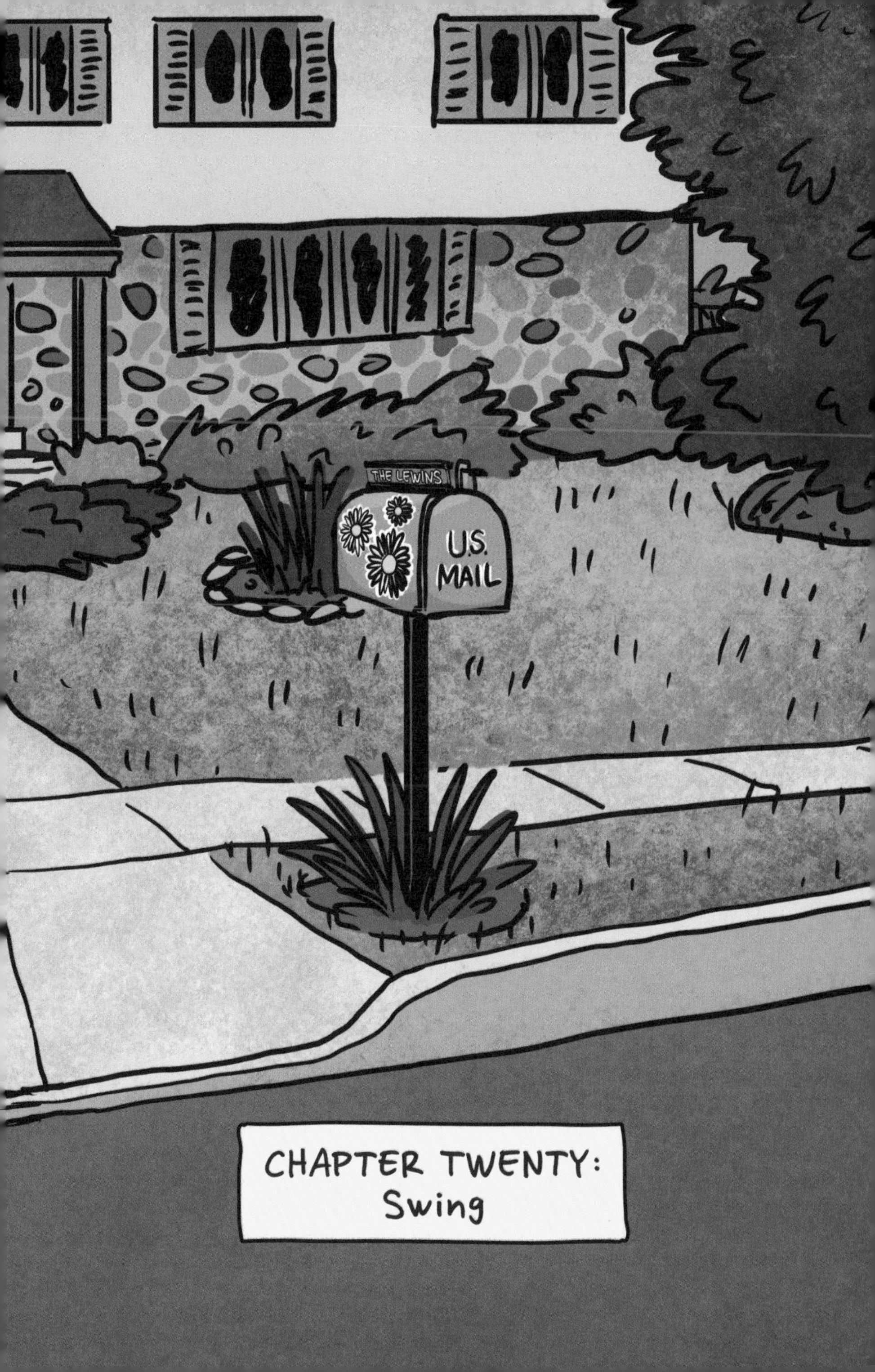
THE LEWINS
U.S. MAIL
CHAPTER TWENTY:
Swing

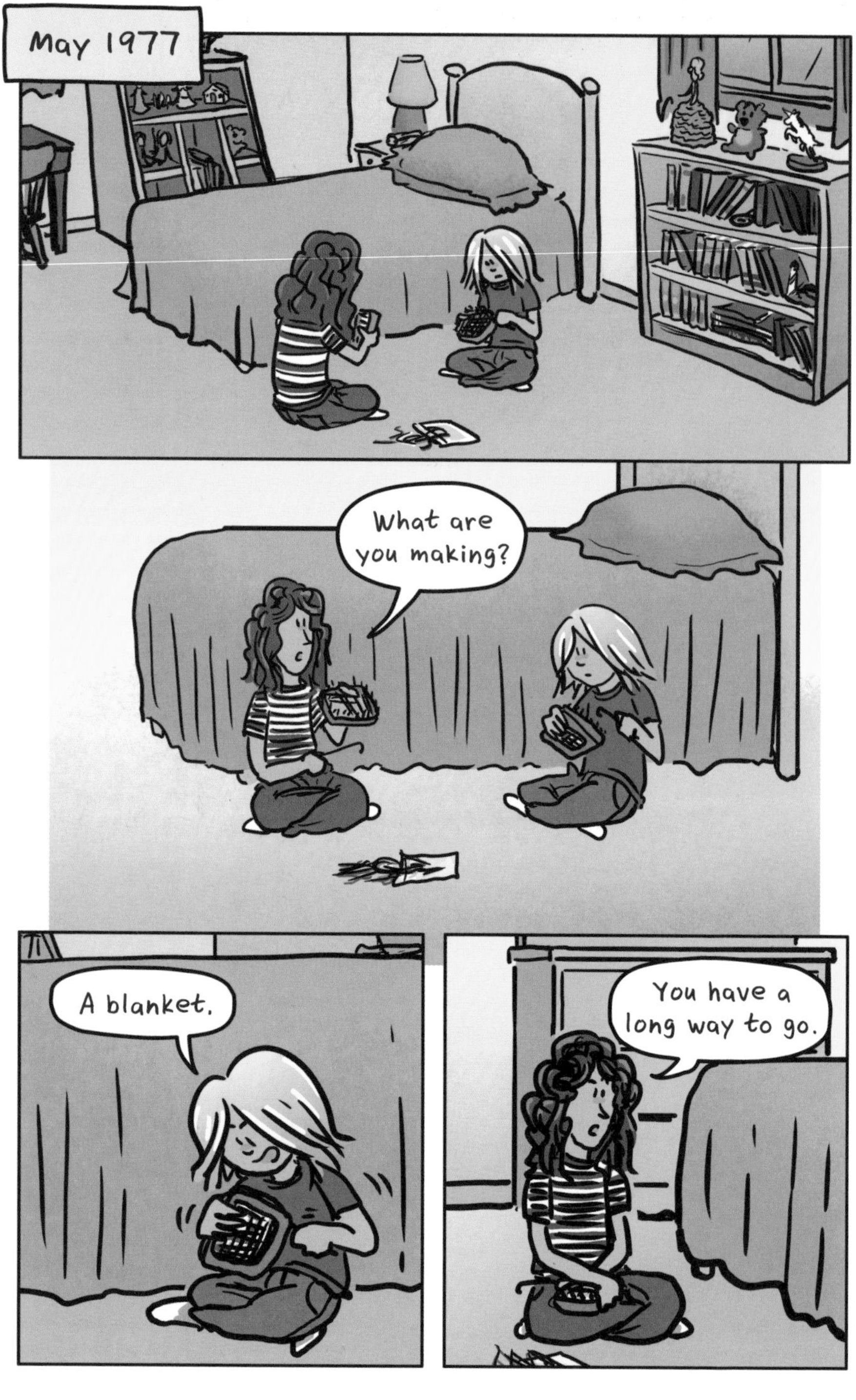
May 1977
What are you making?
A blanket.
You have a long way to go.

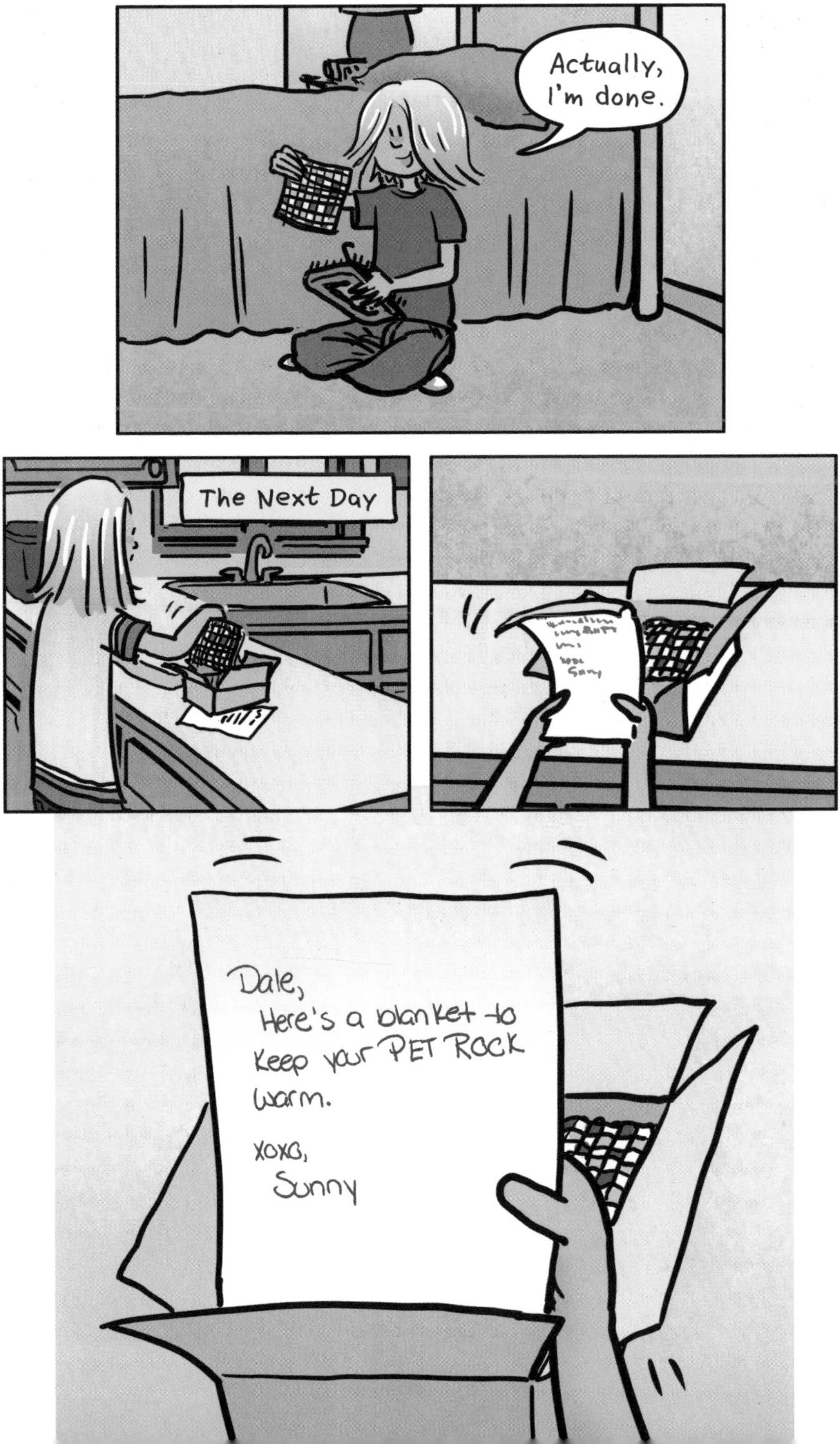
Actually, I'm done.
The Next Day
Dale,
Here's a blanket to keep your PET ROCK warm.
xoxo,
Sunny

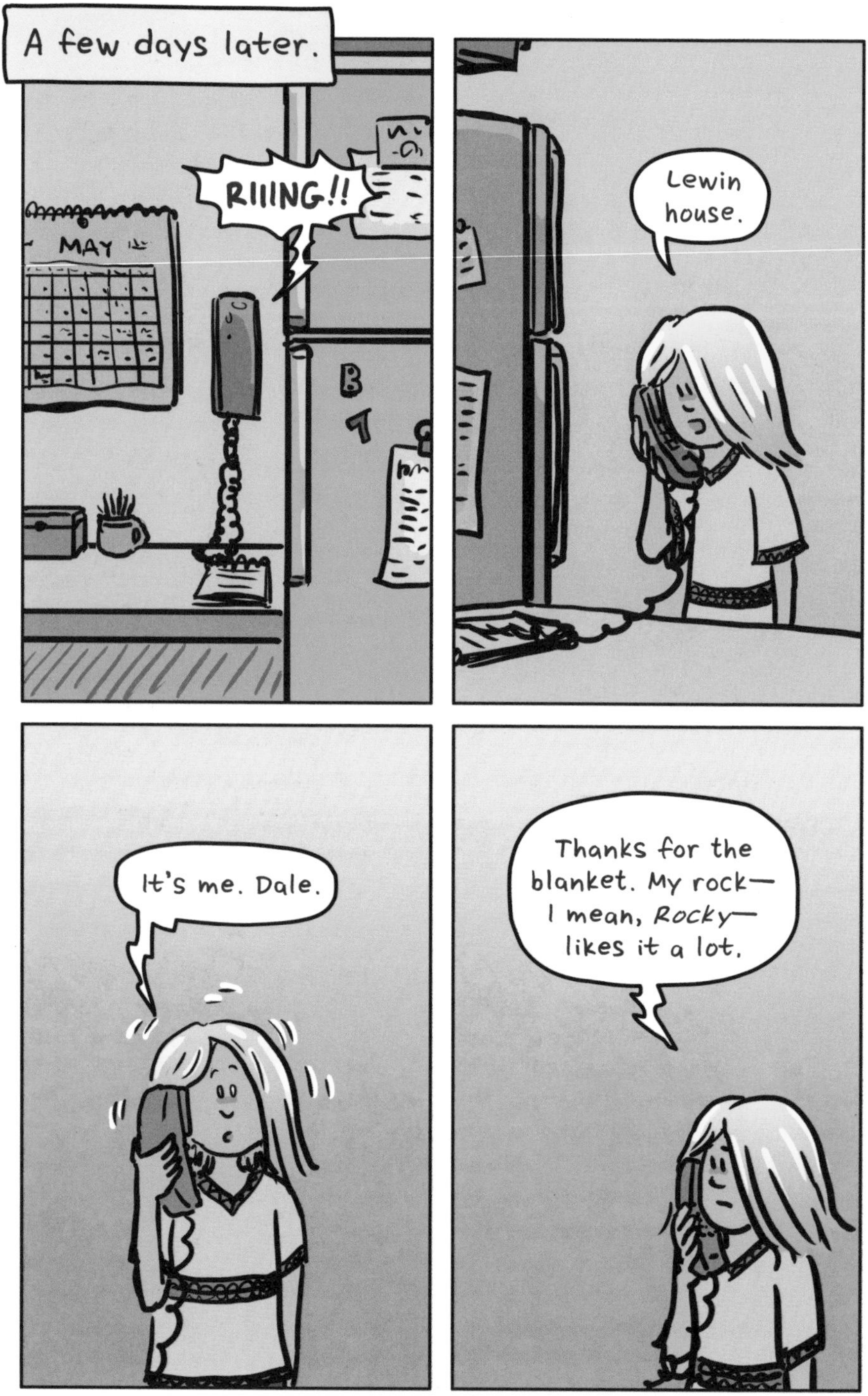
A few days later.
RIIING!!
Lewin house.
It's me. Dale.
Thanks for the blanket. My rock— I mean, *Rocky*— likes it a lot.

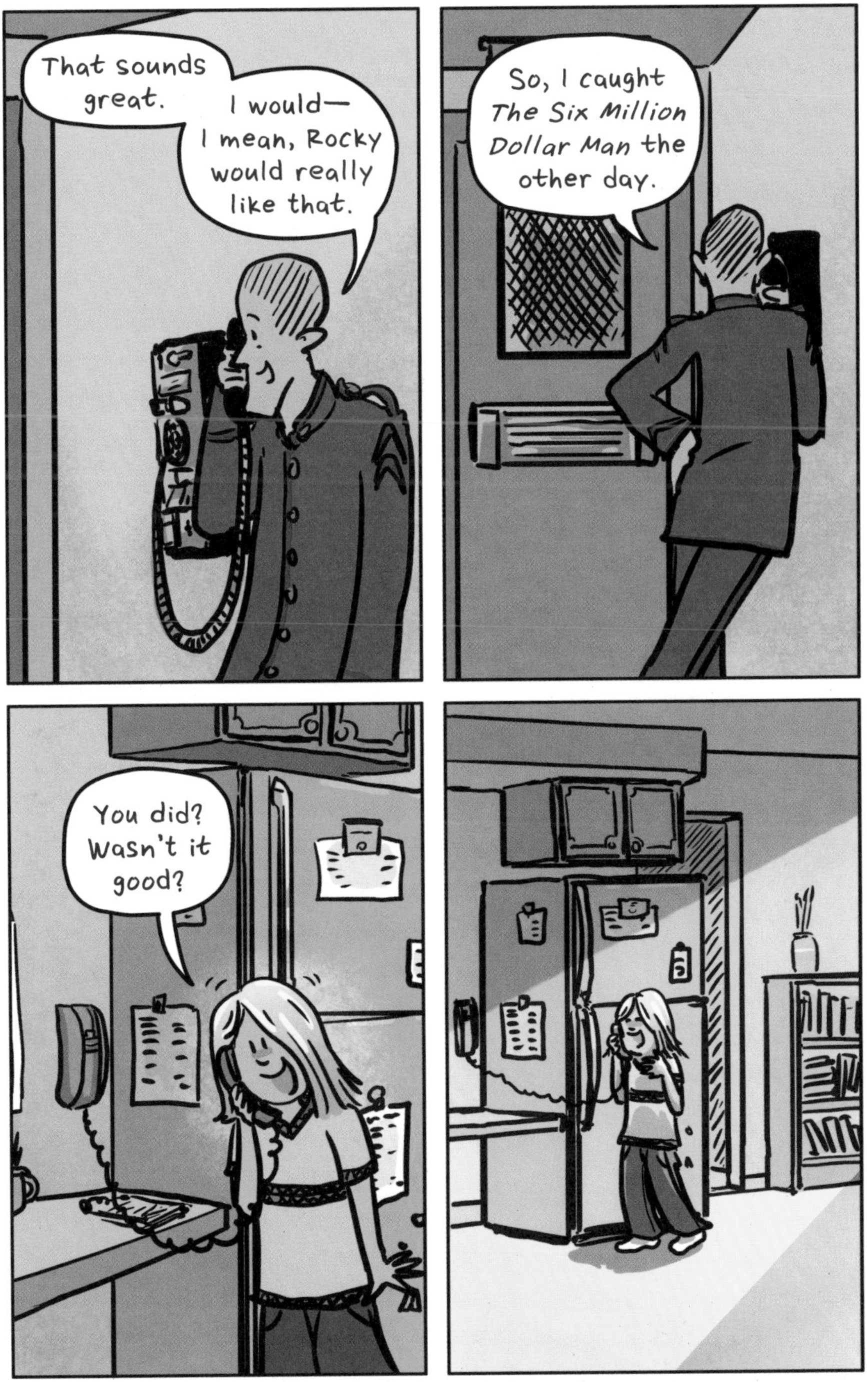

That sounds great.
I would— I mean, Rocky would really like that.
So, I caught *The Six Million Dollar Man* the other day.
You did? Wasn't it good?

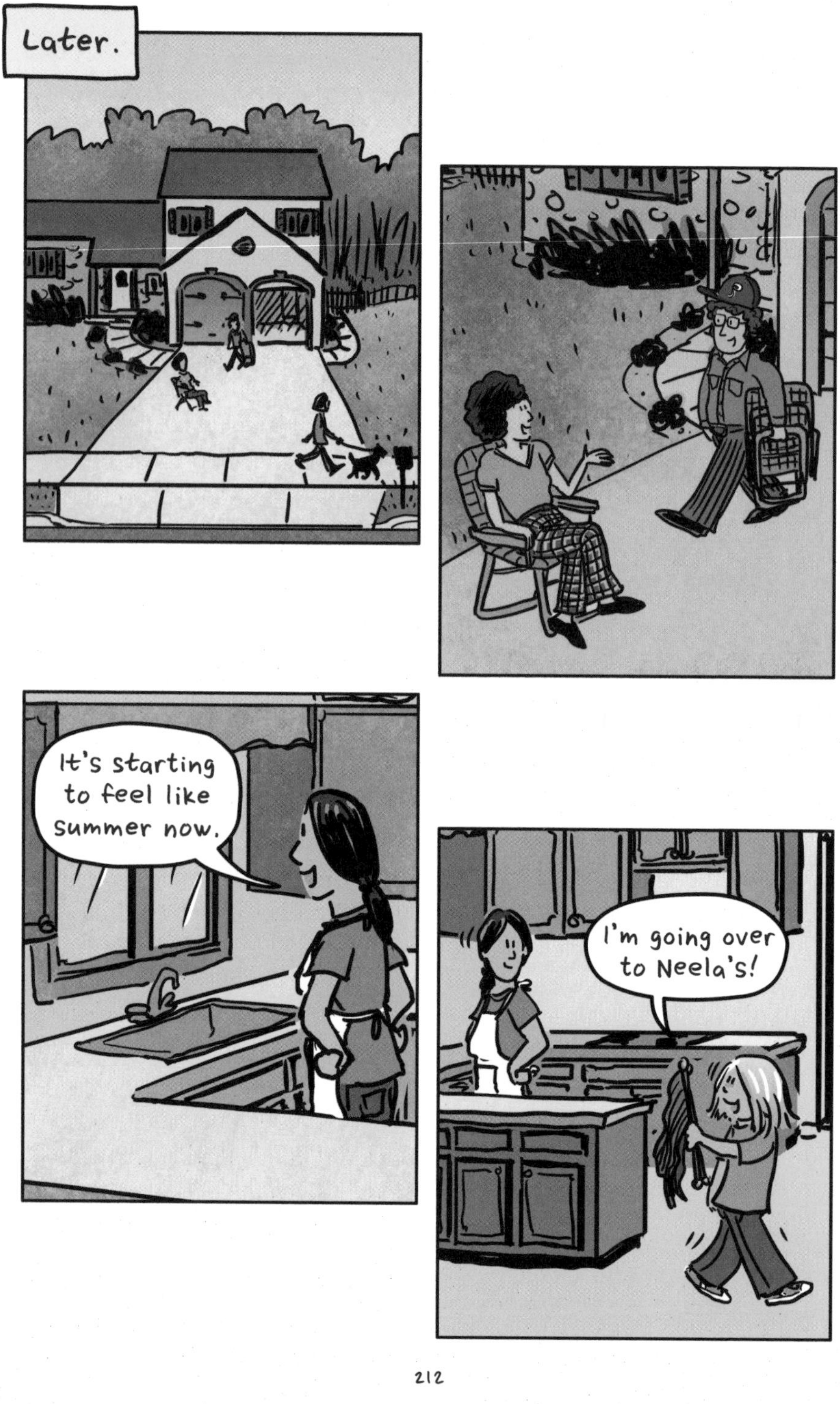
Later.
It's starting to feel like summer now.
I'm going over to Neela's!

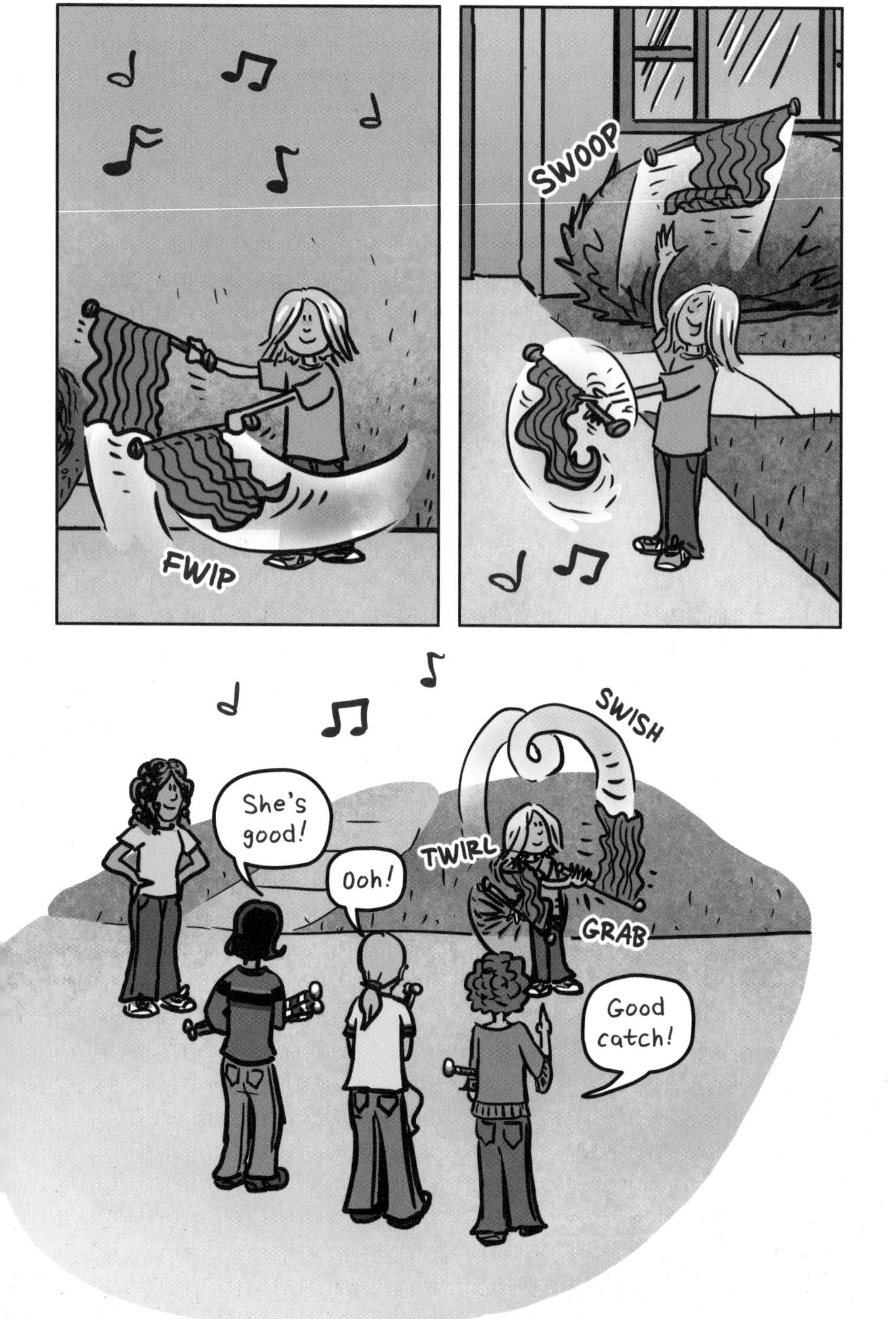
FWIP
SWOOP
SWISH
She's good!
Ooh!
TWIRL
GRAB
Good catch!

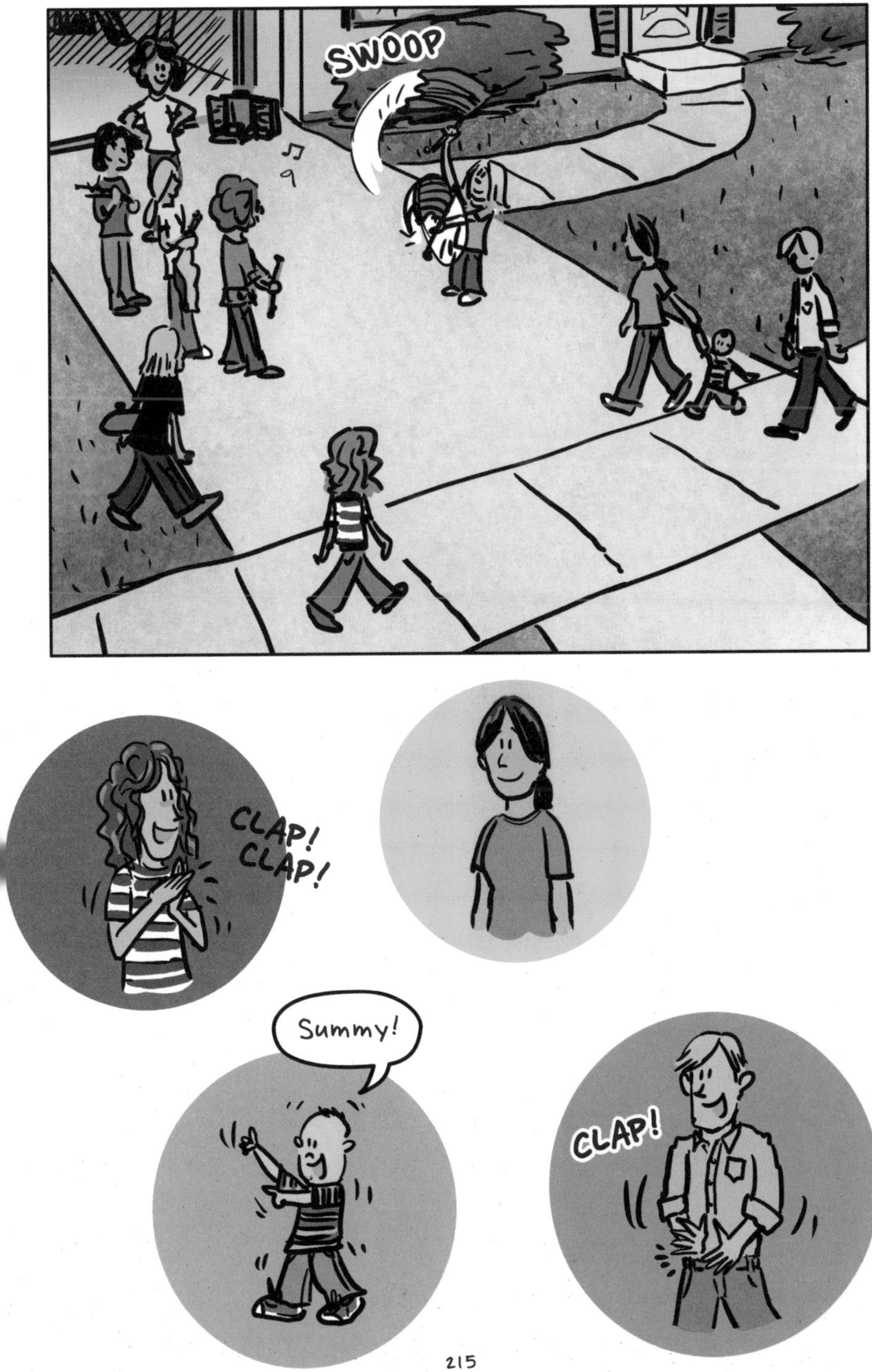
SWOOP
CLAP!
CLAP!
Summy!
CLAP!

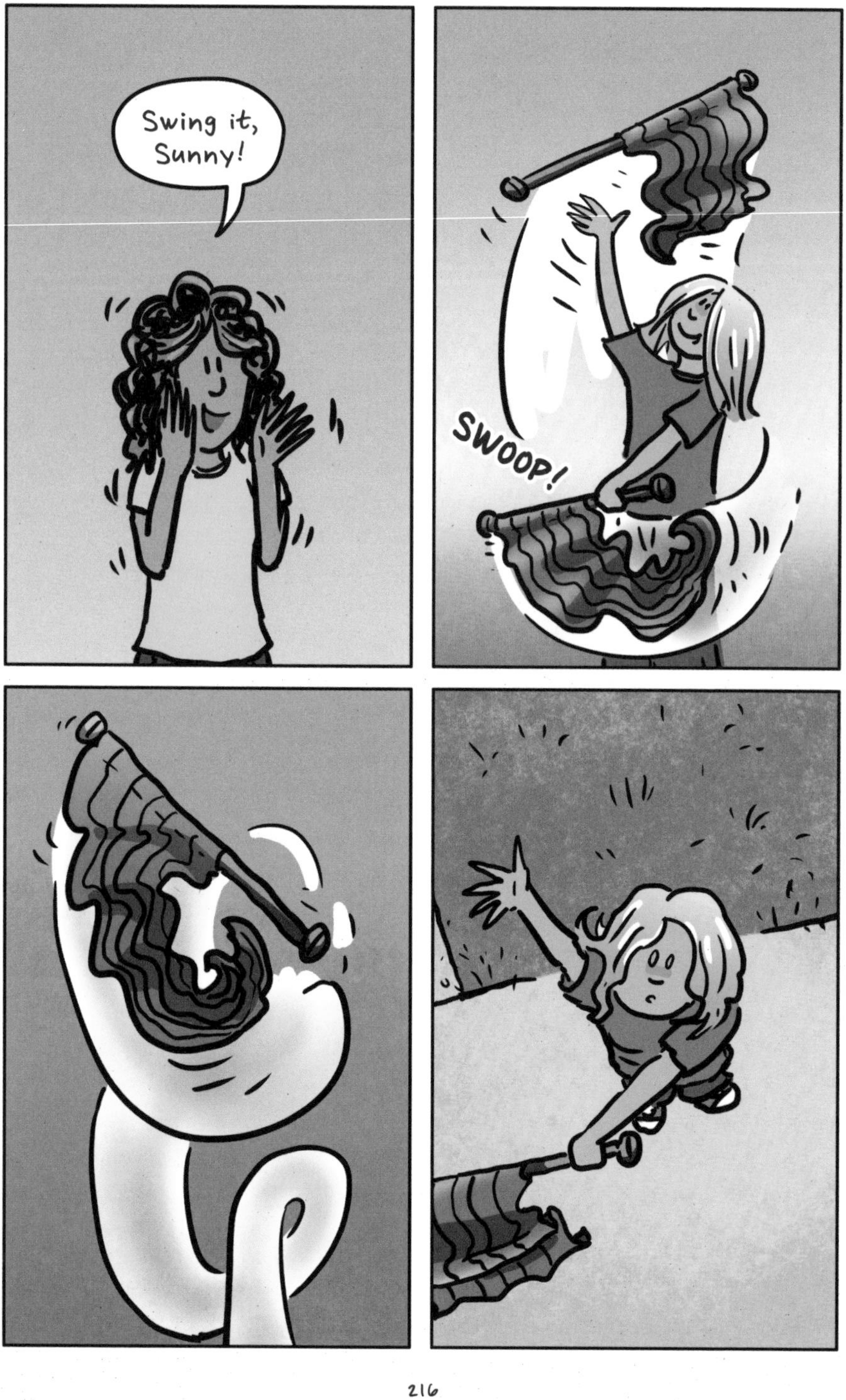
Swing it, Sunny!
SWOOP!

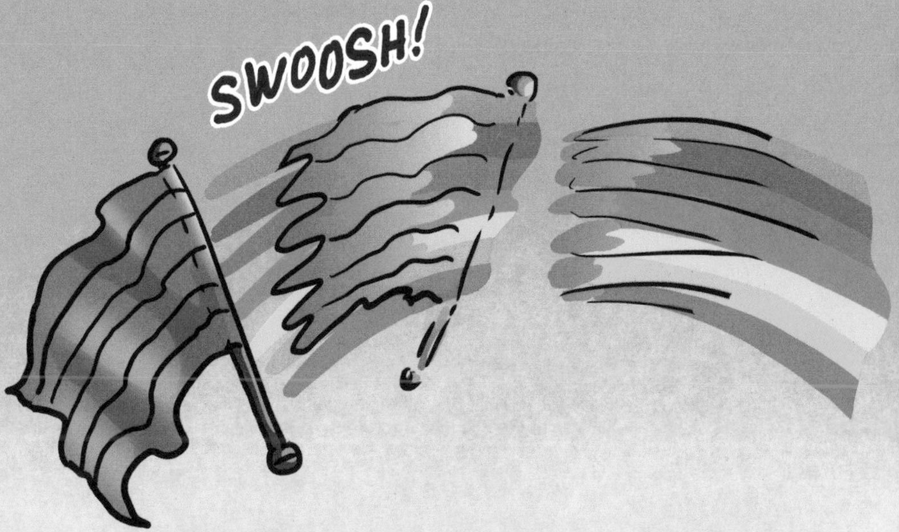
SWOOSH!

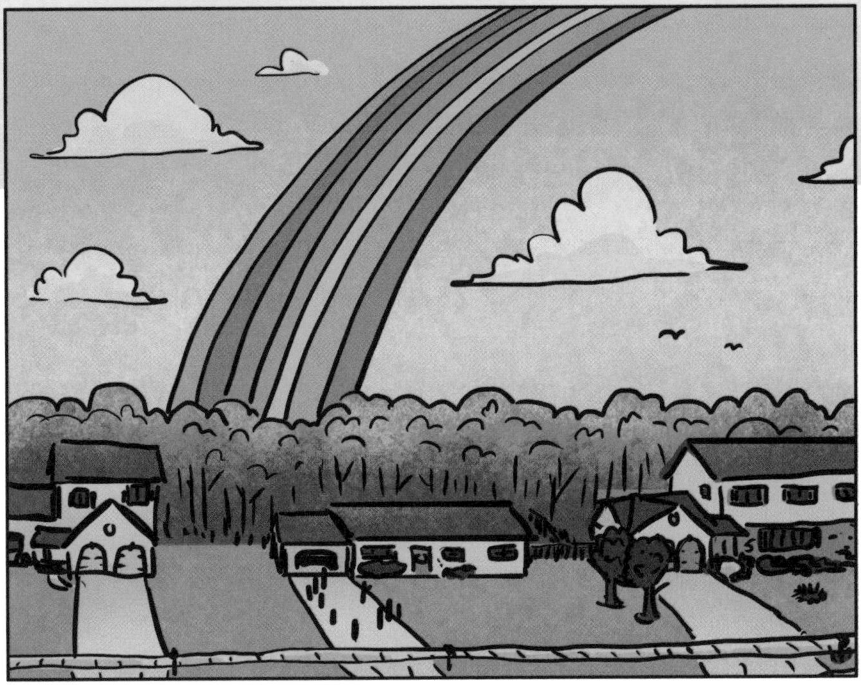

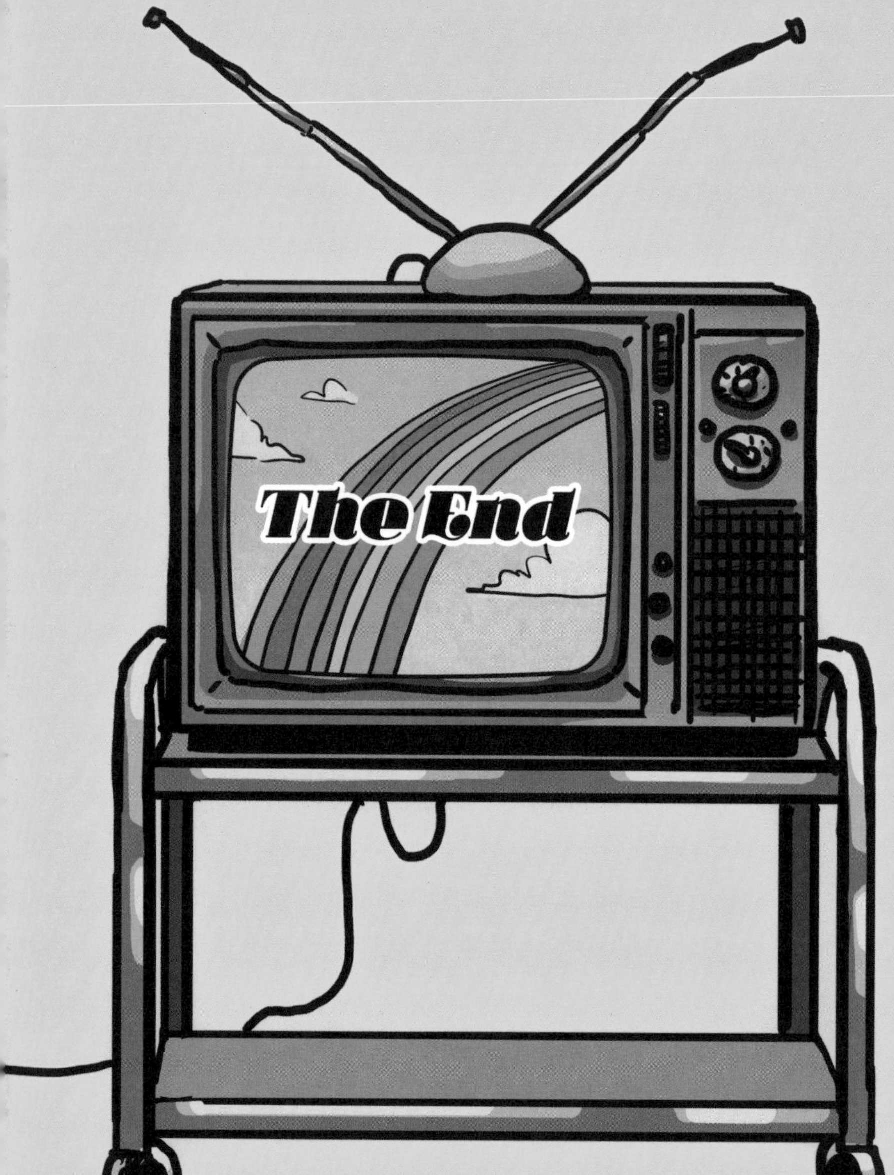
The End

A NOTE FROM JENNIFER L. HOLM & MATTHE

We were inspired to have Sunny learn how
swing flag because Jenni used to do it hers

ACKNOWLEDGMENTS

We are so grateful to all the wonderful pe
us to continue Sunny's journey. With spe
David Levithan, Phil Falco, Lark Pien, F
Koon, David Saylor, Lizette Serrano,
Terry. As always, many thanks to Jill
incredible support.

ER L. HOLM & MATTHEW HOLM

ard-winning brother-sister team behind
use and Squish series, as well as the
ook, SUNNY SIDE UP. Jennifer is also
many acclaimed novels, including
Honor books and the NEW YORK
THE FOURTEENTH GOLDFISH.
ecent novel is MARVIN AND THE
th Jonathan Follett.

orist of SUNNY SIDE UP and
an indie cartoonist from
as published many comics
Printz Award winner
and BOXERS & SAINTS.
ty and Mr. Elephanter
ldren's books.

W HOLM
to use a
elf!

ople who help
cial thanks to
wn Lau, Cyndi
and Alexandria
rinberg for her